BAEN BOOKS BY ESTHER FRIESNER

The Sherwood Game
Wishing Season (forthcoming)

BAEN BOOKS BY ESTHER FRIESNER

The Sherwood Game
Wishing Season (forthcoming)

Chicks in Chainmail

EDITED BY

Esther Friesner

CHICKS IN CHAINMAIL

A Baen Books Original

Baen Publishing Enterprises
P.O. Box 1403
Riverdale, N.Y. 10471

ISBN: 0-671-87682-1

Cover art by Larry Elmore

Printed in the United States of America

Contents

Contents

CHICKS IN CHAINMAIL

Esther Friesner

EN GARDE.

I'll bet you're wondering about the title of this book. Well, I'd like to make one thing perfectly clear right from the outset: It's all my fault.

When I told people the concept I wanted to use for this anthology, the reaction I got everywhere was not just favorable, it was downright enthusiastic (viz: "Cool!").

When I mentioned the *title* I wanted to use, the reaction I got everywhere—from editor, publisher, and potential contributors alike—was: "Are you *sure* you want to call it that?"

But we called it by that title anyway. All my fault. No one else to blame so don't try.

FEINT.

I've never been one to leave sleeping stereotypes lie. It's been my humble opinion for a while now that the Woman Warrior in today's crop of fantasy literature has gone beyond stereotype all the way to quadrophonic. She's strong, she's capable, she's independent, and she's *serious*. She's more than a match for any fighting man. But mostly, alas, she's got a posture problem, either from that chip on her shoulder or from toting around the full weight of an Author's Message.

(Granted, this beats the heck out of her venerable Woman Warrior ancestresses, whose posture problems all came from physiques that made them look

1

like they'd been hit from the back by the proverbial brace of torpedoes. You can still view this less-than-endangered species by opening the pages of *Spandexina! Mutant Babe of the Parallel Universe*.)

Now I'll be the first to admit, today's crop of Ladies Who Lunge (and Parry and Thrust) has it all over their predecessoresses in one department: Wardrobe. In the olden days, when comics still cost a dime and licorice whips wasn't the name of an X-rated movie, if you did have a Woman Warrior she would almost invariably be clothed in some variation on the chainmail bikini. Like the U.S. Postal Service, neither snow nor rain nor heat nor gloom of night would be enough to get her to change into something more sensible, less drafty, and less likely to cause certain strategic areas of the anatomy to freeze or fry on contact. (To say nothing of the unjustly ignored problem of the armored wedgie.)

Indeed, the one advantage of the chainmail bikini was how easy it was to slither out of when the Woman Warrior finally found the one Unspoiled Barbarian Swordsman who could make her a *real* woman.

(I think they sell the kit for that at Wal-Mart.)

It is this image of the Woman Warrior as bimbo-with-a-blade that has caused the stampede in the other direction among fantasy writers. And a very nice stampede it has been, too, except for the fact that once we chucked the chainmail bikini, we also chucked the chance to create a fighting woman who can let down her guard once in a while and just be human instead of an Image.

THRUST.

When I pitched this book, the super-compact capsule description I used was Amazon Comedy.

Amazon Comedy. Yeah, right. What are you, Friesner, some kind of sexist? Oh sure, *you* can get away with this because you're a woman, but just let some man try to write Amazon Comedy and watch him get reduced to a puddle of Politically Incorrect puree!

(This is the same phenomenon that allows members of one ethnic group to tell Those Jokes and use Those Words to one another, but heaven help the outsider who tries.)

Wake-up call time: Not all comedy needs to be cruel. Not all humor depends on ridicule. Most of the best relies on holding up the mirror to our fallible human nature. It lets us laugh at ourselves without making us feel belittled, hopeless, disenfranchised, or dumb. We make mistakes, we laugh at them, and we learn.

All of us. Even strong women. Even Warrior Women.

PARRY.

I once met two dogs.

If you took the Sunday *New York Times* and dropped it on top of the first one, you could probably squash him flat. If you heard how this tiny little flea-with-fur yapped his fool head off at a pitch and volume guaranteed to raise the dead every time anyone trespassed on his Personal Space, you would go right out and buy *two* copies of the Sunday *New York Times* just to be sure you got him good.

The other dog was big and strong enough to play Australian rules football—as his own team—and win. His teeth could punch holes in sheet metal. When his owner played Frisbee with him, this dog got confused and fetched the hubcap off a Monster Truck. With the truck still attached.

This second dog lets babies massage strained peaches into his fur, allows little girls to use his hair and nails when they play beauty parlor, and did not so much as say "Woof!" when his owner's child dressed him up like a clown for Halloween. He really looked silly. Everyone laughed at him. He just sat there with one of those big doggy grins on his face and laughed too.

Try to lay one hand on his food or his family and that's one hand you won't be seeing again in this life.

My point? We're secure enough to take a joke, we're smart enough to tell a joke from a jab, we're human enough to enjoy a good laugh, and we're not going to kill you if you laugh along with us. But try to walk all over us and you're history.

We being the real Women Warriors and our friends.

We do exist, you know. We may not have the chainmail and the swords, but we've got the challenges and the quests and the battles. We can handle them, too.

Remember: It takes a stout heart to hold off a horde of beer-crazed trolls in a dockside tavern, it demands guts of steel to face hand-to-hand combat with the Dark Lord of the Really Ugly in his very citadel. Still, that ain't nothin' compared to the raw courage it takes to be stuck in a car for a four-hour drive with a two-year-old and her favorite Barney tape that she wants to hear *again* or the sheer heroism required to be trapped at an Official Family Function and cornered by a well-meaning relative who demands to know "Why aren't you *settled down* yet, dearie, is something *wrong* with you?"

Come to think of it, maybe we *could* use those swords.

SALUTE.

Now, now, you know what good manners teach us:
Gentlemen first.

LADY OF STEEL

Roger Zelazny

Uttering a curse in his well-practiced falsetto, Cora
swung his blade and cut down the opposing swordswoman. His contoured breastplate emphasized features which were not truly present.

Simultaneous then, attacks came from the right and
the left. Beginning his battle-song, he parried to the
left, cut to the right, parried left again, cut through
that warrior, parried right, and thrust. Both attackers fell.

"Well done, sister!" shouted Edwina, the aging axe-
woman, from where she stood embattled ten feet
away. High compliment from a veteran!

Smiling, Cora prepared for another onslaught,
recalling when he had been Corak the cook but
months before. He had had a dream then, and now
he was living it.

He had thought of being a great warrior, laying
about him in battle, famed in song and story for his
prowess. How he had practiced with the blade! Until
one day he realized he need also practice his walk
and his speech—as well as shaving closely and clan-
destinely every day—if he were ever to realize that
dream. So he did. And one day he disappeared, Cora
appeared weeks later, and a legend was born. Several

months into the campaign now, and he was not only accepted but celebrated—Cora, Lady of Steel.

But the enemy, too, had heard of him, and all seemed anxious to claim the glory of reaping his head. Perspiration broke out on his brow as five warriors moved to engage him. The first he took out quickly with a surprise rush. The others—more wary now— fought conservatively, seeking to wear him down. His arms ached by the time he had dealt with the second. His battle-song broke as he dispatched the third and took a cut deep in his right thigh from one of the others. He faltered.

"Courage, sister!" shouted Edwina, hacking her way toward him.

He could barely defend himself against the nearer warrior as Edwina took out the fourth. Finally, he stumbled, knowing he could not rise in time to save himself from the death-blow.

At the last moment, however, an axe flashed and his final assailant's head rolled away in the direction of her retreating sisters.

"Rest!" Edwina ordered, taking up a defensive position above him. "They flee! We have the field!"

He lay there, clutching his thigh and watching the retreat, fighting to retain consciousness. "Good," he said. This was the closest it had ever been. . . .

After a time, Edwina helped him to his feet. "Well-acquitted, Steel Lady," she said. "Lean on me. I'll help you back to camp."

Inside her tent, the fractured leg-armor removed, she bathed the wound. "This will not cripple you," she said. "We'll have you good as new shortly."

But the wound extended higher. Suddenly, she had drawn aside his loincloth to continue her ministrations. He heard her gasp.

"Yes," he said then. "You know my secret. It was the only way for me to distinguish myself—to show that I could do the work as well or better than a woman."

"I must say that you have," Edwina admitted. "I remember your prowess at Oloprat, Tanquay, and Pord. You are a most unusual man. I respect you for what you have done."

"You will help me keep my secret then?" he asked. "Let me complete the campaign? Let me make a record to show the world a man can do this work, too?"

She studied him, then winked, pinched his fanny, and smiled.

"I'm sure we can work something out," she said.

And you thought you had tax problems ...

AND LADIES OF THE CLUB

Elizabeth Moon

"But you don't tax jockstraps!" Mirabel Stonefist glared.

"No," said the king. "They're a necessity."

"For you, maybe. How do you expect me to fight without my bronze bra?"

"Men can fight without them," the king said. "It's far more economical to hire men, anyway. Do you have any idea what the extra armor for the women in my army costs? I commissioned a military cost-containment study, and my advisors said women's uniforms were always running over budget." The king smirked at the queen, on her throne a few feet away, and she smirked back. "I've always said the costs to society are too high if women leave their family responsibilities—"

"We'll see about this," said Mirabel. She would like to have seen about it then and there, but the king's personal guards—all male this morning, she noticed—looked too alert. No sense getting her nose broken again for nothing. Probably it was the queen's fault anyway. Just because she'd been dumped on her backside at the Harvest Tourney, when she tried to go up against Serena the Savage, expecting that uncompromising warrior to pull her strokes ... the queen gave Mirabel a curled lip, and Mirabel imagined giving the queen a fat one. As the elected representative of the

8

Ladies' Aid & Armor Society, she must maintain her dignity, but she didn't have to control her imagination.

"Six silver pence per annum," said the king. "Payable by the Vernal Equinox."

Mirabel growled and stalked out, knocking over several minor barons on the way. In the courtyard, other women in the royal army clustered around her.

"Well?"

"It's true," said Mirabel grimly. "He's taxing bronze bras." A perky blonde with an intolerably cute nose (still unbroken) piped up.

"Just bronze? What about brass? Or iron? Or—"

"Shut *up*, Kristal! Bronze, brass, gold, silver . . . 'all such metal ornaments as ye female warrioresses are wont to use—' "

"Warrioress!" A vast bosomy shape heaved upward, dark brows lowered. Bertha Broadbelt had strong opinions on the dignity due women warriors.

"Shut *up*, Bertha!" Kristal squeaked, slapping Bertha on the arm with all the effect of a kitten swatting a sabertooth.

"Warrioress is what the law says," Mirabel snapped. "I don't like it either. But there it is."

"What about *leather*?" Kristal asked. "Chain mail? Linen with seashell embroidery?"

"KRISTAL!" The perky blonde wilted under the combined bellow.

"I was only thinking—"

"No, you weren't," Mirabel said. "You were fantasizing about those things in the *Dark Knights* catalog again. This is serious; I'm calling a meeting of the Ladies' Aid & Armor Society."

"And so," she explained that evening to the women who had gathered in the Ladies' Aid & Armor Society meeting hall, "the king insists that the extra metal we require in our armor is a luxury, to be taxed as such. He expects we'll all go tamely back to our hearths— or make him rich."

"I'll make him sing soprano," muttered Lissa
Broadbelt, Bertha's sister. "The nerve of that man—"
"Now, now." A sweet soprano voice sliced through
the babble as a sword through new butter. "Ladies,
please! Let's have no unseemly threats. . . ." With a
creak and jingle, the speaker stood . . . and stood. Tall
as an oak (the songs went), and tougher than bullhide
(the songs went), clad in enough armor to outfit most
small mercenary companies, Sophora Segundiflora
towered over her sister warriors. She had arrived in
town only that evening, from a successful contract.
"Especially," Sophora said, "threats that impugn
sopranos."

"No, ma'am."

"He is, after all, the king."

"Yes, ma'am."

"Although it is a silly sort of tax."

"*Yes*, ma'am." A long pause, during which Sophora
smiled lazily at the convocation, and the convocation
smiled nervously back. She was so big, for one thing,
and she wore so much more armor than everyone
else, for another, and then everyone who had been
to war with her knew that she smiled all the time.
Even when slicing hapless enemies in two or three
or whatever number of chunks happened to be her
pleasure. Perhaps especially then.

"Uh . . . do you have any . . . er . . . suggestions?"
asked Mirabel, in a tone very different from that she'd
used to the king.

"I think we should all sit down," Sophora said, and
did so with another round of metallic clinkings and
leathery creakings. Everyone sat, in one obedient
descent. Everyone waited, with varying degrees of
patience but absolute determination. One did not
interrupt Sophora. One would not have the chance to
apologize. Whether she was slow, or merely deliberate, she always had a chance to speak her mind.
"What about other kinds of bras?" she asked at last.

Mirabel explained the new decree again. "Metal

ornaments, it said, but that included armor. Said so. Called us warrioresses, too." Sophora waved that away.

"He can call us what he likes, as long as we get paid and we don't have to pay this stupid tax. First things first. So if it's not a metal bra, it's not taxed?"

"No—but what good is a bit of cloth against weapons?"

"I told you, leather—" Kristal put in quickly.

Sophora let out a cascade of soprano laughter, like a miniature waterfall. "Ladies, ladies ... what about something like my corselet?"

"He was clever there, Sophora. He doesn't want to tax the armor men wear, and of course some men do wear mail shirts or corselets of bronze. But he specified that modifications to the standard designs—marked in diagrams; I saw them—count as ornamentation, and make the whole taxable."

"Idiot!" huffed Sophora. Then she jingled some more as she tried to examine her own mail shirt. "These gussets, I suppose?"

"Yes, exactly. We could, I suppose, wear men's body armor a size larger, and pad it out, but it would be miserably hot in summer, and bulky the rest of the time. There's always breast-binding—"

"I hate binding my breasts," said someone from the back of the room. "You gals with the baby tits can do it easily enough, but some of us are built!" Heads turned to look at her, and sure enough, she was.

"The simple thing is to get rid of our breasts," said Sophora, as if stating the obvious. The resulting gasp filled the room. She looked around. "Not like *that*," she said. "I have no intention of cutting mine off. I don't care what anyone says about heroic foremothers, those Amazons were barbarians. But we live in an age of modern marvels. We don't have to rely on old-fashioned surgery. Why, there's a plastic wizard right here in the city."

"Of course!" Mirabel smacked herself on the

forehead. "I've seen his advertisements myself. Thought of having a nose job myself, but I've just been too busy."

"That's right," Bertha said. "And he does great temporary bridges and crowns, too: our Desiree had the wedding outdoors, and he did a crystal bridge across the Sinkbat canal, and a pair of crystal crowns for Desiree and the flower girl. Lovely—so romantic—and then it vanished right on time, no sticky residue."

"Temporaries! That's even better. Take 'em or leave 'em, so to speak."

"Let's get down to business," Sophora said. "Figure out what we can pay, and how we can avoid paying it."

"What?"

"Come on in the business office and I'll show you." She led the way into the back room, and began pulling down scrolls and tomes. Mirabel and a couple of others settled down to wait. After peering and muttering through a short candle and part of a tall replacement, Sophora looked up.

"We'll need to kick in two silver pence each to start with."

"Two silver pence! Why?"

"That's the ceiling in our health benefits coverage for noncombat trauma care. It's reimbursable, I'm sure, but we have to pay it first," Sophora said. She had half a dozen scrolls spread on the desk, along with a thick, well-thumbed volume of tax laws. "We might have to split it between a reimbursable medical expense, and a deductible business expense, if they get picky."

"But how?" Mirabel had never understood the medical benefits package anyway. They should've paid to have her nose redone, but the paperpushers had said that because she was a prisoner at the time, it didn't qualify as a combat injury. But since she'd been in uniform, it wasn't noncombat trauma, either.

Sophora smiled and tapped the tax volume. "It's a necessary business expense, required to comply with the new tax code. The chancellor might argue that only the cost related to removing the breasts is a business expense, but the restoration has to count as medical. It's in the law: 'any procedure which restores normal function following loss thereof.' Either it's reimbursable or it's deductible, and of course we aren't paying the tax. With a volume discount, we should be able to get the job done for two silver pence. Bertha says he charged only three for that entire wedding celebration."

Mirabel whistled her admiration. "Very good, dear. You should be a lawyer."

"I will be, when I retire." Sophora smiled placidly. "I've been taking correspondence courses. Part of that G.I.T. Bill the king signed three years ago: Get Into Taxpaying. Now let me get the contract drawn up—" She wrote steadily as that candle burned down; Mirabel lit another. Finally she quit, shook her hand, and said, "See that the wizard signs this contract I've drawn up." She handed over a thick roll. Mirabel glanced down the first part of it.

"It's *heavy*—surely we don't need all this for a simple reversible spell. . . ."

"I added a little boilerplate. And yes, we do need all this. You don't want to wake up with the wrong one, do you?"

"Wrong breast? Ugh—what a thought. Although I expect some of our sisters wouldn't mind, if they could choose which one."

"They can pay extra for full reshaping, if they want. I'm not going to have my children drinking out of someone else's breast, even if it is on my body."

"You want a reversible reduction mammoplasty?" the wizard asked. His eyebrows wavered, unsure whether to rise in shock or lower in disapproval. Mirabel could tell he didn't like her using the correct term for the operation. Wizards liked clients to be humble and ignorant.

"Yeah," Mirabel said. She didn't care if the wizard didn't like smart clients; she wasn't about to let the sisterhood down. "See, there's a new tax on breast-armor. What we need is to lose 'em when we're headed for battle, but of course we want to get 'em back when we're nursing. Or . . . whatever." Whatever being more to the point, in her case. Two points.

"I . . . see." The steepled fingers, the professional sigh. Mirabel hated it when wizards pulled all this high and mighty expert jazz. "It could be . . . expensive. . . ."

"I don't see why," Mirabel said. "It's not like we're asking for permanent changes. Isn't it true that a reversible spell disturbs the Great Balance less? Doesn't cost you that much . . . of course I can find someone else. . . ."

"Where *do* you people get your idea of magery?" the wizard asked loftily. Mirabel held up the Ladies' Aid & Armor Society's copy of *Our Wizards, Our Spells.* He flushed. "That's a popularization . . . it's hardly authoritative—"

"I've also read Wishbone and Peebles' *Altering Reality: Temporary vs. Permanent Spellcasting and Its Costs.*"

"You couldn't have understood that!" True, but Mirabel wasn't going to admit it. She merely looked at the wizard's neck, thinking how easily it would come apart with one blow of her sword, until he swallowed twice quickly and flushed. "All right, all right," he said then. "Perhaps you soldiers should get a sort of discount."

"I should hope so. All the women warriors in the kingdom . . . we could even make it exclusive. . . ."

"Well. Well, then let's say—how much was the new tax?"

"Irrelevant," said Mirabel, well briefed by Sophora. "We can pay two silver pence apiece per year."

"Per year?" His fingers wiggled a little; she knew he was trying to add it up in his head.

"As many transforms as needed . . . but we wouldn't want many."

"Uh . . . how many warriors?"

"Fifty right away, but there might be more later."

"It's very difficult. You see, you have to create an extradimensional storage facility for the . . . the . . . tissue, so to speak. Until it's wanted. Otherwise the energy cost of uncreating and creating all that, all the time, would be prohibitive. And the storage facility must have very good—well, it's a rather difficult concept, except that you don't want to mix them up." But what he was really thinking was "a hundred silver pence—enough for that new random-access multidimensional storage device they were showing over in Technolalia last summer."

Still, he was alert enough to read the contract Mirabel handed him. As she'd expected, he threw up his hands and threatened to curse the vixenish excuse for a lawyer who had drawn up such a ridiculous, unspeakable contract. Mirabel repeated her long look at his neck—such a scrawny, weak neck—and he subsided. "All right, all right. Two silver pence a year for necessary reversible mammoplasties . . ." He signed on the dotted line, then stamped below with the sigil on the end of his wizard's staff, as Sophora had said he should. Mirabel smiled at him and handed over two silver pence.

"You can do me first," she said. "I'll be in tomorrow morning. We'll need proof that it's reversible."

The operation took hardly any time. The wizard didn't even need to touch the target area. One moment the breasts were there, then they weren't. The reversal took somewhat longer, but it worked smoothly, and then they were again. A slight tingling that faded in moments—that was all the side effects. Mirabel had gone in with her usual off-duty outfit on, and came out moments later with considerably more room in the top of it. The other women in the palace guard, who had come to watch, grinned happily. They would all have theirs done at once, they agreed.

Mirabel thought it felt a bit odd when she stripped for weapons practice, but the look on the king's face was worth it. All the women in the palace now displayed an array of admirably flat—but muscular—chests above regulation bronze loin-guards. At first, no one recognized them, not even the sergeants. But gradually, the men they were training with focussed on the obvious—Mirabel's flat nose, Kristal's perky one—and the necessary, like the sword tips that kept getting in their way when they forgot to pay attention to drill.

The king, though . . . the king didn't catch on until someone told him. "That new draft . . ." he said to the sergeant. "Shaping well."

"Begging the king's pardon, that ain't no new draft," said the sergeant.

"But—"

"Them's the ladies, Sire," the sergeant said. "Haven't got no thingies anymore." He knew and had already used all the usual terms, but felt that when addressing the king in person, he ought to avoid vulgarisms. "They's fightin' better than ever, your highness, and that's better'n most."

"Women!" The king stared. Mirabel, in the first row, grinned at him. "And no tits!"

"Uh . . . yes, Sire. No . . . er . . . tits." Not for the first time, the sergeant felt that royalty had failed to adhere to standards.

"No tax," Mirabel said cheerfully, as the king's eyes flicked from her face to her chest and back again.

"Oh . . . dear," said the king, and fled the courtyard. Minutes later, the queen's face appeared at a high window. Mirabel, who had been watching for it, waved gaily. The queen turned her back.

The prince glared at himself in the mirror. The spell was definitely wearing off. The wizard insisted he'd simply grown out of it, but the prince felt that having a handsome throat did not make up for having a . . . face. He left a blank there, while staring at the mirror. Face it was, in that it had two eyes and a nose and mouth arranged in more or less the right places. Aside from that, he saw a homely boy with close-set eyes under a sloping brow, a great prow of a nose, buck teeth, and a receding chin, all decorated with splotches of midadolescent acne. And even if he had outgrown the spell, it was still wearing thin—last week his throat had been handsome, but this week his Adam's apple looked like a top on a string. This spell should have been renewed a month ago. If only his father weren't such a cheapskate . . . he had his own spells renewed every three months, and what did he need them for, at his age. Everyone knew the important time of life was now, when you were a young prince desperately trying to find a princess.

She was coming next week. Her parents had visited at Harvest Home; her aunts and uncles had come for Yule. Now, at the Vernal Equinox, she was coming. The beautiful Marilisa—he had seen pictures. She had seen pictures of him, they said: the miniature on ivory done by their own artist. But then the spell had been strong, and so had his chin.

He had to get the spell renewed. His father had said no hurry, but suppose her ship came in early?

"I think we should return to normal for the Equinox," said Bertha. "Think of the dances. The parties. The prince's betrothal . . . the wedding, if we're lucky."

"But that's when the tax is due," Mirabel said.

"Only if we're wearing breast-armor," Sophora pointed out. "We can manage not to fight a war for a week or so, I hope. Just wear civilian clothes. Some of you are pulling castle duty then—I suppose you'll have to stay flat, at least for your duty hours but the rest of us can enjoy ourselves again—"

"Yes," said Kristal. "I like that idea. . . ." She wriggled delicately, and Mirabel gave her a disgusted look. "You would. But . . . after all . . . why not?"

They presented themselves at the wizard's hall. "All of you reversed at once?" he asked. "That will take some time—the reverse operation is a bit slower, especially as I now have so many in . . . er . . . storage. And I do have other appointments. . . ."

"No," Sophora said. "You have us. Look at your contract." And sure enough, there it was, the paragraph she had buried in the midst of formal boilerplate. She read it aloud, just in case he skipped a phrase. "Because that the Welfare of the Warrior is Necessary to the Welfare of the Land and Sovereign, therefore shalt thou at all times and places be Ready and Willing to proceed with this Operation at the Request of the Warrior and such Request shall supersede all Others, be they common or Royal. And to this Essential shalt thou bind thyself at the peril of thy Life at the hands of the Ladies' Aid & Armor Society."

The wizard gulped. "But you see, ladies, my other clients—the ladies of the court, the chancellor's wife—"

Sophora pointed to *be they common or Royal*. "It is your sworn word, wizard, which any court will uphold, especially this court. . . ."

The wizard was halfway through the restorations when the royal summons came. "I can't right now," he told the messenger curtly. He had just discovered that the newly installed random access multidimensional storage device had a bug in it, and for the fifth time in a row, he'd gotten an error message when he tried to retrieve Bertha Broadbelt's breasts. He was swearing and starting to panic every time he glanced at her dark-browed face.

"But it's the king's command," the messenger said.

"I don't care if it's the king's personal spell against body odor," the wizard said. "I can't do it now, and that's final." He pushed the messenger out the door, slammed it, and tried to calm himself. "Sorry about the interruption," he said to Bertha, who seemed to be calmer than he was. Of course, she had the sword.

"That's all right," she said. "Take your time. Nothing's wrong, is it?"

"Nothing at all," said the wizard. He tried again. No error message in the first part of the spell, at least. He felt the little click in his head that meant the transfer had been made, and glanced at Bertha just as she looked down.

And up. He knew his mouth was hanging open, but he couldn't say a word. She could. "These aren't *my* boobs," she said without any expression at all. "These are Gillian's." He wondered how she could recognize someone else's breasts on her chest just as he realized he was having trouble breathing because she had a vast meaty hand around his throat.

The prince hated being in the throne room with his outgrown spell leaving the most visible parts of himself at their worst. But he'd been summoned to wait for the escort that would take him to the wizard for the spell's renewal, so he'd slouched into the room in a long-sleeved hooded jerkin, the hood pulled well forward and the sleeves down over his awkward hands.

"Stand *up*, boy," his father said.

"Don't wear your hood in the house," his mother said.

"He won't do it," the messenger said, bowing his way up the room.

"Won't do it!" King and queen spoke together, glanced at the prince in unison, and then glared at the messenger. The king waved the queen silent and went on alone. "What do you mean, he won't do it. He's our subject."

"He's busy," the messenger said. "That's what he told me. He said even if your majesty's personal body-odor spell—"

"Silence!" bellowed the king. His face had turned very red and he did not glance at the queen. "Guards!" he called. The prince's escort looked up, with interest. "Go arrest us this pesky wizard and bring him here."

The wizard's shop, when the guards arrived, was open and empty but for the usual magical impedimenta and the mysterious black box with a red light that was humming to itself in the key of E-flat minor. A soldier touched it, and it emitted a shrill squeal and changed to humming in the Lydian mode. "Fatal error," said a voice from the emptiness. The soldiers tumbled out of the shop without touching anything else.

"If you're looking for that there plastic wizard," said a toothless old woman on the street, "one of them there lady warriors took him away."

The soldiers looked at each other. Most of them knew where the Ladies' Aid & Armor society met. A few of them had been guests at the Occasional Teas. But no man went there uninvited. Especially not when Sophora Segundiflora was leaning on the doorframe, eyeing them with that lazy smile. They had started off to the meeting hall in step, and come around the corner already beginning to straggle . . . a straggle that became a ragged halt a few yards out of Sophora's reach. They hoped.

"Hi, guys," she said. "Got business with us?"

"Umm," said the sergeant. And then, more coherently, "We heard that plastic wizard might be around here; the king wants him."

"Probably not," Sophora said. "Not now." She glanced suggestively at the door behind her. No sounds leaked through, which was somehow more ominous than shrieks and gurgles would have been.

"Ummm," said the sergeant again. No one had asked his opinion of the new tax code, but he had one. Anything that upset Sophora Segundiflora and Mirabel Stonefist was a bad idea. Still, he didn't want to be the one to tell the king why the wizard wasn't available.

"Anything else?" Sophora asked. She looked entirely too happy for the sergeant's comfort; he had seen her in battle. The sergeant felt his old wounds paining him, all of them, and wished he had retired the year before, when he'd had the chance. Too late now; he'd re-upped for five. That extra hide of land and a cow wouldn't do him much good if Sophora tore him limb from limb. He gulped, and sidled closer, making sure his hands were well away from any of his weapons without being in any of the positions that might signal an unarmed combat assault. There weren't many such positions, and his wrists started aching before he'd gone ten feet.

"Look—can we talk?"

"Sure," said Sophora. "You are, and I am. What else?"

He knew she wasn't stupid. Word had gone around about that correspondence course. She must be practicing her courtroom manner. "It's . . . kind of sensitive," he said.

"Got an itch?" she inquired. "Down two streets and across, Sign of the Mermaid . . ."

"Not that," he muttered. "It's *state* business. The prince—"

"That twerp Nigel?"

"It's not his fault he inherited that face," the sergeant said. It would have been disloyal to say more, but everyone had noticed how the prince took after his uncle, the chancellor. "Not a bad kid, once you know him."

"I'll take your word for it," Sophora said. "So what about the prince?"

"He's . . . that princess is coming this week. For the betrothal, you know."

"I heard."

"He . . . er . . . needs his spells renewed. Or it's all off."

"Why'd the king wait so long?" Sophora asked. She didn't sound really interested.

"The gossip is that he felt it would be good for the prince's character. And he thought with enough willpower maybe the prince could hold on until he was full-grown, when they could do the permanent ones, and a crown at the same time."

"I see. But he needs a temporary before the princess arrives. How unfortunate." Without even looking at him, she reached behind her and opened the door. The sergeant peered into the hall, where the wizard could be seen writhing feebly in Bertha's grip. "We have a prior contract, you see, which he has yet to fulfill. And a complication has arisen."

A slender woman jogged up the street, and came to a panting halt at the door. "Got here as soon as I could—what's up?"

"About time, Gillian," Sophora said. "Bertha's got a problem with our wizard and your—" she stopped and gave the sergeant a loving look that made his neck itch. "Go away, sergeant. I have your message; I will pass it along."

The sergeant backed off a spear length or so, but he didn't go away. If he stayed, he might find out what happened to the wizard. Better to return to the palace with a scrap of the dismembered wizard (if that happened) than with no wizard at all. So he and the others were still hanging around when a grim-faced group of women warriors, some flat-chested in armor and others curvaceous in gowns, emerged from the Ladies' Aid & Armor Society hall.

The sergeant pushed himself off the wall he'd been holding up and tried to stop them. "The king wants the wizard," he said.

"So do we," Sophora said. Her smile made the sergeant flinch, then she scowled—a release of tension. "Oh, well, you might as well come along. We're going to see that the wizard corrects his errors, and you can report to the king."

She led the way back to the wizard's house, and the others surrounded the wizard.

Inside, it still looked like a wizard's house, full of things that made no sense to the sergeant.

"Someone touched this," the wizard said, pointing to the black box.

"How can you tell? And who could've touched it?" Sophora asked. But they all turned to look at the hapless soldiers.

"We were just looking for him," the sergeant said. "He wasn't here ... we were just looking for evidence...."

"FATAL ERROR," said the voice from the air again. Everyone shivered.

"Can't you shut that up?"

"Not now. Not since some hamfisted boneheaded *guardsman* laid his clumsy hands on it." The wizard looked particularly wizardly, eyebrows bristling, hair standing on end ... Mirabel noticed her own hair standing on end, as the wizard reached out his staff and a loud blue SNAP came from the box.

"SYSTEM OVERLOAD," said the voice from the air. "*REALLY* FATAL ERROR THIS TIME."

"Code!" said the wizard.

"A ..." the voice said, slowly.

"B!" said the wizard. "B Code. B code run." Mirabel wondered what that was about, just as a shower of sparkling symbols fell out of the air into the wizard's outstretched palm.

"NO TRACE," said the voice; the wizard stared at his hand as if it meant something.

"I need a dump," the wizard said. Then he muttered something none of them could understand, nonsense syllables, and a piercing shriek came from the black box.

"NOOOOOOOOoooo." Out of the air came a shower of noses, ears, toes, fingers, and a pair of particularly ripe red lips.

"Aha!" said the wizard, and he followed that with

a blast of wizardese that made another black object, not quite so boxy, appear shimmering on the desk. Without looking at any of them, the wizard picked it up and spoke into it. "I want technical support," he said. "Now."

The small demon in the black box enjoyed a profitable arrangement with others on various extradimensional planes. Quantum magery being what it was, wizards didn't really understand it, and that kept the demons happy. Nothing's ever really lost, nothing's wasted, and the transformational geometry operated a lot like any free market. It was a lot easier to snatch extra mammaries than to create them from random matter. Demons are particularly good with probabilities, and it had calculated that it need keep no more than a fifth of its deposits on hand, while lending the rest brought in a tidy interest income.

"And I didn't do nothin' wrong, really I didn't," it wailed at the large scaly paw that held it firmly. Far beneath, eyes glowered, flamelit and dangerous.

"Subcontractors!" the universe growled, and the small demon felt nothing more as it vanished in universal disapproval.

"It's under warranty," the wizard insisted.

"Shipping replacement storage device . . ." the voice said.

"But my data . . ."

"Recovered," the voice said. "Already loaded. Please stay on the line and give your credit card number—sorry, instruction error. Please maintain connection spell and give your secret name—" The wizard leaned over and said something through cupped hands.

With a flicker, the miscellaneous body parts disappeared, and a black box sat humming in the key of A major; its light was green.

"Me first," said Bertha. "I want Gillian's boobs back on Gillian, and mine on me."

"But the prince—" the sergeant said.

"Can wait," said Bertha.

The royal accountant lagged behind the chancellor, wishing someone else had his job. The chancellor had already given his opinion, and the accountant's boxed ears still rang. It wasn't his fault anyway. A contract was a contract; that's how it was written, and he hadn't written it. But he knew if it came to boxing ears, the king wouldn't clout the chancellor. After all, the chancellor was the queen's brother.

"Well—what is it now?" The king sounded grumpy, too—the worst sort of grumpy.

"Sire—there's a problem with the treasury. There's been an overrun in the military medical services sector."

"An overrun? How? We haven't even had a war!" Very grumpy, the king, and the accountant noticed the big bony fists at the ends of his arms. Why had he ever let his uncle talk him into civil service anyway?

"A considerable increase in claims made to the Royal Provider Organization. For plastic wizardry."

The king leaned over to read the details. "Plastic wizardry? Health care?"

"Sire, in the reign of your renowned father, plastic wizardry to repair duty-related injuries was added to the list of allowable charges, and then a lesser amount was allocated for noncombat trauma—"

The king looked up, clearly puzzled. "What's a reversible reduction mammoplasty?" The chancellor explained, in the tone of someone who would always prefer to call a breast a bosom.

"Those women again!" The king swelled up and bellowed. "GUARDS! FETCH ME THOSE WOMEN!" No one, not even the accountant, had to ask which women.

*　　*　　*

"But your majesty, surely you want the women of your realm able to suckle their own children?" Mirabel Stonefist, serene in the possession of her own mammae, and surprisingly graceful in her holiday attire, smiled at the king.

"Well, of course, but—"

"And you do not want to pay extra for women's armor that will protect those vulnerable fountains of motherly devotion, isn't that right?" She had gotten that rather disgusting phrase from a sermon by the queen's own chaplain, who did not approve of women warriors. Rumor had it that he had chosen his pacific profession after an incident with a woman warrior who had rendered his singing voice an octave higher for a month, and threatened to make the change permanent.

"Well, no, but—"

"Then, Sire, I'm afraid you leave us no alternative but to protect both our womanhood, and your realm, by means of wizardry."

"You could always leave the army," said the queen, in a nasty voice.

Mirabel smiled at her. "Your majesty, if the king will look at his general's reports, instead of his paperpushers' accounts, he'll find that the general considers us vital to the realm's protection." She paused just that necessary moment. "As our customized armor is necessary to our protection."

"But this—but it's too expensive! We shall be bankrupt. Who wrote this contract, anyway?"

"Perhaps I can explain," Sophora Segundiflora strode forward. In her dark three-piece robe with its white bib, she looked almost as impressive as in armor. "As loyal subjects of this realm, we certainly had no intention of causing you any distress, Sire. . . ."

The king glared, but did not interrupt. Perhaps he had noticed the size of the rings necessary to fit over her massive knuckles.

"We only want to do our duty, Sire," she said.

"Both for the protection of the realm, and in the gentler duties of maternity. And in fact, had it not been for the tax, we might never have discovered the clear superiority of this method. Even with armor, we had all suffered painful and sometimes dangerous injuries, not to mention the inevitable embarrassment of disrobing in front of male soldiers while on campaign. Now—our precious nurturing ability stays safely hidden away, and we are free to devote our skills to your service, while, when off-duty, we can enjoy our protected attributes without concern for their safety."

"But—how many times do you intend to switch back and forth?"

"Only when necessary." Sophora Segundiflora smiled placidly. "I assure you, we all take our responsibilities seriously, Sire. All of them."

"It was the tax, you say?" the king said. He glanced at the queen. He was remembering her relationship to the chancellor.

"We'd never have thought of it, if you hadn't imposed that tax," Sophora said. "We owe you thanks for that, Sire. Of course, it wouldn't be practical without the military's medical assistance program, but—"

"But it can't go on," the king said. "Didn't you hear me? You're not paying the tax. You're spending all my money on this unnecessary wizardry. You're bankrupting the system. We can't spend it all on you. We have the prince's own plastic wizardry needs, and the expenses of state visits. . . ."

"Well." Sophora looked at Mirabel as if she were uncertain. "I suppose . . . it's not in the contract or anything, but of course we're very sorry about the prince—"

"Get to the point, woman," said the queen. Sophora gave the queen the benefit of her smile, and Mirabel was glad to see the queen turn pale.

"As long as the tax remains in effect, there's simply nothing else we can do," Sophora said, looking past the king's left ear. She took a deep breath that strained the shoulders of her professional robe. "On the other hand, if the tax were rescinded, it's just possible the ladies would agree to return to the less efficient and fundamentally unsafe practice of wearing armor over their . . . er . . . original equipment, as a service to the realm." She smiled even more sweetly, if possible. "But of course, Sire, it's up to you."

"You mean, if I rescind the tax, you'll go back to wearing armor over your own . . . er . . ."

"Bosoms," offered the chancellor. The king glared at him, happy to find someone else to glare at.

"I am quite capable of calling a bosom a breast," he said. "And it was on advice from *your* accounting division that I got into this mess." He turned back to Sophora. "If I rescind the tax, you'll quit having these expensive wizardy reversals?"

"Well, we'll have to put it to a vote, but I expect that our proven loyalty to your majesty will prevail."

"Fine, then," the king said. The queen stirred on her throne, and he glared at her. "Don't say a word," he warned. "I'm not about to lose more money because of any parchment-rolling accountants or Milquetoast chaplains. No more tax on women's armor."

"I shall poll the ladies at once, Sire," said Sophora. "But you need not worry."

"About *that*," growled the king. "But there's still an enormous shortfall. We'll have to find the money somewhere. And soon. The prince must have his spells renewed—"

"Ahem." Sophora glanced over her shoulder, and the wizard stepped forward. "As earnest of our loyalty, Sire, the Ladies' Aid & Armor Society would like to assist with that project." She waved the wizard to the fore.

"Well?" the king asked.

"Sire, my latest researchers have revealed new powers which might be of service. It seems that the laterally-reposed interface of the multidimensional—"

"His new black box came with some free spell-ware," Sophora interrupted before the king's patience shattered.

"Not exactly *free*," said the wizard. "But in essence, yes, new spells. I would be glad to donate the first use to the crown, if it please you."

"Nigel!" the king bellowed. The prince shuffled forward, head hanging. "Here he is, wizard—let's see what you can do."

The small demon in the new black box received the prince's less appetizing morsels with surprising eagerness. In a large multitasking multiplex universe, there's always someone who wants a plague of boils, and a wicked fairy godmother who wants to give some poor infant a receding chin. Available at a reasonable price on the foreign market were a jutting chin, black moustache, and excessive body hair, recently spell-cleared from a princess tormented by just such a wicked fairy. It spit out those requirements, causing a marked change for the better in Prince Nigel's personal appearance. A tidy profit, it thought, and turned its attention to retrieving the final sets of mammary tissue.

The princess in the rose garden was as beautiful as her miniature; Nigel could hardly believe his luck. Her beauty, his handsomeness . . . he kept wanting to finger his new black moustache and eye himself in any reflecting surface. At the moment, that was her limpid gaze.

"I can hardly believe I never met you until this day," the princess said. "There's something about you that seems so familiar. . . ." She reached out a delicate finger to stroke his moustache, and Nigel thought he would swoon.

Across the rose garden, Sophora Segundiflora smiled at the young lovers and nudged Mirabel, whose attention had wandered to her own new nose job.

Mirabel was bored, but Sophora didn't mind chaperoning the young couple. Not with the great gold chain of chancellor across her chest. The previous chancellor had made his last confession the day the wizard tried out his new spells—the other had been a Stretched Scroll, which highlighted certain questionable transactions, such as the withdrawals to the chancellor's personal treasure chest. The fool should have known better. To embezzle all that money, and then choose women warriors as the group to make up the revenues . . . she hoped the wizard had done something to enhance Nigel's wits. Certainly his mother's side of the family hadn't contributed anything.

Meanwhile, the Ladies' Aid & Armor Society would continue to flourish; other older warriors had decided to follow Sophora's example and study law. Girls who hitherto had hung around the queen pretending to embroider were now flocking to weapons demonstrations. Even Kristal had been seen cracking something other than a whip.

After reading this, I will never look at politics or opera in the same way, provided that I can tell them apart.

EXCHANGE PROGRAM

Susan Shwartz

A headache the size of her healthcare plan—no, better make that the size of the national deficit—was turning Hillary Rodham Clinton's skull into the local percussion section. One moment, she and her staff sat reviewing policy notes as the Washington/New York Metroliner rattled along. There'd been some grouching that ice had grounded Air Force One, but the benefit at the Metropolitan Opera couldn't very well be called on account of weather.

Her gown was hanging up, ready for her to put on about the time the train reached Trenton; and her hairdresser was heating the rollers in what was probably another futile attempt to soften her image, if not her chin line. It wasn't as if she *cared*, mind you, but she had enough troubles without adding yet another Media Bad Hair Day to them. So far, so good. But, in the next moment, a *WHAM* that had to have shattered every noise-pollution ordinance in the country and probably every bone in her body jolted the club car off the tracks.

In one horrible moment, she had time to review all the crazies who might want her out of the picture. Someone who probably wasn't Secret Service snatched her up. *If I see Rush Limbaugh's puffy face,*

31

I'll know *I'm in hell.* On that encouraging note, she
blacked out.

"Do you think she needs something to drink?"
Unmistakably, the voice was female, concerned, very
young, and with a lilt in it that reminded her of the
president of Iceland.
"Let her wake up first, why don't you?"
"Why'd you have to bring *her*? You're going to get
us all in trouble again!"
"No one put you in charge, so there!"
"Stop pinching, or—"
"You can't draw that in here!"
Sounds of a scuffle followed. Hillary suppressed an
undignified groan—no one from Marilyn Quayle to
Empress Michiko should see her at a loss, thank you
very much—and opened her eyes in time to get a
face full of water, dribbled onto her by a girl hardly
older than Chelsea.
Thank god it was an opera, not a ballet Hillary had
been scheduled to attend at the Met, or Chelsea, bal-
let-mad, would have pleaded to come along, and Bill
would probably have leaned on her to allow it. Her
eyes filled with relief. At least Chelsea was safe. She
struggled to sit up. Even a whole White House staff
wouldn't be able to keep the worst of the stories of
the accident away from her daughter. Chelsea would
need *her.* Maybe she hadn't been hurt that badly.
"Lie still," said the first voice.
Hillary's vision cleared. Now she would watch the
scuffle—no, the *scrum.* She hadn't seen that many
husky, fair-haired young women . . . very young
women . . . fighting since Wellesley and intramural
field hockey. The undergraduates had worn short,
pleated skirts and hacked violently at a ball with
wooden sticks. These women, just as painfully ener-
getic and noisy, had swords, not hockey sticks. And
what was that thing the youngest girly had on? A
bronze *training* bra?

There might be some dignity in being kidnapped by terrorists, Hillary Rodham Clinton decided. But she was damned if she'd be kidnapped by the Society for Creative Anachronism. She remembered them from Wellesley: even longer hair than hers, a fondness for garish costumes, and not a sensible pre-law major in the bunch.

"Stop that! Can't you see she's awake?"

What had to be the weirdest field hockey team she had ever seen amused itself with a few last shoves and some nervous laughter. Having had Quite Enough of this, Hillary fixed them with the Look she had developed, perfected on her husband those painful years when he tiptoed late into the Governor's Mansion, and used to advantage on Congress. As she expected, they subsided into whispering attention, waiting for her to speak.

She sat up. Thank you very much, she was not about to perpetrate the cliché of "Where am I?" She found her back resting against a pine tree; and wouldn't that just snag hell out of her pink St. John jacket? The countryside reminded her of her visit with Chelsea to the Olympics. How had she gotten from the Washington corridor to Scandinavia?

Horsehooves stomped the snow-covered ground. A gust of wind, laden with salt, made her raise her head. She was near the sea, was she? Not too far away, rocks jutted out into great cliffs. She could not see the water of the sea, or the fjord, or whatever, for the giant rainbow that dominated the horizon.

She remembered the medievalist from Maine in her dorm, senior year. The woman's notion of student activism had stopped at the Children's Crusade, and she read a lot of Tolkien, but she had made junior Phi Bete and could spin a fine yarn when everyone was already giddy from pulling all-nighters. She had even conned Hillary into going to Boston Symphony Hall to hear that improbable woman with a face like

Hillary's own heroine Eleanor Roosevelt and a voice like nothing on earth.

If the fact that the Met was going to put on Wagner—*Das Rheingold,* her itinerary had said—had sunk in, she'd have thought three times about going to this damned benefit. She could just see having to explain this to the FBI. "I'm not making this up, you know!" she'd tell them. That is, if she got the chance; and a terrible chill in her stomach made her realize that she wouldn't.

If place and people reminded her of Scandinavia, her old classmate, and hearing Anna Russell retell the Ring Cycle, these noisy girls had brought her to Valhalla; and that was strictly a one-way ride.

Maybe Bill could win a second term on a sympathy vote. While that was nice, the idea of not getting to see Chelsea grow up hurt worse than the train crash that put her into this mess; and the possibility that he might set some smoking bimbo in her place *really* ticked her off.

Give me a minute, she wished at the seated Valkyries, who looked as if they were in their early teens. *It isn't every day that you wake up dead.*

"Those noisy girls," Anna Russell had described the Valkyries. But they weren't noisy now. They watched her with what she identified as apprehension. Chelsea had looked that way when she'd made her pitch to keep Socks after her dog had been hit by a car, even though Chelsea knew that she and Bill were both allergic. Hillary was a sucker for kids in trouble, and these kids looked as if they'd bought themselves plenty.

How? By rescuing her? She'd be glad to go back; she had policy to push through. But there was no way she wanted to go back if it meant reconstruction in Walter Reed, or a sheet pulled over her face.

Hillary Rodham Clinton stood up, pulling the cloak on which they had placed her up around her shoulders. With the ease of years in public life, she smiled and gave each of them a handshake—firm enough, but careful of her fingers, which had to last the whole campaign.

"I thought your choices had to be strictly single sex," she remarked, to put them off-balance and see how they'd react. As she recalled, Valhalla bore a remarkable resemblance to Dartmouth Winter Carnival.

The girls looked down at their booted feet. One or two fiddled with her weapons. One kicked at the snow.

The soprano chorus erupted again.

"It's happened before," one of them said.

"Brunnhilde . . . she brought in . . ."

"Oh, do you remember how she could *sing?*"

"They could both sing. . . ." The youngest girl was crying.

"She looked nice, that Sieglinde. I liked her."

"She was going to have a baby, and Brunnhilde took pity on her. Even if she was supposed to bring in her brother instead."

"Wasn't he our brother too?"

"Quiet. He'll put you in a ring of fire too if you talk about that!"

"What does it matter, anyhow? It's been years since spring anyway. The hall's crowded, and do you see how Loki grins?"

Hillary almost raised a hand for quiet, but the chorus was winding up dismay loud enough to reach the highest rows of an opera house.

"If Allfather punished Brunnhilde, and she was his favorite . . ."

Hillary couldn't quite remember what happened next. She'd been too busy laughing at Anna Russell's words. But there was nothing funny about the tears in the youngest Valkyrie's eyes.

Hillary put her arms about the girl. Why, for all her primitive militaristic trappings, she was scarcely older than Chelsea.

"It's all right, honey," she said, glad that her time in Arkansas had softened the flatness of her Midwestern birthspeech into something more like comfort. "You just cry it out, you can tell me, I have a daughter, too. Maybe I can help."

The girl gulped and looked up. "Oh, *could* you?"

Hillary removed the child's absurd helmet (at least it didn't have those preposterous phallic horns on it) and smoothed the tumbled blonde hair, even thicker and untidier than Chelsea's after a soccer game.

Bad enough she'd found herself in an eternal version of the Ring, not *Peter Pan*; and she was the last person on Earth (only she wasn't on Earth now, was she?) to play Wendy to a bunch of lost boys. But these were lost girls, and she really rather thought that the Valkyries had saved her in defiance of orders—of unjust, sexist orders—to stand in for Brunnhilde, their exiled sister.

She promised herself that she would do her best. After all, how much harder could the Father of the Norse gods be to deal with than a Republican Congress?

Heimdall wound his horn, and Bifrost glittered as Hillary Rodham Clinton marched into Valhalla. Her borrowed cape trailed behind her, and her Ferragamo pumps squished on the floor. Skillful questioning of her adolescent witnesses and memories of her college classmate had produced more information. Valhalla was a long hall, wrought of wood, its beams intricately carved with beasts gripping and biting each other. Feasting boards running the length of the building were crammed now with hungry blond men. They ate with an appetite that positively made Bill look picky. Despite all the meat they were washing down with ale, they hadn't started to acquire the gut her husband was getting on him, and it didn't seem to hurt their arteries any. Maybe it had something to do with a warrior hero's metabolic level, or you didn't have to worry about cholesterol once you were dead. She had never given the matter much thought, and she didn't think Colin Powell had, either. At least they had stacked their weapons outside. One or two slammed horns down on the board.

"Uh oh," said the oldest remaining Valkyrie. "It was my turn to serve. See you."

"Stay right here, young lady!" commanded the First Lady. Only women were serving, and she was certain that the trays they carried exceeded OSHA weight regulations. Besides, the Valkyries were clearly underage—or, being immortals, were they? She noticed that the men did not harass the girls. That, at least, was something.

Valhalla's central firepit cast its flame up into a kind of atrium (okay, so that was Roman, not Norse, but she was a lawyer, not some SCA weirdo). Nevertheless, the hall still reeked from fatty foods and secondhand smoke.

At the opposite end of the hall from the entrance where she stood, Wotan Allfather, ravens on his shoulders, slumped on his throne. Well, thank goodness, they were ravens, not spotted owls. Still, Hillary wondered if he had a permit to own wildlife. Leaning near him sat a man or god or whatever with red hair. He grinned and winked at her in a way that made Hillary wonder if he'd heard the latest Foster jokes.

Hillary handed her cloak to the youngest Valkyrie and strode forward. With no Chief of Protocol around, she'd have to wing it. She remembered how Jacqueline Kennedy had curtseyed to Prince Philip after JFK's assassination. What was the protocol for greeting gods if you were the wife of a head of state?

Seeing a grown woman who wasn't a Valkyrie and underage and who wasn't a goddess, one of the warriors reached out and made a grab at her. Hillary grabbed up a drinking horn and brought it down firmly on the man's blond head. Pity he had nothing between the ears but testosterone poisoning. He was rather a hunk, otherwise, and she had a definite yen for light-haired men.

"Straighten up, soldier!" she snapped, relishing the unfamiliar speech. "You think you're at Tailhook? This is Valhalla, not the Las Vegas Hilton!"

The man shook his head. Too many blows on the skull, Hillary decided, and too much ale or mead or whatever had made him punchy. She walked toward Allfather, nodded formally, then advanced with her best candidate's-wife smile and handshake. The girls clustered in behind her. How sad that they were afraid of their father. Hillary only wished that she were able to see her own father again, now that she had apparently Crossed Over. She made a tart mental memo to add, in her prayers, that this was hardly her idea of heaven.

"I am Hillary Rodham Clinton, First Lady of the United States of America," she announced.

"Fine. You're not supposed to be here, but grab a pitcher and give the girls a hand," said Loki. "After dinner, we can discuss what to do with you. I've got some ideas." He leered.

The man was worse than Clarence Thomas. Hillary flared her nostrils in disgust.

"Sir, I want to talk to you about your daughters," she said firmly. "The President and I believe that children are our most precious gift. I am very concerned about your daughters' welfare. Where is their mother?"

"Erda?" Under the hat he had not removed in the hall, Wotan focused a bleary eye—he only had the one—upon her. "Oh, here and there. Mostly underground."

"Are you divorced?"

Somehow, Hillary couldn't see Wotan having married an activist. Ever.

She stood and waited to be offered a seat. When no such offer was forthcoming, she waited Wotan out.

"Their mother . . . yes . . . we never quite got

around to making things legal. But I just talked to her before the Fimbulwinter started. More bad news. She always was a downer."

"Is there a stepmother?"

Wotan grimaced. "Not so loud, lady, please! Or we'll have another fight on our hands. Nag nag nag. The goddess's always *right!* I tell you, it's enough to make a god pray for Ragnarok."

Asgard trembled underfoot. Hillary heard the lashing of branches as the World-Ash creaked. *When the bough breaks, the cradle will fall; and down will come Asgard, Wotan and all.*

"I didn't mean it!" Wotan shouted. "Everybody eat, drink, whatever. I didn't mean it!"

The feasting warriors pounded on the boards, waiting for the girls at Hillary's heels to serve them. Hillary turned and shouted at them.

"Gentlemen, you're not homeless, and this isn't a soup kitchen. Help yourselves or take turns serving."

The ravens squawked at her. "Oh, nevermore to you, too," she retorted.

Behind her, a Valkyrie giggled. Wotan merely blinked.

"Siddown, lady," said Wotan. "Loki, get up and give the lady your seat."

"She can sit on my lap."

"Like hell she will," said Wotan. "You want me to call my sister?"

Loki got up fast and disappeared from the hall.

"He's probably going to run straight to the Frost Giants and tell them I'm losing it."

"Foreign policy isn't my strong suit, sir," said the First Lady. "But it might be possible to send Secretary of State Christopher out here—wherever here is—or establish diplomatic relations. Maybe NATO ..."

She was out of her depths, she knew it. However squalid this Allfather was, he was a god, *the* god here, and therefore her only chance to return to her world.

Again, a Valkyrie giggled. Launching itself into the

smoky air, one of the ravens pecked the girl on the face, returned to Wotan's shoulder (his cloak was white with traces of the bird's tenancy), and began to preen its ruffled feathers. The young Valkyrie cried out as much in anger and shock as in pain.

And Hillary lost it. "This is no fit place to bring up innocent girls," she said. "Child labor, an awful environment for their self-esteem, and too much alcohol consumed while their father abuses them and has already driven their eldest sister away."

"That's not all," whispered the youngest Valkyrie. She scratched at the rim of her bronze training bra.

"If I were their mother's lawyer, I'd advise her to sue you for custody."

The raven uttered a shrill cry. Was it Huginn or Muninn, thought or memory—and how had Hillary remembered *that*? Wotan leaned forward, setting down his drinking horn.

"*You're* a lawspeaker? You?"

"Yale Law," said Hillary Rodham Clinton. "I taught at the University of Arkansas. And I was a partner in the Rose Law Firm, Little Rock, Arkansas."

"I can use a good lawspeaker," said the Allfather.

Hillary thought of mentioning her hourly rate, then wondered if the Arkansas Bar had reciprocity with Asgard.

"Girls," Wotan spoke to the Valkyries who had huddled behind Hillary for protection, "I think we can overlook this little oversight on your part. In fact, here!"

From the depths of his dark cloak and garments, he produced rings and bracelets that he tossed, one to each girl. They squealed in gratitude, then oohed and aahed over each other's trinkets.

"You're *buying* those girls' affection!" Hillary accused Wotan. "They need your care, not trinkets!"

"Woman, don't you ever shut up? The last woman with a mouth like yours, I married, and I've been sorry ever since."

Inappropriate words slipped from Hillary's mouth. "Life's a bitch, and then you marry one." She flushed, appalled at herself.

But Wotan roared with appreciation. "Here's to you, lady! You can teach the girls some of your spunk. Oh, they're good enough on a battlefield, but can any of them tell a saga or unlock the wordhoard and produce a well-wrought verse? Not a bit of it."

He detached the gold torque from about his neck and tossed it to her, "Consider this as your retainer."

Hillary caught the torque, hefted it, considered the current price of gold, and set it down. She'd only have to account for it anyhow, and Al D'Amato was enough of a pain as is. Still, she nodded thanks. No point in being rude. Or, she thought, with the beginning of inspiration, ruder. If she couldn't think of a way out of here, she was stuck for good; and judging from Wotan's comments about Frost Giants, an endless winter, and the twilight of the gods, goodness had nothing to do with it.

Wotan toasted her with his drinking horn and motioned one of his daughters to fill one for her. Fastidiously, she sipped.

"Good, isn't it? Ah, it's not the mead of knowledge, but good, strong brown ale. . . ."

An idea blossomed in her head. The Valkyries pressed closely around her, basking in their father's approval and in their success in acquiring Hillary to tend them. Well, they would just have to learn otherwise. She'd bet that this Wotan wouldn't even file his 1099s, let alone the forms that a U.S. citizen with foreign income must file; and she was in enough trouble without being on either side of a Nannygate scam. They seemed like nice enough girls. But she didn't want to be their mother. She wanted to be Chelsea's mother. And Bill's wife. And a policy honcho and a law partner and all the other things that made her the person she hoped to be.

To her horror, her eyes filled. She wanted to be home, or at least at Camp David!

The Valkyries, bright in their new ornaments, took over the job of serving in the hall. One plied her with beef and lamb, with never a bit of broccoli; another filled her drinking horn, and Hillary forebore to ask for mineral water or decaffeinated iced tea.

Temporarily, at least, she was at a standstill. Time to regroup, she thought, and thank goodness she'd sat in on the military briefings that his staff had insisted Bill attend. What a useful, sneaky way of thinking. Almost like being a politician.

"Tell me about your daughters, Wotan," she purred with the smile that had won her applause when, in this very suit, she had testified on Capitol Hill. "They seem like such healthy, pretty girls. One of them's away, you said . . ."

"Brunnhilde." Wotan leaned his chin on his hand. His one eye drooped, but not before Hillary saw the sorrow in it. "She . . . disobeyed me. Brought a woman here, too. But it was a family matter, and we're keeping it in the family."

Hillary decided to table that for the moment.

"Now, you mention that the younger girls cannot write poetry. Considering that you yourself are a poet . . ." no, what was the word? A *skald*. ". . . What arrangements have you made for their education?"

In the days—this being eternity, time was flexible—to come, she pushed Wotan as hard as she could, but Allfather resisted admirably. The Valkyries' stepmother must have more brass about her than her breastplates; most men caved in long before this under the sort of pressure that Hillary could bring to bear. But he agreed that she could spend time with the Valkyries. They grew more and more assertive, laughing when the warriors they had rescued protested at KP. Hillary had to mediate one minor crisis when Rossweise called the goddess of love and beauty

a bimbo—and then defined the word. (Memo to self:
Speak somewhat more discreetly.) Just because Hillary said she looked like Gennifer Flowers, only with
real blonde hair. Egil sneered, wanting to know how
Hillary knew Ms. Flowers was a *real* blonde, so Hillary had to threaten a slander action. She'd had hopes
of that, but Wotan only laughed.

Still, no one would tell her about Brunnhilde. Hillary started to rack her brains. What had happened
to the eldest Valkyrie? Damn, she wished she had
listened to that medievalist her senior year; but who
would have thought Old Norse would have proved
at all relevant? Wotan said something about a family
problem. That could cover a lot of things, including
child abuse—which in this family wouldn't surprise
her one single bit.

The Valkyries coaxed her out of her knitwear into
a gown. Nothing could be done about her hair, and
she hoped to be gone before it grew. *God in heaven,
how long have I been here?* She would wake in the
darkness before Bifrost's glow shone down on Middle
Earth and worry about that. Maybe weeks here were
but the twinkling of an eye back in her world. The
idea made her break into a cold sweat and work even
harder for a way back.

Gradually, she got the Valkyries to exchange their
kirtles and wholly unsuitable metal bustiers for the
homespun equivalent of jeans. Now they looked more
like teenagers than some fascist soccer team. Maybe,
if they worked out a trade agreement (Norway might
have turned down European Economic Union, but
Hillary knew there would turn out to be more reasons
why GATT was a godsend), she'd be able to get the
girls running shoes. Those greaves had to be uncomfortable. She didn't anticipate much trouble on the
trade front: Vikings seemed to have specialized in free
trade, didn't they?

Give her a couple weeks, and she'd present Wotan
with a plan for task forces on the Fimbulwinter.

Weather mapping might give NASA something to do, and Asgard clearly had enough gold to pay for some satellites. That looked hopeful: NASA would drive a hard bargain, but if Wotan sent *her*, she would use what influence she had. . . .

Medicine didn't look hopeful at all as a grounds for getting home. The Swedes had superb socialized medicine, and Hillary rather thought Wotan was a skilled healer himself. Damn.

She anticipated a little more success as the Valkyries grew more and more assertive. Egil, in the apron they insisted he wear to protect his chainmail, made her choke on her ale. To her horror, she realized she was beginning to enjoy its taste. By contrast, Rutger— the hero with the gray eyes, the cheekbones, *and* the buns she had covertly admired—had taken a certain amount of pride in cooking the stag he had slain, then carving it. She rather thought Rossweise had brought him in. Now, the two of them spent a lot of time nudging each other and whispering; and Hillary kept her eyes on both of them. If this went on, she'd have to get the Surgeon General to talk with them. Must be the Asgard air. Exercise had never made Bill look that good.

She had her elbows on the table, leaning over a draft of a plan on how to postpone Ragnarok by means of shuttle diplomacy, reviewing the plan with Wotan, when thunder pealed.

"After all," she told Wotan, "there is simply no reason for Sleipnir just to lounge around on his eight legs eating his fool head off when someone like Heimdall could ride him across Bifrost and talk with the Frost Giants. It's not as if he requires an inordinate amount of fuel, not like Air Force One." (If only she had waited for a flight, rather than taken Amtrak! She wouldn't be here. She'd be home and alive. Better not think of that.)

"Now, I'd suggest," she said, "Heimdall to go speak to the Frost Giants. I take it that Loki . . ."

"He's likelier to betray me, if he hasn't already," said Wotan.

"For Niflheim," she went on, "I'd suggest sending me. I think I could work very effectively with Hela. I gather that she represents a sovereign state?"

In the next moment, Hillary realized how stupid she had been. Hela probably ran a theocracy. Religious zealots: oh joy.

Wotan rubbed beneath his eye patch as if his scar hurt. Then he turned and looked up. His gaze traveled to his daughters, then to Hillary.

At that moment, Heimdall blasted his great horn. At least it wasn't a saxophone. The warriors feasting in the hall set down horns, knives, and flagons, then looked up at Wotan. Was this the summons to mortal combat they had been brought here to await? Where were the Geneva observers? That was what Hillary wanted to know. She had no desire to participate in a Dark Age Bosnia (which, come to think of it, was redundant), and she was damned if she'd let Wotan's daughters fight either. After all, she was pretty sure that the Army still didn't allow women in infantry or cavalry positions, and she didn't think the Valkyries' horses qualified as fighter planes.

A rapid pounding made the doors of the halls shake. Thunder pealed out again, then subsided. As Hillary grew more apprehensive, the warriors grinned. Even Wotan's face brightened, which took considerable doing when you realized that he considered himself and his whole cosmology to be living on borrowed time.

The doors burst open. Wotan's ravens cawed in welcome, and the god himself jumped up, knocking over a bench that a serving woman was entirely too quick to replace. In walked a one-man parade of a man, bigger and blonder than any opera heldentenor would even dream of becoming. The newcomer wore a red silk tunic that would have drawn wolf whistles on Christopher Street, until the whistlers had seen the cold gray eyes above his jolly, just-one-of-the-guys grin. Even as he marched in, he flexed his muscles unconsciously, making Rutger look like a wimp. A huge, phallic-looking hammer hung at his side. Carrying a thing like that on a belt would have pulled anyone else sideways. Thor wore it as easily as Chelsea would have hung a Swiss army knife at her belt, assuming Hillary and Bill would have let her have one, which they wouldn't.

"Thor!" bellowed Wotan. "My son!" Hillary narrowed her eyes at the disgusting display of family favoritism as father and son tried to crack each other's ribs in the most macho hug she'd ever seen, and Thor's sisters scurried to bring him enough food and drink to have fed an entire homeless family for a week. It was positively archaic, especially after she'd shown them better.

To her annoyance, she found that she too had gotten to her feet, drawn, she told herself, by the desire to examine the torque, wristlets, and belt buckle that Thor wore and that were obviously not museum replicas.

He detached his hammer from his belt and laid it on the table.

"I thought they were supposed to stack all weapons except eating knives outside," Hillary allowed herself to be heard to remark.

Thor glared at her. *Oho.* She had seen that before, on the Marine recruiter who had preferred not to answer her questions on the judge advocacy program in the Marine Corps in favor of giving her the bozo treatment, letting his eyes scan her from glasses to heels, then fill with contempt. *What? Do you think I'd actually let a girl into the Corps? Do you think I'd even be civil?*

She'd told the story at a Wellesley reunion, and a classics professor had snickered and said something rude about the Sacred Band of Thebes. As homophobic as the remark was, Hillary's own ox had been gored (oops—better not say that around Tipper, assuming Hillary got lucky enough ever to get back to D.C.) sufficiently that she had snickered back.

Hillary allowed herself to examine Thor the way the Marine Corps recruiter had eyed her. Obviously, she decided, he was a parody of a hero, overcompensating for a lost or distant mother by deeds of heroism and hostility to women.

As Wotan watched him fondly, Thor drained his drinking horn, saw it refilled, then leaned massive elbows on the table.

"What in Niflheim is going on here?" he demanded politely of his father. "I'd been practicing throwing my hammer at the Midgard Serpent when I ran into Loki, who looked as cheerful as if he'd gotten soused on my grave-ale. He laughed and said he didn't *need* to go to Jotunheim to start trouble; you already had more of it here than you could get out of, this side of Ragnarok."

The earth shook at mention of the fatal word. Thor brandished his fist at the offending Middle Earthquake. "Stop that!" he yelled. "It's not Ragnarok until we say it is."

He glared at his father. "I have a mind to try pest control on that Nidhogg. If it keeps on gnawing the World-Ash, that tree's going to die."

"That's the point," Wotan said.

Hillary pursed her lips. As she recollected, wasn't there just *one* Midgard Serpent? Then this overage, hypermasculine juvenile delinquent was persecuting the last member of an endangered species.

Allfather passed a hand over his bearded lips, forestalling her next protest. "Fru Clinton here is attending," he said with suspicious mildness, "to your sisters' education."

"You got those brats a *nanny?*" Thor sounded as if he wanted to spit up all the ale he had already drunk. Hillary braced herself. Alcohol abusers frequently turned to family violence, and this one didn't look as if he needed much encouragement.

"They already know how to ride and choose and fight, if they have to, and to serve at table. What do Valkyries need with more knowledge, unless you give 'em a good hiding so they know how to obey? Look at Brunnhilde. You actually talked to her and taught her to read, and what happened? She started trying to use her judgment—that's a laugh, and wound up asleep on a mountaintop surrounded by fire and waiting for the first hero with the balls to come and claim her."

Hillary suppressed a hiss of pure rage (after listening to Phyllis Schlafly, Randall Terry, Jesse Helms, Orrin Hatch, and the other Neanderthals, you got good at that) because of an exultation that suddenly washed through her, making her feel taller and stronger than Thor.

Buddy boy, she thought, *I think you just gave me my ticket home*.

"You just pass me that gavel, mister," she demanded suddenly. "You're not chairing this meeting. Your father delegated it to me."

She pointed assertively at Thor's hammer. The girls watched, eyes round, appalled, but somehow hopeful.

"Now!"

He passed it over, so reluctant to have her touch it that you'd have thought it was Lorena Bobbitt's knife—or what it cut.

Wotan shrugged his shoulders. "She's good with the girls," he admitted. "They like her."

Hillary leaned forward, planting small fists on either side of Thor's hammer. "You bet they like me. I'm the only one around here who listens to them. Maybe you can tell me what happened to their oldest sister. *They* just cry. You didn't even let them grieve."

Thor glared at Hillary. "Gods don't grieve," he said.

Hillary glared back. "Tell it to the Marines," she suggested.

"Ask *him*," he grunted.

"*Him* is hardly a polite way to refer to your father and Allfather, I believe he's called," she informed him. "The girls ... I mean, your sisters ... told me that Brunnhilde was your father's favorite. Never quite forgiven her for that, have you? And that she disobeyed him and brought a woman into Valhalla. So what? *I'm* here, aren't I?" *And I wish I were home!* Dammit, if she kept that lament up, she was going to sound like E.T.

"It wasn't just any woman, woman," Thor snarled. "It was *Sieglinde.*"

Hillary waited him out. "I wouldn't know Sieglinde from Jessye Norman," she told him. Since she knew very little about Jessye Norman and Thor knew nothing at all, the score in this particular game of one-upmanship was tied.

"She ran away from her husband Hunding. Honestly, I don't know what Middle Earth's coming to," Thor grumbled.

"Did Hunding abuse her? If he did, I think your sisters did a very brave thing in giving her refuge." Hillary might not know how to embroider, but she certainly knew how to needle.

"You just don't get it, do you, woman? She ran off with her own brother Siegmund Walse's son, whom she hadn't seen for years. Hunding followed them and killed him. Very properly."

"That poor woman. And you stood for this?" She flashed a Look at Wotan with both eyes, and he deflected it with his one. Then, to her astonishment, he looked down, ashamed and saddened.

"My wife insisted. Uh ..."

Hillary hadn't led her class at Wellesley for nothing. "Ah," she said. "You go in for a spot of wandering around among mortals from time to time, do you? And maybe under an assumed name like Walse? In the name of god, Wotan, how could you allow your children to suffer like that?"

"It gets worse," Rossweise put in from the dubious shelter of Rutger's arm. "Sieglinde was going to have a baby."

"You get away from him!" Thor bellowed. "Just because your sister's lying out on the hill for the first comer—" Hillary managed not to laugh in a way that might have distracted him "—doesn't mean you're not still a virgin goddess. Does it, missy?" He strode over to the Valkyrie and her chosen hero. The two of them, standing together, were enough to face up to him. Barely.

Adultery, two generations of it. Incest. Murder. This wasn't an afterlife, Hillary decided, it was a Scandinavian soap opera! And it had just gotten Worse: Brunnhilde abandoned on a hill until some rapist in chainmail decided to step through a fire and grab her; Rossweise and all the others forbidden education, autonomy, control even of their own bodies, just because some *men* decided for them what they should do about them.

"This didn't have to happen," she said with a tone that even to herself sounded nauseatingly self-righteous, "if you had decent birth-control centers for women to go to.

"*You!*" she flared up at Wotan. "You stuck your eldest daughter on a rock because she disobeyed you to protect her own half-sister. You're keeping these poor girls ignorant, violent, and noisy. You encouraged your son to become an arrogant, bullying brute, and you even feast with a man you know is going to betray you. Call yourself a god, let alone the father of the gods here. You're a poor excuse for it. I've got a good mind to start Ragnarok just to give this place a good cleaning."

Where, oh where, was Newt Gingrich when she needed him? Let him get his teeth into a scandal like this, and he'd never have time for the White House.

"Woman, you go too far!" Thor bellowed.

"I haven't gone far enough!" Hillary shouted back. "Now, you're out of order."

Whereupon she picked up the hammer and brought it down sharply on the table for order. That is, she would have brought it down sharply on the table if the thing hadn't been so heavy it weighed her shoulder down and she dropped it.

Boom! The earthquakes that accompanied each mention of Ragnarok were nothing to the crashes that followed as the hammer broke the table, broke through the floor, and probably the sound barrier, as it emerged outside the hall. Thunder pealed again, and from the rain and lightning that lashed down outside, you'd have thought Hurricane Andrew had come again. Most likely, a couple branches broke loose from the World-Ash.

Do you suppose Wotan budgeted enough for disaster relief? I'm sorry! *But all I want to do is get out of here.*

Thor whistled and raised his hand. The hammer flew back to him, and he brandished it at her.

But Hillary was drunk on adrenaline. "Go ahead," she challenged him. "Make my day."

To her astonishment, she heard footsteps, felt the support of the Valkyries at her back. Post-feminism be damned, she thought. Sisterhood *was* powerful.

"I told you before," she said to Wotan, "you have *fine* daughters, and you don't deserve to have custody of them."

"Enough!" Thor roared. "You get her out of here, Allfather, or so help me, when Naglfar sets sail and Ragnarok begins, you're going to be fighting without your chief of staff."

Unmistakably, Wotan's eye closed at Hillary in a wink. She thought of her own father, of his pride in her. She thought of how she and Bill went rushing to Chelsea's defense in anything from a gang of reporters tormenting Socks to *Saturday Night Live* making jokes about her. And here was Wotan, facing up to his own mistakes as he faced up to the end of his world. It was too late for Brunnhilde, just as it had been too late for Sieglinde and probably a host of other women he had lost. But these girls might yet have their chance.

"Are you going to let your generals boss around the commander in chief?" Hillary demanded. "Truman fired MacArthur when he tried that."

"Get her *out* of here! Out! Out!"

"He sounds like the Fenris-wolf, yelping," whispered Rossweise. She giggled. Thor turned the red of imminent apoplexy.

Wotan stood up. He swirled his cloak back from shoulders that, despite his age, were still massive. Unerringly, he reached behind him for his spear and banged upon the floor for attention and order. The ravens mantled, then subsided.

"Where shall I send her?" Wotan asked his son. "The girls brought her here, and you know what that means."

"Send her to Niflheim for all I care."

"You know I can't do that to Hela, son. And have you thought what might happen if the two of them liked each other?"

"Then send her *back*."

"You know that breaks the pattern. And anything that breaks the pattern . . ."

". . . brings Twilight closer."

The fires sank in the central firepit of Valhalla. Outside, the light seemed to diminish as if the Twilight of the Gods advanced like sunset in December. A wind blew about the great hall's eaves, picking up volume until it rose into a howl.

"That's right," said Wotan. "If I send her back, it brings . . . *it* just so much closer. I'll need my best warriors with me then. In that case, are you with me, or are you going to go off again and sulk?"

"Get her out of here," Thor pleaded, "and I'll do anything you say."

"Your daughters too." Well, she and Bill had always
wanted more than one child. Hillary caught Wotan's
eye and held it. *Their last chance, old man. For once
in your life, make the right choice. In the name of
God.*

"Well, girls?" Thor raised his hands in holy horror
as Wotan actually asked the Valkyries their opinion.

"Get them *all* out of here!" he wailed.

"I'll make sure someone grooms the horses," Wotan
promised his daughters. Then he banged his spear
thrice upon the floor of Valhalla.

Smoke swirled up, then clouds, then more smoke.

And before Hillary or the Valkyries could sing "hoi-
otoho" (which Hillary couldn't, not even on her good-
voice days), she found herself lying beside a buckled
railroad track somewhere between Wilmington and
Philadelphia.

She had the mother of all headaches, especially
with those ambulances shrieking like the winds of
Ragnarok in her ears. But her heart sang, even if she
couldn't. She had survived. She had made it back
home. She'd be able to hug Chelsea again. She would
even pet Socks, no matter if he made her sneeze
or not.

Secret Service and aides clustered about her, barely
letting the doctors through.

"There are others in the train," Hillary murmured.
"Young, innocent girls." And a tear that Peggy Noo-
nan would have envied slid down her face. Someone
raced down the track and into a car, then emerged
to shout in a voice that that wretched Thor would
have envied, that the Scandinavian tourist group was
just fine, and so was everyone else.

She thought, before she allowed herself to yield to
the painkiller, that that made even better news than
"I, William Jefferson Clinton, do solemnly swear . . ."

Hillary never did get to hear *Das Rheingold.* She
had talked under influence of the painkillers, and her

near-death experience and some truly godawful photographs filled the tabloids and prompted a whole rash of "I saw an angel" stories. It even had the Christian Coalition inviting her to testify at prayer breakfasts. The White House had to hire more staff just to handle the cards and letters; and bulletin board service providers suffered temporary crashes as people started flame wars about what *really* happened.

Here is what is known for certain. The picture of the First Lady, bravely leaning on an aide's shoulder and asking about the health of the Norwegian exchange students as a doctor tended to her chased all other pictures from page one of the leading papers. Even the *Washington Times* carried a human interest story dealing with how often she visited the students, how she invited them to the White House to meet her daughter, and how she made herself responsible for their education.

Here is what else is known for pretty certain. The soccer and field hockey coaches at Sidwell Friends and Wellesley College are ecstatic, and the First Lady's approval ratings have never been higher.

the end

This story is for Trent Telenko, who has only himself to blame for giving me the idea of writing it.

This really happened. No, honestly, it did. Well, most of it. You could look it up.

GODDESS FOR A DAY

Harry Turtledove

The driver held the horses to a trot hardly faster than a walk. Even so, the chariot jounced and pitched and swayed as it rattled down the rutted dirt track from the country village of Paiania to Athens.

Every time a wheel jolted over a rock, Phye feared she'd be pitched out on her head. She couldn't grab for the rail of the car, not with a hoplite's spear in one hand and a heavy round shield on the other arm. The shield still had the olive-oil smell of fresh paint. Before they'd given it to her, they'd painted Athena's owl over whatever design it had borne before.

Another rock, another jolt. She staggered again. Peisistratos, who rode in the car with her, steadied her so she didn't fall. She was almost big enough to make two of the *tyrannos*, but he was agile and she wasn't. "It will be all right, dear," he said, grinning at her like a clever monkey. "Just look divine."

She struck the pose in which he'd coached her: back straight so she looked even taller than she was (the Corinthian helmet she wore, with the red-dyed horsehair plume nodding above it, added to the effect), right arm out straight with the spear grounded on the floorboards of the chariot (like an old man's stick, it helped her keep her balance, but not enough), shield held in tight against her breast (that took some

55

of the weight off her poor arm—but, again, not enough). She stared straight ahead, chin held high.

"It's all so *uncomfortable*," she said.

Peisistratos and the driver both laughed. They'd really fought in hoplite's panoply, not just worn it on what was essentially a parade. They knew what it was like.

But they didn't know everything there was to know. The bell corselet they'd put on Phye gleamed; they'd polished the bronze till you could use it for a mirror. That corselet would have been small for a man her size. Mashed against hard, unyielding metal, her breasts ached worse than they did just before her courses started. The shield she carried might have been made of lead, not wood and bronze. One of her greaves had rubbed a raw spot on the side of her leg. And of course she stared straight ahead; the cheekpieces and noseguard on the helmet gave her no other choice. The helm was heavy, too. Her neck ached.

She itched everywhere.

A couple of people—a man with a graying beard and a younger woman who might have been his daughter or his wife—stood by the side of the track, staring at the oncoming chariot. Phye envied them their cool, simple mantles and cloaks. A river of sweat was pouring down her face.

Peisistratos waved to the couple. He tapped Phye on the back. They couldn't see that. She couldn't feel it, either, but she heard his nails rasp on the corselet. "The gods love Peisistratos!" she cried in a loud voice. "The gods ordain that he should rule once more in Athens!"

"There! You see?" the man said, pointing at Phye. "It *is* Athena, just as those fellows who went by the other day said it would be."

"Why, maybe it *is*." The woman tossed her head to show she thought he was right. "Isn't that something?" She raised her voice as the chariot clattered by: "Hurrah for Peisistratos! Good old Peisistratos!"

"It's going to work," the driver said without looking over his shoulder.

"Of course it will." Peisistratos was all but capering with glee. "We have ourselves such a fine and lovely goddess here." He patted Phye on a bared thigh, between the top of her greave and the bottom of the linen tunic she wore under the corselet.

She almost smashed him in the face with her shield. Exposing her legs to the eyes of men felt shockingly immodest. Having that flesh out there to be pawed showed her why women commonly covered it.

She didn't think she'd given any sign of what was passing through her mind, but Peisistratos somehow sensed it. He was no fool: very much the reverse. "I crave pardon," he said, and sounded as if he meant it. "I paid your father a pound of silver for you to be Athena, not a whore. I shall remember."

The village lads made apologies, too, and then tried to feel her up again whenever they got the chance. After that once, Peisistratos kept his hands to himself. Whenever the chariot passed anyone on the road—which happened more and more often now, for they were getting close to Athens—Phye shouted out the gods' love for the returning *tyrannos*.

Some of those people fell in behind the chariot and started heading into Athens themselves. They yelled Peisistratos' name. "Pallas Athena, defender of cities!" one of them called out, a tagline from the Homeric hymn to the goddess. Several others took up the call.

Phye had not thought she could get any warmer than she already was under helm and corselet and greaves. Now she discovered she was wrong. These people really believed she was Athena. And why not? Had she been walking along the track instead of up in the chariot, she would have believed it was truly the goddess, too. To everyone in Paiania, the Olympians and other deities were as real and close as their next-door neighbors. Her brother, for instance, swore he'd seen a satyr in the woods not far from home, and why would he lie?

But not to Peisistratos and his driver. They joked back and forth about how they were tricking the— *unsophisticated* was the word Peisistratos used, but Phye had never heard it before, and so it meant nothing to her—folk of the countryside and of the city as well. As far as they were concerned, the gods were levers with which to move people in their direction.

That attitude frightened Phye. More and more, she wished her father had not accepted Peisistratos' leather sack full of shiny drachmai, even if that pound of silver would feed the whole family for a year, maybe two, no matter how badly the grapes and olives came in. Peisistratos and his friend might imagine the gods were impotent, but Phye knew better.

When they noticed what she was doing, what would *they* do—to her?

She didn't have much time to think about that, for which she was grateful. The walls of Athens drew near. More and more people fell in behind the chariot. She was shouting out the gods' will—or rather, what Peisistratos said was the gods' will—so often, she grew hoarse.

The guards at the gate bowed low as the chariot rolled into the city. Was that respect for the goddess or respect for the returning *tyrannos*? Phye couldn't tell. She wondered if the guards were sure themselves.

Now the road went up to the akropolis through hundreds upon hundreds of houses and shops. Phye didn't often come in to Athens: when you used a third of the day or more walking forth and back between your village and the city, how often could you afford to do that? The sheer profusion of buildings awed her. So did the city stink, a rich, thick mixture of dung and sweat and animals and stale olive oil.

"Athena! Pallas Athena!" the city people shouted. They were as ready to believe Phye was the goddess as the farmers outside the walls had been. "Pallas Athena for Peisistratos!" someone yelled, and in a moment the whole crowd took up the cry. It echoed and reechoed between the whitewashed housefronts that pressed the rutted road tight on either side, until Phye's head ached.

"They love you," the driver said over his shoulder to Peisistratos.

"That sound—a thousand people screaming your name—that's the sweetest thing in the world," the *tyrannos* answered. "Sweeter than Chian wine, sweeter than a pretty boy's *prokton*, sweeter than anything." Of the gods, he'd spoken lightly, slightly. Now his words came from the heart.

Men with clubs, men with spears, a few men with full hoplite's panoply like that which Phye wore, fell in before the chariot and led it up toward the heart of the city. "Just like you planned it," the driver said in admiration. Peisistratos preened like a tame jackdaw on a perch.

Phye stared up toward the great buildings of wood and limestone, even a few of hard marble, difficult to work, that crowned the akropolis. They were hardly a stone's throw from the flatland atop the citadel when a man cried out in a great voice: "Rejoice, Peisistratos! Lykourgos has fled, Megakles offers you his daughter in marriage. Athens is yours once more. Rejoice!"

The driver whooped. Unobtrusively, Peisistratos tapped Phye on the corselet. "Athens shows Peisistratos honor!" she called to the crowd. "Him Athena also delights to honor. The goddess brings him home to his own akropolis!"

At the man's news and at her words, the cheering doubled and then doubled again. From under the rim of her helmet, she looked nervously up toward the heavens. Surely such a racket would draw the notice of the gods. She hoped they'd note she'd spoken of Athena in the third person and hadn't claimed to be the goddess herself.

Past the gray stone bulk of the Hekatompedon, the temple with a front a hundred feet long, rattled the chariot. At Peisistratos' quiet order, the driver swung left, toward the olive tree sacred to Athena. "I'll tell the people from the rock under that tree," the *tyrannos* said. "Seems fitting enough, eh?"

"Right you are." The driver reined in just behind that boulder. The horses stood breathing hard.

Peisistratos hopped down from the chariot. He *was* nimble, even if no longer young. To Phye, he said, "Present me one last time, my dear, and then you're done. We'll put you up in the shrine for the night"— he used his chin to point to the plain little wooden temple, dedicated to both Athena and Poseidon, standing behind the olive tree—"get you proper woman's clothes, and send you back to Paiania in the morning." He chuckled. "It'll be by oxcart, I fear, not by chariot."

"That's all right," Phye said, and got down herself. She was tempted to fall deliberately, to show the crowd she was no goddess. But she had taken on the outer attributes of Athena, and could not bring herself to let the goddess fall into disrepute from anything she did. As gracefully as she could, she stepped onto the rock.

"See gray-eyed Athena!" someone exclaimed. Phye's eyes were brown. The Corinthian helm so shadowed them, though, that people saw what they wanted to see. Thinking that, she suddenly understood how Peisistratos had been so sure his scheme would work. She also discovered why he spoke of an adoring crowd as sweeter than wine. Excitement flowed through her as the crowd quieted to hear what she would say. She forgot the squeeze and pinch of armor, the weight of the shield, everything but the sea of expectant faces in front of her.

"Athena delights in honoring Peisistratos!" she cried in a voice so huge it hardly seemed her own.

"Let Athens delight in honoring Peisistratos. People of Athens, I give you—Peisistratos!"

She still had not said she was Athena, but she'd come closer, far closer, than she'd intended. She got down from the boulder. The *tyrannos* hopped up onto it. Most of the roar that rose from throats uncounted was for him, but some, she thought, belonged to her.

He must have thought so, too. He leaned down and murmured, "Thank you, O best of women. That was wonderfully done." Then he straightened and began to speak to the crowd. The late-afternoon sun gleamed from his white mantle—and from the crown of his head, which was going bald.

Phye withdrew into the temple and set down her spear and shield with a sigh of relief. She was out of sight of the people, who hung on Peisistratos' every word. She did not blame them. If he accomplished half, or even a fourth part, of what he promised, he would make Athens a better substitute for Zeus than Phye just had for Athena.

He must have memorized his speech long before he returned to the akropolis. It came out as confidently as if he were a rhapsode chanting Homer's verses. He made the people laugh and cheer and cry out in anger—when he wished, as he wished. Most of all, he made them love him.

Just as the sun was setting, Peisistratos said, "Now go forth, O men of Athens, and celebrate what we have done here today. Let there be wine, let there be music, let there be good cheer! And tomorrow, come the dawn, we shall go on about the business of making our city great."

A last cheer rang out, maybe louder than all those that had come before. The Athenians streamed away from the akropolis. Here and there, torches crackled into life; when night fell, it fell sudden and hard. Someone strummed a lyre. Someone else thumped a drum. Snatches of song filled the air.

Phye waited in the temple for someone to bring

her a woman's long mantle. She wanted to go forth,
not to revel but back to her quiet home in Paiania,
and could hardly do that in the panoply of the goddess. Peisistratos had promised one of his men would
take care of her needs. She waited and waited, but
the man, whoever he was, did not come. Maybe he'd
already found wine and music and good cheer, and
forgotten all about her.

The akropolis grew quiet, still—deserted. Down
below, in the agora, in the wineshops, people did
indeed celebrate the return of Peisistratos: no *tyrannos* had ever given a command easier to obey. The
noise of the festivity came up to Phye as the smoke
of a sacrifice rose to the gods. Like the gods, she got
the immaterial essence, but not the meat itself.

She muttered under her breath. Tomorrow, surely,
they'd remember her here. If she spoke to Peisistratos, she could bring trouble down on the head of
whichever henchman had failed her. She sighed. She
didn't care about that. All she wanted was to go home.

Her head came up. Someone up here on the akropolis was playing a double flute—and coming closer
to the temple where she sheltered. Maybe she hadn't
been forgotten after all. Maybe Peisistratos' man had
just paused for a quick taste of revelry before he took
care of her. She wondered whether she should thank
him for coming at all or bawl him out for being late.

He played the flutes very well. Listening to the
sweet notes flood forth, Phye marveled that she didn't
hear a whole band of men—and loose women, too—
following, singing to his tune and stomping out the
rhythms of the *kordax* or some other lascivious dance.

As far as her ears could tell, the fluteplayer was
alone. Cautiously, she stepped forward and peered
out through the entryway to the temple, past the
sacred olive and the boulder on which she and then
Peisistratos had spoken. She remained deep in
shadow. Whoever was out there would not be able to
spy her, while she—

She gasped, gaped, rubbed at her eyes, and at last believed. Daintily picking his way toward her, his hooves kicking up tiny spurts of dust that glowed white in the moonlight before settling, was a satyr.

No wonder he plays the flutes so well, Phye thought dizzily. He looked very much as her brother had described the satyr he saw, as the vase-painters showed the creatures on their pots: horse's hind legs and tail; snub-nosed, pointed-eared, not quite human features; phallos so large and rampantly erect, she wanted to giggle. But neither her brother's words nor the vase-painters' images had come close to showing her his grace, his strange beauty. Seen in the flesh, he wasn't simply something made up of parts of people and animals. He was himself, and perfect of his kind.

He lowered the double flute from his mouth. His eyes glowed in the moonlight, as a wolf's might have. "Gray-eyed Athena?" he called, his voice a slow music. Phye took a step back. Could he see her in here after all? He could. He did. He laughed. "I know you are in your house, gray-eyed Athena. Do you not remember Marsyas? You gave me the gift of your flutes." He brought them to his lips once more and blew sweetness into the night air.

"Go away," Phye whispered.

No man could have heard that tiny trickle of sound. Marsyas did, and laughed again. "You gave me a gift," he repeated. "Now I shall give you one in return." Altogether without shame, he stroked himself. He had been large. He got larger, and larger still.

Phye groped for the spear and shield she had set aside. The shield she found at once, but the spear—where was the spear? She had leaned it against the wall, and—

She had no time to search now. Past the boulder Marsyas came, past the sacred olive tree, up to the threshold of the shrine. There he paused for a moment, to set down the flutes. Phye dared hope the power of the goddess would hold him away. Athena was a maiden, after all, as Phye was herself. Surely Athena's home on earth would be proof against—

Marsyas stepped over the threshold. "Goddess, goddess," he crooned, as easily befooled as any Athenian, "loose yourself from that cold hard bronze and lie with me. What I have is hard, too, but never cold." He touched himself again and, incredibly, swelled still more.

"Go away," Phye said, louder this time. "I do not want you." Would Athena let a woman, a virgin, be raped on the floor of her temple? *Why not?* a cold voice inside Phye asked. *What better punishment for a woman who dared assume the person of the goddess?*

And the satyr Marsyas said, "But I want you, gray-eyed Athena," and strode toward her.

Almost, Phye cried out that she was not the goddess. She would have cried out, had she thought it would do any good. But, to a satyr, female flesh would be female flesh. Even in the deep darkness inside the temple, his eyes glowed now. He reached out to clasp her in his arms.

She shouted and interposed the shield between them. If he wanted her maidenhead, he would have to take it from her. She would not tamely give it to him. All right: for Peisistratos' sake, she had pretended to be Athena. Now she would do it for herself. She'd have to do it for herself. Plainly, the goddess was not about to do it for her.

Marsyas shoved aside the shield. Phye's shoulder groaned; the satyr was stronger than a man. Marsyas laughed. "What have you got under that armor?" he said. "I know. Oh yes, I know." Like an outthrust spear, his phallos tapped at the front of her corselet.

"I do not want you!" Phye cried again, and brought up her leg, as hard as she could.

In her grandfather's time, greaves had covered only a hoplite's calves. These days, smiths made them so bronze protected the knee as well. She was a big woman—Peisistratos would never have chosen her had she been small—she was frightened, and, if not so strong as a satyr, she was far from weak.

Her armored kneecap caught Marsyas square in the crotch.

Just for an instant, his eyes flamed bright as a grass fire seen by night. Then, all at once, the fire was quenched. He screamed and wailed and doubled over, clutching at his wounded parts. His phallos deflated like a pricked pig's bladder.

"Go!" Phye said. "Never think to profane Athena's temple again." When the satyr, still in anguish, turned to obey, she kicked him, right at the root of his horse's tail. He wailed again, and fled out into the night.

That was well done.

Phye's head swiveled round. Had the thought been her own, or had it quietly come from outside her? How could it have? She was all alone, here in Athena's temple. But if you were alone in the house of the goddess, were you truly alone?

Peisistratos would think so.

"Thank you," Phye whispered. She got no response, real or imagined. She hadn't expected one.

A little while later, a man bearing a torch in one hand and carrying a bundle under his other arm came up onto the akropolis. He lurched as he walked, as a man with a good deal of wine in him might do. Almost like a windblown leaf, he made his erratic way toward the temple where Phye waited.

"Lady?" he called—he could not be bothered remembering Phye's name. "I've got your proper clothes here." He jerked the bundle up and down to show what he meant. "I'm sorry I'm late but—*hic!*" To him, that seemed to say everything that needed saying. "Here, what's this?" Just outside the temple, he bent and picked up the double flutes Marsyas had forgotten in his flight. "Are these yours, lady?"

"They are Athena's," Phye answered. "Close enough."

Need I say that this is *not* your ordinary fairy tale?

ARMOR-ELLA

Holly Lisle

Once upon a time—
Which is to say there are still living descendants,
so we can't name names.
There was a beautiful young girl—
Six feet tall, twelve stone, with shoulders like a
blacksmith's from swinging a two-handed sword for
hours on end—but beautiful. Really beautiful. Call
her El.
Who fell in love with a handsome prince.
An avaricious, land-grabbing, double-crossing,
sneaky young prince; but he looked like a male model,
and he had a lot of land—most of it recently acquired
by treacherous means—and a whole lot of money. You
may call him Charming if you like. No one else did.
And the bit about the glass slipper was pure fiction.

The prince decided the house he'd found was perfect. He'd been riding for hours, looking for just such
a property, and he was delighted his journey was over.
The house he'd discovered was half hidden in the
Enchanted Forest, facing onto a flower-filled, sun-
speckled glade; its cut-stone walls were covered with
ivy and its well sat out in front at the end of a charm-
ingly landscaped little path.
Solid construction, he thought. The miniature ramparts
atop the stone walls came complete with miniature

crenellations—too small for bowmen to hide behind,
but they added a nice touch. Arrow slits decorated
the second floor—they were glassed over, though, so
no one could actually shoot out of them. The machico-
lations above the main doorway looked real, however—as though someone inside might consider
pouring boiling oil onto the proselytizers and door-to-
door salesmen who came calling. He approved. The
place was definitely a concept house. He would bet
the builders had pitched it to the family by saying,
"Think castle. Your own little castle."

A battering ram would go through it in an instant,
of course; it wasn't a *real* castle. But it would be a
grand location for intimate little parties, it would serve
as a strategic garrison for some of his troops in the
event of activity in the area . . . and it would extend
his territory about fifteen leagues directly south into
what was currently Queen Hilde's kingdom.

Location, location, and location—the real selling
points when acquiring property.

He turned to his aide. "We'll use the usual story.
Go up, see who lives there, and let's find out how
difficult they're going to be to get rid of."

"Somebody get the door!" El's stepmother had
incredible lungs.

El, busy sharpening her sword, didn't even look up
from her whetstone.

However— "I'm doing something," Carol shouted,
and a beat behind her, Martha yelled, "El's downstairs! El, get the door!"

The doorbell clanged again.

El rolled her eyes and put down her blade and
went to see who was there.

She found a lean, whippet-faced man with mourn-
ful eyes waiting on the front step, cap in hand. "Your
prince requires your assistance, madam. Our hounds
chased a stag while we were hunting, and became lost

in the woods. We have been searching for them for days, without luck. Have you seen or heard them?"

She looked down at the man—his eyes didn't meet hers when he spoke, and she disliked the way he twisted his cap; also, she didn't think he looked dirty or tired enough to have been hunting lost hounds for days. He was lying about the hounds—she'd bet on it. She glanced across the yard to where the prince waited on his fine white steed. The horse looked like he'd been freshly bleached and starched; for that matter, so did the prince.

Worse—although she didn't follow politics closely, she'd had a queen, not a prince, the last time she heard. She doubted that had changed without anyone mentioning it—she also doubted that the flunky's identification of the prince as *her* prince had been in innocent error.

Hunting their dogs, she thought. Of course they are. But she smiled at the man on her doorstep, walked past him out into the yard, and curtsied to the prince.

She clasped her hands and tried to look shy. The prince was gorgeous, and gorgeous men didn't make it into El's stretch of woods often. Not even gorgeous slime. She figured she was probably doing a pretty good imitation of a bashful, blushing maiden. "I did hear hounds, your majesty," she told him, "only last night. But I mistook them for the Hell Hounds that so often hunt these woods after dark."

She glanced away long enough to let him consider the import of her words, then glanced up to see how he was taking her news. She noted that he had paled. His gaze flicked nervously to the sun, which had passed its halfway point earlier and was steadily creeping down the sky. "Hell Hounds?"

El ducked her head to hide her smile. "Certainly you know of them, my lord. This is the forest of the Folk. Even during the day it is a tricky place, but at night, I would never ride through it. Besides the

Hounds, there are also bogles who hunt in the darkness, and the fey folk that try to lead riders astray. Those who wander into the forest at night are rarely heard from again."

The prince looked down at her, then over her shoulder toward his toady, then back to El. "Well," he said thoughtfully. "How interesting. Do you have a spare room where we could spend the night?"

"Alas, sir," she lied, "it would compromise our honor when my brothers returned home from hunting, if they were to find strange men in the house with their women. Worse, when they come back we will have no room to stable your horses—and left outside, I fear the bogles would eat them before morning."

His face fell at the mention of brothers, and further at the mention of bogles. "Bogles, eh? Could you describe these bogles for me."

Ella thought fast. "Of course, your lordship. Well, none who see them live, of course. Still, they followed me through the forest once, so I can tell you how to recognize their sign. When first they notice you, you'll feel them watching. You'll see nothing, no matter how you look around for them, but you'll know they are there. Next will come the sound of rustling leaves, though you will feel no wind. You'll see tree branches sway, and know they have begun to stalk you. As they get closer, you'll hear whispering, though you won't be able to make out words—bogles are mad, and talk to themselves. And when they prepare for the final lunge, all the animals near you in the forest will fall silent." El shivered. "*No* one can tell what happens after that."

The prince's nostrils pinched in and his lips thinned to a hard line. "I see." He studied her, and she saw curiosity and some darker emotion warring on his face. "How, then, do *you* live here, fair maid?"

El made her face woeful, and hung her head. "My

father made a pact with the lord of these woods that his family could live here in safety."

"A pact, hey?" The prince's face brightened. "Maybe I could make a pact with this lord."

El nodded. "Perhaps, though I think you would not want to. My father's pact was to exchange our safety for his life."

El listened until she could no longer hear the receding thudding of horses' hooves—then she turned away from the well to go back into the house. The danger—and she had no doubt but that it had been a danger—was gone.

Something giggled softly nearby, then said, "I liked the way you described bogles. Very frightening. The prince didn't quite believe you, though, you know." The voice was high-pitched and raspy.

El moved back to the well and said, "Who's there? Who said that?"

The chuckle again. "When he left, he said to his flunky, 'We'll check at the first village, and see if anyone else knows of bogles in the Enchanted Forest. I *want* that house; I don't want some stupid country girl's superstitions to stand in my way.' But you should have seen the way he near flew out of the forest when I began rattling branches just behind him." The chuckle again. "Set him up good, you did."

She was pretty sure the stranger was hiding in the clump of rosebushes and clematis to the side of the house. She intentionally turned her back on the spot, picked up a bucket that hung on the rope crank, and took the end of the rope in hand, as if she intended to draw up water. "Well, of course he was suspicious," she said. "Everyone knows there's nothing enchanted in the Enchanted Forest. That's just the name real estate agents came up with to sell scrubby wooded lots out in the middle of nowhere to fools."

She heard breath sucked in.

She added, "Every stupid country girl knows there are no Folk," and smiled.

The hidden visitor shrieked. "What?!" The piping little voice shot up at least an octave. "No Folk? Nothing *enchanted*? Just look at me and tell me there are no Folk in the Enchanted Forest!"

A little creature materialized out of the gathering gloom—his rough, weathered skin could have been the bark of an old oak tree, his eyes glowed as red as the jaunty cap he wore, and he stood no higher than her knee. He leaned against a rosebush at the edge of the clearing, arms akimbo, chin jutted out, clearly furious.

El looked around and right through him and then beyond him; she pretended puzzlement. "I don't see anything at all."

He darted closer, and as she continued to stare through him and around him, closer still. She suppressed the smile that twitched at the corners of her mouth.

"Are you blind?!" the creature shouted, and danced up and down in front of her. "Idiot *peasant*! I'm right *here*!"

El clapped the bucket down over his head. "Every stupid country girl knows there are no Folk," she said softly, "but *I'm* not stupid."

The creature under the bucket screamed and fought; he scrabbled for El's hands with long, pointed fingernails, but she held on. He turned into a huge black cat that spit and scratched and bit; when he did, she threw the bucket away and grabbed him by the scruff of the neck. He became a snake, cool and dry and papery in her hands, with strong coils that whipped around her arm. She hung on, gritting her teeth—and he became a fish, slimy and slippery, with barbs at the tips of his spines that stabbed and scratched. He flopped and she lost her grip, and he almost got free, but she caught him in her apron and wrapped him in the cloth—and still she held on.

"Let me go!" he yelped. He was once again the tiny manlike creature she'd first seen, though now he was tangled in her apron.

"No." She got a firm grip on the back of his neck and unwrapped him.

"Dreadful big hulking ox of a girl," he muttered.

"With good reflexes," she agreed, and grinned at him.

He glared at her—those red eyes gave him an impressive glare. "Why aren't you afraid of snakes?"

"I'm not afraid of anything," she told him, and grinned wider, showing her teeth.

He shivered and looked away from her. "You might as well let me go. I don't have any gold," he said.

He was lying. They all had gold—and if she hung on to him, she could make him give it to her. But she said, "That's all right. I don't need your gold."

He brightened instantly. "You don't *need* my gold? Really? I don't suppose you'd care to put that in writing?"

She shrugged, but didn't loosen her grip. "I don't mind."

A sheet of parchment and a huge plumed quill pen appeared in his hand. "Oh, marvelous. What luck." He scribbled for a moment, then presented her with the results of his labor. "Here—this says, 'I voluntarily forgo all right to the gold belonging to Widdershins, both now and in perpetuity, both for myself and all heirs and assigns.' Write your name there—or you can just draw your mark if you can't write."

She winked at him and said, "I can read *and* write . . . Widdershins." She giggled when she said his name. "But it doesn't have the second part of the agreement here, so I can't sign it."

"Second part?" His gnarled brow furrowed, and he shook his head. "That covers everything."

"No. It doesn't cover what you're going to do for me, in exchange for my giving up my right to the gold to which I am entitled."

He looked at her, obviously appalled.

"You don't think I left out that bowl of milk every night—with the cream still on, no less—just to get you to stay around, or that I went through the trouble of catching you and hanging on to you just for the pleasure of your company. Did you?"

"I'd hoped."

"I'll bet."

"You left that milk out for me? Just for me? I thought you'd left it for your cats."

"We don't have cats. I put it out for you every night."

"Oh. Well . . . thank you. It was very nice. I'm awfully fond of milk—and the cream was especially good." He sighed. "So what do you want, since you don't want my gold?"

"Which you don't have anyway," El teased.

"Er, right."

Ella sat on the grass and held Widdershins firmly on her lap so he couldn't escape. His cool skin, rough as oak bark, scraped her hands; his pungent leaf-mold scent surrounded her. "When my mother died, Dad and I managed well enough for a while. I missed my mother, but my father loved me. Half the time he treated me as a cherished daughter, and the other half as the son he'd always wanted."

"I didn't *think* you had any brothers," Widdershins interrupted.

"Of course not. But you don't think I'd tell some land-grabbing Haptigan prince that, do you?"

"Oh. I suppose you wouldn't."

"Anyway," El said, dragging her story back on track, "then Dad brought Georgia and her two daughters home with him, and Dad didn't have time to teach me to ride or fight anymore. He was too busy working so his new wife could spend the money he earned. And ever since Dad died, things haven't been too good for me. I want happily ever after, you know—

and I don't think I'm going to get it living here with them. We don't get along too well."

"Well—that's too bad," Widdershins said. "But I don't see what I can do to make things any better."

"I need a fairy godmother," El said.

"What?!" the little creature shrieked. "Excuse me, pardon me—you'll notice perhaps that to be your fairy godmother, I'd have to have a sex change . . . and I don't intend to—not for any reason. I like all my parts *where . . . they . . . are.* So the fairy godmother idea is out. Got it? Out."

El shrugged. "So you can be my fairy god*father.*"

"I could, could I?" He snorted and crossed his arms tightly over his chest. "And what duties would a fairy godfather have, pray tell?"

"You would have to help me catch a prince—and keep him. I'm strictly a marriage kind of girl—I don't want any of that living-together nonsense, and I'm not at all interested in becoming a mistress."

"A prince? You want a *prince?* Like that two-faced scoundrel who wants to steal your land? You *want* someone like that?"

"Not even someone *like* that. He'd be fine, actually," El said. "On my terms, of course. I wouldn't want him on his."

"Yes," Widdershins replied after a thoughtful moment. "I can see where you're big on your terms."

"Is it a deal, then?"

Widdershins stared into the distance. "A deal . . . Would it be over when I finished helping you marry that prince?"

"I thought perhaps you'd care to stay on in my employ—for a full pitcher of milk with the cream on every evening, say, and free run of the castle for yourself and your own offspring. In exchange, you could be my luck. I think a long-term deal would be beneficial to both of us."

"Milk—" He sighed again, and closed his eyes. "One of those big metal pitchers, the kind with two handles? About yea tall?" He raised an arm over his head.

"Good heavens," El said. "A milk can? I'd need a dozen or so cows to keep one of those filled. For that much milk, I'd have to insist on a daily update of what you'd heard around the castle—and occasional extra favors, as agreed upon by both of us."

The wee man looked at her through narrowed eyes. "What exactly did your father do?"

El's smile became positively gleeful. "He was a lawyer."

"Of *course* he was."

So they signed their bargain, and El and Widdershins set to work to implement El's plan.

Nor were they any too soon, for a week after the prince's first visit, the mailman brought a gilded invitation in a lovely handmade paper envelope to the door.

Carol opened it at the breakfast table. "Oh, incredible," she murmured when she saw what it contained. She handed it to Martha, who read it with increasingly wide eyes. *She,* in turn, passed it off to her mother.

Georgia read the card, smiled brightly, then sighed and handed it to El. "You ought to at least think about going," she said. "This would be an excellent opportunity for you to get away from the horses and the swords and do something ladylike for once."

El looked over the card.

"By order of the King of Haptigia, who seeks a wife for his son, there shall be a ball on the third Friday of this month, from seven p.m. until dawn. The presence of your entire family, especially all unmarried daughters, is requested—please plan to attend. Formal attire."

"He's looking for a wife," Carol whispered. She hugged herself, then stood and twirled across the floor.

Martha laughed and said, "Oh, Mama—just think—one of us might have a chance to marry a prince."

"That would be wonderful," their mother said. "I think I'm about ready for a house in town. Convenient shopping, a level of civilization, entertainment . . . a chance to meet a nice widower, perhaps . . ." She nodded firmly. "Yes. You girls need to do your best to interest this prince."

"Has it occurred to any of you that we don't *have* a prince?" El asked. She crossed her arms over her chest and watched her two petite stepsisters stop their dancing. "We have a dowager queen with a single daughter, Fat Lucy."

"*Princess* Lucy," Georgia said with a sniff.

"*Princess* Fat Lucy." El compromised.

"Perhaps the borders have moved," Carol said. "That happens sometimes."

El raised an eyebrow. "It happens all the time around the Haptigan kings. They've been expanding their borders for over a hundred years."

Georgia rolled her eyes. "Well, even Haptigan kings—or their sons—have to marry. And they might as well marry into our family."

El looked from one petite, lovely, dark-haired stepsister to the other, and felt the old envy rise. Neither Carol nor Martha could swing a sword or ride a horse . . . or read a legal brief, for that matter. And neither of them would ever need to. Men fell all over themselves protecting and cosseting dainty little creatures like the two of them—but let a tall, strong Valkyrie of a girl like El come along, and suddenly every man around was too busy to help. "Don't get your hopes up," she said, and glowered off to her room.

"Are you sure you aren't going, then, Ella, dear?" Georgia was checking her own makeup and making sure the stays in her corset were all lying flat—she was primping in the mirror as badly as either of her daughters.

"No. Sorry. I'm going to oil Dad's armor tonight, I think—and maybe go out and polish Thunderbutt's hooves."

Martha made gagging noises in the background. Carol rolled her eyes and said, "Ooooh. That sounds more thrilling than I could stand."

Both Carol and Martha settled their toques on their heads and tucked the corners of their outer skirts into the clips at their waists. Nobody, El thought grimly, should have an eighteen-inch waist. Both of her stepsisters looked fabulous enough that if this ball was on the level, either had a more-than-even chance of snatching the prince away from any other contenders. El was throwing away what little chance she might have had—and with those two in the arena, that was a mighty little chance indeed.

Of course, El suspected the ball was a ruse. The timing was just too unbelievable for it to be anything else. And if she was right, *only* she had any real chance of acquiring the handsome Haptigan prince as a husband.

Her sisters and her mother rolled away in the rented carriage, and El went out to the stables.

"They're gone?" Widdershins sat on the stable gate, grinning.

El nodded.

"Well. Then I suppose we ought to get ready."

El nodded again, and swallowed hard. She found herself suffering from a bad case of nerves.

Widdershins studied her through slitted eyes. "Second thoughts? By my very bones, I'd have them if I were you."

"I'm worried," El confessed.

"With reason. If you fail tonight, you'll likely die—but even if you succeed and catch your prince, you lose, to my way of thinking. I can see no reason why you'd want to keep him."

El bit her lip and sighed. "Part of my reasoning is horribly mercenary and self-serving," she confessed.

"With his power behind me, I can do what I want to do. With his money, I can own the things I desire." She stared at her callused hands, turning them over and over. "I'm tired of hard life and hard work. I want to try luxury."

The creature chuckled. "Well, that's pragmatic. I'm relieved. I was afraid you were going to spout poetry and nonsense, and go all dewy-eyed on me. If all you're looking for is a business arrangement, then I think even with that prince, you'll get your 'happily ever after.' "

"That's *part* of the reason I want him," El said, and there was a sharp edge in her voice. "The other part, unfortunately, is that I have been able to think of nothing and no one else since I first laid eyes on him. My pulse flutters like the wings of a hummingbird when I imagine his face, and I yearn to feel his lips against my skin."

"Oh, dear." Widdershins groaned and rolled his eyes skyward. "And the moment after you feel his lips against your skin, I'll bet you feel his teeth sinking into your throat."

"The possibility has crossed my mind."

"With good reason. What a pity I cannot protect you from yourself."

El looked up at the darkening sky and straightened her shoulders. She took a steadying breath. "Well, you can't. But you can help me win. Did you tell your friends about my offer?"

The little man clucked his tongue. "Of course—and they've promised they'll be here when the time comes. Just remember that if you double-cross them, they can do terrible things to you."

"I meant every word I said." El began putting on the padding she would wear under her father's suit of armor.

"Your majesty might wish to come take a look," the soldier at the drawbridge said quietly. "I think these are your . . . guests."

The prince went to the secret window, where he could watch without being seen. Mounted soldiers had stopped the carriage, and were asking for identification.

An older woman—obviously the mother, though still good-looking—leaned out and handed a card to the soldier. "My daughters and I were invited to the prince's ball," she said.

Two dark-haired, sloe-eyed young women looked out the windows and smiled fetchingly at the soldiers. The prince frowned. "This isn't all of them. There are supposed to be brothers—and the blonde girl I talked to, as well. Find out where *they* are."

The soldier walked out, whispered something to the guard at the gate, then stood and waited.

"All of us?" The mother frowned. "Well, no . . . my stepdaughter Ella stayed home. She . . . wasn't, ah, feeling well."

"What of your sons, or stepsons?"

The woman's face became genuinely puzzled. "I have no sons, and no stepsons either. We four women are—" Her face clouded and she fell silent. The prince realized she didn't like admitting four women lived in the house alone, unprotected. He didn't blame her. There were a lot of wolves who would willingly prey on a house full of poor, defenseless, beautiful women.

He grinned, and his grin stretched until he felt his face would split.

He rang a bell and the soldier, hearing it, returned to the guardhouse.

"Your majesty?"

"Have these three and their driver detained in the—oh, the west wing, I suppose. Do make sure Father doesn't see them. I'll be along sooner or later to explain things to them. First, I have to let the men know there is still someone at the house, and that I want her brought back here."

He frowned as he turned away, though. He suddenly

realized that the girl he'd spoken to had mentioned brothers with enormous confidence. She'd met his eyes when she spoke of them and she hadn't flinched or flushed. Either she was a superb liar, or these people were on to him, the brothers were waiting at home, and his men were riding into a trap.

He considered the possibilities.

The girl was almost certainly lying—and probably to protect her virtue. Four women alone with no one to protect them . . . two strange men. Oh, he could see it. The poor girl had probably been terrified he'd want to exercise *droit du seigneur,* and had been hoping to scare him off. He chuckled at the delicious yet typical inconsistency of a woman lying to protect her virtue.

He'd planned to remain at the castle while his men claimed the house. But that lovely girl was waiting . . . at home, no doubt in bed, with her covers tucked up to her chin. Not feeling well, her mother had said.

All alone, with no brothers and no "bogles" to protect her—helpless.

But something did come after us as we were leaving . . . his inner voice worried.

He listened to it only enough to decide to take a few extra men with him, then rationalized that decision by telling himself the soldiers were only in case the hypothetical brothers turned out to be not entirely hypothetical.

The idea of claiming his new property in person pleased him.

He headed for the stables, where his men waited.

El looked down at her father's armor in dismay. "It's exactly the same as it was!"

What it was was ill-fitting and heavy. Her father had never actually worn it—he'd inherited it from his father, who had apparently been stout, short . . . and fat-headed. The long-sleeved hauberk sagged and bunched under El's arms; the mail hood gapped beneath her chin, exposing her neck to cutting blows; and the acorn helm so completely covered her eyes that she had to give up wearing it entirely. While she could have put both her legs into one of the chausses, she could only draw the mail leg armor up to her knees. She tried to imagine them completely covering her grandfather's thighs, and snarled, "Good God in the Heavens, was Grandfather a *dwarf?*" The chausses weren't going to do her a bit of good, but Widdershins had insisted she wear them anyway. She'd had to hold them up with bits of baling twine, because the leather straps intended to do the job didn't reach anywhere near her waist.

And now Widdershins stood in front of her and swore on a long string of Folk gods that he had transformed her into the perfect picture of a mighty warrior—while she could see perfectly well that he hadn't. She looked like a tall girl in her short, fat grandfather's armor.

She could no longer hope for her first plan to succeed; it had depended heavily on Folk magic and a bit of deception. If she were right and the prince was up to no good, El was probably going to end up in an honest-to-god pitched battle. She wondered how the Folk were with swords.

A winged pixie no bigger than a mouse zipped into the stable and fluttered in front of El's face. It glowed dully in the deep shadows—a flash of wings, a faint, dark sheen. It smelled of marigolds, with the faintest hint of summer grass; it hung on the air in front of her face, wings moving without creating even the tiniest perceptible breeze. Its red eyes glowed as they stared into hers, and its pointed teeth gleamed. If El had not first seen it in daylight, she would have found the creature frightening.

"They're coming," the pixie told her.

"You're certain?"

It nodded. "Men in armor riding horses—about fifteen of them, coming down from the north."

"So I was right." El felt a tiny thrill of satisfaction at that, which fear immediately buried.

Another pixie darted in and shrilled, "They're coming!"

"We already know," El said.

"You knew?"

El nodded, but Widdershins interrupted. "Weed was waiting in a different part of the forest, El. Weed, what did you see?"

The second pixie said, "Men, perhaps twenty, coming around from the southeast."

"Oh!" El looked from the first pixie to the second, and her eyes went round. "Nearly forty men. That's a lot."

She glanced over at Widdershins, who shrugged. "To be expected."

"Do we have enough Folk waiting to beat them?"

"Beat them? The plan was never to beat them, missy."

"But we're going to have to beat them—fight them into the ground and take them prisoners. My plan can't hope to work—look at me! I look ridiculous."

"To yourself, and," the hint of a smile twitched across his face and was gone, "to the Folk, perhaps—but you won't to the people you need to convince. You're going to have to trust me; you're going to have to trust all of us."

El shook her head, but mounted up. Outside the stables, she began to hear the low moans and eerie howls of her advance troops. "I hope I can," she muttered. She couldn't help but wonder how seriously the Folk would take her signature scratched on a promissory note, once things got nasty—or if they would consider what she promised in exchange for their help good enough.

Something was definitely going on.

The prince, traveling with the soldiers who crept through the night toward the house along the main path, had just decided the blonde girl's stories of bogles had been, like her story of brothers, designed to frighten him off. He and his men were already within a longbow shot of the house, and nothing untoward had happened.

Then the wind died, and the normal nighttime sounds with it. In the stillness and the hush, he heard leaves rustling, and then something howled. His men stopped and drew weapons. Without the creaking of saddles and the soft clank of armor, he could hear another sound—a low, steady, garbled whispering.

"What was that?" the soldiers muttered among themselves.

"Nothing," the prince said. "Dogs. And the leaves on the trees. Keep moving." He hadn't bothered to relay the story the girl had told him about the forest— he didn't want his orders questioned.

The men started forward, but his captain dropped back to his side long enough to say, "I believe I heard men in the undergrowth up ahead. That sounded like whispering to me, not leaves rustling. I fear we may be riding into an ambush."

The prince frowned. "We're heading to a house where one sick girl is all alone."

"Then why did we bring all these men?"

"Because I want to convince her that we're holding her mother and sisters hostage, and that she *wants* to give me her land. I don't want her to try any—"

He broke off in midsentence, as he noticed that pairs of glowing red orbs surrounded him and his soldiers, just above their heads. He pointed them out to the captain. "Do you see those?"

"Yes." The captain did not sound enthused, exactly. In fact, his voice squeaked out the word, with the tiniest quaver at the end.

"Do you know what they . . . are?"

"No."

They drew closer, those floating spheres—and the prince had a bad moment when he noticed that they blinked. Then another, when he realized the lowest of them was easily twelve feet off the ground. He began to believe he could make out the hulking, hairy shapes attached to those eyes. "Bogles," he whispered.

His men packed in around him, riding close and slow. He shuddered as something warm and wet licked along the back of his neck. He jerked around in the saddle, but nothing was there—except that something breathed hot, stinking breath into his ear and laughed a horrible, whispery laugh.

Then the screams began. Those were his men screaming—the men in the flanking party whose job had been to surround the back of the house and cut off escape. The soldiers with him flailed out at the whispering, invisible enemy. The prince drew his own sword, and in tight quarters hit only one of his men, who screamed.

The soldiers in the front shouted, and turned back to flee whatever lay ahead.

"Advance," the prince shouted. "Advance. Keep at them!"

The fleeing men froze—then they began pointing and shouting at the place from which they'd just come.

The prince's gut knotted, and he turned, only to find himself staring right into a pair of red eyes the size of grapefruits, inches from his own. And something warm and wet licked along the back of his neck again. "Yum. Tasty," it whispered in his ear.

The prince, howling, spurred his horse forward, shoving his men and their horses out of the way, and cantered into the clearing in front of the house, then sawed back on his reins so hard his horse reared and he nearly fell off its rump. It was well that he did not, for his men, racing after him in a panicked throng, would surely have trampled him.

He stared, jaw hanging, heart throbbing in his throat. In the circle, the moonlight illuminated a cast of shaggy horrors so terrible he thought he would have scratched out his eyes to save himself from ever seeing them again—except that in the center of those terrors, astride a radiant milk-white horse, a glowing creature of surpassing beauty waited and watched. Her hair, white as moonbeams, swirled around her face. Her armor, every inch of it hand-hammered gold, glowed as if it reflected the light of the noonday sun. Her face was perfect, heartbreakingly beautiful, terribly fierce. He knew her. He'd met her in daylight in this very clearing, and mistaken her for something other than she was. Now he saw her in her own element.

The men who'd made up the second half of his pincer cowered in front of her, on their knees with their foreheads pressed against the grass. Only a real woman could make armed warriors grovel in the dirt like that. Oh, she was a real woman—tall and proud and dangerous. She unsheathed her two-handed sword with a smooth movement, and lifted it easily over her head with a single hand, and he fell hopelessly in love. Even as he slid out of his saddle to kneel in front of her, he found himself wondering if she knew what to do with a whip, too.

I would give anything to find out, he thought.

It was working! El watched the prince dismount and drop to one knee in front of her. His expression held a mixture of worship and fear—so the illusions of the Folk were holding. She wondered what he and his men saw—and was almost relieved she didn't know firsthand. They all seemed so afraid.

She still saw nothing but a line of pixies floating above her to either side, and another line behind the prince, forming a most insubstantial wall.

She wanted to make her deal, but she wasn't sure the prince was softened up enough yet. El considered the special swordsmen's tricks her father had taught her, the ones guaranteed to wring a plea for mercy from even the fiercest opponent.

She began tossing her sword from hand to hand, catching it easily—the famed Alternating Strokes of Flying Death. She was its master. Then she swirled the blade one-handed in a figure eight that crossed over her horse's ears—the lethal Doom Loops. Executed perfectly, as always. She saw the prince's eyes grow round as he watched her, and she prepared herself for the Whistling Two-Handed Circles, when an irate voice broke her concentration.

"What are you *doing*?" Widdershins snapped. He rode double behind her, with his little claw-tipped hands gripping her belt.

"The Alternating Strokes of Flying Death." She snapped right back at him. "Then Doom Loops. If you hadn't interrupted me, I was going to go for the terrifying Whistling Two-Handed Circles."

"The *what*?"

"Whistling Two-Handed Circles," she whispered impatiently. "They're a master swordsman's prize strokes. They're guaranteed to terrify even the best opponent."

"Into thinking he's fighting a lunatic." Widdershins waved one hand in the general direction of the prince, and the prince and his little band yelped and went forehead to the ground like the other batch. "There," the little creature said. "I gave them a new illusion. Now they just think you were making mystic passes or somesuch."

El was still seething from his comment about lunatics. "How dare you say that! My father taught me those strokes."

"Your father . . . the lawyer?"

"Well . . . yes."

"When you said you were a master swordswoman, I took your word for it. Whom have you fought?"

"My father . . . well, when I was little. I've been practicing on the woodpile and the stuffed practice dummy since then."

"Oh, dear." Widdershins sighed deeply. "Lucky you

didn't actually have to use that thing tonight. I want you to follow my advice for a moment here. Just hold your sword high overhead—in either one or both hands. It doesn't matter. Whichever you prefer will be fine. It looks dramatic and impressive, and those soldiers see the sword as a glowing magic one. None of your master strokes though, please. Concentrate on looking fierce and proud, and say your little bit, and we should get through this yet."

El bit her lip and nodded. No more Alternating Strokes of Flying Death ... no more Doom Loops ... no more Whistling Two-Handed Circles.

El wasn't happy with what she was hearing. But she knew about the value of advice. Her father had always said, "Never take advice from people you aren't paying to give it to you, and never ignore the advice of the people you are paying." She was paying—or planning to pay—quite a bit to Widdershins if she got what she wanted.

So she held her sword high above her head—one-handed—and tried to look noble, and then she took a deep breath. "Hear me, O Prince," she said, and was impressed by the way her voice echoed. Probably proximity to the well, she decided. The prince looked up. "These are my demands, if you and your men would leave my forest alive."

Much to her amazement and everyone else's, it all worked out.

Ella moved into the castle of her Haptigan prince, and put her stepmother and her stepsisters up in the east wing. The castle was big enough she rarely saw them, so they didn't drive her crazy. El's husband, the prince, settled down—more on that in just a moment—and, at her request, added on a dairy farm to the establishment, though for reasons he could never figure out, he got less milk out of his cows than any other dairy farmer in the kingdom. He didn't get away with anything, either—his wife knew exactly what he intended to do from the instant he first came up with any idea. From time to time, he thought he saw some of those glowing red eyes around the castle, but he never dared ask. For one thing, El was not the sort of woman to press on issues she didn't want to talk about.

For another, she did know how to use a whip.

The Whistling Two-Handed Circles were his favorite stroke.

Widdershins and all his friends loved their new home.

So.

Once upon a time, there was a beautiful young girl who fell in love with a handsome prince. And the bit about the glass slipper was pure fiction.

But the happily ever after part wasn't.

What does Mommy do all day? Oh. *Oh!* Oh my goodness,

CAREER DAY

Margaret Ball

The damn beeper went off just as I was parrying the two big guys' swords at once. I've seen Vordo do this in the arena, and it's a neat trick; if you work it right you can catch them with their own blades crossed at your guard, give a little *zotz* to the pommel and they're both disarmed. Of course it doesn't work unless you can arrange to be fighting two big stupid swordsmen who get in each other's way. And it doesn't work at all if Call Trans-Forwarding distracts you for a crucial split-second. I bungled the parry badly; sliced one man's hand off and had to shove the point of my sword into the other one's throat to keep him from toppling onto me.

I guess I can't really blame it on the call. Vordo never lets himself be distracted by *anything*. I'd love to take lessons from him, but he doesn't teach. Actually I'd love to do just about anything you name with Vordo. Not only is he the greatest fighter on Dazau, he's also a hunk: golden hair and thews to die for.

Duke Zolkir would not be pleased. He'd specifically said to bring them back alive for questioning. Well, there were still three left, and the one with the missing hand might make it if I got it bound up in time; and at least I had time to push the bronze stud on my right wristband that activated the vocal transform and stopped the beeping.

"May I speak with Riva Konneva, please?" chirped the voice on the other end of the link.

"Speaking," I snarled. The thief whose hand I'd lopped off was bleeding to death in the dust. His three buddies weren't helping him, but they weren't backing off enough for me to safely help him, either.

"Riva, this is Jill Garner? With the PTA Volunteer Committee? It's about the field trip to Shady Brook Stables? We need another driver, and I thought that since you don't work . . ."

"I do work," I told the wristband. "I'm working *now*, as a matter of fact." One of the three remaining thieves was trying to circle around to my left.

"Oh. I just thought, since the only number listed for you is your home phone . . . Do you work at home?"

"Sometimes." That was more or less true. Dazau *was* my home; Jill's planet was just a temporary address. The man behind me on the left was moving in now, confident that I hadn't noticed him.

"I suppose I'll have to call Vera Boatright, then." Jill sounded depressed. "She's about the only mother left who's at home, because her church disapproves of women having careers."

The little sneak was close enough now. I hooked one foot behind his leg and brought him down with a thump. He tried to curl up from the ground with his dagger out, but that sort of move is hard to do if you don't keep your abdominals in shape. I stomped on his knee. It crunched and he collapsed back in the dust, moaning slightly. I really hate the sound of a breaking kneecap.

"Disapproves of women working? Will the church pay my rent if I quit?" I asked. At the moment I wasn't all that crazy about my job.

The other two thieves backed off and made comments about Unfair Use of Wizardly Devices.

Jill sighed. "It doesn't work that way. She probably won't do the field trip, either, because I think they also disapprove of girls riding horseback. Say, I've got an idea! Instead of driving the field trip . . ."

The skinny one in the purple robe dived forward, scattering something like sand in front of him with both hands. I squeezed my eyes shut just in time and struck out, blind, in the direction where the sharpies felt thickest. Tiny needles stung all over my arm, but my sword whacked into something yielding that moaned.

"Spellsharpies," I said. "That's dirty fighting."

"What?" said Jill.

The air felt clear again. I squinted through my lashes and saw part of the purple robe lying on the sand at my right side. The other half was wriggling and flopping in front of me.

"You cheated first," said the last thief. "Calling up them there wizardly advice spells outa the air."

"I didn't call her, she called me."

"How would you like to take the class to your workplace for Careers Week?"

"I'm gonna tell Duke Zolkir you cheat."

"That's perfectly fine with me. Come back right now and tell him in person."

"Perfectly fine? Oh, wonderful!" Jill chirped. "I *knew* I could count on you, Riva. Will next Wednesday be all right?"

"I didn't mean you, I was talking to him. Wait a minute. *Wait a minute!*" I yelled at the last thief as he started to sidle away.

My wristband clicked. Jill had hung up. I snarled and threw my dagger at the last thief. The idea was to slow him down, but I was mad and my aim was off. It slid right between two ribs and stuck out of his back, quivering, while he collapsed and coughed up blood.

Never in a million years could I have made a throw

like that if I'd been trying. It had to happen when I
didn't *want* to kill the bastard.

I looked around the back alley where we'd been
fighting. Wasn't there one left? Let's see, I'd got one
in the throat, sliced one in half, accidentally stabbed
this one in the back, and the one with the missing
hand had bled out while I was busy. Oh, yeah. The
guy with the smashed kneecap. He shouldn't be dead,
and he wasn't going anywhere.

He shouldn't have been dead, but he was. Two
corpse-rats had slunk out of the gutter and slit his
throat while Jill rattled on about field trips. I just saw
their gray robes whisking around the corner when
I turned.

The dead man's pouch had been neatly cut from
his belt, probably with the same knife the corpse-rats
had used to slash his throat.

All five thieves dead. And I hadn't even retrieved
the tokens they'd stolen from the duke.

Zolkir was *not* going to be pleased.

Especially when I told him I had to take next Odnstag off.

After cleaning my sword, I decided not to tell Zolkir
directly. I'd leave a message with Furo Fykrou
instead. It was almost time to pick Sally up from
school, anyway.

Furo Fykrou charged an extra ten zolkys for deliv-
ering the message, claiming he'd have to do it by
voice-transform because he wasn't about to traipse up
to Duke's Zolvorra on my business. I suspected that
meant it had also cost me ten zolkys to take Jill's call.
On top of the monthly fee for keeping the voice-
transform link active across dimensions, *and* the
monthly fee for the Al-Jibric transformations that took
me back and forth from Dazau to the Planet of the
Piss-Pot Paper-Pushers. And the fee for translating
my pay into the flimsy green stuff the Paper-Pushers
considered money. What with the costs of commuting
plus the fact that I could only take on contracts during

school hours, I was slowly going broke. The fact was that I couldn't *afford* to live among the Paper-Pushers and work on Dazau.

As I stepped into the transform zone and felt my molecules going all squoogy the way they do just before you solidify in the destination locale, I vowed that I'd find a way to make it work. At least for another few years. Maybe I could get a night job on Paper-Pushers, bouncer in a bar or something. . . . No, Sally was too young to be left alone at night. Well, I'd think of *something*. Sallagrauneva's education was too important to give up on that easily. The kid had brains; I wanted her to qualify for something better than a bronze-bra job when she grew up.

Maybe I could get together with some of the other single mothers with kids at Sally's school. A lot of them, like me, had moved into that nice yuppie suburb so their kids could go to a good school. A lot of them were also struggling to make ends meet on a part-time salary and a high rent. I should talk to them, maybe arrange to share a house or something to cut down expenses. After all, I wasn't all that different from them.

It was just that I'd moved from a little farther *away*.

Next Wednesday/Odnstag I stuffed my fighting gear into a tote bag, slipped an old shirt and some jeans over my armor, and walked up to school with Sally. There were seventeen fourth-graders, Vera Boatright, and some tall dweeb with black-rimmed glasses waiting at the front door.

"Wait a minute," I said while Sally shrieked with glee and ran off to join her best friends in a little knob of giggling girls. "I contracted to take the kids, not the adults." And Furo Fykrou's transfer fees for the kids, even at half price for children below sword-age, had just about wiped out my credit with him. I'd have to get a loan from him for the two adults, and at his interest rates I'd never get paid off again.

94   *Chicks in Chainmail*

Sally emerged from the crowd of short people. "Miss Chervill can't come," she informed me. "She called in sick, too late to get a substitute."

Smart Miss Chervill. If I had to face this roomful of brats every morning, without even a sword and shield, you can bet I'd call in sick as often as I thought I could get away with it.

"So Mr. Withrow offered to be our teacher chaperone for the trip."

The long drink of water in glasses blushed right up to his black eye-gear. "Dennis to you," he said. "I've seen you at the PTA meetings, Ms. Konneva, and I've been looking forward to meeting you in person."

"Mr. Withrow is the eighth-grade math teacher," Sally said, "and I hear he's an absolute fiend in class."

Dennis turned red again. "Sallagrauneva!" I said sharply.

"A lot of children feel that way about algebra," Dennis said. "I try to persuade them it can be fun."

"Yes. Well." I cleared my throat. "Look, the transport for this trip is kind of tight, and I'm not sure I can squeeze you two in." I looked at Vera Boatright, hoping she'd take the hint.

Vera did not take hints. She swept her daughter into her arms. "No one takes my little girl on these Godless excursions without me to watch over her!" She did her best to look like a protecting mother, but it was hard work; at ten Becky Boatright was already taller and broader than any other kid in the class. Vera looked like a banty hen trying to protect a half-grown duckling.

"And Brian and Erin and Byron and Arienne all have the flu," Sally added. "That's why there's only eighteen of us."

Only?

"You really don't want to be the only adult in charge of eighteen fourth-graders," Dennis told me. "Trust me. I've been there."

"I didn't want to do this at all," I muttered,

recalculating quickly. Take off four half-fares, add two adult fares, it should come out even—although doubtless Furo Fykrou would find a way to squeeze a little extra out of me for the last-minute change. "Okay, listen up, all of you. The place where I work can be kind of dangerous. You should be all right if you stay right behind me and don't go wandering off or anything. Oh, and don't talk back to anybody; my, er, colleagues are kind of short-tempered, and I'd hate to bring any of you back minus a hand or a foot."

Peals of laughter from the children.

"Where's our bus?" Vera Boatright demanded.

"Don't worry," I told her, "it'll be here any minute. If you'll all just gather around me out here in the parking lot—"

"I'm not supposed to walk in the street without a grown-up holding my hand," piped up one midget.

"Me neither."

"It's not a street, it's a parking—oh, never mind. I'll hold your hands." But I also had to manage the carryall with my sword, shield, and beeper. Dennis came to my aid, grabbing one whining kid with each hand and towing them to the center of the parking lot, where I'd arranged with Furo Fykrou to pick us up.

"I think I forgot to take my medication this morning," another kid said.

"Well, you can't go back for it now, you'll miss the field trip," I said, just as the squoogy feeling hit my insides.

When we went solid again, a couple of the kids looked kind of green, but nobody had actually thrown up.

It was a perfect day on Dazau—balmy, not a cloud in the sky, and no wars within walking distance; I'd checked. We were standing in a grassy field just outside Duke's Zolvarra. The gray battlements of the outer town wall encased a huddle of red-tiled house tops and stone towers, clustering up the hill to the duke's own keep at the very top.

"Wow," said Becky Boatright, "it looks just like Disneyland!"

"Now, darling, you know the church doesn't approve of Disneyland," Vera Boatright said automatically. She shot me a suspicious glance. "What happened to the bus?"

"I think you had a dizzy fit, Ms. Boatright," Dennis said.

"Mrs.," she snapped. "*I'm* a decent married woman." She gave me a dirty look.

"Why don't you all follow Mr. Withrow and me to the town gates?" I suggested. "Mrs. Boatright, would you please guard the end of the line and make sure there are no stragglers? I'd hate to lose anyone before we even begin the tour." I also liked the idea of having eighteen fourth-graders between me and Vera Boatright.

"You owe me one for distracting that woman," Dennis muttered out of the corner of his mouth as we marched up the slight slope to the town wall. "What exactly *was* our transport, anyway?"

"You wouldn't believe me if I told you." I smiled sweetly and he backed off a step. Men on Paper-Pushers often do that when I smile; I can't understand it.

"Let me take you out for a beer after the field trip and you can try explaining," Dennis suggested. "We can compare Vera Boatright stories. Did you know she wants to censor the math textbooks for Satanism? I'm supposed to teach geometry without five-sided figures, because the pentagram is used in Satanic invocations."

"Well, it *is* a powerful figure to be teaching eighth-graders," I allowed, trying to look as though I understood mathemagics.

"I *know* I forgot my medication," wailed the kid who'd been complaining when we took off. "I'm getting hyper. I can feel it coming on."

"Shut up, Jason," said half a dozen other children at once.

"But I get distracted without my medication. I can't stop watching everything all the time. What are those little purple weeds? How come all their flowers are different shapes, like snowflakes? Flowers aren't supposed to do that. And another thing—"

I turned and smiled at Jason. He backed off too. "This isn't Nature Study, it's Career Day." I said as sweetly as I could. Actually I'd never noticed the different shapes of the brakenweed flowers. There really was something strange about the kid. "Come along for a nice demonstration of my work."

Just how true that was I didn't realize until I got my new orders from the Duke's house wizard.

"I told you," I protested, "I'm not taking any jobs this Odnstag." Had Furo Fykrou failed to deliver that message? No, the house wizard was nodding. "Understood. This isn't a new job, though. It's a follow-through on that assignment you screwed up last Thorstag."

Thorstag? Nearly a week ago. What had I been doing around that time, apart from letting Jill Garner talk me into herding the fourth grade around Dazau for Careers Day? Oh, yeah. Those scumbags who snuck into Duke's Zolkarra and snitched his magic tokens. Okay, I had royally screwed up the retrieval job, presenting the duke with five corpses and no tokens, but he'd already blistered my ears and refused to pay me for the day's work. How much worse could things get?

A lot worse.

"Baron Rodograunnizo says those were five of his loyal guard," the house wizard informed me, "and you lured them into the alley for the express purpose of killing and robbing them. And there being no witnesses to the contrary, *and* one of them had his belt-pouch slit off, *and* you didn't bring back the magic tokens that would enable us to argue they were common thieves—"

"Right. So the Duke is not happy. I knew that. What's this follow-on business?"

It seemed the Duke had agreed that Baron Rodograunnizo was entitled to send his champion against me in single combat to settle the truth of their quarrel.

Today.

Well, it wasn't quite the peaceful tour of Duke's Zolkarra that I had planned, but what the heck. These kids saw worse every day on TV. In color.

"Guess what, kiddies," I said as brightly as I could, "the Duke has arranged for you to see a demonstration of actual sword-fighting as part of the Career Day tour." If Rodograunnizo's champion was as incompetent as his hired thieves, I figured this bout should kill half an hour, max. Maybe with luck I could drag it out to two hours and then take them to the Blue Eagle Inn for lunch.

"Come on," I said, "this way to the combat arena!"

"Can we stop at a drugstore?" Jason asked. "I really need my medication."

"I need to go to the bathroom."

"When's lunch?"

I ignored all of them. I had enough trouble getting eighteen fourth-graders into one of the roped-off spectator areas and making sure they understood that they were not to move outside the ropes for any reason. I didn't have time for potty trips. Vera and Dennis could handle the whines; wasn't that what they'd come along for?

Then I found out who Rodograunnizo's champion was.

"*Vordokaunneviko?*" I gasped. "You're kidding. He wouldn't work for Rodizo the Revolting. Particularly not in a trumped-up cause like this one."

"Vordo," said Rodograunnizo's house wizard smugly. He was a new one, a flashy dresser like Vordo.

He smoothed down purple sleeves that dangled over his fingertips and stroked the gold embroidery on the cuffs. "Want to reconsider? Concede?"

If he hadn't smirked, and if Vera hadn't come up with one of her nifty quotes about the woman being subject to the man in all things, I might have had the good sense to do just that. There was no way I could take Vordo in a fair fight. I'd seen the man in action.

Besides, that wasn't how I wanted to take him.

But Sallagrauneva was watching. How could I back down in front of her? And Vera Boatright? And what would I use for zolkys if the Duke decided to fire me for refusing challenge?

I figured Vordo and I could work something out once the fight started, when we were out of earshot. He couldn't really want to champion a phony like Rodograunnizo. Not Vordokaunneviko the Great, the undefeated champion of all Dazau. It must be some mistake, or else Rodograunnizo had tricked him into taking on the job. I'd explain the setup, we'd put on a nice show of swordplay for the audience, and then I'd let him defeat me in some showy maneuver. The Duke wouldn't be happy about that either, but he couldn't really expect me to win against Vordo.

That theory lasted about fifteen seconds into the match.

When Vordo marched into the arena, there was a wave of applause from all around. Even though most of the spectators were Duke Zolkir's people and theoretically on my side. Well, I couldn't blame them. Hells, I'd have applauded him myself if I hadn't been the next course on the chopping block. Eighteen hands tall, golden from his crested helmet to his gilded shin-guards, his stern face and icy blue eyes striking terror into the hearts of malefactors everywhere—who wouldn't have cheered? I made a sorry show in comparison, shucking my jeans and shirt and fishing around in the carryall for my equipment.

Vordo and I circled each other sidewise a couple

of times while the crowd roared and stamped their
feet. One good thing about the constant cheering,
they couldn't possibly hear what we were saying to
one another.

Vordo started out with a couple of casual warm-up
insults, the kind of thing you throw out to distract
your opponent while you're figuring out which is his
weak side and how you're going to open.

. "Cut it out, Vordo," I said. "You don't understand.
Cousin Rodo's lying, My Aunt Graunneva always *said*
that branch of the family had no honor. He hired a
bunch of incompetent thieves to steal some of Duke
Zolkir's magic tokens, and he's mad because I kind of
accidentally sliced them up a little more than I meant
to when I went after the tokens. You don't want to
take this too seriously. Now look, we both know I
can't take you out, but I've got this bunch of kids
watching, see? I don't want to get all dirty and bruised
just before lunch, and neither do you. Let's put on a
nice show, two or three bouts of flashing swords, and
then I'll let you 'defeat' me and everybody will be
happy."

"Nobody *lets* Vordokaunneviko the Greatest defeat
them, stinking camel-dung face," Vordo snarled. He
lunged at me and I sidestepped.

"Uh, right. Poor choice of words. But you get my
meaning? No need to make a big deal about this. I
don't really want to fight you anyway, Vordo. I'd much
rather—"

"Nobody *wants* to fight Vordokaunneviko the
Greatest." He bared his beautiful white teeth at me
and flexed his arms. For a moment I thought about
all the things we could be doing instead of this play-
fight. Then his sword came whistling down at an angle
that would have removed my left leg if I hadn't moved
fast and fancy. It certainly removed my hopes of keeping this fight neat and simple.

For the next few minutes I was fully occupied in
staying alive. Speed and accuracy, my strongest points,

weren't doing me any good this time. Vordo's defenses felt like hitting a brick wall. He was one sneaky swordsman. Looked big and slow and easy, but every time I thought I saw a perfect opening and went for it, I felt like I'd hit that wall. He could have taken me five times in the first clash, but he always held back. Almost as if he were playing with me. Could he be reconsidering my offer? I hoped so.

Behind him, on Rodo's side of the arena, I saw that new wizard dancing from one place to another to get a good view of the fight, purple sleeves flying.

"I thought she was such a great fighter," Jason whined, "she isn't even touching him!"

"She is too!" Sally defended me.

Unfortunately, Jason was right.

He said something I didn't catch. I hopped backward on one leg and barely saved my hamstring from one of Vordo's slashing blows; evidently he'd decided to get down to business. From the corner of my eye I saw Sally punch Jason.

"Is not!"

"Is too!"

"Children, stop that this minute!" Vera Boatright shrieked.

She was too late. Half the fourth grade was in the fight. Somebody got knocked against the ropes at the boundary of the arena and suddenly there were little screaming kids all over the place.

"See? See?" Jason yelled at Sally. "Watch when she tries to hit at him. He flickers all over for a second."

I wasn't, at that moment, trying to hit anybody. I was trying not to step on children. Vordo knocked over two kids to get at me and I swung at him again. Jason squealed and pointed. "See? It's just like the magic shield you gain on the third level of Defenders of Doom!"

I almost thought I could see the flicker. Hmm. That gave me an idea. But first we had to get the fourth grade out of danger. I backed away from the kids as

fast as I could, until Vordo and I were in the far
corner of the arena, with the kids milling around
between us and Rodo's spectators. Specifically, they
were ruining that new wizard's view of the fight.

This time, when I lunged, the tip of my sword
found Vordo's shoulder. He backed off, but instead
of parrying, he turned around and screamed, "Do
something!"

"Get those damned kids out of the way!" shouted
the wizard. "I can't see you!"

"Ha! Thought so," I gasped (I was gasping for air
anyway). "You two come as a package deal, do you?
What's he do, give you magic shields? Vordokaunneviko the Cheat!"

Vordo screamed at the wizard again. I took a small
nick out of the inch of exposed skin at his knee. Vordo
threw his sword at me and ran, trampling a few more
children, and shouting obscenities at the wizard.

"Idiot!" the wizard yelled back.

"Get back there and fight," Baron Rodo yelled at
Vordo, and then, at the house wizard, "*Do
something!*"

The wizard waved both arms and shouted something in Jomtrie. A small monster with seven legs and
purple skin and green warts appeared in the arena. It
was about as big as a puppy and could have been cute
if it hadn't been spitting acid.

Before I could clear the kids out of my way and
get at it, Becky Boatright had picked up Vordo's fallen
sword. Staggering under the weight, she raised it in
a two-handed grip and let the blade drop onto the
monster. I got there just in time to pick her up and
throw her out of range. Some of the blood spattered
me, but not enough to do any major damage.

"Why'd you stop me?" Becky howled. "I want to
fight evil just like you!"

Vera Boatright screamed and fainted. "Pick her up,
Dennis!" I shouted, bracing myself for the next wizardly attack. "Get out of the arena, kids!" The places

where the monster's blood had spattered me burned like fire-ant stings.

The kids scattered, but Dennis left Vera where she was. "No time!" he shouted back. He tried to jump over the last standing rope barrier, caught one foot at the top and went sprawling in the sand.

"C(A+B)=CA+CB!" screamed the wizard.

"Oh, no," I groaned, "he's using Al-Jibber."

More little purple monsters started growing out of the sand.

"It's the Distributive Law," Dennis muttered as he scrambled to his feet. "So it Distributes his magic. Symmetry ought to turn it around. A = B => B = A!" he called out.

The monsters shrank down into squirming purple patches of sand.

"d/dx cos(x) = −sin(x)," the wizard called. Green specks of light danced through the air, buzzing and circling us.

"Now he's using K'al-Kul," I groaned.

"Yeah, but it's only derivative. esin(x)dx = −cos(x)!" Dennis called, and the green things coalesced into a curving shape that slowly dissolved.

"d/dx tan(x)=sec² (x)!"

A ring of purplish flames surrounded us.

"Not to worry," Dennis said calmly, "I can integrate anything he can throw at us. esec² (x)dx = tan(x)!"

The flames died down.

"ecsc(x) cot(x) dx = −csc(x)!" Dennis added, and the wizard's robe caught on fire. "Gosh," Dennis said, "and some people say higher math isn't relevant."

That ended the fight. While the wizard was rolling on sand to put his fire out, Rodograunnizo fired him and Vordo both, not that Vordo had stuck around to hear the formal severance of contract.

"Looks to me like you lost big," Dennis said. "Don't you owe Riva something? False challenge . . ."

"I need a new house wizard," Rodo said, looking at Dennis meaningfully.

"Cheating by use of magic in a physical contest . . ."

"I can pay well."

"You pay Riva," Dennis said. "I don't want your job; I like the one I've got."

"Who're you working for? Zolkir? I can double whatever he's giving you."

"I *like* teaching," Dennis said. "Now about Riva's compensation . . ."

Furo Fykrou told me that the sum they eventually settled on would convert into enough Paper-Pusher's money to keep Sally and me solvent for a couple of years. He tried to hire Dennis, too. When Dennis turned him down, he mentioned to me that he could use an apprentice who knew something of these strange Paper-Pushers variants of Jomtrie and Al-Jibber and K'al-kul, and it wouldn't hurt if she were handy with a sword. Regretfully, I confessed to him that I didn't know anything about the formulas Dennis had been throwing around.

"I could teach you," Dennis volunteered.

"You would? Oh, that's . . ." I looked down at the little stack of green bills that Furo Fykrou had turned my challenge compensation zolkies into. Enough to keep Sally and me for two years . . . but not if I squandered it on wizardly teaching fees. "I can't afford it," I said sadly.

Dennis grinned. "Haven't you heard of free public education? I like teaching, Riva. You'd be a nice change of pace from those giggling little eighth-graders."

"You'd teach me for *nothing?*"

He took my hand for a moment. "I wouldn't exactly call it nothing," he said. He was blushing again. "It's a privilege to spend time with a lovely woman like you, Riva."

Really, the glasses weren't so bad, once you got used to them. On a man who'd hurled himself and his Al-Jibber between me and wizardly monsters, they looked pretty good. As for Vordo . . . well, I'd learned *that* lesson. Mighty thews are nice to look at, but they're not so impressive when your last sight of them is the back view of the champion running away.

Jill Garner called me the day after the field trip. Fortunately I was still on Paper-Pushers, studying *Make Friends with Mr. Euclid,* so I didn't have to pay Furo Fykrou for Call Trans-Forwarding.

"What's this I hear about you taking the kids to Fiesta Texas instead of to work?" she demanded.

"I didn't take them to a theme park," I said. "I took them to my workplace."

"Well, one parent said it sounded like a science fiction convention to him. Except those are mostly on weekends. And it couldn't have been the Renaissance Faire, because that isn't until October. Riva, you were supposed to show them what the real world of work is like, not take them to a theme park and play games about purple monsters and wizards!"

"Believe me," I said, "they weren't games."

"Well, I want you to know that Vera Boatright is very upset about the whole thing."

"That's too bad," I said. "Sorry, but I have to go now. I'm working." Dennis was coming over at four o'clock to go over the first chapter of the geometry book with me, and I wanted to go through the problem sets before he got here.

A couple of years of Jomtrie and Al-Jibber and K'al-Kul, and I might even be able to take Furo Fykrou up on his offer of an apprenticeship. That is, if I go back to Dazau at all. Paper-Pushers Planet has its attractions.

Like I said, mighty thews aren't everything.

There are all sorts of armor . . . and if you don't believe me, there is a lovely museum in Worcester, Massachusetts, that has a few of these on display.

ARMOR/AMORE

David Vierling

Sighing, Edaina twined her slender arms around Cromag's sinewy neck. The sun-bronzed warrior caught her in his massive, scarred arms and lifted the lush Princess easily, carrying her over the variously dismembered bodies of the twenty-seven temple guardsmen. Cromag's brown eyes smoldered as he noticed how the torn silk of the sacrificial robe showed more of her voluptuous figure than it concealed.

Kicking open the door at the end of the hallway, Cromag strode across the courtyard of the mountain-top temple to his horse, then tossed the raven-haired maiden unceremoniously across the saddlebow. Into his saddlebags he dropped the bag of gems he had looted from a secret niche behind the altar. Grinning, he prepared to swing his massive frame astride the horse and ride off into the dawn.

"Hold it!" barked Edaina, sliding down from the horse. "If you think you can just have your little fling, then conveniently dump me, you can forget it."

"Huh?" replied Cromag the Barbarian, dumbfounded.

"Girls talk—I know how it is with you macho barbarian types," said Edaina. "You ride off with the grateful, eager girl at the end of the adventure, but she always conveniently vanishes before the next one, left behind, no doubt, to explain to her family about the horned-helmeted baby she's carrying.

"Girls today want *relationships*," continued the Princess. "Commitment. Something lasting. We want to be wooed. You know, flowers, romance, that sort of thing. Dinner and drinks would be a good start."

Born in the midst of a mighty battle (well, really a cattle raid by a neighboring tribe), the first sounds Cromag ever heard were those of warfare: the ring of sword on shield boss, the crunch of axes splitting horned helmets, the bleating of captured sheep. He'd never heard much about relationships. "Ale and a joint of beef?" Cromag ventured hopefully.

Edaina snorted, wrinkling her pert nose. "Hardly. Someplace nice, with real atmosphere, like that new Kleshite place on the Street of the Tinkers."

"All right," agreed the Barbarian, grateful that a decision had been made. Lifting Edaina, he once more threw her across the saddle.

"No, no, NO!" she shouted as she slipped again to the ground. "Style, that's your problem. You've got tons of charisma, but no *style*. At least Gag-Anun had style, in an evil sort of way. *He* wouldn't have thrown me across his saddlebow."

"He was sacrificing you to the demon snake-god Dadoo-Ronron!"

"I didn't say he was perfect, or even that I'd go out with him, just that he had *style*." Edaina shot back defensively.

"His style is kind of flat since I threw him off the parapet," said Cromag smugly.

"Yeah," agreed the Princess, a little too wistfully for Cromag's liking.

Cromag reversed the subject again. "Maybe you're right. Perhaps I *should* settle down."

"Go on, I'm intrigued."

"I'll make you my mate. You shall bear and raise

strong sons for me in the wilds of the dusty, frozen
North-East, and when they're old enough, the boys
can join me on adventures. . . ."

"Hold your iron-thewed horses—after I do all the
work of carrying and bearing the children, *I'm* the
one who'll need to go adventuring—unwind, lose
weight—you know, fight postpartum depression."
Cromag, who certainly did *not* know, nodded sagely.

He mulled it over for a moment. "This is getting
too complicated for me," he said, leaping into the
saddle. Edaina ducked under the stallion, jerked loose
the saddle girth, and tipped Cromag sideways off
the horse.

Before the Barbarian could recover, Edaina darted
in cat-quick and snatched one of the half-dozen knives
at his belt. "If you think you're getting out of this *that*
easily, you're out of your sun-bronzed mind," she said,
brandishing the poniard.

Rising, Cromag drew his sword. Edaina laughed.
"You're bluffing, toots. Everybody knows your 'Barbarian Code' won't let you fight a woman."

Cromag scrunched up his almost nonexistent forehead, so that his single eyebrow briefly met his
square-cut, black bangs. Then he brightened. "Wrong.
The Barbarian Code says it's all right to fight a woman
if I disarm her without hurting her. Then she always
swoons into my arms, making my corded muscles
stand out in stark relief." He stepped forward,
swinging.

The longer reach and greater weight of Cromag's
sword soon drove the Princess back through the door
they had exited a moment earlier. A mighty blow from
Cromag's sword knocked the dagger from her
numbed fingers. Raising the back of one hand to her
forehead, eyes rolling upward, Edaina began to pitch
forward toward the already-flexing arms of the eager
victor. As soon as Cromag's sword clattered to the
ground, she straightened and punched him with both
small fists simultaneously, one to his bull-like Adam's

apple, the other to the nerve cluster just above his xiphoid process. Cromag hit the floor like a ton of sun-bronzed bricks.

As she tossed Cromag's sword out a window overlooking a 400-foot precipice, Edaina commented, "All members of the royal family of Hyccupia-Zambonee are trained in the ancient art of Trackshu-Jitsu." Cromag heaved himself to his feet and lurched toward her. "The first lesson of Trackshu-Jitsu is: 'Scared as Shit' runs faster than 'Madder than Hell,'" she finished, sprinting nimbly down the corridor, vaulting over slain guards. Over her shoulder she called, "That sword's pretty big—are you compensating for something?"

With an inarticulate roar he followed her fleeing form, thoughts of riding off without her forgotten. Rounding a corner, Cromag saw the Princess duck into the temple's library. The Barbarian stopped just inside the door, staring at the shelves packed with dusty books and ancient scrolls of arcane and evil knowledge.

He never saw what hit him: the largest, heaviest volume in the temple's collection, the pop-up, action *Kama Sutra*. The embossed leather cover left position LXIX imprinted on his cheek. Dropping the tome on Cromag's foot, Edaina said, "I know that's the closest you've ever been to a book, so I hope you learned something. At least it made an impression."

Before he could grab her, she was gone again, racing down a hallway and into the temple's kitchen. This time, Cromag came through the doorway more cautiously; hence the cast-iron frying pan caught him only a glancing blow before he tore it from Edaina's grasp and hurled it across the room. Cromag raised his fist.

Again Edaina laughed. "You won't hit me—your Barbarian Code won't permit it!"

It was Cromag's turn to laugh. "The Barbarian Code's very clear: I can cold-cock a woman 'for her own good,' usually to keep her out of danger. For you I'll make an exception." Then he unloaded a haymaker that would have smashed her like a bug on a chariot's windscreen, if it had connected.

Ducking Cromag's ham-fisted swing, Edaina grabbed a cup of pepper from a table and hurled it in his face. As he clawed at his eyes, she kicked his feet from under him, dropping him flat onto his back.

Edaina knelt between his legs, yanking another knife from his belt. Eyes still tightly shut, Cromag felt a tickling sensation he identified as a knife point *there*. Sighing heavily, he said, "You win. I will marry you. This I swear by Chrome, my patron god who never listens to humans' prayers anyway." The dagger was tossed aside and Cromag rose to his knees. "Now you will reward me with your virtue." He pulled aside the tattered remains of her sacrificial robe, then snatched back his hands as if he'd been burned. "What sort of armor is this?" he cried, staring aghast.

"My, but you *are* provincial. It's called a 'chastity belt,' and it prevents . . ."

"I CAN SEE WHAT IT PREVENTS! But I can also see that I'll tear it off with my teeth if that's what it takes to . . ."

Edaina smiled, patting the Barbarian's head. "That's sweet, darling, but the belt's magical, and the only key is at my family's castle. I'll send a carrier pigeon asking my mom to bring the key when she comes to live with us."

"Your mother? Live with us?" gasped Cromag. "But my reward . . . ?"

"It'll take a week for mom to get here. Think of it as foreplay."

"Foreplay?"

"A man with your looks and reputation doesn't know about foreplay?"

Cromag shrugged as she helped him to his feet. "Women usually just swoon into my heavily-muscled arms. I thought *that* was foreplay. Lots of swooning."

A thought struck him. "How do you know so much? You're supposed to be a virgin."

Gazing at his broad shoulders, deep chest, lean waist, sinewy arms, long legs, wide hands, powerful fingers, and adamantine fingernails, she breathed, "I am. But girls talk, and even virgins have ears . . . and imaginations."

Cromag nodded, pleased with the implications. "You are worth the wait. Never before have I met a woman who was my equal in battle."

"You still haven't met a woman who's your *equal*," Edaina corrected her fiancé.

Students of Chinese history will know I mean it when I say that something very like this really happened too. The rest of you: Enjoy it first and then . . . look it up!

THE STONE OF WAR AND THE NIGHTINGALE'S EGG

Elizabeth Ann Scarborough

If you ask me, a empire ought to act regal and not pretend to be his own jester. Jokes aren't proper or fitting for royalty—especially not when they're played on somebody smarter than the monarch.

And that Sun Zoo fellow, he was plenty smart. Never seen any smarter. It was because of him and his teachings that I was there to begin with—his last patron was a better pupil than my poor lady and with the help of Sun Zoo's teachings managed to conquer my people entirely, though we had been barons of the burren for some time.

Even I'd have to say we were always better at raw courage and combat than we were at cunning and treachery. Sun Zoo was the one who coined the phrase about all being fair in war—meaning he had no honor, which was practical of him, since honor is of very little use to the vanquished.

It's an out-and-out disability in a slave, which is why it's more a property of officers, who are ransomable, than enlisted personnel, who are more likely to endure captivity of a more permanent nature, if they're not killed outright. Footsoldiers tend to be

112

pragmatic, yours humbly, dishonorably, but viably included.

In some ways, harem life made a fine retirement for me. I was getting on in years for the rough stuff, toward the time when perhaps I ought to think about settling down and having what family it remained to me to have. Much past twenty-five and you start to lose your edge for battle.

I was lucky enough to be sold to the emperor himself, who was skeptical about the practice of keeping eunuchs to look after his ladies. And while it was true enough that the ladies had their jealousies and intrigues, I was used to being in an all-female outfit and catfights were nothing new to me. These women got to share one man among them, after all, whereas my comrades and I got none whatsoever until we were demobbed. The women among my people live and fight together in separate units from the men, you see, since we're bound to refrain from becoming mothers until we've ceased being warriors. Enemies have speculated that this practice is what made our warriors of both sexes so ferocious.

The emperor's newest concubine arrived the same day I did. We were both brought before the Tai-Tai, the number one wife. The concubine was a fourteen-year-old from the Caucasus, with delicate coloring, masses of hair, and a body of the pneumatic type common in the emperor's harem, by which I took it that Himself preferred it. I fit the type, as well, and had always required special adjustments in my armor to keep my bosom out of my bowstring.

"So," said Tai-Tai, "a barbarian child, a barbarian hag—no doubt you will be good company for each other. You, woman, have you a name?" she asked me.

"Madame, I do, madame." I pulled myself upright and at attention in more ways than one. You didn't want to be inattentive around this one. She had about her the look of a lazy leopardess with all the world as her prey. She was also the mother of the emperor's eldest daughter. So far he had no sons, but he hadn't been emperor very long.

"Well, then, what is it?" she asked.

"If it please you, madame, Boadecia."

"A stupid name, and ugly," she said, evidently never having heard of the queen for whom so many of my generation were named that we had to assign numbers and nicknames to keep ourselves straight. There was Big Boadecia and Blond Boadecia and Bloody Boadecia, who was our captain before her death. I myself was actually surnamed for those impediments to archery which had landed me my current position.

Tai-Tai seemed to be expecting an answer so I added, "As you say, madame." I tried to think of my captivity as just another change of command, you see, and her as just another officer.

"I do say, but it suits you. Boadecia, you will be maid to—excuse me, urchin, what is your name?" This was a deliberate insult, you see, that I, the slave, was asked to introduce myself before my superior. Fortunately for me the new girl wasn't the hoity-toity sort.

"Karoly, Tai-Tai," the Caucasian urchin said and, evidently mistaking her new overlady for the maternal type, offered her one of the dimpled smiles that would soon endear her to the emperor.

"Another stupid name, unfit for a concubine of His Majesty. You shall be called Lien—Lotus." She let it sink in and then said with a laugh that included every other woman there except Karoly/Lotus. "A lotus, after all, comes from the mud just as this person comes from nowhere of any consequence."

It wasn't much of a joke but the other women apparently knew better than to refrain from laughing, while the girl grinned foolishly.

Karoly/Lotus and I got on well enough considering that in my opinion she had been weaned too early and was eager to please to an extent that made her look more foolish than she was and frivolous enough that she was almost as foolish as she seemed. In her opinion, I was deficient in the arts of wardrobe maintenance and hair dressing.

"Bodie, His Majesty adores long hair. Why do you persist in wrapping mine around my head like some outlandish turban instead of making it look longer and fuller?"

"Mistress, loose hair is a weapon in the enemy's hand," I told her, repeating the aphorism I had learned at my mother's knee. "Women of my people cut ours when we begin our courses and it is never longer than our helmets throughout our careers."

"We are not among your people," she reminded us, "and far from being an enemy, His Majesty is exceedingly friendly to me and I *wish* him to put his hands in my hair."

In the bath she would say, "Bodie, do not scrub so hard. I am so raw when you're done that when you splash on my perfume it stings my skin."

"Mistress, a good scrubbing eliminates fleas and lice and smells which would reveal you to your foes. It is bracing, or at least, my horse and I always found it so."

"Bodie, I have never had fleas or lice in my life and His Majesty says my essence is like unto the heady fragrance of a Persian garden. Besides, I trust my skin is more delicate than that of your horse—and certainly more so than your own."

I trusted she would in time overcome her objections, however, and benefit from the wisdom of my ministrations. Certainly she had objected loudly enough to the makeup and wardrobe I had selected for her.

"Bodie, you stupid woman! This looks like war paint! And all this black leather and net look as if I have a date with a condemned man, not an emperor."

"But, mistress, leather is durable and easy to maintain and the net keeps it from being overly warm." I didn't even attempt to answer her slander about the makeup. I had copied that pattern from the one I beheld on the face of the Queen herself before her fall.

"But I am chosen because of my youth and freshness and this makes me look like a, like a, well, not like the other ladies. Observe."

"Indeed, you do not look like those hussies," I whispered—but very carefully, as the walls had ears and I did not wish my own to join them, separated from my body. "They all look the same in their wafty silks and brocades and bright colors. I wonder that the emperor can tell who's in his bed so alike are they! But very well, I'll find you a change. . . ."

"No time, no time!" she had said, and shooed me out as His Majesty came in.

Later, she reported that His Majesty found her countenance exciting and required that I invent some similarly unusual aspect for her every time he visited—which was more and more often. She acquired at this time a great deal of jewelry, and there, at least, she could not fault me. My armor always got the highest commendation from my officers and was an example to my subordinates. I polished the emerald collar he sent her, and the golden torque. I even shined up the bars on the cage of the mechanical gem-studded nightingale that came complete with life-size ruby egg.

As you may surmise from his generosity, the emperor was so pleased with my mistress that he spent a great deal of his time with her and I heard, in passing, that the Tai-Tai was alarmed lest this newcomer who got herself up in such "masculine" array might have a son by His Majesty and gain favor above all of the other ladies.

Thus, the coming of Sun Zoo played right into her hands.

He swept into court one day, looking austere and dangerous, his black eyes dancing at the opulence surrounding him while his false smile showed many teeth and his voice held the heat of a sacrifice in wicker knickers on Midsummer Eve, which I wished he was, the bastard. "Your Majesty, Ladies and Gentlemen of the Court, I have come to present to your eminences my sublime new and improved, tried and tested and one hundred percent guaranteed methods of conducting warfare. To prove to you how extraordinary my formula is, Your Majesty, I will, as a free demonstration with no obligation to yourself, turn any member of your court into a model soldier within a week."

The emperor laughed. Unfortunately for him and for my poor lady, Sun Zoo's fame had not preceeded him. "A week! Impossible. Why, it took me years to train for the field myself, not that I've ever had to use it."

"Nonetheless, a week."

Naturally, I knew when he said this, if not by his very aspect, that sorcery definitely had to be involved in such a promise. I burned to learn what his secret might be, since he was the downfall of my people and the cause for me being consigned to this stagnant backwater of femininity where preferred conversation was what one should eat to ensure that one would give birth to a male child rather than what one could wield to ensure the death of someone else's.

I was soon to get my chance, for once the emperor had had Sun Zoo settled in the Court Astrologer's wing, he could contain himself no longer and laughed aloud. "Imagine that fellow! Make a soldier of anyone in a week, he says! What does he think my guards are? Women?"

Before I had time to resent that, the Tai-Tai was leaning into his ear and whispering, giggling. He laughed uproariously at that. "Even so, my love! A perfect test! Put that fellow properly in his place!"

Some taunted me that it was the costume I devised for her that made His Majesty think of my poor Lady Lotus as Sun Zoo's impossible "test case" for his theories. I knew better, of course, that it was Tai-Tai, more afraid of Lotus than of all the other ladies and determined to put an end to her.

That evening when the court was gathered for dinner, the guest at the empire's right hand, Tai-Tai on the left, myself attending Lady Lotus as the other maids attended their own ladies, the empire made his announcement with many a wink and barely controlled chuckle. "Master Sun, I've been considering your offer and I have decided that you may have a chance to demonstrate your skills."

"You will not be sorry, Your Majesty. Only show me who you wish me to train!"

"You're sitting next to her," the King replied. "The Lady Lotus will be your trainee. In one week you must turn her into such a fine soldier that she can best ten of my ablest guardsmen."

Sun Zoo cast a lascivious eye on Lotus. "Her? Come, come, Majesty, she looks to me as if she could take them on right now."

I should have poisoned his wine then and there.

Since I did not, the next morning the whole court turned out to watch Sun Zoo turn little Lotus into a soldier. I could have told him it was a lost cause.

He very much looked the part of the martial instructor—black leather armor, black leather gauntlets and a helm with menacing nosepiece with a red stone set in it about the size and color of the egg in the nest of the jeweled nightingale His Majesty had given Lotus the week before. He exuded menace and authority but it was lost on Lotus.

She couldn't even lift the sword. Her breasts got in the way of the box, as I could have told him, and she blushed and dissolved in giggles when he tried to teach her hand-to-hand combat, and cried when he dumped her on her shapely behind.

She was such a disgrace to womankind that even His Majesty began to feel disgusted with her, though it was on Sun Zoo that he vented his disgust. "Bah!

Your claims are worthless. You can't make even a young girl follow your orders!"

"That is because she is undisciplined, Majesty. Such lack of discipline, as you know, can only be remedied by absolute authority."

"You have it."

"Did you hear that, Lady?"

She giggled.

In despair he tore off his gauntlets, and threw up his hands. "Very well, go to your quarters and consider your duty to your master, if not me. I will expect better of you on the morrow or there will be dire consequences."

Poor little Lotus couldn't stop blushing or giggling. The Tai-Tai and the others looked smug. I couldn't understand why, if Sun Zoo had the magic to do as he said, he would embarrass himself and her by not using it right away. Therefore, I resolved to find out because I could see this encounter was going very badly for Lady Lotus. She, who had heretofore faced nothing more unpleasant in her life than being given to a potentate for carnal tasks she was only too willing to perform, had little idea just how nasty some people could be. I blamed the Tai-Tai entirely and used her own weapons against her that night.

When my poor little lady was fast asleep in her chamber, exhausted by making such a poor showing throughout the day, I put to use all of the things I had learned from her and the other ladies that were pleasing to men of a certain type. I lined my eyes with Lotus's kohl cake and rubbed red berry juice into my lips and cheeks. I fluffed out my hair, by now grown to rather luxurious length, as she liked hers done and braided flowers into it. Then I borrowed one of the sheer silky robes she liked to wear around the harem. It cast a rosy glow over my flesh but did little else to conceal it. Over all of this I drew one of the black capes the women use to protect their finery and their identities when abroad on the palace grounds. Thus attired, I made my way to the astrologer's tower, the location of which I had earlier ascertained while in conversation with one of the guards.

The sorcerer was in. "Ah, what is this, a little gift from the emperor to apologize for sending me such an inept pupil?" he asked when I presented myself, having left the cloak outside the door.

"Something like that," I said with the smile I reserve for wounded enemies. "I have come, great one, on behalf of my mistress."

"That stupid girl! She's embarrassing me in front of the entire court. My methods have worked beautifully on entire armies but I have never before had an army that blushed and giggled or wept and refused to meet my gaze."

I let my fingers walk up his sword arm. "My lady is young and pampered and with strong female urges that only respond to a man of your power in one way, and that is not an appropriate way for her to respond, to you while her husband is looking on, if you take my meaning? But I'll meet your gaze, master. What exactly do you want me to look at?"

He laughed. "Bold piece, aren't you? Just a moment."

I pretended not to look while he found his magic implement—it seemed to be connected with the helmet he wore for training. "Meet my gaze then, wench," he ordered.

I carefully avoided looking at the red gem in the middle of the nosepiece, and gave him a sidelong glance first, and gasped. "Oh. Oh, my. Well, sir, I can certainly see my lady's problem. The sheer raw masculine power you exude when you put that on is just too much for a woman to withstand. However, if you can offer a girl a drink, I'll see if I can bear it long enough to convey your message."

He was more than willing to provide that drink and the next and the next. I'm a good drinker. He was not, particularly. "So, master," I cooed in the manner

I had heard Lotus use with His Majesty, "I think I'm ready to gaze into your eyes now."

I wouldn't need to look up since his gaze was firmly locked on the bodice of my gown.

"Yes, my dear. I have much to teach you."

"I have learned much already," I said, and I had, though not from him. Prior to coming into Lotus's service I would never have thought to use such a subterfuge and could not have imagined it would work.

"Look into my eyes," he commanded, and as we locked gazes, he suggested that I assume a position most often assumed by small boys in the captivity of Greeks and Romans.

Magic implement or no magic implement, I had absolutely no wish to do so. "That's amazing," I said. "And naturally I can't wait to satisfy your every command." Then, while he licked his lips, I snatched the helm from his head and ducked playfully away from him, evading him long enough to put it on my own head.

"Give that back, you vixen!" he demanded, but not angrily. I'm sure it looked rather fetching with the gauzy gown that was half-falling off me anyway.

"Certainly, my lord. But first you must look *me* in the eye and say 'please.'"

Still laughing, he looked me in the eye and I said, "You will recline on that couch and close your eyes and when you open them again, all your most exotic and depraved desires will have been fulfilled."

He went straight to the couch and lay down with a silly smile on his face and his eyes closed. I hit him over the head with the helmet.

I had to trust my own instinct, but I guessed that you had to use the gem to command he or she who looked into it to do or become something they wished to do or become anyway. Most men Sun Zoo faced would truly wish to become great warriors, so it worked well enough to give him both confidence and reputation. I had no wish to become a slave boy in addition to being a slave girl, so the gem had no influence on me. I wasn't sure how it would work on Lotus if she dared look at it, so I'd have to try it out.

With the helm under my cloak, I hastened back to her chamber and woke her up. Placing the helmet on my head, I said, "Do me the favor of looking into my eyes, my lady."

"Bodie, you look ridiculous. Have you no fashion sense whatsoever? That hat is absolutely the wrong accessory for that ensemble."

"But the jewel is nice, isn't it?" I asked. "Take a close look." She did and I said, "Now, go kiss the Tai-Tai's behind."

"What?" she asked.

"Aha! I thought so. You don't really *want* to kiss the Tai-Tai's behind, do you?"

"Bodie, are you quite well?"

"Never better, my lady, never better. But tell me, seriously, have you ever had any desire to be a soldier at all?"

"None. I seek only to win the emperor's favor and bear him many sons."

"Commendable. Now then," and I looked her straight in the eye. "Go back to sleep."

Then I went to work on the helmet and the nightingale, slipping back up to the Chief Astrologer's chamber just before cockcrow to slip into the room of the still-sleeping Sun Zoo, where I deposited both the helm and the dress I'd worn on my earlier visit.

The next morning the court assembled once more to observe the defeat of Sun Zoo and the humiliation of Lady Lotus. I was well dressed for the occasion in a tasteful collection of red handkerchief-sized veils, sheer trousers, and a little bolero concealing the jewel dangling from my bodice. If caught with it, I could be cut to pieces for stealing what would be assumed to be the nightingale's egg from my lady's trinket. The activities of this day were no more satisfactory

than before. "Lady Lotus, look into my eyes," Sun
Zoo commanded.

"Tee hee."

"At once."

"Tee hee heh heh hee."

"I have absolute authority over you. You will look
into my eyes."

She peeked up at him.

"March."

"I beg your pardon?"

"March."

"Tee hee. You must be joking!"

"I will tell you three more times and then you will
face the consequences of a disobedient troop."

"It isn't nice to yell at people."

"March!"

"You're frightening me."

"March!"

"Your Majesty, this horrid man is being very mean
to your little pomegranate."

"See here, Sun . . ."

"Your Majesty, by your own tongue you gave me
authority over this woman. We mustn't set a bad
example for others. Now. Lady Lotus, one last time,
MARCH!"

At this she broke into tears, threw herself on the
ground, and began screaming that she wouldn't, she
wouldn't, she wouldn't and nobody could make her,
so there!

"Your Majesty, this is not my failure to teach but
this woman's failure to obey my instructions, despite
your order that she do so. Thrice have I given her
direct command and thrice has she failed to execute
it, therefore I shall execute her, that she be an example to all others who would defy your wishes."

Lady Lotus wailed while the Tai-Tai and the other
ladies looked gratified. His Majesty looked horrified
and very sad, to give him credit, but I knew emperors

and he would do what Sun Zoo instructed to preserve his own royal dominion.

The emperor was appealing directly to Lotus. "Little Pomegranate, will you not do what this man commands or must I allow him to kill you."

"I *can't,* sire, I just *can't.* Please don't let him kill me, please please. You said . . ."

The time had come for me to attack.

Slithering out to comfort Lotus in the best harem style—my, I *had* absorbed a lot being around these ladies!—I turned to face the emperor and spoke. Normally, this would have been enough to cost me my life because slaves don't chat up the monarch any time they feel like it in the regular order of things. However, at the present time the emperor was so distraught he would be glad to hear a suggestion of how to save face and Lotus at the same time even if it came from her mechanical nightingale.

"Your Majesty, this man is a fraud and because he has not been able to prove his boast, he seeks to take the life of my lady. She is not disobedient to Your Majesty. Indeed, she worships you. It is simply that this man has no idea how to lead women."

"And you do, I suppose?" Sun Zoo asked with an arched eyebrow and a wink that implied he'd been leading me pretty well the night before.

"Not in a week—which is ridiculous for someone who has not hardened their thews and sinews, who has been kept sequestered throughout her life, who has no protective clothing, much less armor, and weapons too large for her stature. All of that can be improved in time, and yes, I could lead not only Lady Lotus, but all of the ladies in the harem, given six months, freedom to requisition that which is necessary, and the same authority His Majesty has given this would-be murderer of his adored concubine."

"I promised a week!" Sun Zoo said.

"You promised to train one lady, which you have failed to do. I offer to train the entire harem."

The Lady Lotus looked even more horrified at the idea of spending six months training as a soldier than she had at being executed. Tai-Tai's nose went so far into the air that, had it eyes instead of nostrils, it would have been quite as useful as any hawk for aerial surveillance.

"Six weeks," the emperor said. "I shall give you six weeks. That is all."

"Of free rein to train these ladies as I see fit with the help of the armorer and stables and—" I shot a look at the disdainful nobles who were finding my performance almost as diverting as the senseless execution of a young girl, "—absolute privacy."

"She asks for everything, Your Majesty, and I asked for nothing but a pupil."

"Yes, and you failed." His Majesty beckoned me forward. "I do want it understood that if *you* fail, my dear, I will not be expected to execute my entire harem."

A most reasonable request. I began to appreciate His Majesty as a most reasonable man, for an emperor. I approached him and said in a voice too low for any to hear but himself, "The test, Your Majesty, though the ladies know it not, shall be a pitched battle between them and an equal number of your own palace guard. I do promise, unlike the learned gentleman, that in the event that any of the ladies fail and are slain, I shall be slain as well."

"I command it," the emperor said.

"Majesty!" exclaimed Number Two Wife, who was pregnant.

Tai-Tai was beside herself with anger. "How can you think of giving this barbarian slave hegemony over me, my lord?"

But the emperor gave her a balky look and simply repeated, "I command it."

First I approached my Lady Lotus, who was still in a groveling position. She shrank back from me as if I'd gone crazy but I said, "My lady, here is your chance not only to live, but to gain His Majesty's favor above all others and to be the first to bear him a son. Only do as I instruct and all will be well."

I did not order anyone around at that moment, but allowed all to see that there would be no more diversions that day; while I proceeded to the armorer's hall and the stable to make arrangements to equip my reluctant unit.

On returning to the harem, I found that everything had returned to normal and the ladies were practicing peeling grapes and being fanned with peacock feathers and working on their abdominal exercises for the dancing they would do to assist Number Two Wife when she gave birth in another five months.

My lady was resting, but I just had time to replace the ruby egg in the nightingale's nest before she awoke. "Oh, it's you, Bodie. I don't know what all that nonsense was about out there on the field, but you made that awful man spare my life. For that I owe you anything, anything at all, which I can give."

"My lady, your cooperation will be the most valuable gift you can give us both in the weeks to come, but I shall need the loan of one of your material possessions as well."

"It is yours."

"The egg of the mechanical nightingale—will you give it to me for now?"

"For now and always, and the nightingale as well. The emeralds and diamonds and gold work are worth far more than that ruby."

"Thank you, mistress, but the ruby will do nicely."

I spent that afternoon going visiting among the ladies of the harem. They were inclined to snub me, of course, until they saw my new bauble.

Tai-Tai was the toughest nut to crack, but I knew what she wanted. I also positioned the ruby so that the moment she looked at me, she saw it. "Tai-Tai, you will gain even greater influence over His Majesty if you are also commander of his elite guard. This is

well within your abilities as a forceful and determined
lady. By doing everything I say, you will achieve this
power and will increase your chances of having a male
child. However, that may not even be necessary. Once
His Majesty sees how a woman may rule and defend
her rule, he is quite likely to allow his daughter by
you right of succession."

Now, this was utter and complete horse shit, as we
both very well knew, but that was where the jewel
really worked—because she wanted to believe that
such goals were attainable, she wanted to believe what
I said was true. When I added, as I did to them all,
"Also, our maneuvers will give you the opportunity
and the right to knock the smirk off the face of the
lady . . ." She filled in the lady's name most hated
by her.

To some I said that being tough and strong was a
way to the empire's slightly perverted heart, to others
that this was their chance to redress slights, to others
that they might actually have a chance to defend
themselves next time instead of watching helplessly
while their homes were despoiled, their families
killed, and themselves sold into bondage.

By the end of the day, with the jewel's assistance,
I had the promise of each lady that she would do her
utmost to learn what I had to teach her in the next
six weeks.

The following day, to keep interest up, we went to
the armorer's. There, each lady took her turn at
archery and her endowment was altered with special
garments to maximum functionality. The armor itself
was then tailored to the lady, and set with little jewels
to make it more attractive to each. Each lady was to
be issued helm, breastplate, shield and leather gauntlets and sandals with shin guards, a similar costume
to the one favored by the empire's guard.

I knew I would meet with resistance if I required
the ladies to cut their hair, so we formed teams to
braid it and had the helms made to fit over the

braided mass, which formed extra cushioning. Swords
and daggers were made short and lightweight, though
strong, and both longbows and crossbows were tailored so that they were somewhat more than the
ladies could manage presently.

This quickly changed as the ladies began sinew
strengthening, endurance training, and unarmed
hand-to-hand combat. Here their exercises varied
from those of the men and of the women I had
trained with, for while these women were not particularly strong or fit, they were quite agile, quick and
slippery and from the harem dances knew well how
to move one group of muscles in total isolation from
others. Their hips and legs were also quite strong and
well adapted for bumping a taller, stronger opponent
well below his center of balance, knocking him off his
feet, and stomping a mudhole in his most sensitive
and unarmored areas while he struggled to regain
his feet.

We practiced these new tactics by first allowing
each lady to spar with her most despised enemy,
which quickly showed them the wisdom of restrained
hairstyles and simplicity of line in costume.

It also got much of the personal rivalry out of their
systems, which was good, since the next step was to
tie the former sparring partners together back-to-back
and have them circle while defending themselves
against two other similarly bound opponents, then single opponents free to move. Thus did each lady learn
to work with each of the other ladies. The emperor's
little daughters meanwhile had a wonderful time emu-
lating their mothers.

We practiced riding, which some of the ladies
already knew how to do in some measure, though
others were accustomed only to being carried in
palanquins.

Then we coupled weapons with hand-to-hand
fighting, followed by weapons and hand-to-hand with
riding, followed by riding with archery and spear

throwing. The stone worked well in that they were highly motivated and kept trying until each was doing her utmost at all times—a much better percentage than you get in most outfits.

But was it enough? They were still gently bred ladies and six weeks could not harden them enough for them to face seasoned soldiers with any degree of success in the ordinary way of things. Their swords and daggers were suited to them and they used them well, their arrows hit the mark as well as the arrows of most troops, but their spear throwing was hopeless. Also, in the evening they ate too well, despite some cooperation from the palace kitchens, and slept too long on their silken sofas. The one concession I was able to acquire from His Majesty was that he visited none of them during this period.

"Absolute privacy, you promised, my lord," I reminded him at Lotus's threshold.

"But the poor girls will be lonely!" he protested.

"They'll be dead otherwise, sire. Besides, think of the privation they are enduring for your sake—is it not a noble thing for you to undergo a slight deprivation for theirs—and will it not make your reunion all the sweeter?"

"Well, I suppose I can find a few affairs of state to become involved in. Or perhaps I'll go visit my vassal Lord Chuski of the Steppes. I understand he has triplet daughters who are just turning fifteen."

"Of course," I said, "if they should return with you, they would need to be included in the battle with your guards—and quite without the benefit of the training your other wives are getting."

He sighed deeply. "Yes, I suppose that would be the only just thing to do and I *am* known as a just ruler."

As the end of the six weeks neared, and the ladies sat around the common table they liked to eat at now to tend each other's wounds of the day and supply each other with unguents and oils guaranteed not to leave scars, I dreaded the battle to come on the morrow.

"Lotus," Tai-Tai said. "The next time an opponent swings her spear toward you, slide from the saddle to the side as you did earlier today, and avoid the blow."

"I will, Tai-Tai. I am sorry for your split lip and loosened tooth. There is a remedy our healer once taught me for loose teeth. . . ."

"I must say, I feel better," Number Three Wife said. "It's been rather fun having something to do instead of just lying about all day. I shall miss our times together."

"Somehow, I feel that we need a campfire," Number Four Wife said.

"Not in the middle of the fourth-century carpet," Tai-Tai said. "The brazier will have to do. A bit of music would be nice, however."

"I'll bring my flute, shall I?" asked Number Four Wife. "Back in a jiff."

"Oh, I wonder if she knows that old Mongolian song about the Valley of the Red River. . . ." mused Number Two Wife.

"I have the strangest urge to write home to my mother," mused Number Fourteen Wife, "but I see her every second Thursday and she can't read anyway."

For now that the ladies were at war during the daytime, evenings in the harem had become much more peaceful. Tai-Tai, far from being the bored and cynical, grasping autocrat she had appeared, was actually an aristocratic lady with great skill in commanding. Fighting with her co-wives had taught her their worth and somehow, knowing it, she was no longer afraid that it lessened her own. Even Lotus had begun to look up to her.

And Lotus herself, while possessing very little aggressive spirit, was quick and playful and mad in the way of many small and merry people whom the evils of war and the world never seem to penetrate

very deeply. She was very fond of suddenly sinking to
her knees and onto her back in battle and dealing
damage to the underside of her foe. Those who
thought she was showing her belly and making herself
defenseless thus reckoned without her ability to twist
herself round and bob up for a new attack.

Number Two Wife was probably the most ferocious
of all, defending her belly.

I was almost sorry for the things I had to say the
night before the test. "Ladies," I told them, the jewel
strung on a fine gold chain and dangling between my
eyebrows, accentuating my gaze as I looked into each
of their faces in turn, "I have something disturbing
to tell you. I know that you all have felt these past
few days have been simply to please your lord and
gain various benefits for yourselves. But the fact is,
the emperor only agreed to allow this experiment
because your new skills will soon be needed. There
has been revolt brewing among the Palace Guard,
inspired by that brigand Sun Zoo, who has told them
that they can overthrow His Majesty and throw the
kingdom into chaos and yourselves into bondage and
fates worse than death and I'm sure you all know
what that's like and wouldn't care for it to happen
now that you're on the verge of—you know," I said
meaningfully to each one so that she would believe
we alone shared the secret of what she would become
to the emperor when this little charade was over.
"The point is, if the emperor and kingdom and your
own positions are to be preserved, your honor and
the lives and honor of your daughters saved from
these upstart ruffians, you will have to fight in earnest.
Intelligence has informed His Majesty that there will
be an attack on the harem on the morrow. This is not
a drill. I repeat, this is not a drill. This is an actual
alert of an impending battle, the only one you'll
receive. Fight well, comrades, or all will be lost."

Tai-Tai said, "In that case, Bodie, I think we should
post a guard."

"Excellent idea, Number One Lady. I'll stand first watch while you ladies get some sleep. I'll wake you, my Lady Lotus, for second watch. . . ."

"I'll stand third myself," Tai-Tai said grimly.

That suited me very well.

I knew, of course, that the battle wouldn't take place until morning, so I felt safe in donning my cloak, and bundling myself out to the wall where the night watch was on duty.

No one recognized me. Not only was I well cloaked in a cloak, I was also well cloaked in darkness.

"Nice night," I said to the bloke on duty. It was only raining a little.

"In't it?" he replied, pulling his cloak close about him. "What're you doin' out so late then, darling?"

"Couldn't sleep," I said. "I'm too worried about the outcome of the battle tomorrow."

"Battle?"

"You *know*, when the Palace Guard take on the emperor's harem."

He laughed, "Oh, that. I wouldn't go so far as to call that a *battle*. Not a proper battle. I mean, they're a bunch of the emperor's pampered houris for all their struttin' about in armor. Be more like a massacre, I should say."

"Yes," I said. "I know. That's what has me so worried. You see, I cherish a secret passion for the Captain of the Guard. . . ."

When the conversation was over and I returned to the harem to wake Lotus, I felt rather ashamed of myself but then, I had to remember, my people had been tricked by cunning when courage alone wasn't enough. Honor is for those who have the wherewithal to survive defeat.

The ladies and I staged a preemptive strike the next morning.

"There's not a moment to lose!" I told them after a quick foray into the castle to make sure my ploy had worked. "Our foes have surrounded the emperor's bedchamber," I told them.

"Oh, my poor Papa Panda Bear!", Lotus cried. "We must save him!"

"Ladies," Tai-Tai said, "I think it best we use that strategy Bodie described to us wherein some of us come from the right, and some from the left, while some drop down on our foe from the rafters. . . ."

The guards at first appeared absolutely bewildered, but when they realized the ladies in armor, fighting in earnest, dealing real cuts and blows, were their appointed foes, they rallied somewhat.

His Majesty poked his head out of his chamber long enough to say, "Oh, it's begun, has it?" and ducked back in to get his own crowned helm, which provided him some protection during the fray.

Sun Zoo showed up too, and stood on the sidelines with folded arms and a smirk on his face, until he saw that the guards were not automatically winning.

In fact, they were on the point of being annihilated. Three had made the mistake of cornering Number Two Wife and she was parrying for all she was worth. Meanwhile, Lotus dropped down from the rafters onto the shoulders of one of the attackers, ripped off his helmet and began bashing him on the head with her shield. Tai-Tai and Number Two Concubine closed in on the other two, fighting off their own attackers.

Blood was quite satisfyingly everywhere and none of it seemed to belong to my ladies.

Lotus's victim collapsed under her and she pounced upon another one, using the maneuver wherein she slid under his legs and . . .

"Majesty!" wailed the Captain of the Guard. "Can I kill her? She's about to unman—stop that, you minx," he swore something less repeatable and tried to kick her away but she was like a leech. "Me!"

"No, no!" the monarch cried. "Call it off, call it off.

I can stand this no longer! All you men, go away, stop looking at my harem. Surrender!"

"Hearing and obeying, Majesty. We'll turn ourselves in to the brig immediately," the Captain of the Guard said, laying his sword gingerly across Lotus's abdomen, which was still quivering at floor level, though her dagger was no longer raised to endanger his future children.

The emperor meanwhile was jumping up and down, clapping his hands and crying, "All my lovely ladies, attend me. Seeing you in all your sweating, sinewy glory after all this time without you has made me feel very excited. Enough of this bloody combat. I have a more congenial use for you all. . . ."

It was lonely in the harem the rest of the day and that night.

I felt distinctly left out. Wandering the chambers alone, with no sound of the flute, the lute, or the strains of "The Aura of Lady Lee" sung round the brazier, no one tending anyone else's bruises or saddlesores, it was very lonely.

"A Pyhrric Victory, eh, Madame Spy?" said the voice of Sun Zoo. He wasn't sneering now, however, or even leering.

"Not at all," I said. "My ladies are all alive, including the one I saved from your heavy-handed tactics, the emperor is happy—or so I imagine him to be—and the guards were none of them seriously wounded and will live to guard again."

"And none of them will lose their retirement pay or be demoted after all, eh? In spite of the rumor going around last night to the effect that any guard who actually maimed or killed one of the emperor's ladies would not have much of a career left to him. I can't think where such a tale would have started."

I shrugged. "If it isn't exactly honorable to undermine the enemy's morale in any way you can, it's at least sensible. In another six months, or a year, perhaps, at the same level of training, the ladies would have needed no edge. They were excellent. But your week's worth of training is good only if you're talking about hotheaded pot boys who want to be soldiers and already have the muscles and are not with child, are fit, and have no womanly scruples."

"Yes, I could see your charges were very much hampered by womanly scruples," he said dryly.

"You should also see that the rumor was the simple truth. The emperor would have thanked no one, you least of all, for killing his ladies. Everyone is better off. Even the guards have been put on their mettle—"

"Well . . . yes. I don't think they expected quite such fierce resistance. But if the guards could have fought to wound . . ."

I shuddered. "But it is at least a draw, wouldn't you say?"

"At least. I saw some excellent fighting technique there and some of it from that hopeless little twit I attempted to teach. How did you?"

"Professional secret," I told him. I wasn't about to tell him I was already an experienced soldier when I began watching him teach Lotus and learned a tremendous amount from his pontificating.

When I returned to the harem, the ladies were already beginning to file back in, spent, smelly, and quite happy. In the bath they told me that the emperor was so taken with their performance—and his own, afterward—that he decided to form a special, very personal, bodyguard from their ranks, a guard to which it would be a very high honor to belong. The training, therefore, was to continue, on condition that His Majesty got to watch this time.

Sun Zoo was allowed to slink off, and graciously, I even captured his helm long enough to prise my lady's nightingale egg from it and replace it with the magic ruby.

The odd thing was, it turned out that all of the tales I told various people while I wore the red stone were reasonably true. The emperor *did* like his women a bit on the Amazonian side, and so the ladies gained favor and power from it. Also, many of them had male babies, though I can claim no credit for that, nor can the stone, or can it? In addition, a guard who killed or maimed one of the ladies would certainly have lost His Majesty's favor, for as he proved, he was very fond indeed of his ladies. So fond, in fact, that he never again chose another wife. Which many said showed he was a wise and prudent man, if not a brave one.

One more thing proved true as well. When, for my services, I was offered my choice of all of the gentlemen of the court to be my husband, I chose the Captain of the Guard, for whose bulging sinews and reluctant gallantry I found I held all the admiration I had earlier confided to his subordinate. It is my intense pleasure to report that Lady Lotus's knife did him no damage whatsoever.

Sometimes a woman just doesn't feel like herself.

THE GROWLING

Jody Lynn Nye

"You have used up the last of the birch moss, Honi," Dahli complained, a frown on her heart-shaped face. She tipped up the earthenware container to prove the truth of its emptiness, then dropped it to the dirt floor. Her strong hands, more used to clenching a sword than a broom, clamped down on her hips.

"Why not? My need is the same as anyone else's." Honi pouted, flexing a bicep until her apron sleeve split, showing her bronzed arm. In a moment, the shield-sisters might come to blows over an increasingly petty argument. Their chief flung herself between them.

"Enough!" cried Shooga, her voice filling the small supply hut. "Peace between you. Since there is not enough birch moss, I order that you two shall go out and seek more, and furthermore, you shall not raise your voices again. Now, apologize," she said, patting her palms against the air as if pushing the two women together. "You are warriors and sisters in combat."

Dahli looked at Honi, who eyed her with suspicion.

"I apologize," Honi said at last.

"So do I," Dahli said, tossing back her mane of brown hair. "But you did use up the moss." Honi's face turned a deeper shade of tan.

"I needed it!"

137

"And what am I supposed to do? Watch where I sit for a week?" Dahli breasted up to Honi, her fists clenched. Honi went on guard with her basket, as if she was about to belabor her shield-sister over the head with it.

"Girls! Girls!" Shooga shouted, pushing them apart in truth this time. The warrior women dodged to glare at one another over her head, making faces. Shooga was fed up with the lot of them. Her back hurt, too.

The time of the Growling had come again. Thank the Goddesses such times were rare in the history of the village of Hee Kwal, or there would be no unity, merely widely spaced houses full of woe. The fault lay with Mother Nature herself. Women of bearing age had children, with only a few turns of the moon between birth and conceiving anew. With men gone so long, though, the last of the children had been born months ago, leaving wombs idle. It was as if all the women returned to the time of their earliest nubile season, before they had bargained between themselves for husbands. As was the way of the Mother Goddesses during the time of creation, each of the women's cycles had gradually returned, joining the pattern until they were identical in timing and duration. When the girls who had reached womanhood but never been with a man were numbered alongside the grown warriors, that made the Red Time very strong. Woe betide the unwary stranger who wandered into the village during the Growling. True, it only lasted a day or two in every moon, but it sorely tried Shooga's patience.

The men of Hee Kwal had gone to the capital of Sen Setif, to serve their year's time as honor guard to the king and queen. Next time Shooga would see that it was the women who went to represent Hee Kwal. The men had been away so long Shooga's youngest baby was already fourteen moons old, and she was feeling the lack of male comfort. So were all the others, though they didn't precisely want them *now*. Her mate, Brohne, usually made himself scarce during this time of the moon anyway when he *was* at home, preferring to be out of range. Yet the women's patience was wearing thin at the men's absence. Their anger was never so obvious as at this time of the month. The Growling released fierce, wild, magical energies, and lent strength to female warriors' arms.

The seeress Wysacha hobbled up to them and raised her rheumy eyes to Shooga. "The Hen of Night laid the Day Egg hours ago. This argumentative one," she pointed a chipped nail at Honi, "has her appointment when the Egg reaches its highest. If she is not at my hut by the time it hatches into the red Rooster of Evening I will take the next patient."

"I will be there!" Honi said, glaring at the old woman. "You shall take away my pain, Wysacha. I receive no relief and no respect either in this village. If my husband was here . . ."

"If your husband was here you'd be with child, and there'd be no Growling," Wysacha said, with a grin that showed her toothlessness. "Thank the Goddesses I'm past all that, but I thank you for the extra magic I can draw upon."

"I think the men stay away deliberately," Dahli said, shoving her dark hair behind her and working it into a rough braid. "Why resume the responsibility of home and child when they can be away, free to hunt and fight?"

"My husband will pay when he gets back, that I promise you," Honi said, hoisting her basket on her hip and tossing her golden hair. "I'll be with you very soon, Wysacha."

"Good, good," the old wizardess said, turning in a swirl of dark red robes to totter back toward her hut. "Bring some food. The Day Egg needs nourishment to grow. Huh! Goddesses pity the first man to set foot in this village: the whole place is set against you."

* * *

"The Night God spat the Gob of Light hours ago," Pex, chief of the Buh Bah, admonished his spy. "How lies the land?"

The man grinned, his white teeth gleaming in the blackness of his beard. "You'll like this, chief. The whole place is empty of men, except for boys not old enough to grow peach fuzz. The women are alone, and for a long time, I wager. The village has deteriorated. Gardens are untended, and above all lies the fume of an unfamiliar smell."

"No men? Do you say so?" demanded Abbs, chief of the Ma Cho and Pex's second-in-command.

"I swear, brother," the spy said, slapping his hand on the other's well-muscled buttock in testament of a good oath.

"*Hur hur hur*," laughed Pex, diabolically. "It shouldn't take much to conquer them, and then— Par Tee!"

The scared rite of Par Tee involved the consumption of much fermented spirits, followed by the ingestion of well-greased meats, and then fertility rites, the more vigorous the better. As Pex looked around at his cohort, he saw that every man's face wore a grin wide enough to swallow the ears of the man on each side.

The tribes of Buh Bah and Ma Cho had once been at war. The battling had lasted for many seasons until peace had grudgingly been proposed. It seemed that the two sides would rather sneer at one another over the bargaining table until one wise soul pointed out that if they united forces they could go and pick on smaller tribes. A treaty was suggested, and both sides agreed at once.

The most defenseless of Buh Bah's neighbors were the Sen Setif. Sen Setif males were objects of derision in both the Buh Bah and Ma Cho lands because the Sen Setif valued male and female alike, both in the arts of war and of peace. The Buh Bahs and the Ma Chos knew well that a woman's place was in a man's bed. Any woman's place. How convenient it was that they wouldn't have to fight the Sen Setif for their females.

Honi was grateful for her close-fitting leather armor as she brushed past the waist-high, stinging nettles to get close to the birch trees. She spotted a lush clump of moss and began to pull it off the white bark. Such dull work.

She heard the clink of metal near her. It must be Dahli threshing through the reeds on the bank of the stream, looking for wide lily leaves to pack the moss in. Honi wished she would hurry up. She wanted to get back to the village and have Wysacha work her magic on Honi's aching lower back. Though her skin felt as if it itched on the inside, she discovered that the irritation that had dogged her all day disappeared as soon as she set foot outside the village wall. Wysacha was right: the place was packed full of magic. Perhaps in the rite of the Third Day they could wind the whole package into a spell and send it to bring their men home safely—so she and Dahli and the others could beat them with sticks for having been gone so long.

She sighed and rested her back against the nearest tree bole. Mytee was a good man. He'd hardly know their son, who had grown up enough to walk and wield a play spear already. She'd even taught the little one to say "Surrender or die!"

Honi knelt to yank one more chunk of the absorbent moss off the handiest birch. Almost enough now for ten women, she told herself, looking down at her well-filled basket. The metallic clank came nearer. It must be Dahli. She looked up, expecting her shield-sister. Instead, she had one moment's glimpse at a tall, well-muscled, handsome, but greasy, unshaven, and dirty man before hands grabbed her from behind and clamped over her eyes and mouth.

*   *   *

"Ow! Gods damn her, she bit me!" Gluetz howled. The eight men trying to hold onto the blond woman paid him no mind. Their captive was refusing to cooperate. She struggled and kicked, even managing to work a fist loose now and again to punch a man in the face. Pex signalled to the warriors to drop their burden and sit on her so he could tie the woman's hands and feet. Most of them sported scratches and bruises before he was finished.

"A fine one," Abbs said, running his eyes up and down her body. "Spirited. I like that. She'll be a worthy object for the rite of Par Tee."

The female glared at them over the gag made of a wad of birch moss and her own belt. Pex grinned down at her. Suddenly, her body relaxed, and her eyes closed.

"The force of my personality," Pex said, certain that it was true. "Pick her up. Let's see if the rest of them are so easily subdued."

The men shouldered their burden, but not before Pex saw the woman's eyes open again. In them he saw hate, and the promise of retribution. That look would change to love once he gave her his personal attention.

"Soon, my pretty, soon," he said, patting her on the thigh. The woman kicked at him with both legs, almost throwing herself off Abbs's and Gluetz's shoulders.

Across the meadow, Dahli straightened up from the mass of lilies, her hands full of dripping leaves. A sharply painful impulse had hit her right in the guts. She thought it was belly cramp, returning earlier than Wysacha had promised, but no. It was a warning, the kind she felt when there was to be a battle.

"Honi?" she said out loud. Her friend didn't answer. Dahli threw away the water lilies and reached up over her shoulder for her sword.

The noise of feet threshing the reeds made her drop to one knee, on guard and out of sight.

A group of men passed her by. At first she was gladdened by the sight, thinking it was their husbands returning from their travels. The next puff of wind swiftly disabused her of the idea. These men stank like months-dead offal. Their tunics and trews bore so much soil and grease at first Dahli didn't see the rips. And besides, the garments didn't match. No Sen Setif man would let himself go so badly.

Between them, two of the men carried a struggling bundle. Honi! Dahli thought at first of leaping up and charging in to save her friend, but realized she was well outnumbered. Better to sneak back to the village and get help.

"They've got Honi?" Shooga asked, but she was already buckling her sword harness over her black body armor. She added her favorite war hammer to a loop on her belt. "How dare they?"

"*Who* were they?" Wysacha asked, wringing her thin hands together.

"Buh Bahs," Dahli said, pacing up and back over the chief's carpets. "And Ma Chos, too, unless I mistake the smell. There's at least forty of them, all filthy."

"By the Goddesses, they will pay," Shooga said, slapping one hand into the other. "Muster all the women. Put the children in the central barn with the beasts, and put a heavy guard on all the doors. Attack our village, will they?" The chief felt herself getting hot, as if the air around her had caught fire.

"Careful," Wysacha said, holding out her palms to sense the ether. "The magic is packed around us like bomb-powder. A forceful thought could set the whole place off."

Shooga stopped three paces before charging out the door and made herself calm down. The heat died away to a warning of warmth. She turned to nod at the wisewoman.

"I'll save that for the right moment, old one. In the meantime, I must see to our defense. Get to a safe place, and watch out for us."

"I'm already weaving spells," Wysacha said, tottering out the door as fast as she could.

Pex had his hand on the hilt of his sword as he swaggered into the village square, followed by his men and their captive. Nice place, this. Houses in good repair: all of them even had *roofs*. Plenty of trees to lounge beneath, lots of wood for fires. Good grass for herds. They were going to like it here. He surveyed the village as if its surrender was a mere formality.

Abbs carried a sheep he had killed. It would make a fine barbecue for the Par Tee. He threw it on the ground in front of the group and stood next to Pex. In the doorways and courtyards, women went nonchalantly about their tasks: drawing water, weaving cloth, milking cattle, pulling weeds.

"They can hardly contain their enthusiasm," Gluetz said, looking around him.

"Perhaps they haven't noticed us," Abbs whispered.

"How could they not?" Pex asked, thumping his chest mightily. "Do we not have the appearance of warriors? Do we not reek of manly musk? They ought to be grateful to us for coming. Look around you. These might not have had a man in months. Some will feel the lack."

"And how good could a Sen Setif man be anyhow," Delts snickered, "with his foolish ideas about equality? A woman gets just as much pleasure from a rough tumble as she does from slow wooing."

"Hah!" Gluetz said, slapping his leg. "And a man can get in three or four women in so much time. Why waste a nice, warm day like this one getting all hot over a single roll in the straw?"

"*Hur hur hur*," Pex laughed. "So true. Ladies!" He

raised his hands on high, turning so every woman could look upon his masculine splendor. The women turned disinterested eyes toward the group in the center of the grassy square. "Greetings! I am Pex of the Buh Bah! You will be glad to see us. My men and I here claim title to this land and everything that grows or walks on it. We are your conquerors! Surrender to us easily, and you may even enjoy our attentions. We are bold and experienced lovers, and I promise none shall go without. What do you say?" He stood with his hands outstretched and a broad smile on his face, waiting for the gratitude of the village maidens.

"Aaaaaaaaaaaaahhhhhhhhhh!" The voices from a third of a hundred female throats were raised in a shrill war cry that caused the hair on the nape of his neck to stand straight out. From behind looms, from under milking stools, from flower baskets, from the folds of dresses came swords, spears, and maces. The loose robes fell away, revealing armor and ringmail.

For just a moment, the Buh Bah were paralyzed. Then Pex swept his sword out of its scabbard just in time to meet a blow aimed at his head.

"Oh ho! So you want it rough?" Pex chortled, beating back the attack with ease. "Wonderful! My men prefer it that way."

Dahli led the first wave of ten Hee Kwals. At her side was Timayta, Honi's younger sister, eager to redress the wrong done to her family's honor. Eight of them charged straight into the midst of the men, forming a shield for the two who swung bludgeons at the knees of the men guarding Honi. While the erstwhile guards were jumping up and down clutching their legs, Dahli's squad surrounded Honi, cut her bonds, and guided her out again. As soon as her hands were free, the blond warrior drew her own sword and waded in against the invaders.

"Cooperation," Shooga had said over and over

again, when teaching tactics. "Cooperation—and hit them where they live." Honi took that advice.

Meanwhile, the other two waves of ten closed in on the mob of Ma Chos from both sides. Dahli, the last to withdraw, took a swipe at Pex himself. He disengaged her blade expertly, and countered with a hard blow that vibrated her arm to the shoulder. Gritting her teeth, she swung again. He laughed, parrying her sword and Timayta's with a single cunning move.

Dahli let out a frustrated scream between her teeth and rained blows on him from every angle, only to meet a counterstroke each time. Her own sword turned in her grip, and she had to hold it with both hands. She couldn't hold out long against such a forceful attack. An arm encased in black leather slid past her and caught the next blow on the shaft of a war hammer. Shooga shouted at her.

"Together, now!"

Dahli nodded shortly. Around them, men and women battled fiercely. Dahli saw with despair that the women were not up to their best fighting trim. It had been so long since they'd had a genuine conflict that they'd let themselves go soft. She vowed to the Mother Goddesses that if they survived this battle she'd train her muscles every day, instead of twice or thrice a week. As she began to tire, she recalled Wysacha nagging her to follow the Way of Ayrao Bix, the first and most tireless of Hee Kwal's female warriors. How she wished she had heeded that advice.

"Are you all right?" Timayta asked Honi, as the two of them hammered on the sword and shield of a blackbearded male.

"My hands are numb, my back aches, and the smell is making me sick to my stomach," Honi said, punctuating each phrase with a sound strike on their enemy's sword or leather shield. "Other than that, I am fine."

"Don't get yourselves all tired out," the man said,

leering at them over the edge of his shield. "You should be looking forward to the Par Tee."

"Par Tee? With you?" Timayta cried. "How barbaric!"

"Yeah." The man grinned. "Ain't it great?"

Honi was infuriated by the big man's arrogance. She struck again and again at him, but knew her blows were not connecting with flesh. He turned them all back; not easily, but steadily. She was good, but where skills were evenly balanced, weight and height would always win. Honi was suddenly afraid that her village would fall to these disgusting invaders. They would . . . touch them. She panted with fury, and was made even more angry when the man watched her breathe with open admiration. Honi saw red.

She didn't know at first whether there was something in her eyes, or if the whole world was disappearing in a crimson mist. Around her, fellow warriors were falling, and the men, with fewer opponents to face, were ganging up on single women. Warriors were vanquished one after another, knocked out or tied up by the invaders. She tried to fight her way toward them, but it was getting harder and harder to see. The sun was a red lens in the sky.

Pex turned away the puny blows of the females. His men wielded the greater strength, and their cause was just. It was only a matter of time before they had worked all the fight out of the women. When they were exhausted, they'd be that much easier to convince to serve the Buh Bah. And the Ma Cho. This equal sharing stuff was too advanced for him. Normally he would just tell his men to take the ones they wanted, and leave the rest for the other tribe. Numbers weren't his strong suit, but even he could see there weren't enough women to go around.

"Don't kill any of them!" he shouted. The big woman in black and the sexy woman in ring armor pressed their attack on him as if they really knew what they were doing. For a moment he felt sorry for their fathers. If these girls had been sons, he could have made warriors out of them.

Suddenly Abbs and Delts were beside him, a red-headed woman slung between them, unconscious.

"How goes the day, brothers?" Pex asked, parrying a double blow with both hands on his sword hilt. The woman in black showed all her teeth, and slammed a hammer blow at his arm. He shrugged it off with the edge of his hide shield.

"Over soon," Abbs said, cheerfully. "This is number ten plus two to go down. Only some more to go!" Abbs wasn't too good with numbers either, but he was a good judge of a battle.

"Fine," Pex said. "I'll just finish off these two." His brother chief pushed by behind him, leaving Pex with his opponents. The women were tiring at last. He was pleased to see that the fire in their eyes was undiminished. The Par Tee would be a good one.

And yet, Pex thought, it was strange. The day had been fair, but now there was a low cloud gathering around the battle like rising mist. It wasn't dust; no one was coughing. Besides, the dirt here wasn't red.

With a skilled twist of his sword, he disarmed the big woman of her hammer. She reached over her head for the sword on her back. Pex chopped at her arm, and connected with the tricep muscle. It didn't cut through the leather, but he could tell it hurt by the tears that sprang to the woman's eyes.

"Give up now," he suggested, almost kindly. "Save us all some time."

"Never," the woman gritted. She shrugged her sword free, and engaged him again. The cloud around them grew more palpable, cutting off the sight of the other warriors around them. She slashed at his chest with the point of her blade. Pex turned it away, but just barely.

The chief of the Buh Bah began to think something was very wrong. The women should have been getting weaker, but instead, they seemed to be drawing strength from somewhere. And he, puissant fighter, felt himself growing tired. How could such a thing be? The woman in black was saying something.

"How *dare* you invade our village!" she shrieked, chopping deeply into his shield. "How *dare* you capture one of my warriors and truss her up like a roast! How dare you kill one of our prize ewes! How dare you offer to rub your greasy, smelly bodies against ours! How dare you insult us and the honor of our husbands!"

With every slash of her sword, Pex found himself retreating a step. He blundered backwards over a loom. Another woman-joined the attack on him, her eyes ablaze.

"You ruined my weaving!" she shrieked. "A moon's work, destroyed!" She brought a mace crashing down on him, but only hit him in the head. A mere scratch.

"You should be glad we offered to conquer you," Pex pointed out to the three women confronting him. "We will appreciate your beauty, and you won't have to wear those confining garments any longer."

"You arrogant cretin," the woman in ringmail snarled. The thrust she aimed at him actually passed through Pex's defense and rammed him in the chest. If the sword had had a point, he'd have been done for. That thought struck him just as he bumped into something.

"That you, chief?" Abbs's voice asked.

"What is happening?" Pex asked, dumbfounded, turning his head just enough to see his fellow chief, at bay. His arm moved mechanically, parrying one blow after another. Out of the corner of his eye Pex saw that every one of their men was now back-to-back in the center of the village square, fighting for their lives against a brood of women. "This is impossible!"

The invaders were overwhelmed by the circle of female fighters. One by one, the men dropped, and the women clustered around the next warrior, beating him until he submitted or fell unconscious. Soon, there were only a few standing: Pex, Abbs, Delts, and Gluetz.

"And now," cried the blond woman that they had captured out in the field, "*kill!*" She raised her sword arm over her head, and charged.

The women, only just visible through the red fog that now blanketed the village square, responded with their shrill war cry. The four invaders, as one, cowered and dropped to the ground with their arms over their heads.

"No!" a little old crone shrieked, appearing out of one of the houses. She pushed herself into the midst of the women and stood in front of the chiefs. "Don't kill. The power of the Growling will rebound back on you the way their attacks have on them!"

"Then I've already paid for this!" Honi said, striding forward to Pex. She grabbed a handful of his greasy hair and hauled him to his feet. There was incredible strength in her slender arm. Pex couldn't have stayed down if he'd wanted to.

"This is for sitting on me," Honi cried.

"I'd hate to see what would happen if your men were here," Pex said, weaving back and forth. He tried to lift his hand to brush her away, but it was too heavy.

"If our men were here," Honi said, cocking back her gloved fist and aiming carefully, "they'd watch and applaud!"

With the full force of the Growling magic behind her, Honi swung. Her fist connected with the man's chin. He flattened out on the air, and sailed a dozen yards over the heads of his men before crashing into a tree. Curious birds, disturbed from their nest, sailed down to fly around his head in a circle, twittering to one another.

* * *

As soon as the last of the invaders was defeated, the air cleared. The red mist vanished, leaving the sky a pure and sparkling blue.

"The Growling is over," Wysacha said, with a pleased nod, as if she had arranged the whole matter herself.

"Thank the Goddesses," Shooga said. She reached up to sheathe her sword and stopped in surprise. "My back has stopped hurting!"

"All you needed was some exercise," the old woman said, coming over to pat the chief on the back. "I have told you this before. Exercise and good nutrition, just as it is said the great one Ayrao Bix practiced."

"Is this the answer?" Shooga asked, only half joking. "Next time the Growling comes, we should go looking for a fight?"

"No, no," Wysacha chided her gently. "By then I hope the men are back again. The magic was so strong this time. We won't always find so easy a way to dissipate it."

"Easy?" Abbs asked, staring up at the sky. He lifted his head, then dropped it to the earth again. The village females all walked away from them, the Ma Cho, leaving them lying on the turf as if they were of no importance whatsoever. If he had the strength, he'd ... he'd ... he'd better leave before he found out *what* he would do. Some mysteries were better not investigated. He rolled over onto his belly and hauled himself to his feet with surprising difficulty. The other men were all scattered nearby like heaps of dirty rags.

"Come on," he said, swaying as he gestured with one arm. He hadn't felt so bad since the time they brewed liquor out of mushrooms. Abbs gathered up those of the tribes who were conscious, and assigned them to carry the ones who weren't. It took four of them to haul the mighty Pex away from the tree where he was resting.

The men boldly slunk out of the village of Hee

Kwal. No one attempted to stop them, which Abbs attributed to the reputation of the Ma Cho. And if they told their story first around the pubs in the great cities to the north and east, that reputation would not suffer.

"You forgot the sheep," Delts told Abbs. "We could at least have had the barbecue."

Abbs glanced behind them at the ragged file of warriors. Some of them were walking in a delicate fashion to avoid chafing bruised body parts. Those women did *not* fight fair.

"Bugger the sheep," Abbs said. "No one is in the mood for any kind of Par Tee."

Honi looked down at her knuckles. "Ech! Look at that, will you?" she said, holding out her hand to her friends. "That brute had enough grease on him to light a lamp."

"Filthy," Dahli agreed, shaking her head over the ugly smudges. She offered the edge of her own tunic to her shield-sister and best friend to wipe off the grime, then something occurred to her. "Honi, where is the moss? I really need it now."

"Oh, I dropped it near the birch trees," Honi said, pointing up the hill. "I'll go with you to gather it up. At least now I am certain we won't be disturbed."

Mine humble and o'b't Correspondent informs me that something like *this* really happened too. As she is also a Penwoman of some Authority and Reknown upon the subject of Regency texts, I perceive small reason to doubt her.

THE NEW BRITOMART

eluki bes shahar

It was entirely the fault of the book which that great enchanter, the Wizard of the North, had made, to begin with; for once Sir Arthur Mallory obtained his copy of that eagerly-awaited tome from Hatchard's, the damage was done past all repairing.

"Hello, Wilfred," Miss Rowena Spencer said, opening the top half of the kitchen door on a brisk March morning. "Have you come to do Papa's accounts again?"

Rowena Spencer was a damsel of that blonde buxomness long celebrated by the less-respectable English poets, though Rowena herself was a young woman of impeccable probity. Her birth was the result of a delicately disregarded *mesalliance* between Lady Letitia Burroughs, only daughter of the Viscount Greystoke, and the village blacksmith, young Weland Spencer. Upon the occasion of the Viscountcy's devolution upon the broad shoulders of a distant cousin raised entirely in foreign parts by wildly unsuitable persons, Lady Letty had announced that rather than remain one more instant beneath Cousin John's roof,

153

she would marry the first man she saw, the subject of her vow being the fellow who was shoeing her horse at the time.

There were times at which Rowena Spencer wished that her late mother had been a shade less precipitate, but she was a stout-hearted English girl who embraced her present station with a stalwart heart while dreaming of better things.

One of those better things was Wilfred.

Wilfred Roland Oliver Charlemagne Lancelot Mallory was the only son and principal heir of Sir Arthur Mallory, a robust gentleman whose fortune obtained in equal measure from Scottish sheep and Birmingham mills. Young Wilfred had scarce nineteen summers to his credit, and—though his hair and eyes could charitably be called blond and blue—to name them so would be the most definite thing about Mr. Mallory's person.

"Hullo, Rowena," Wilfred said gloomily. "No, that isn't until the end of the week." He drooped endearingly upon the doorsill, reminding Rowena of a desolate dandelion. "Is your father in?" he pursued, for he was a polite young man, and cognizant of the social necessities.

Mr. Wilfred Mallory's greatest desire was to be an accountant: he had first salved that burning hunger in his maiden soul by preparing so rigorous a catalog of his father's extensive library that his work was quite the envy of the entire county. There had been numerous offers tendered for his services, but Sir Arthur had angrily rejected them all, saying that one in whose veins burned the immortal blood of the greatest of English kings (Sir Arthur having conveniently forgotten that he had purchased his title in 1807) would not stoop to clerking drudgery.

As Wilfred found himself without many outlets for his natural talents at Camelot Court, and the recipient of little peace within its walls, he had endeared himself to the tradespeople of Miching Malicho by a positive

yearning to handle their accounts and billing, and for this reason he was much seen in the shops on High Street around the fifteenth of each month.

"He's at the smithy, of course," Rowena said. "But come inside, Wilfred—there's new bread made and the cloth laid for tea. Is it about the tourney?"

"So you know, then," Wilfred said despondently. "Does everyone know?"

"Only everyone in the county," Rowena said, in an attempt to be consoling. "And possibly London," she added.

Sir Arthur Mallory had taken up the new Gothic fashion embraced by Horace Walpole seventy years before, and with the inspiration of Strawberry Hill before him, Sir Arthur had taken the fruit of many successful years in the wool trade and erected his own homage to medieval chivalry and his own hotly-mooted ancestors. The erection of Camelot Court in the otherwise undistinguished border town of Miching Malicho (located between the Whiteadder and the Tweed, and of very little earthly import whatever) was far more than a nod to the current interest in the Gothic style: it represented, in fact, the first flowering of Sir Arthur's greatest obsession—to prove his descent from the legendary King Arthur himself, and, failing the seizin of the throne of England by genealogical means, the restoration of the Court of Camelot at the very least.

That Sir Arthur had not been invited to dine among the peers of the realm last year, when Prinny had finally legitimately assumed his father's dignities and the style of King George IV with all the medieval pomp and splendor that a blithe disregard for financial economy could muster, had been a crushing disappointment to Sir Arthur's medieval ambitions, it is true, but in all probability that gentleman would merely have retreated to the sanctuary of his anachronistic

crenelations to lave his psychic wounds in the salt of resentment, were it not for The Book.

Ivanhoe.

Sir Walter Scott—the Wizard of the North, the Great Enchanter—was a noted *romancier* who could always be counted upon to produce something ornate and dramatic about the many injustices suffered by his beloved Highlanders, but, sales having fallen off on the *Waverly* series of late, he had turned his mind and his pen to a time and a place he hoped would be dearer to the hearts and pocketbooks of his reading public.

He called it *Ivanhoe*, and it burst upon the literary scene in December of 1819.

In February of 1821, Sir Arthur Mallory, cheated of the greater ceremony beyond his touch, determined that Camelot Court would be the site of a tourney that very summer.

"This is the outside of enough," Sir Arthur's son said forlornly. He seated himself at Rowena's well-scrubbed kitchen table and regarded the corn-gold curls, coral-pink lips, and gillyflower-blue eyes of his hostess without any particular approval. If the truth were told, Wilfred liked numbers much better than girls, although some girls—Rowena being one—were slightly less objectionable than others.

Rowena placed a mug of hard cider in front of him, along with the end of a hot loaf fresh out of the oven. He was, she felt, too thin, and wanted feeding. "A tourney," Wilfred repeated, just in case either of them had forgotten the cause of his depression.

"Perhaps it will be amusing," Rowena suggested hopefully. "The banners, and the horses—and the armor."

"Do you know how to wear a suit of armor?" Wilfred moaned. "Do I? Do any of the half-mad antiquarians Papa is inviting? We have had nothing but the tourney for breakfast, nuncheon, and tea since he

took this maggot into his head—the winner of the joust is to crown whom he will the Queen of Love and Beauty and ask what boon he will, and I am sure Papa would award Elaine's hand in marriage to the victor, did he think he could manage it without her turning him into a toad!"

"Ah," Rowena said. An idea was beginning to take strong possession of her, and she felt her heart beat faster. "And may anyone compete in this tourney?"

Wilfred—who had finished one large mug of alcoholic apple juice and was beginning on the second—laughed as harshly as so indefinite a young man might.

"Oh, aye—anyone who shows up with horse and armor will doubtless be invited—the more mysterious, the better! But there is one whom you will not find in the lists on the Feast of St. John, and that one, Miss Spencer, is I!"

It should not be particularly difficult, Rowena told herself, looking about the now-deserted smithy (Papa having gone for his usual three-tankard lunch at the Bell and Candle, the local coaching house), *and it is my only chance to fix my interest with Wilfred.*

Rowena gazed about the Miching Malicho smithy with a practiced eye. Through this well-built structure at the edge of town came every horse, cart, and hinge in the county requiring shoeing or maintenance. Rowena had helped her father here on many an occasion. Now she was going to help herself.

Wilfred said that anyone might compete. And that he would not. And that the winner could crown the Queen of Love and Beauty—who would sit beside him at the feast that Sir Arthur will hold thereafter.

She picked up a crested helm that was lying in the corner, awaiting removal of its dents. Most of the armor gracing the halls of Sir Arthur's castle had been made here, there not being enough available from Samuel Pratt's fine antiquarian show rooms in Bond Street to nurture Sir Arthur's anachronistic mania.

And if what Wilfred—and local gossip—said was true, orders would soon be flooding in from all over the nation for improvement and custom-fitting of ancestral armor. In such confusion, it would be simplicity itself to add one more requisition.

So all I have to do is win the tourney—and crown Wilfred. That should make him notice me!

Nobody will notice me. Elaine Mallory sat in the window seat of her tower laboratory, her battered green kerseymere dress wadded up around her knees as she sat curled up in the window seat. The heat from the athanor nestled in its straw-filled cradle did little to palliate the chill of the room, likewise the small alcohol-fed flames beneath certain of her other experiments.

If it was Wilfred Mallory's curse to have been born an ordinary chap into a family of monomaniacal eccentrics, Elaine's curse was to wish to have everything both ways.

Elaine Guinevere Astolat Mallory was a well-grown damsel of three-and-twenty, the pleasing effect of her black hair and brown eyes—and a most agreeable countenance for one whose marriage settlements were known to be so large—marred only slightly by a certain randomness of toilette and a tendency to slouch. While her dowry ensured no lack of eligible suitors for her hand, her lamentable tendency to quiz young hopefuls upon their Latin and Greek made it likely that she would be keeping house beneath her father's roof for many a year to come.

This did not normally cast Elaine's spirits so far into the dismals as it might be supposed, as Elaine was the recipient of a generous allowance, the entire North Tower to her personal use, and a strong tendency to follow in her father's footsteps: she was studying sorcery.

However, what was tolerable and even agreeable when it was unknown to those whose regard must

always be solicited became far otherwise when it was
to be held up to consideration before an audience
drawn from half the persons of *ton* resident in the
counties of England.

There would be a Queen of Love and Beauty chosen at the Mallorean Tourney, and it was, after all,
only reasonable that the daughter of the tourney's
host should receive this encomium.

And she wouldn't. No matter who won. Even if by
some miracle Wilfred were to win (unlikely in the
extreme, as he was so far refusing even to ride in the
opening procession) he would be unlikely to remember to choose her, no matter how black-and-blue she
pinched him the night before.

Oh, if only *she* had a champion to ride into battle
for her!

Elaine's gaze sharpened, looking not to the meters
of glass tubing and flasks of bubbling reagents, but to
the bookshelf beyond. Slowly she got to her feet and
crossed the room.

There, between a copy of Francis Barrett's *The
Magus* and John Dee's *Talismantic Inteligencer* was a
copy of The Book. She flipped it open and began to
read, her lips moving as she told over the familiar
description of a knight, raven-haired and ebon-eyed,
his skin burnt black in the fires of Outremerian suns.
The most puissant, the most ascetic, the most able
knight and Templar in all Christendom.

All she had to do was find some way to get him.

News of Sir Arthur's entertainment was broadcast
across an England desperate for diversion and uneasy
beneath the rule of their new (and most unsatisfac-
tory) king. All over England, the thought of dusting
off great-grandfather's armor, borrowing the tenant's
best plowhorse, and going off to tourney, took on a
lustre that no sensible pastime could match.

Sir Arthur spent lavishly. There was the venue of
the event itself to be constructed: tilt-yard and melee

field, as well as the grandstands from which the entertainment was to be watched. There was the small
army of seamstresses, at a half-shilling a day, needed
to sew up the cloaks, tabards, surcoats, shield covers,
pavilions, banners, bannerets, pennons, gonfalons, and
the ornamental swagging that would decorate both
the tourney field and the banqueting hall.

The banquet itself had grown to a feast with covers
for five hundred souls, three hundred of whom would
have to be accommodated at trestle tables on the
south lawn, their revelries lit by torches. And that was
only the beginning.

In fact, if not for the *chere amie* who had been (so
she said), drawn to Miching Malicho by news of the
tourney, Sir Arthur might have given it up altogether.

Sir Arthur, in short, had met a lady.

Mrs. Titania Underhill's vague personal antecedents
were more than offset by her opulent personal
charms. The young widow (Mr. Underhill having
exited the scene in a manner equally inexplicit) had,
upon inspecting it, found Camelot Court so quaint,
so charming, yet so comfortable and modern, that she
had quickly extracted an invitation from Sir Arthur to
hold herself his guest for the indefinite future.

"It's disgusting," Elaine had said.

"It isn't quite the thing," her brother had
responded, and the siblings had found themselves as
close to agreement as they had been any time these
past two decades.

What neither of them suspected was that Mrs.
Underhill reciprocated their feelings, and felt that she
could certainly dispense with both of Sir Arthur's
inconvenient children before settling into a domestic
arrangement with their father.

The Mallorean Tourney would be the perfect
opportunity.

By day Rowena Spencer aided her father at the
forge. By night she first crafted a suit of armor, and

then   sword and shield. Once these items were hers, her evening hours were devoted to practice, since to bear away the prize at the tourney she had to win against all comers.

In these solitary hours, wielding sword and shield against an anonymous army of straw opponents, Rowena found true happiness and avocation. It was a great pity that there was no employment for female soldiers, much less for soldiers of any kind who fought with sword and buckler, for the sense of liberation their use gave her was not one she would lightly set ˉe when the tourney's day was done.

Ah, but to sit beside Wilfred at the High Table, to address to his ear alone the appropriate courtly speeches (for Rowena's later evenings and Sunday afternoons were devoted, like those of many of the other townsmen who had received free copies from Sir Arthur, to reading out loud the stirring or uplifting segments of The Saga, until Rowena felt herself— semantically at least—more than a match for the linguistic wiles of such an one as Sir Brian de Bois-Gulibert) would recompense her for a lifetime spent without the thrill of live steel in her hand.

Or so Rowena told herself.

At the moment, Sir Brian might have agreed with her.

Although she was an efficient sorceress and housekeeper, there had been times that Elaine despaired of finishing her preparations in time. While a simple evocation was child's play for one who had studied as she had, this was not quite a simple evocation.

There was, for one thing, the difficulty of providing a corporeal body once she had summoned the spirit.

At first she'd thought of stealing a corpse from the local cemetery, but none of the locals had been obliging enough to die at a time that suited her purposes— and then there would have been the added difficulty of transporting the body all the way to her tower.

She next thought of dispatching one of the servants, but in addition to the fact that Papa would surely miss any of the footmen whom her choice might fall upon, there was the possibility that the departing spirit of the slain domestic might interfere in her conjurations.

In the end, both for practicality and ease of transport, Elaine had settled upon a hundredweight and a half of mutton chops from the butcher, suitably interlarded with talismans particularly subject to Hermes Psychopompos, the Conductor of the Dead, and the addition of a Spell of Transmogrification to her enchantment. As during the last few weeks she had also succeeded in creating the Philosopher's Stone (at least, the black residue in the bottom of her athanor *ought* to be the Philosopher's Stone, if everything had gone properly), she felt a certain certitude of success.

Thus, at the appropriate hour, she chalked a Solomon's Seal upon the floor of her tower, filled three copper braziers with suitable herbs and resins, lit thirteen beeswax candles stolen from the local church (Elaine was always especially generous to the parish poor box to make up for her thefts, and would not have made them at all save for the inconvenient fact that her recipes demanded them), draped a white silk pall over the mutton chops, and began her conjuration.

As she chanted, pausing at intervals to throw more incense into the braziers, the air grew thick, the room grew dark, and the temperature dropped to near-Hyperboreal levels. A wind blew up—seemingly from nowhere—ruffling the pages of The Book to which she had turned for last-minute inspiration. At last the shape beneath the silk flowed, coalesced—and moved.

"You're no angel," Brian de Bois-Gulibert remarked, regarding his conjuror critically.

And that, he discovered, was only the beginning of his troubles.

* * *

The day of the Mallorean Tourney dawned gloriously fair, and—unlike the preceding three months—blessedly calm. The innkeepers and tradesmen for miles around blessed Sir Arthur's name, for their inns were full and their storerooms empty, so great were the numbers of those who came—with invitations or no—to view Sir Arthur's entertainment. The Earls, Viscounts, Barons, and Knights who vied one with the other over their precedence in the opening procession were enough to gladden a sterner epigone's heart than Sir Arthur's, and the resurrection of their ancestral duties for such men as the Knight Marshall of England and the Master of the College of Heralds was enough to ensure that Sir Arthur's tourney was *the* social event of the Season.

But Sir Arthur's elevated spirits upon this St. John's Day were not due entirely to these felicities, but to the fact that he had recently asked Mrs. Underhill to become his wife, and that lady had assured him of her answer at the banquet this very night. He was perhaps not perfectly aware of the fact that Mrs. Underhill had no intention of enacting even a bigamous liaison until all of Sir Arthur's progeny were extinct.

With that end in mind, it was a simple matter for Mrs. Underhill to see to it that Wilfred, too, competed in the tourney. She'd had a suitable suit of armor ready for weeks, and through the addition of a simple philtre to his morning tea, the opening of the tourney found young Wilfred Mallory seated upon the back of his confused and skittish hunter in a gleaming suit of 14th century enamelled German plate, wearing a silk surtout with the salvaged arms of the Mallorys upon it and a helm extravagantly plumed with egret feathers pillaged from Elaine Mallory's best Sunday bonnet.

Observers laid young Wilfred's silent abstraction at the door of pre-tourney nerves, and it was true that the company gathered here at Camelot Court upon this bright June day compassed the bluest blood and scatteredest brains of all England—plus one.

"Now remember what I told you," Elaine hissed up at her champion, who was seated upon a raking grey from her father's stables.

"This mock combat likes me not," the knight growled. He glared down at the woman standing at his stirrup.

"I don't care *what* you like—all you have to do is go out there and *hit* people! You're the best knight in England—The Book said so!"

"Aye. All save Richard, and no man knows now in what dungeon the Lionheart respires."

"Well he won't be *here*, so what has that to say to anything?" Elaine snapped. The difficulties attendant upon clothing and concealing an irritated Templar for ten entire days would have been enough to ruin a sunnier disposition than Elaine Mallory had ever possessed.

"And crown thee Fairest of the Fair. Woman, wouldst bargain with the honor of Brian de Bois-Gulibert?"

"I don't give a fig for your honor!" Elaine cried in exasperation. "Win—and crown me—or it's back in The Book for you!" The fact that she had no idea of how to accomplish this was a fact she conveniently chose to forget.

"To die for the love of some wench I've not yet met," the dark knight growled. "It seems a poor recompense for such service as I have rendered Christ and His church."

"Oh, go on—the line's starting to move!"

Considering that the last tourneys to be held on English soil had taken place some two centuries before, the flower of English chivalry did passably well. The day began with tilting at the ring and the quintan, and after a few passages of that, the jousting itself.

The dark man with the device of the skull and raven issued no challenges at first, and, seated in the stands between her father and Mrs. Underhill, Elaine worried first her handkerchief and then the ribbon at the end of her braid into tatters.

What was taking him so long? If she didn't get the crown after all this, she'd— She'd try out some other spells she knew, that's what she'd do! To make things worse, her disobliging brother hadn't even bothered to show up at all, leaving her to swelter alone in her unseasonable velvets.

Elaine tried to look on the bright side—maybe she could get Papa to disinherit Wilfred after this!

At Elaine's side, Mrs. Underhill—who was not only more familiar with these clothes than any here but had possessed the wit to have her outfit run up in summer-weight fabrics—was equally vexed. While young Wilfred should receive his quietus in the melee if not earlier, the plans she had made for his sister, and predicated upon the arrival of a certain Sir Robin from the continent, had not come to fruition, due entirely to the continued absence of the so-disobliging Sir Robin.

Put a girdle round about the earth in forty minutes, but never around when you want him, oh, no—

She would have to improvise.

Staring up at the cloudless sky, Titania Underhill began to hum a soundless tune under her breath.

It was fortunate, thought Miss Rowena Spencer some hours earlier, that everyone in the county would be at Camelot Court today so that no one would be left to remark on her suspicious departure from or dramatic return to Miching Malicho. As soon as she was certain that the village was quite deserted she slipped out to where her horse and armor were hidden.

Since the smithy itself had offered no concealment
of her aims, Rowena had concealed her armor—and
since last night, her horse—in an old tithing barn just
outside the village. The Bell and Candle did not yet
know of the new career being taken up by this one
of its equine hirelings, and Rowena only hoped that
ten years as a change horse on the coach roads of
England would translate to a certain nimble-foot-
edness on the tourney field.

With the speed of long practice Rowena donned
first the leather padding, then the armor to top it,
until she was habilimented from hauberk through
gambeson and onward to spurs. Once the last buckle
was secured, Rowena saddled and bridled the burly
white gelding, his pedestrian leather harness covered
over with gaudy satin and bullion in the approved
style.

After that, all that remained to do was to climb
carefully to the top of a stack of hay bales and let
herself down carefully onto the animal's back. Her
shield—blank and virginal, just as Romance demanded—
was already hung from his saddle, and, once her feet
were in the stirrups, she leaned over gingerly to
retrieve her lance.

She was ready. And tonight Wilfred would be hers.

The last thing Wilfred Mallory remembered with
any clarity was the odd taste of his breakfast tea.
When he came at last to his senses, Wilfred was standing in the shade of a pink and blue pavilion, leaning
on a pennoned lance and watching other people get
hurt.

By accident or design, no one had challenged him
yet—not the neighbors, whose quarterings made their
shields more resemble polychrome antique lace than
grants of arms, and not the stranger, whose skull and
raven on a field gules was disturbingly unambiguous.

The first thing to do was to remove himself from
the armor—and then, from the tourney field. It might

next be necessary to remove himself from Scotland entirely, but Wilfred felt it was best to deal with one thing at a time.

Making certain the pavilion he stood before was deserted, Wilfred ducked inside, as quickly as one may who is wearing fifty-five pounds of jointed steel plate, and began searching for the buckles.

The Knight of the Skull and Raven, about halfway through the morning (and following a furious written message from the grandstand), began challenging—and unseating—his brother knights with depressing regularity. So monotonously had he unseated everyone against whom he had ridden, that a number of the wilder sparks were suggesting evening the odds by the addition of a pair of Purdys shotguns to the permitted weaponry of the lists. This would have disturbed Sir Arthur far more had he been awake to see it, but his paramour, concerned that her hopeful familicide might disturb her intended, had made certain that the malmsey flowed thick and fast in that quarter, and now Sir Arthur slept the sleep of the spifflicated.

The marshals, harassed, were about to declare Sir Brian the winner against all comers—mendacious as that might be—and break for lunch when the stranger appeared.

The stranger rode a white horse and bore a white shield, and the heralds (who had very little experience with the actual exercise of their hereditary office) were entirely at a loss to define him.

"An Unknown Challenger!" the nearest herald finally shouted, and the White Knight rode up to the line of waiting combatants. The Knight of the Skull and Raven put his mount forward, and thus was the first to accept the challenge of the stranger.

"Do I know you?" Sir Brian asked curiously of the impassive metal countenance before him. "You have the look of Saxon scum about you."

The White Knight—Saxon scum or not—chose not to answer, and Sir Brian, who had been unhorsing the squirearchy all morning with monotonous regularity, thought this new challenger would be more of the same.

He was wrong.

An English coach horse is nobody's fool, and an English blacksmith's daughter is stronger than she looks. Rowena's lance point took Sir Brian at just that point in the shoulder where the necessity of jointure makes the armor weakest with the predictable result. Sir Brian went flying. The spectators (saving Sir Arthur) surged to their feet with a roar.

This, thought Mrs. Underhill, *is BEYOND boring*. While Bois-Gulibert had looked like a plausible candidate for removing the tedious Wilfred, it seemed far too probable that the White Knight just arrived would turn out to be some distressed nobleman who would befriend Wilfred Mallory and swear eternal fealty, saving Wilfred's hide as well as adding one more person to a household that Mrs. Underhill thought already overlarge. And there was Elaine to consider, after all, as Sir Robin, Mrs. Underhill's constant cicisbeo, had failed her in this matter upon which she had most required him.

And so Mrs. Underhill—who had a husband still living, although she saw him only rarely—twisted a certain ring about on her finger, and sketched a certain symbol in the air. And above the tourney field the summer sky darkened as if with summer thunder. But the darkness wasn't clouds, not at all.

The darkness was a dragon.

Sir Brian had gotten to his feet to continue the combat afoot with live steel—the knights-marshals not having the wit to stop it—and as Rowena gazed down at the impassive armored figure in the blood-red surcoat, she felt a strange stirring in that part of her anatomy previously occupied with thoughts of Wilfred.

While it was true that she'd never seen her opponent's face, any man who would assume the arms of the wicked yet romantic Templar Bois-Gulibert, that dark paraclete who had imperiled Wilfred of Ivanhoe's life and happiness, in a company of this sort must surely be such an one who would not scorn a lowly blacksmith's daughter—especially since she'd just unhorsed him.

It was at that moment that Sir Brian looked skyward, and relieved himself of an oath as blasphemous as it was authentically archaic. Rowena, puzzled, followed the direction of his gaze.

It was a dragon.

As fanciful as the Wizard of the North's works might be—though only later generations would compass the full extent of their whimsy—he had stopped short of introducing dragons. Nevertheless, Sir Brian and Rowena were both conversant with—though disbelieving of—what they saw.

Its wings covered the sun. The surface of its hide shone like hammered metal, and the scent of hot iron preceded it upon the summer air. As Rowena watched in spellbound disbelief, she saw sunlight flash across the smooth skin of its wings as it banked.

It was going to land.

"You!" Rowena addressed her erstwhile opponent. "Get back on your horse! Someone catch it for him!"

No one mentioned the egregious breach of tourney etiquette that this was, possibly because while she was speaking, the dragon landed at the far end of the tourney field, and a number of the erstwhile combatants took flight—including, alas, Sir Brian's mount.

The dragon, Rowena noted despairingly, was much, much larger than Farmer Graythorpe's prize Black Angus bull, although it certainly seemed to share that animal's disposition. Head weaving and tail lashing—resembling nothing so much as a maddened housecat grown to enormous size—the heraldic and impossible beast dominated the foot of the lists.

Her horse, having seen, in its opinion, far worse, remained where it was, tail switching in boredom.

"It seems, then, that only we two remain to face the beast," Sir Brian said.

Rowena—who, until that very moment, had only considered retreating in good order, the experience of Graythorpe's bull firmly in mind—suffered a reversion of feeling.

"Indeed we do, Sir Knight!" she sang out gaily. "And mayhap this day, by God's grace, we shall win victory over the nightmare beast and such glory for ourselves as shall show us to be the most true knights in Christendom."

"I had rather trust me to a good sword," muttered Sir Brian, drawing his blade.

The dragon roared, and a jet of pale flame appeared about a foot from the end of its muzzle. Rowena couched her lance and urged her horse forward, wondering precisely how one *did* slay a loathy worm with a lance, Sir Walter having failed to cover that matter in his otherwise superior volume. Sir Brian walked at her stirrup.

In the stands, a genteel retreat was in process, less abrupt than that occurring upon the field due to the feeling among the spectators that this was merely another refinement to Sir Arthur's entertainment.

Elaine Mallory, however, doubted that the dragon was another of her father's fabrications. She pulled the unfashionably full skirts of her medieval costume tight about her and stood.

"Oh, don't go, dear," Mrs. Underhill cooed. "After all, we do want it to go away again, don't we? And to arrange that requires a *virgin* sacrifice."

"But I'm not—" Elaine began, and then stopped, in mortified confusion.

Although there was no point in trying to put a gate between herself and something that could fly, Rowena did her best to lure the dragon away from the stands and toward Camelot Court's south lawn. Using her lance against it was like teasing a barn cat with a piece of straw: fortunately, this was something not unique in Rowena's experience.

Following in her wake, Sir Brian—intemperate, luxurious, and proud, yet with a good backswing—rained blows upon the creature's haunch, producing no result save a sound like an axe blade being applied to stout English oak.

Eventually, however, this activity went far enough toward claiming the dragon's attention that it withdrew its consideration from Rowena and swung its head around to regard its hopeful tormentor. That the resulting side sweep of wing knocked Rowena from her saddle—and that her mount took the opportunity to leave the scene of an activity which held no further interest for it—was an entirely irrelevant side effect.

The dragon fixed Bois-Gulibert with one baleful orient eye.

"You," it announced, "are a *fictional character.*"

"Not a virgin?" Mrs. Underhill snarled, holding fast to the wrist of her future daughter-in-law.

"Well, you see—" Elaine began.

"Never mind that now, you appalling chit! *Find me a virgin!*"

The dragon's voice reverberated all across the east lawn of Camelot Court. It had a surprisingly loud voice for something that oughtn't have been able to talk at all, although since it was an entirely mythological beast the consideration of its ability to talk was, in a certain sense, moot.

"*Fictional!*" it repeated, outraged.

"And you," said Sir Brian, who had had time enough to adjust to stranger things than this, "are a

vile and mannerless caitiff villain. If human speech is
vouchsafed you, knave, then declare your name and
your condition, that I can recall them ere my sword
drinks deep of your heart's blood."

"But I— But you— Now look here—" the
dragon sputtered.

"Your name," Sir Brian repeated, as implacably as
he could manage while listening with every fibre of
his being for the faint sound of clashing ironmongery
in the background that meant his ally, the Knight of
the White Shield (about whom Sir Brian had, at this
moment, a certain number of irrelevant suspicions),
was regaining his—or possibly her—feet.

"Mauvais de Merde, of a very old and still very
well regarded lineage, much good may it do you!" the
dragon snapped. "But I have no intention of con-
testing with *fictional* characters of whatever stripe,
kidney, or ilk—and I'm behind in my job search program as it is—so you might as well just find me the
virgin now and let me go home!"

With that, it sat back on its haunches and glared
about itself, tendrils of smoke rising up from its
nostrils.

Wilfred stumbled out of the pavilion wearing his
underclothes, his surcoat, and a cloak held tightly
about himself for personal modesty's sake. His entire
universe at the moment consisted of an intense desire
for three fingers of brandy and a quiet bed.

"Ah," said the dragon, with satisfaction, "there he
is now."

"*Wilfred!*" shrieked his sister. "*Wilfred's a virgin!*"

At any other time the boldness of this unsolicited
declaration might well have brought a blush to the
cheek of any unwary listeners, but in the disorganized
chaos currently obtaining, it passed without comment.
Oblivious to the necessity of anything other than providing an alternative candidate for dragonbait, Elaine,
with Mrs. Underhill in tow, advanced upon the dragon

Mauvais de Merde, who was at this present dividing its attention between the inattentive Wilfred and the resupine knights before it.

"Wilfred!" Elaine said, grabbing his surcoat. "You're a virgin!"

Her sibling's eyes focussed on her vaguely; Wilfred had a pounding headache. "Really, Ellie, this is hardly the time . . ."

"Well, get his clothes off; I'll just eat and run," Mauvais said resignedly. "Oh, not that it's *necessary*—but what would I do with him once I got him home? It isn't, after all, as if he knew anything useful—like the general rules for cataloging, for example."

"Don't be silly," Mrs. Underhill snapped. "Nobody does. Melvil Dewey won't be born for another thirty years. We have other problems right now."

"As for that, dearie," the dragon camped, "did anyone in particular give a thought to *my* problems when they whistled me up? Sixty-five thousand volumes, new books coming in at the rate of a dozen a day, and who have I got to process them? Gnomes and tree-spirits, that's who—and don't even *talk* to me about OCLC!"

"I warned you about those book clubs," Mrs. Underhill said.

At last Wilfred appeared to notice the dragon—at least slightly.

"Did you mention cataloging?" Wilfred said with interest. "You must have a catalog, don't you know—without one you'll never know what your holdings are. Accession numbers, that's the ticket, and the sooner, the better."

Everyone stared at Wilfred.

"I've changed my mind," said Mauvais. "I won't eat him. Just hand him over and we'll be on our way."

"There's just one slight hitch," Mrs. Underhill said.

Some quarter of an hour later, matters, though quieter, were at even more of an impasse.

The dragon Mauvais de Merde was entirely willing to take Wilfred as its *teind* and depart—and even, at a stretch, willing to devour Elaine—but there was nothing at all it could do about the presence of Sir Brian de Bois-Gulibert.

Elaine Mallory, approached with the possibility of putting Bois-Gulibert *back* into the book she'd taken him from, tearfully confessed she had no idea how she'd taken him out of it in the first place.

"I only wanted to be Queen!" she wailed, causing her complexion to become even more unbecomingly blotched.

"This doughty knight is the only true soul of chivalry among you," Sir Brian snarled, resheathing his sword and removing his helm. He glared at them all, including Mauvais, in a fashion suggesting he'd be trouble wherever he was.

The doughty knight he'd spoken of, relieved both to be alive and to not have to kill a dragon, removed her helmet as well. Cascades of guinea-gold hair spilled about her shoulders.

Sir Brian stared.

"It's Rowena!" Wilfred bleated. "Rowena, what are you doing here?"

Rowena blushed prettily. Wilfred gulped. Sir Brian put his hand upon his sword.

"I'm not giving him back, that's all *I* have to say," snarled Mauvais.

"If I might lend a hand?" a new voice suggested.

The newcomer was dressed in the height of Town fashion, from his Moroccan leather slippers to the lustrous surface of his curly-brimmed, high-crowned beaver. His coat of bottle-green superfine perfectly complemented his butter-yellow waistcoat, which article was discreetly ornamented with a pocket watch whose dial held thirteen numbers and a carved malachite fob of Triple Hecate, as well as being of the only possible shade to harmonize with his biscuit-colored pantaloons. Overtopping all this subtle sartorial rainbow were collar points with which one might have sliced bread and a cravat whose folds fell in the starkly ornamental simplicity of the difficult "Labyrinth" style.

His elegant gloved fingers toyed with a walking stick that seemed to possess, for its knob, the largest diamond that most of the onlookers could conceive of.

In short, Sir Robin Goodfellow had arrived.

"It took you long enough to get here," Mrs. Underhill said.

Sir Robin bowed. "When one has as many engagements as I, dear lady, one may see that celerity, while always devoutly to be wished, is not in all things possible. I am delighted, however, to be able to offer you a path out of your current difficulties."

The look that Mrs. Underhill turned upon Sir Robin was marginally more baleful than that of the dragon Mauvais; Sir Robin hurried onward.

"And while it is also true that the lady Elaine cannot in any wise affect Sir Brian," Robin paused to make a slight bow in Elaine's direction, "the same is certainly not true of our gentle colleague." Here a bow to Mauvais. "Let Mauvais de Merde put Sir Brian back into his book, and take Wilfred away with her, and there's an end to it."

"There's still the matter of the girl," Mrs. Underhill said doubtfully, regarding Elaine. "Although I suppose I could simply—"

"Leave the girl to me," Sir Robin said briskly. "She wishes to be Queen? She shall be—until Your Majesty should choose to return, of course," he added diplomatically.

"No fear of that," Mrs. Underhill muttered. "Do you think I enjoy getting nothing but lukewarm bathwater and having a bunch of damned elves yodeling under my window every night? Even English plumbing is preferable to the Court's, and the nights are quieter."

"And what if I choose not to condole in the plans of

fiery serpents and losel wights?" Sir Brian demanded. "Having been told something of this book whereof the lady speaks, I have no desire to go back there."

"Go to another one, then—it's all the same to me!" Mrs. Underhill snapped, her good humor fraying with the likelihood that Sir Arthur might awaken at any moment.

"Not without me you don't!" Rowena said.

It may well have been the dragon, or perhaps the sight of Sir Brian's sun-bronzed countenance, but Rowena Spencer was the only one of the day's participants who still felt any affection whatsoever for the days of chivalry.

"Fine," said Mauvais, who was getting bored. The dragon raised a claw.

Suddenly, where the two knights had stood, appeared a leather-bound book with golden clasps.

"We'll be off, then," said Sir Robin hastily, and hustled Elaine toward a waiting carriage drawn by six milk-white horses with ninety-nine silver bells per horse braided into their manes and tails.

"Well, now that I've got my virgin *I* don't see any more reason to stick around," Mauvais said. "Unless as there's something else?" it asked politely.

Mrs. Underhill assured it that there was not, and that, furthermore, Mauvais was entirely welcome to visit Camelot Court on any occasion when she herself was in London.

There was a pause.

Wilfred (whose only certainty was that, no matter what else had happened this day, he was going where there were thousands and thousands of books to be organized) picked up the book from where it had fallen to the greensward.

"Well," he said, "I suppose I'd better take this along and, er, catalog it, shall I?"

He opened the book, and in the moment before Mauvais de Merde swept him off, such spectators as there might be supposed to be could have beheld a colored frontispiece, upon which a knight in a scarlet surtout knelt at the feet of a blonde lady in shining armor.

But that's another story.

He tells me he beheld the lady of his heart arrayed for gardening as if for battle. The rest followed naturally.

ON THE ROAD OF SILVER

Mark Bourne

It was shortly after Mrs. Batchett left the planetarium that she saw the fairy, the elf, and the gnome. Which was probably kismet, because by five o'clock it had already been a bad day at the planetarium.

While the final group of fourth graders was herded through the exit doors—leaving another flurry of museum programs and school handouts littering the seats and floor—Mrs. Batchett reset the star projector for that evening's feature show. When the exit door shut behind the final youngster, she dimmed the house lights to make sure the Spring constellations were in the correct part of the sky. Artificial night flooded the domed room. The familiar routine of placing Boötes and Virgo and this season's planets just so in the scaled-down sky never failed to ignite a bone-deep spark within Mrs. Batchett. Even after twenty years as a science teacher, and ten more here at Portland's Northwest Museum of Science and Technology, the planetarium sky filled her with a pleasing, serene sense of awe. The artificial sky wasn't as good as the real thing, but it would do for a daytime, all-weather stand-in. She could never tire of sharing that sense of wonder, of seeing it sparked in the minds of the children who came to the planetarium. Mrs. Batchett

178

wheeled the stars into position, made tonight's full moon rise with the turn of a dial, checked her pointer (the bulb had been flickering lately), and brought up the lights.

Sam Peterson approached from the opposite side of the room.

"Good afternoon," Mrs. Batchett called. "Did you enjoy the show?" She tried to keep the surprise out of her voice.

He smiled. "Very much, Roberta." Then crooked a finger at her. "May I see you in my office?"

She followed her department manager upstairs.

Though he had been at NMST for only six months, Sam Peterson was the very model of the modern museum manager. His stylish suit enclosed a middle-aged athlete's body and accented his *GQ* good looks. His pristinely ordered desk had a corner—near the leather-cased, gold-embossed EverOpen™ dayplanner—dedicated to the latest magazines and journals for "the 90's executive." On the wall facing the desk, four different calendars hung like prisoners in a dungeon. Framed certificates, awards, and a photo of Peterson coming in second at the city-sponsored Jog-o-thon hung in descending order of size. Nearby was a poster proclaiming The Seven Cardinal Virtues of a Great Boss, cheerily illustrated with specially researched colors designed to elicit comfort in all employees who gazed upon it. Against another wall was the expensive sofa dedicated to the power naps taken from 1:15–2:15 P.M. daily. The air was sweetened by hidden cakes of "spring garden" air freshener. If this office was a shrine to the latest trends in corporate efficiency and appearances, Peterson was its high priest. Mrs. Batchett took the chair that might as well have been labeled Sacrificial Altar.

"Now, Mrs. Batchett—Roberta," Peterson said, sitting in his tan leather chair. "Would you like something? Cappuccino? A latté?" Charm oozed from him like yogurt through a colander.

"No thank you."

"Roberta, you've done fine work here in the planetarium. School group attendance is strong—" *Even though you cut the new programs I hoped to produce,* Mrs. Batchett replied silently. "—and we keep getting splendid thank you letters from the kids and their teachers. The volunteers say you've done a fine job teaching them the ropes of performing the shows. That shows teamwork, Roberta, and teamwork is important. Especially now in the museum's current fiscal reevaluation." *Crisis, you mean. I don't like this. He just got out of a meeting. I can smell it.*

"Roberta, I just got out of a meeting with the other senior managers. All departments are being forced to cut themselves to the bone and find new sources of income. The Exhibits staff is scrapping their interactive evolution exhibit for a traveling show called DinoMania. I'm afraid that we too have to restrategize our paradigms. It's my job to analyze operational priorities in regards to revenue enhancement."

Which means?

"Which means that we're forced to make some changes on our end also."

Such as cutting the Senior Managers' "Effectiveness Enhancement Retreat" at Timberline Lodge ski resort?

Peterson put on his face that said I'm Really Really Sorry To Have To Say This But. "Roberta, I'm really really sorry I have to say this, but I'm afraid we're forced to let you go. It's nothing personal and it doesn't reflect on your outstanding job performance. The team simply has to cut back somewhere. Because you've been so valuable to us, you'll receive two weeks' severance pay, which not all the other layoffs around the museum will be getting." He looked pleased with himself about that.

Roberta said nothing. She had expected this for weeks. Ever since the subject of, oh Lord . . . *it* first came up.

Peterson leaned toward her. His hair was as

perfectly sculpted as a topiary. "You'll be glad to know that the school groups will still be coming. Don't you worry about that. Starting next week, we'll be replacing the educational programs with laser light shows. We just hired Lazer Euphoria, Inc. to set up shop in the planetarium."

There it was—*it*. Peterson opened a slick color brochure and handed it to Mrs. Batchett. *Since when do you spell "laser" with a "z,"* Mrs. Batchett wondered.

"They guarantee to increase our revenue by eighty percent with a gate-share contract. See! They do it all—*Lazer MetalDeath, Lazer Pink Floyd, Lazer Grunge, Lazer Dead Rock Gods*. Their biggest hit right now is *Lazer Cowboys*. It has this animated Garth Brooks that's supposed to be really something. All the major planetariums are contracting them."

One "contracts" the plague. Mrs. Batchett chewed the inside of her left cheek.

Peterson removed the brochure from her hand. "Their staff rep will be moving into your office day after tomorrow, so if you could, um . . ."

"Yes sir," Mrs. Batchett said. She stood and turned toward the door.

"Oh, Roberta." She pivoted toward him. "Roberta, if you please, don't mention the severance pay to anyone. Might look bad, you know." He opened a drawer in his desk. Mrs. Batchett noticed how silently the desk operated. He withdrew a slip of colored paperboard and handed it across the desk to her. He smiled warmly and his eyes by God twinkled. *I bet he learned that at a seminar*.

"Here," he said. "Have a free pass to the gala premiere. *Lazer Yanni*. I hear it's kind of like space music. You'll love it."

She took it. "Thank you," she said, then cursed herself for it. The door shut behind her on noticeably well-oiled hinges.

*   *   *

"*mumblemumblemumblemumble*Hello dear," Prof. Lawrence Batchett said. He didn't even glance up from the stack of final exams he was grading at the dining room table. He resumed mumbling incoherently, though Mrs. Batchett heard the phrases "It's *not* Chaucer's 'Cantaloupe Tales'!" and "William Shakespeare did *not* defeat King Harold at the Battle of Hastings!" bubble up from his murmuring drone. Prof. Batchett pushed his glasses up his nose, ran a hand through hair that had not existed for ten years, and stroked his graying goatee. It was his ritual signifying the urge to commit murder most foul against yet another year's worth of Brit Lit students. He had even removed his favorite tweed jacket—the one with the leather patches at the elbows—and the necktie decorated with hand-painted images from the Bayeaux Tapestry. A sure sign of distress.

Mrs. Batchett placed her purse and the Teddy-Bear-in-a-spacesuit a second-grade class had given her onto the coffee table. She studied the back of her husband's head from across the room. His hair was now reduced to a silver crescent moon that barely managed to cover the skin between one ear and the other. He frequently claimed that he liked looking the part of the distinguished Reed College English Professor, but Mrs. Batchett had once seen him in the bathroom trying on hairpieces borrowed from Dr. Stengler in the Physics Dept. He pounded a fist on the table, said something about King Arthur *never* meeting the Knights of Ni in the book, and continued mumbling and shaking his head.

"I got laid off today," she announced. "Enhancement stratagems were datatized. Paradigms were reassessmentized. 'The Universe Around Us' is now *Lazer BrainDamage*."

Lawrence scribbled red revenge across the face of an exam. "No thank you, dear," he said into the papers. "I just had some."

Mrs. Batchett sighed. She went upstairs, changed

clothes, returned downstairs wearing her broad-brimmed gardening hat, and exited through the back door.

"Titania and Oberon were not invented by Neil Gaiman!" was the last thing she heard as the door slammed shut behind her.

It had rained the night before, so the garden smelled of earth and green. Mrs. Batchett relished the feel of moist soil between her fingers and against her knees, and the sound weeds made when she pulled them up. The irises were doing well. So were the foxgloves. New clusters of magenta and white rhododendrons had bloomed. Nearby, a bee hummed a relaxed mantra. The world of lazers-with-a-z and Beowulf seemed far from here. With Robby and Sylvia grown and living in distant cities, these were her children now. Here was her private world, where she was in control and esteemed for her efforts.

With a satisfied hand-brushing, Mrs. Batchett looked across the yard at her other garden. *Oh, damn!*, she huffed and stood too quickly. Her knees complained loudly to her. After the first fifty years, some things didn't happen as easily as before.

Slugs had been in the garden again. What had once been healthy daylilies were now ragged, stripped leaves and ravished, chewed buds. The primroses and hostas were also destroyed. Narrow trails of slime laced through the remains.

"God damn it!" Mrs. Batchett did not swear often. She had laid down a new box of Corry's Slug Death (Original English Formula) just last week. She began pulling the useless stems from the slime-tainted dirt. As she yanked and tugged, she felt the tears well up in her eyes and slide down her face. She shredded a handful of stems in her hands, then sat in the dirt and let herself cry. No one could hear her in the garden. Prof. Batchett *wouldn't* hear her.

Soon she was cried out, but the pent-up anger still sat like a rock in the pit of her stomach. She sat with her eyes shut and a headache pounding behind her eyes. *I'll probably start menopause today, too.* When at last she opened her eyes, the first thing she saw was the fairy staring at her. The second thing was the lithe, ethereal elf standing on the coil of garden hose. The third was the gnome squatting on a wicker lawn chair and picking its teeth.

"Weep not, my Mistress," said the fairy, fluttering off the ground. Its voice was rich and feminine, though its naked body was smooth and genderless. It was no taller than the daylilies had been. Delicate, leaflike wings stroked the air soundlessly and the being lit on the ground next to Mrs. Batchett. Its wide blue eyes were level with hers. Mrs. Batchett felt its gaze as it frowned mournfully at her. "Mistress, the mortal world has surely changed you. No longer do you bear the scars from when you spilt Fir Bolg blood onto the Plain of Pillars." Its voice had an Irish lilt. "Your face no longer glows with the wine of victory, nor your arms hoist the wizard-forged weapons engraven in gold with your true name." It smiled at her and touched her sleeve with a long, slender hand. "But all this is mere appearance, rough-hewn human glamour. We bring you a gift from those of Tir na n-Og who knew you in your life of glory."

During all this, Mrs. Batchett remained still, unflinching. Her heart pulsed in her chest, though, and she felt dizzy. *Oh, great. First I hallucinate. Then I have a stroke. Or maybe I've already had the stroke and that's why I'm hallucinating. It's nice to die in the garden but only if the slugs are gone. Lawrence won't notice I'm dead until it's time to rake leaves in the fall.*

The elf—she recognized the beings, though she didn't know why—strolled gracefully to her and removed her sun hat. Its fingers were cool against her forehead. Mrs. Batchett suddenly knew with crystal certainty that she wasn't hallucinating. She knew that these beings meant her no harm, that their presence in her garden was as natural as the moon in the night sky or slugs in the flower beds or the feel of a mighty bejeweled steed between your legs and a sword in your hand.

"Remember," the elf said with a voice like wind through trees. "When you cleaved the skulls of the Fomorii in the Second Battle of Magh Tuiredh. Remember how you saved my people by defeating the Roth Hugar on the icy shores of Thambulir."

Mrs. Batchett remembered, and shivered at the memory of cold seaspray against bare, flayed flesh.

The fairy sat cross-legged in the air before her. "Remember," it said, "when your father Lluta Orgetlann the Tireless gave you his armor and shield, created in the Oldest Times by Goibniu himself. Remember the sword, Dagda's Arm, and its power over all earthly beings."

She remembered her father. Not the car salesman from Montana, but her father before in a former life: the warrior king who loved her and taught her the warrior's arts by the time of her first bloodmoon. Her mother wasn't the schoolteacher who died from a lifetime of sucking cigarettes, but a queen of the line of Arianrod who first taught her about the stars and the quiet power of the moon.

"Remember," the elf continued, "your training by the very hand of Scathach on her warrior's isle. And your achievements in the ways of magic and inner arts on Emhain, the Isle of Women. Remember when you were of our kind, the Daoine Sidhe, not of this mere mortal world, and the powers granted to you at your birth. When Faerie and the Earth-realm touched one another. Before we were driven away by cross and machine. Before you left us for the love of a mortal warrior."

Her lover: the great, learned Ton n'Uthara, who had fought against her, then alongside her, before they bedded and wedded each other on the cliffs of Scathach's isle. All the Tuatha De Danaan had attended the wedding. Even Finvarra, King of Eirinn Faerie, had kissed her goodbye with a tear in his eye after the ceremony.

"Yeah," piped up the gnome who, throughout the foregoing, had been clipping his toenails. "And don't forget the time you saved my village by conking that ol' dragon Ruadherra on his bean with your bare fist!" The gnome grabbed his knees and rocked with laughter. "And then you commanded all the birds in the land to peck off his golden scales and rain them down on us to make up for the damage that ol' fire-farter had caused! Hoo!" He fell off the wicker chair and rolled guffawing into the rhodies. The elf gave him a reprimanding stare.

She remembered it all, as if it were a recurring dream first dreamt long ago. She sat there in the garden, watching the fairy, the elf, and the gnome, and remembered a former existence as Nnagartha of the Golden Strength, a fairy warrior princess clad in dragon-hide leather and magic-fired armor. Who fought beside fellow warriors of Faerie and of Earth. Who could command the creatures of land and sky. Who forsook her faery nature for the love of a man like no other man, and had been condemned to remain in the human world after her people left it for Tir na n-Og—land of joy, of everlasting youth and flowers, where hydromel flows in the riverbeds and where warriors eat and drink of fairie dishes in the companionship of their own kind.

I've been reading too many romances and fantasy novels, she mused. But her copies of *Love's Forceful Sword* and *Mistress of the Dragon's Quest* ("First Book in the Dragon's Quest Trilogy") lay unopened on her nightstand, a forgotten gift ("You just gotta read 'em!") from that annoying Marge Tarkelson next door.

I'm kidding myself, she realized. Because she remembered. Because the fairy, the elf, and the gnome were in her garden. Because even the gnome stared at her worshipfully while he scraped out the crevasses between his bulbous toes. She reached out her arms to her old friends. She was strong enough in the inner arts to not be embarrassed by the loose, weak flesh that hung where a warrior's muscles should have been.

"You said something about a gift," she said, taking the fairy's hand.

"Since when did Beowulf fight NanoMan?" Prof. Batchett had reached the stage where he forgot to remove the pen from his hand when he rubbed his head. So his scalp was crosshatched with thin red lines. Though the sun had set behind the hills in the west, he obviously had not budged from his chair since Mrs. Batchett had last seen him. A growing pile of red-slashed exams littered the floor beneath the dining room table. An equal-sized pile of ungraded papers still covered her place at the table. No matter. She had other things to do. Tonight was a warrior's night! Still, thanks to two decades of marital courtesy, she turned on the overhead light for Prof. Batchett.

One-hundred-watt radiance reflected off the rune-embossed golden armor hemispheres that shielded her breasts. Shards of rainbow light danced across her mail of dragon's scales. Perhaps that was her own shimmering aura she saw in the chrome of the toaster. Her helmet in one hand, the frightful steel of Dagda's Arm in the other, Mrs. Batchett approached Prof. Batchett.

"Don't wait up for me, Lawrence," she declared. Such power in her voice! She hadn't heard that in a long time. Centuries, actually. "For tonight, for as long as the full moon gazes upon this earth, I, Nnagartha of the Golden Strength, shall strike terror once again in the hearts of evil! My people still remember me and have thus granted me this solitary reprieve from the dull shackles of the mortal world. Beware, dark denizens of the nether-realms! Stand guard,

dragons and wyrms who despoil the lands of the inno-
cent and virtuous! Take flight, ye host of the Unseelie
Court, ye bogles and banshees and blood-devouring
Leanan-Sidhe who torment those weaker than myself!
This night you shall remember she who defeated you
before!" With a mighty lofting of Dagda's really big
Arm, she carved a neat slit into the dining room
ceiling.

Prof. Batchett wrote CHAUCER, NOT DAUMER!
into a margin. "That's nice, dear. Tell them I said
hello."

He didn't notice the fairy and the elf following his
wife out the back door. Or the gnome raiding the
refrigerator and rescuing a pint of Häagen-Dazs from
merely mortal consumption.

Twilight darkened into true night. The real Boötes
and Virgo faded up in the sky's tranquil dome. Moonlight shone on armor and glittering dragonflesh. Mrs.
Batchett felt her power strengthening. It returned to
her from the moon, from the stars, from the magic
of a world removed from this mundane, new world
of dayplanners and Brit Lit 101. Though it would take
three stout men to lift Dagda's Arm, she brandished it
with ferocious grace, tracing the memories of ancient
battles through the night air. From up here on the
roof, the city lights of Portland glimmered like the
jewels in the Castle of Ragnok Rur, where she lost
her best bowmen to the bloody blade of Redcap. By
the time her vengeance was through, the hideous gob-
lin's infamous cap had been re-dyed in its own blood.
Between her and the city snaked the Willamette
River. Wavering moonlight blended with electric-
borne sparkles across its surface. Its waters led to the
Columbia a few miles to the north. And from there
to the Pacific. Mrs. Batchett thirsted again for the
roar of the sea and the crash of waves on rocky shores.
She had been the one to tame the Aughisky, the kel-
pie sea-demon that had murdered hundreds before it

met Nnagartha of the Golden Strength. The moon rose higher. Dagda's Arm cut through the air. Mrs. Batchett moved with a dancer's ease on the angled rooftop. Her foes did not come. Above the lights of Portland, that pair of flying glowing eyes was a jet descending toward the airport, not a dragon seeking her out for its bloody revenge. No warrior hordes advanced from suburban Beaverton. Not a single Black Wizard hurled flaming magic death at her from the condominiums behind the marina. Mrs. Batchett wiped a tear from her cheek when she realized that the mighty Ton n'Uthara was not at her side to help her protect the people in another hour of need. *Progress is boring,* she snarled. There was no need for her kind in the world these days. With a stroke of her blade, she sliced the stainless steel rooster cleanly from the weather vane.

She looked to the lights near the river. Yes! There! There was a final place that needed her. Between here and the river, standing proud along the nearest shore, was a besieged castle. It was a fortress of good that was being usurped by a dark prince who fought with cowardice, armored in data displays and meeting agendas, who hoisted false banners made of spread sheets and revenue reports—who sought to replace the true magic of knowledge with pandering to the dull demands of the local peasantry and their ill-spent gold. She would be the citadel's rescuer. Generations of grateful searchers for truth would never forget this night.

She leapt to the ground, landing smoothly on her feet in a crouching stance. *If the evil won't find you, it is necessary to find the evil.*

By the time the enchantment was finished, even she had to rest. She sat in the wicker garden chair and noticed the position of the moon. Nearly midnight. It had taken two hours to gather and focus her strength and to remember how to direct it through Dagda's

Arm. The sword still glowed with silvery luminescence from where she had stuck it into the earth near the slug-ravaged flowers. She was satisfied. She hadn't felt such power since she helped that nattering Christian, Patrick Somethingorother, drive all the snakes from her people's land. That had been toward the end, though, just before her people left the earthly realm forever. She wondered for the first time what part, if any, the Christian's "miracle" had played in that. This time, things would be different. This miracle was all hers.

First, she heard them coming. A soft rustling among the earth and leaves. Then greater movement beneath the soil caused it to ripple like living flesh. There! In the moonlight, small glistening things were moving through the grass toward her sword. And there! Several more wet, rubbery things emerged from the earth, drawn to the force emanating from Dagda's Arm. And from out of the rhododendrons came an advancing surf of more writhing wormlike gastropods as fat and round as dismembered brown fingers. The thick trail of slime behind them glittered like liquid silver in the moon's light.

"Dis*gust*ing!" the gnome muttered, spitting out a mouthful of Häagen-Dazs Irish Cream Splendor.

Mrs. Batchett took Dagda's Arm and hoisted it skyward and toward the river. It was time to march.

The slugs came to her. Through the wealthy East-moreland neighborhood, she drew them away from the manicured lawns, out of the professionally-serviced gardens, and into the streets in front of the stately homes. Their path was marked by a sheen of silver that glistened beneath the street lamps. She gathered more as she led them through the Reed College grounds, across the local golf course, and through the famous Crystal Springs Rhododendron Gardens. Night noises gave way to the sounds of moist slithering behind her.

At her side, the fairy, the elf, and the gnome accompanied her in awestruck silence.

By the time she took a left turn at 28th and Holgate, her army covered the width of the street and, at its center, was as high as her waist. The midnight moon added a lustrous sheen to the growing mass. Her sword lit their way, a beacon summoning them from near and far, bringing them to her by the power that once called birds to peck gold from a dragon's flesh and pushed a million snakes to a watery doom. Occasionally, a late-night traveler was forced to steer his automobile away from the invisible shield Dagda's Arm projected in front of Mrs. Batchett. A jogger, her suit aglow with reflectors, stopped stunned by the side of the road. Mrs. Batchett ignored the sound of the poor waif's retching. She felt young again and strong. She was ridding this world—or at least several neighboring counties—of an old enemy. And she would use this enemy to bring vengeance on another.

As she marched, she smiled at the slimy noises that grew behind her. She would lay a road of silver through the tyrant's gates.

The sparse traffic halted on McLoughlin Boulevard. Engines died and headlights faltered at the intersection where Dagda's Arm erected its invisible wall. Mrs. Batchett marched on. The mindless mass following her spread itself across all four inbound lanes. Still it grew. Four lanes of slick mucus remained in its wake.

At McLoughlin and Clay Street she turned left. Cars were frozen at the unchanging traffic lights. She took a shortcut through the Burger King parking lot. A group of teenagers, partying on the hood of a decaying Galaxie 500, put down their beers and their joints. Three of them swore to never touch the stuff again. Four more wondered where to get more of it for tomorrow night.

Soon she reached Clay and Eastbank Avenue. From

there she could hear the Willamette brushing against its shoreline. She could smell the river. Across the water, downtown Portland was alight with a million artificial stars. It would be a short path from here to the water and the destruction of the slogging mountain behind her. But not yet, not yet. The moon was low in the sky. She must act quickly, before her powers—and her true self—vanished. She turned left and proceeded past the huge glowing sign that named the corrupted lair of her last unvanquished foe: NMST. Lights were on inside the complex. As she approached the main entrance doors, she licked her lips at the sound of the dragon's pulsing roar. Tonight was obviously *Lazer Metalhead* night.

Mrs. Batchett found her husband in the dining room, reading the morning paper. He wore the same clothes she had last seen him in. His head was a red maze of crisscrossed lines. Morning sunlight slanted through the venetian blinds and spilled onto a tidy tower of exams on the floor. The uppermost page had *Try again next year* scrawled across the top. Prof. Batchett turned a page of the newspaper.

"Morning, dear," he said sleepily. "Take an early walk? Good idea. They say it's going to be a lovely day." If he had looked up, he might have noticed what she was wearing: her gardening clothes and sun hat. The knees of her work pants were caked with day-old earth. He might have noticed how tired she looked, and how the wrinkled flesh beneath her eyes carried what he might have recognized as dark folds of regret, as if his wife had recently lost something special to her. But he didn't. He did, however, slightly nod the paper in her direction.

"You should read the front page, dear. You'd find it interesting." He made sure she got a good view of the banner headline:

SLUGS MIGRATE TO THE WILLAMETTE
SCIENTISTS BAFFLED BY SLIMY SUICIDE

The article included color photos of the NMST lobby. It looked as though someone had spilled a truckload of silvery mayonnaise across the floor and ticket counters. Another headline caught her eye.

NMST ON MIGRATION ROUTE
SLUGS COULD BE ATTRACTED TO LAZER VIBRATIONS, SAY EXPERTS

Mrs. Batchett found the strength to smile. "Sounds logical. Does it say, um, if there were any witnesses?"

Prof. Batchett flipped to an inside page. "Not really. There was a, let's see, 'lazer rock show' in progress—since when does one spell 'laser' with a z?—but the ticket taker was out smoking in the new DinoMania exhibit. The only one who saw anything was some kid on his way to the planetarium from the men's room."

"And?"

"And he says he saw—where is it?—'This cool warrior chick like off Deathbreath's latest album cover.'" Prof. Batchett put on the voice he used to imitate his most culturally damaged students. " 'It was really cool. Had a glowing sword and everything. There was these three little dudes with her, man, and a zillion radical slugs just squooshing behind her. Bogus promo. Can't wait to see the lazer show, dude.'"

Mrs. Batchett tried to hide the worry in her voice. "Did he say anything else?"

"Only that he just went back to the planetarium. He claims it was his third rock-and-roll hallucination. A 'head trip,' I believe is the common vernacular. By the time the show was over, the slugs were out the opposite doors, on their way to the open sea, and the lobby was unfit for human habitation. Seems quite a few of the revelers lost their Jack Daniels when they exited the planetarium. It'll take the museum a week just to clean up. They're going to create an interactive exhibit from some of that slug slime, though, to explain what happened as soon as they can think up something convincing. The city's going to be washing down the streets all day. They say the whole thing might have started in our neighborhood. Yuck."

"Were all the slugs killed?" Mrs. Batchett had to know. She also wanted to prolong what was already the longest conversation she and her husband had had in weeks.

"Almost," he said. He indicated a photo at the bottom of the page. It depicted an office. Hundreds— no, the article said *thousands*—of dead slugs covered the desk, dripped from the formerly tan leather chair, and blanketed every inch of floor and shelf space. A local biologist posed with the coated remains of an EverOpen™ dayplanner.

SOME SLUGS DETOUR
"THEY MUST HAVE LIKED THE AIR FRESHENER," EXPERT CLAIMS

Mrs. Batchett let herself smile. It had been difficult getting them all piled onto the desktop.

She placed a hand on her husband's shoulder. Silently he flipped through pages to the book review section. She felt his shoulder tighten beneath his shirt. "A comic book adaptation of *Paradise Lost*? That's an outrage!" He flattened the newspaper against the table top and lowered his head toward the offending article.

"I'm going out back," Mrs. Batchett sighed.

Prof. Batchett mumbled something and pounded his fist on the table.

"You cannot come with us, Mistress." The fairy wiped a tear from its eyes, then flew to where Mrs. Batchett sat in the dirt. It brushed away the larger tears it found on her cheek. "It is sad. Your father and mother asked us to tell them about you after we've returned. King Finvarra would love to have you

beat him in a royal chess match again. You have
friends there who miss you. We all miss you."

"But why can't I go?" New buds were already
appearing on the tattered daylilies. They were safe
now. That wasn't enough.

The elf placed a hand on her knee. "It's the law
you agreed to in your former life. You married a mortal warrior. True, he was a great and powerful man,
a man of learning and a friend to all in need. When
our world and theirs split in twain, you chose to be
with him forever. You are condemned to this mortal
realm—" The elf paused and look thoughtful for a
few heartbeats. "*Unless* you can persuade him to
accompany you to Tir na n-Og. Only then may both
of you live together as you once did, as who you
once were."

With strength born of frustration rather than
Faerie, Mrs. Batchett tossed a handful of weeds out
of the garden. "But how can I do that?" she shouted.
"That was another life. He's dead and gone now."
And so am I, she almost said out loud.

The fairy looked at the elf. The elf looked up at
the morning sky. It seemed to be contemplating
deep mysteries.

"Hoo!" The gnome was clutching his feet, rocking
with laughter. "Tell her!" it said, gasping for breath
between bouts of gnomish hysteria. "Go ahead! Sod
the rules! You know you want to!"

"Tell me what?"

The fairy stepped toward the elf. The gnome held
its breath and grinned. The elf chewed its lower lip.
It glanced around, then looked Mrs. Batchett in the
eyes. "When you married Ton n'Uthara, it was for all
time. Just as you are here now in this mortal form,
so too does he walk the solid earth."

Mrs. Batchett felt her heart beat quickly behind
her breast, and for the first time in years that did not
worry her. "He's alive? Now? Where?"

The gnome was unable to contain himself. He told her.

After Mrs. Batchett got over the shock, she turned her head and cupped her hands to her mouth.

"Oh, honey!" she called. *"Could you come out here? I want to discuss British mythology!"*

In which the lady doth not protest too much and strikes yet another blow against becoming a real Fashion Victim.

BRA MELTING

Janni Lee Simner

She came to my shop with a gash in her thigh and blood seeping out of a wound in her stomach.

"Full battle armor my ass," she said. Then she fainted.

I could tell this was one unhappy customer.

Fortunately, it's not very hard to find a healer around here. We're near the Darian border, and that means we see plenty of injured from the front. There are almost as many healers here as warriors, and that's saying a lot. I'm told the same is true in Ryll. Not that I have much interest in understanding Ryllian ways. They're the ones we're protecting our border from, after all.

So I found a healer—the usual sagely type, white beard trailing halfway to the floor. While he worked on the unconscious woman, I set my apprentice, Jarak, to mopping the blood off my floor. I can't stand the sight or smell of blood. That's why I became an armorer, rather than a fighter or healer myself. That and the lack of competition; it's just me and Millicent's Fine Armour, at least for ladies' styles. There are a few others working on the menswear, of course.

I glanced at the injured woman. Her stomach wound had already faded to a pale scar. The healer

197

had his hands over her thigh, his eyes closed, his face intent. The blood had stopped flowing, so I could stand to look.

Her armor was from my fall line; I'm particularly proud of the design. Bikini style, of course: braided spaghetti straps up top, cut high at the bottom to show off the hips. Her long red hair set off the bronze links; her tan skin was sleek and attractive beside the darker mail. Except where the wounds were, of course.

The healer's eyes stayed closed. I left him to his work, set Jarak up at the register, and went back to the forge to hammer out some heavy-duty plate mail for the boys at the front.

When the woman regained consciousness, she was as angry as ever. I offered to pay the healer for her, but she refused.

"What I want is my money back for that armor."

"Your armor looks fine to me, Miss—"

"Myra," she snapped.

"Myra." The links were rust free, unbroken—good as the day I'd sold it. "It's in perfect condition."

"You call this perfect?" She pointed to the scar across her stomach.

"I'm not responsible for injuries—"

"Not even if your armor is the cause?" Her voice held as much fire as her hair.

"I'm afraid I don't see what my armor has to do with it. As for skill on the battlefield—"

"I killed the man who gave me those wounds." Her voice turned sharp as steel against stone. "If I'd been wearing half the armor he was, his sword wouldn't have drawn blood at all. But all anyone in this town will sell me are chain mail bathing suits!"

"We do offer a matching floral shield." I kept my voice calm, reasonable.

"Your shield cracked the first time it met a sword! It's solid wood!"

I shrugged. I'd tried sheathing it with bronze, but metal didn't hold the purple floral paint; wood did. "We don't offer refunds, but you can exchange it if you like. Perhaps something from our Leather and Lace Assassin line."

She spoke through gritted teeth. "What I want is something that will protect me in battle. Plate or scale mail, full-length leather, *something*."

"Our full-body armor is reserved for—" I spoke as delicately as I could "—for our larger sizes."

She jumped to her feet, glaring at me. The healer must have do :e a good job. "Just find me some men's armor that fits, then!"

Men's armor? Why would she want that? "Surely an attractive woman such as yourself—"

The fire in her eyes turned up another notch. "Then I'll have to take my business elsewhere!" She tore off her armor—the spaghetti straps snapped easily enough—and flung it to the floor in front of me.

I stood there, staring. Myra's lucky I'm an honorable man. Good as she looked with that armor on, she looked even better with it off. I swallowed. We were still doing business, after all. "You won't find better armor at Millicent's," I said.

Myra didn't answer; she whirled around and left my shop. Outside, someone whistled. At least it was a warm day.

I picked the armor up off the floor. The straps needed to be welded again, but otherwise it was sound. "Fix this up," I told Jarak. "We'll put it back on the rack come morning." If Myra didn't want my armor, after all, there were plenty of women with more taste who would.

None of those women came to my shop the next morning, though. Or the next day. Or the next week. And seven days after Myra's visit, I smelled smoke. It was salty and metallic—like a forge on fire.

I left Jarak in charge and raced outside. There are

some things a smith doesn't ignore. I had to offer whatever help I could.

Following the scent didn't lead me to a burning forge, though. It led me to the town square. A crowd had gathered there; beyond them, flames leapt into the sky. When I pushed forward, I found a wood fire—with a huge group of women gathered around it. A woman ran up and threw something into the flames. Chain mail, bikini style. The flames leapt higher, and the stench of burning dirt and blood filled the air. The cheers grew louder.

The woman who'd thrown the armor in stood there, grinning. She wore scale mail, I realized—men's scale mail. What fool had sold her that? The armor looked bulky and unattractive on her small frame. Many of the women were dressed that way. Fire reflected off their heavy mail.

"Strangest damn thing I've ever seen!"

I turned to see Millie, of Millicent's Fine Armour, standing beside me. Her gray hair was tied neatly above her head; her flowered dress brushed the ground. Normally, we don't get along too well. But I looked at her and asked, "What are they *doing*?" Besides throwing away good armor, I meant.

"Bra burning," giggled a girl beside us. She was stout and buxom, in a tavern maid's skirt and low blouse, not the sort one would ever see in armor at all.

"Bra melting, more like," Millie muttered.

By the fire, I heard more cheers, then something that sounded like chanting. I couldn't make out the words.

I looked back to the women and the flames. A flash of red hair caught my eye; I saw Myra standing with the others, yelling wildly. Her bulky leather armor hid her curves and tan skin; she looked no different than a man.

She must have felt me watching her, because she whirled to face me. "There they are!" she yelled, raising one fist into the air. "Get the armorers!" someone else cried. Myra ran towards me, a group of screaming women behind her.

"I think we should leave now," Millie said.

I couldn't argue with that. I walked away, as fast as I could without running. I wasn't scared, you understand. I had a business to run, though, and I'd already wasted too much time.

Behind me, the women were still chanting, louder than before. Now I could make out the words.

"What do we want? *Battle armor!* When do we want it? *Now!*"

I scowled, suddenly angry that I'd imagined a real emergency here.

When I woke the next morning, the faint scent of smoke still lingered in the air. By then, I'd decided the madness in the square might be good for business. Those women were going to need my armor more than ever, once they finished destroying what they had. They couldn't keep what they'd worn last night, after all. No woman really wants to look like a man. And most men don't want them looking that way, either.

I whistled as I walked down to the shop, expecting a busy day. I wondered how many women would already be there, waiting to buy.

Myra stood by my door, alone.

I let her in. She wore a tunic and loose breeches now; the clothes made her more mannish than ever. She had a sack slung over one shoulder. Her leather armor, I guessed.

"Would you like to trade that in?"

"Trade?" She threw her head back and laughed. "What makes you think I'd trade with you?"

"What's in the sack?"

She kept laughing. The sound grated.

"If you're not here to trade or buy, you'll have to leave my shop. There are plenty of women who'd be happy to pay for my armor."

"I wouldn't be so sure of that." There was a glint in Myra's eye. "Any woman worth her weight in battle has gone south by now."

"Back to the front?"

More laughter. "Oh, further south than that."

Darian's border runs farther south here than anywhere else, but still, it took a moment to figure out what she meant.

"The traitors!" They'd crossed the border, into Ryll.

"You see? There are people willing to sell us decent armor. You just have to know where to look."

I glared at her, trying to understand how a matter of mere fashion justified such treachery. Anger made my face hot. We still had the men, so of course we'd be safe—but I thought of the size of the crowd by the fire, and I felt uneasy.

"Why are you still here, then? Aren't you heading south with the others?"

Myra smiled, swinging the bag from her shoulder to the floor. It jangled; there was more than leather armor inside.

"I have other plans. I hear you and Millicent need some competition." She reached into the bag and pulled something out. A small piece of metal, shaped into a cup and dangling from a string.

"What the hell is that?"

"It's part of my new fall line." A wicked grin crossed Myra's face. "I call it the thong bikini codpiece."

The greatest challenge every young careerwoman must face: making Mother understand.

THE OLD GRIND

Laura Frankos

Fenia dumped a huge sack of rock salt into the magic quern Grotti as her mother Menia set the millstone to grinding. The old giantess stood on the rocky shore, waves lapping over her enormous feet. Menia stretched her hands over the enchanted quern as she cast the spell.

"Waters quick, waters deep, grind these stones—" She broke off suddenly, arms dropping to her sides. "Daughter! Not so fast! Pour them in slowly, or the quern will overflow. Your haste has caused me to ruin the spell. I must begin again."

Scowling, Fenia took a tighter grip on the mouth of the sack and slowed the shower of rock salt. Her mother nodded approvingly and began the spell once more.

"Waters quick, waters deep, grind these stones, the salt to keep." Menia pointed a stubby finger at the gray ocean and at once a channel cut through the waves. Water gushed through the eye of the millstone; it began rotating, slowly at first, then with greater speed. A whirlpool formed as the flow of water increased. The seas all around became more and more turbulent.

Fenia pointed at the whirlpool. "The humans won't

be pleased with us if they sail their ships through that Swelkie, Ma."

Menia sniffed. "Humans! What do we *gygers* care what humans think? They'd be unhappier still if we neglected to grind the salt and all their precious fishes died." She looked into the quern to make sure it was grinding evenly, then turned her gaze on her daughter. "What has gotten into you, daughter? You're edgy as an axe." Her gray eyes narrowed. "Are you with child? I know that Cubbie Roo's been hankering after you, but after that last row you had with him . . ."

"Oh, *him*." Fenia dismissed the giant with one wave of her hand and sat down on the shore. "He may be the biggest giant here in Orkney, but I can best him in all the things that matter. Did you see what happened when he and Tostig of Kiepfea Hill quarreled last month? Cubbie heaved a boulder and missed Tostig by fifty yards. Disgraceful."

Menia clucked her tongue. "There's more things important than good aim." She picked up the bag by Fenia's feet and dumped the rest into the quern.

Fenia snorted. "What about all his work at building a bridge between the islands because he doesn't like to get his feet wet? Time and again he tries, but he always overloads his basket, and the stones spill into the sea. And besides, how could he help us with Grotti if he won't get his feet wet?"

She succeeded in shocking her mother. "Grinding the sea salt is *gygers*' business! You never saw your father help with Grotti, did you?"

"I never saw Father do anything except fish and poke holes in rocks with his thumb, which never struck me as a useful talent. Assuming I did marry, which is assuming a great deal, why couldn't my mate help with the work? Maybe not with the spells, but dumping in the rocks and carrying the salt to the sea doesn't take anything special."

"It simply isn't done!"

"That's no answer," Fenia retorted. "But it's a

pointless argument, anyway. I've no intention of marrying." She gazed across the Pentland Firth at the dark smudge that was the island of Britain. "I want to leave Orkney, Ma. I went to travel, see the world. I want adventure and excitement. Most of all, I want to get away from this endless grinding."

They had been speaking loudly; the roar of the whirlpool and the thunderous pounding of Grotti made normal conversation impossible. Fortunately, giantesses have loud voices. Fenia's last sentence, however, came just as Grotti finished grinding the salt, and boomed over the gurgling hush of the water trickling back to the ocean.

Her mother looked at her blankly. "You can't mean it. There's nothing for you out in the world. It's cluttered full of humans. You're better off here, with your own kind. What on earth would you do, anyway? You're not trained for anything save tending Grotti."

Fenia stood up and emptied the ground salt into a basket. "I thought I'd try my hand at fighting. I'm so big any human army would be glad to have me."

Menia decided to use guilt to sway her daughter's mind. "If you leave, what will I do? I'm not getting any younger, and Grotti must be tended every day. How my poor old bones ache."

"You're full of fishheads, Ma. You're only two hundred and twenty-eight, the prime of life."

"Two hundred and *thirty*. I've lied to you the last couple of decades."

"Whatever." Fenia lifted up the basket and began trudging up to the high cliff from which she would dump it into the sea. It would have been far easier to pour it right there on the shore, but Menia was a perfectionist, and insisted that the salt dispersed better this way.

"You will need some help, though, when I'm gone," Fenia added. "I thought I'd hire a couple of dwarves."

"Dwarves!" Menia howled.

"Maybe trolls. There're plenty in the hills, but dwarves are more reliable."

"Trolls!" Menia clutched at her head. "I can't believe my ears! My own flesh and blood! We *gygers* have always had a respectable business!"

"So I'll hire respectable dwarves." Fenia reached the top of the steep hill and flung the salt over the edge. The ever-present Orkney wind caught it and scattered it over the crashing surf below, a white, crystalline shower.

Menia stood watching it fall. She resorted to a mother's last tactic: delay. "We'll talk about this later." Without another look at Fenia, she began the trek back down the hill to their home.

"We'll talk, Ma," Fenia said under her breath, "but all your shouting will only add to the strength of the wind."

Gygers have more sense than their male counterparts, who tend to believe everything can be solved with a few tossed boulders. When Menia realized that her daughter's ambitions could not be swayed, she fought for a compromise. Fenia would go out into the world for a year, then come back to Orkney for an unspecified length of time. The younger giantess assumed it would be a brief stay; her mother hoped otherwise.

Fenia had few possessions, so packing was easy. Harder was finding suitable dwarves in the islands. At last she found a married pair selling woolen goods on Fair Isle and tempted them with the promise of a regular salary.

"Ma, this is Alberich and his wife, Erka."

Menia studied the dwarves. "At least they don't smell. Alberich, you say? Wasn't that name in the news not long ago?"

"A distant cousin who was in the jewelry trade," Alberich said hastily. "We're weavers, got some lovely sweaters. Unfortunately, not in your size."

Menia heaved another sigh. "I suppose they'll do. The gods know what the neighbors will say."

"Ma, we haven't got any neighbors! I'm leaving before you say another word! See you next year." Fenia hugged her mother, collected her gear, and went out into the world.

Contrary to legends, giants cannot hop from one island to another; if they could, it would have made Fenia's journey much simpler. After swimming the Pentland Firth, she found little of interest in the Highlands save a few haggard, tattooed warriors who ran away as she approached. *Slim pictings here*, she thought.

She pressed southwards, and marveled how quickly the English ran away from her. "Almost as if they'd been practicing," she mused. "What I need is a way to get to the Continent; Britain is nearly as boring as home. Maybe there's something going on beyond that ridge; I smell smoke." Cresting the hill, she saw several buildings in flames. More Englishmen, long black robes kirted about their waists, were fleeing for the safety of the hills. "No wonder they're good at running, even with those short legs! Hey, you!" she called to one of the men. "Shouldn't you try to put out that fire?"

He stared at the giantess emerging from the woods. "Gleep," he said, and fainted.

Another man hurried to the fallen body. "Brother Ethelred!"

"I'll help you," Fenia offered, bending over.

The second man went pale. "Th-thanks. With all the commotion of the attack, I fear poor Ethelred was unready for a visit from a giantess."

"I'm just passing through."

"That's what the Vikings said," the man said darkly. "But they're still down there."

"Vikings? Why, I've seen some near my home; nice

big ships. Maybe I can get *them* to take me to the Continent!" Fenia clapped her hands in glee.

"*Deus vulut*," said the second man, casting his eyes skyward.

Fenia pelted down the hill to the cluster of buildings. A human, long blond hair showing under his helmet, dashed out of a doorway and ran right into Fenia. He dropped a sack which fell with a metallic clank.

"I'm so sorry," Fenia said. "Let me help you with that."

The human backed away. "No, no, I don't vant it anymore. I vas choost leaving."

"Leaving? Are you one of the Vikings?"

For some reason, this made some of the fear leave his blue eyes. He stood up straighter, and nearly reached Fenia's bellybutton. "Ja, I go viking. I am a Norseman."

"Good. I want to come with you. On your boat."

The Viking made a noise rather like the one Brother Ethelred had made. "I'd better take you to my chief, Ganga-Hrolf."

"Hrolf the Walker? Why's he called that?"

The Viking hesitated, measuring Fenia with his eyes. "Because he's so big, no horse can carry him."

"Good! We have something in common."

Ganga-Hrolf was big, for a human. He was taller than her navel and considerably wider than most humans. He was delighted to learn that Fenia wished to join his men, but balked at crossing the Channel.

"What's the point? We got plenty of good stuff to loot here in England; been looting it for years. Why not keep on wi' it?"

"But Ganga-Hrolf . . ."

"Call me Rollo. Somehow I feel less big in same room as you."

"Rollo, then. Consider the opportunities on the

Continent! It's many times the size of England. Just look at your map."

They were sitting in what Rollo called a church. It had been one of the burning buildings, but Fenia herself put out the blaze because she liked its great, high ceiling. It reminded her of home.

"It's a big gamble," Rollo muttered. "Who knows what these Franks got? Maybe not'ing! Maybe I should just sail west and see what the gods placed on the edge of the world!"

"Oh, don't go that way. My uncle, who suffers from an unfortunate hair condition, went that way years ago. He says it's rather cold and unpleasant."

"So is Denmark. Well, maybe we go there nodder time." He folded his arms and looked up at her. "I take you to Francia. What you do?"

She shrugged. "Whatever you say. I'm your *gyger*."

He slammed his fist in his open hand. "We fight! How can I lose wi' genuine giant on my side?"

Fenia felt his enthusiasm. She smiled, and felt better than she had in days. Preparing to invade a country was far more interesting than grinding salt.

Rollo's longboats were much larger than the tiny fishing boats of the humans in Orkney, but Fenia was still cramped. She couldn't squeeze through the cabin door, so the Norsemen rigged a canvas cover for her on the deck to shield her from the wind and rain while they headed back to Denmark to drop off the latest loot. The crew, under their chief's orders, accepted her and were even pleasant. Her capacity for mead mightily impressed them. She wished her mother could see her getting outfitted for a chainmail hauberk, or singing with the crew by lantern's light. Humans could be very pleasant when they weren't shrieking.

They spent a few weeks in Danish towns, making preparations, then headed south to invade Francia. Fenia was glad. She had not liked staying in the towns; though the Vikings accepted her, their relatives, especially their female relatives, did not. The bolder women ignored her or made magical signs at her; the others fled. Small, daring Danish boys tossed rotten fruit at her and darted into doorways too narrow for her to follow.

Rollo's ships landed without incident, and he led his army inland. Fenia trooped along loyally, studying the countryside. It looked very different from her windswept rocky home. The ground was dark and rich, the summer crops plentiful. Fenia marveled at the large orchards; there were few trees in Orkney. The men admired them, too: Many times Fenia heard men murmur they wished they had such grand farms.

After several days' plundering, Rollo returned to the ships to plan. "My scouts say the Franks are gathering an army; we should have company by the end of the week. Ready for battle, Fenia?"

"Ready," she answered, but as the time drew closer, she worried how ready she might be. She had a shield, but the master armorer had barely begun her hauberk. Without it there was going to be a lot of *gyger* exposed to Frankish weapons.

Her fears were not unfounded. The Frankish army, though fighting defensively, concentrated their attack on the largest Norse target: Fenia. At the end of the day, she had endured dozens of cuts and punctures, and her shield resembled Menia's pincushion. To her credit, she tossed a few boulders at the Franks, and her aim was true, unlike Cubbie Roo's. She never got to use her axe; her best use, it seemed, was making the enemy flee.

Afterward, Rollo called it a victory, and planned to use the Franks' rivers against them, sailing into the heart of Frankish territory and pillaging whatever they could. The men celebrated through the night. Fenia put vinegar on her cuts and went to bed. She didn't want to admit to anyone, much less herself, that she did not enjoy her first battle. It was much more exciting than tending Grotti, but she could not call it fun.

Summer stretched into fall, with the same routine. The Danes ransacked the countryside, fought skirmishes, and enjoyed themselves immensely. Many of them suggested to Rollo that they stay permanently in this bountiful land. Rollo considered it, "We could make it a Norseman's land, bring down our families from Denmark. . . ."

"Who needs that?" someone roared. "These Frankish and Breton maids are better looking than my wife!"

Rollo grinned. "Then it's settled! Let's winter here. Come spring, we'll confront King Charles. We will make this land our own!"

The Vikings shouted with approval and beat their shields. Fenia ate a pot of porridge in silence and wished, for the hundredth time, that the cook used more salt. She was tired of marching, tired of battles, and especially tired of Frankish arrows. She looked up only when Rollo mentioned her name.

"We'll lay siege to Chartres! We'll build engines and catapults, and hammer its walls! But greater than any catapult is our own giantess, Fenia, who shall personally attack the front gates!"

The Vikings cheered again. Fenia had wearied of heaving boulders, too. At least when Orcadian giants threw them, they tossed a couple and were done, the point taken. These humans thought if one was good, fifteen were better. She hoped she would get plenty of rest over the winter; she feared she would need it.

The siege of Chartres was not successful. Charles the Simple had defended it well, and Rollo's style of lightning-quick attacks was not suited to this type of drawn-out contest. Fenia dutifully threw rocks when she could; unfortunately for Rollo, there weren't many to be had.

Several weeks into the siege, the Vikings were

startled at dawn by a surprise attack. Frankish cavalry had come down from Paris to harass the invaders. Fenia was cut off from Rollo's main body of fighters, and nearly all the Norsemen with her overwhelmed. The Franks, as usual, kept their distance from her, but one knight threw a rock that caught her on the cheek. Dazed, she stumbled. When she looked up, a fine red haze seemed to cover the battlefield. She blinked, trying to clear her view. Then she blinked again, harder.

Flying through the mist on white horses were nine warrior-women in armor far better than her plain hauberk, long blond tresses flowing under their gleaming metal helmets. They swooped low over fallen Danes, touching them with spears. At each touch, a shimmering form rose up from the body and took a place behind the woman on the horse. Then the horses and riders vanished back into the clouds.

Fenia staggered forward, unsure which way to go. Two ravens swooped over her head, and someone impossibly strong grabbed her by the arm. A voice rang in her ears. "Lost your steed, daughter? Shameful! Mayhap we'll find him back at Valhalla."

Fenia was jerked upwards and deposited on the back of a huge flying horse with eight legs. An old man with a long beard and a blind eye sat before her. He craned his head around and squinted at her with his good eye. The horse looked at her, too, in a rather critical manner. "Putting on weight, daughter?" the rider asked.

Fenia didn't know what to say, for she realized with dread that this must be Odin, greatest of the gods . . . one who didn't get on well with giants.

Fortunately, he did not expect an answer. "Sleipnir, away!" Odin cried, and the mighty horse climbed higher into the sky. The ravens flew like black arrows before them, crowing so raucously it sounded like laughter. Moments later, Fenia saw a magnificent hall with a sparkling silver roof, impossibly situated among the clouds. Sleipnir landed, if one can call the action of setting hooves to clouds "landing." They dismounted, and Odin began leading Sleipnir to a building near the great hall. He gestured to her. "Come, daughter, perhaps one of your sisters has brought your lost steed to the stables."

One of the warrior-women emerged from the stables and gasped at Fenia. "Father, what *have* you brought from the field? This giantess is not ready for the mead of Valhalla!"

"Giantess? What's that you say?" Odin turned to peer at Fenia. The ravens alighted on the stable roof and cawed again. This time, Fenia was sure they were laughing.

"By my good eye!" Odin shouted. "You're right, Brynhild! I mistook her for one of you girls!"

Brynhild looked insulted. "Your 'good eye' is failing, Father. She's too big and ugly to be a Valkyrie. Besides . . ." She stalked closer to Fenia, her nose almost twitching. ". . . *we* are all maidens, and she is *not*."

Fenia stammered, "Well, you see, Cubbie Roo was over one night and he . . ."

"We don't want the disgusting details, giantess," snapped Brynhild. "Father, what are you going to do with her? She can't stay here. *She's not one of us*."

Odin tugged at his beard. The two ravens clicked their beaks, watching. "In times past, I've had to deal harshly with giants, but I own the error here and must remedy it. What is your name? Fenia? Shall I take you back to that battlefield, Fenia? Or would you rather go to Jotunheim, the realm of the frost giants?"

Fenia thought quickly. Brynhild's last disdainful sentence rang in her ears. The Valkyrie was right: She didn't belong here with the gods, but neither did she truly belong with humans. It was tempting to think of living in fabled Jotunheim with distant relatives of far renown, but what would a simple Orcadian *gyger* do there? The best place for her was ... home. She hated to admit it, but Menia was right.

"If it please my lord Odin, I'd like to go home to Orkney, but for one thing: I was fighting in the army of the human, Ganga-Hrolf the Dane, and I feel badly at leaving his service so abruptly. I worry he may fail without me, though I truly wish to go home."

"Tut! Huginn and Muninn here—" Odin nodded at the ravens "—have been keeping their bright eyes on your Norseman. He'll do well enough without you. That land will be in his family for many generations to come, I promise you. Brynhild, fetch the mead for our latest arrivals; I'll be there to welcome them soon. Come, Fenia, mount again. Sleipnir can bear your weight, for he is the offspring of a giant's steed."

Fenia had barely time to cast one last look at mighty Valhalla, a view partially spoiled by Brynhild's sour stare. Then Sleipnir plunged through the clouds again, whistling towards the earth.

"Some fun, eh?" Odin yelled. Fenia gulped.

Moments later, the eight-legged horse landed on the rocky headland of Fenia's own island. Odin bowed politely after she dismounted. "Do forgive my error, Fenia. I don't usually pick up pretty giantesses on battlefields." The one eye gleamed. "Humans occasionally, but usually in their bedrooms. Good fortune to you."

Then he and the horse were gone. Fenia walked along the shoreline. She could hear the familiar crashing sound of Grotti grinding the sea salt, though she could not see the magic quern yet. She clambered over a high, rocky spit, eager to see Menia again, though less eager to hear her gloating.

She looked up, and stopped in her tracks. There was Menia, tending Grotti, with Alberich and Erka by her side. And there, carefully pouring a huge sack of rock salt into Grotti, was Cubbie Roo, his feet in the roaring surf.

"What are you doing there?" Fenia bellowed.

They all stopped working. Grotti stopped grinding. Menia stood with her hands on her hips, waiting for Fenia to approach. "I might ask you the same thing. I didn't expect you back so soon."

"I meant him." Fenia pointed at Cubbie, who was blushing.

Menia's face grew sly. "Och, Cubbie's been helping me ever since you left. These dwarves are hard workers, but not so strong as a giant!"

"What about his *feet*?"

Cubbie hoisted a leg. "Made some sealskin boots. Works pretty well."

"What of you?" Menia asked. "Did you find adventure and excitement?"

Fenia thought back over her months with the Vikings. It had been an adventure, and some of it had been exciting. But other parts were boring or painful or unpleasant. "Yes, I did," she answered slowly. "I've had my fill of them, and decided to come back to the old grind."

Menia looked smug, but Cubbie Roo was worried. "Does that mean I shouldn't help anymore?"

"Oh, no," Fenia said hastily, realizing how much nicer looking Cubbie was then any of the humans she'd been with for so long—even Rollo. "Not when you've gone to the trouble of making boots and all."

"If you like," Cubbie said, "you can help me drop the salt from the cliff."

"I'd love to," said Fenia.

They walked off together. Menia laughed to herself. "Well, you can find adventure and excitement at home, if you'll only look for them."

Alberich tugged at her sleeve. "Now that she's back, are we out of work, too?"

"Wait a bit," said Menia. "How are you at baby-sitting?"

It's not how well you do the job, it's how well you
dress for success.

THE WAY TO A MAN'S HEART

Esther Friesner

Talona the Terrible folded her sinewy arms across
her mighty armor-plated bosom and glared at her
opponent. "Just what do you mean by coming to class
at *this* hour, young lady?"

Amaryllis pressed her lips together, forcing back
the same words which had gotten her into trouble a
good twenty-eight times since her arrival at the school.
Every single one of those times she had been
reproved before all her fellow students *and* made to
slop the school pigs. Therefore, instead of the angry
retort "I am *Princess* Amaryllis, you muscle-bound
crone!" she meekly replied, "I'm sorry, Swordmistress,
but on the way to class I thought I heard a cry for
help coming from Rushy Glen, so I went to investi-
gate, for extra credit."

"Ah!" said Talona, uncrossing her arms and leaning
forward on the podium which creaked and cracked at
the joints in protest. "And did you think, child, that
I am unaware that the only presence in Rushy Glen
at the moment is one Hamid, a travelling merchant
and master of Hamid's Caravan of Discounts?"

Amaryllis cringed and blushed, mortified, while her
classmates sniggered. "I—I was only looking at the
daggers. He has a fine selection of the new models for
distant Goristan, and at prices that just can't be beat!"

Talona sighed. "Shopping. I might have known. You can take the princess out of the castle, but you can't take the urge to shop out of the princess. Well, shopping is not the proper occupation for any serious swordswoman, let me assure you."

"But I'm *not* a serious—"

"*Hush!*" All the instincts of a seasoned fighter snapped into action as Talona leaped the length of the classroom to clap a sword-calloused hand over Amaryllis's mouth. Darting her eyes to left and right as if seeking skulkers in the shadows, the veteran hissed, "Do you want the surviving princes to hear you? Their agents are everywhere. These are cut-throat times."

"Mo mah miff may *mid*?" Amaryllis said as well as she was able.

"So what if they did?" Talona echoed. "Mark my words well, lass: If they did, I promise you that you would face the deepest doom, the saddest fate, the most dreadful curse that ever can befall a woman." She lowered her voice so that it sounded even more portentous: "You would have to stay single *forever!*"

A gasp of involuntary horror shook the assembled student body, causing chainmail-clad bosoms to heave until the jingling sounded like the charge of a bellringers' choir, out for blood.

As for Amaryllis, at the very mention of possible spinsterhood she collapsed in a dead faint.

She awoke to the sounds of a heated argument between Talona and one of her fellow students, a lady named Gethina.

"—Sovereign Essence is the best remedy for swoons available without a wizard's prescription, that's why!" Gethina was saying, waving a small yellow bottle dangerously near the Swordmistress's face.

"Vorn's Sovereign Essence can bring back the dead for all I care," Talona shot back, smacking the unlucky bottle out of Gethina's hand. "I still would never have it under my roof. It is manufactured solely by the

Witches' Auxiliary of the Council Sorcerous as a fund-raising item. One of the principal ingredients, as any ninny knows, is consommé of frogskin. Out of simple good taste and sensitivity I refuse to stock it in the school infirmary, and I am surprised that you—a princess born!—would be in possession of such filthy brew, let alone suggest *using* it!"

"Oh, don't be surprised, Teacher." Santorma's nasty, insinuating voice came scraping at the edges of Amaryllis's returning consciousness. "Gethina never had a hope of finding a decent husband before the great disaster, so why should she care a fig for the rest of us now; *or* for good taste?"

"That's a lie!" Gethina flashed a scathing look on Santorma. "Before the disaster I was engaged to be married to Prince Reston of Beverlita."

Santorma's scornful laugh was every bit as nasty and insinuating as her voice. "More like Princess Beverlita of Reston, if you get my drift, and don't you just. I hear tell that he looked so much like a frog to start with that the witches didn't need to cast more than half the frog spell over him before boiling him down for consommé."

Gethina let loose a bloodcurdling shriek and threw herself on Santorma. Swords flashed and met in mid-air. The classroom rang with the alarm of steel biting steel, and the grunts and curses of the combatants.

Talona clapped her hands rapidly to get the attention of the other girls. "All right, ladies, you know the drill: Papers out, pencils flying; I'll be collecting your observers' notes on this skirmish afterwards."

Pucina, lately princess of Treb, raised her hand. "Will we be getting graded on this?"

"Only if both of them survive," Talona replied. "If one or both dies, you will write a five-page essay on the winning strategy, due tomorrow."

Pucina's eyes widened. "For the love of all the gods, you two, *don't die!*" she shouted.

By the time Amaryllis had managed to pick herself

up off the floor and borrow a pencil, the set-to was over. Both combatants had survived, though both were also bleeding from a number of superficial wounds, besides which Santorma sported a shiner. Their teacher observed them with an expert's eye and pronounced, "Not bad. Neither one of you would have lasted five minutes against one of the girls from my old regiment, but you fight well enough to deceive a prince who wants to have a swordmaiden for a wife."

Santorma did not accept her teacher's praise graciously. She spat a gob of blood studded with a couple of her smaller teeth and decreed: "I *quit*." She touched her blooming black eye and added, "If our remaining princes have gotten so cursed finicky about having to wed a swordmaiden, then I say to the netherpit with them! I'm going home. First I'm going to have a nice, hot bath, then I'm going to marry my father's swineherd, and *then* I'm going to bribe as many minstrels as it takes to spread some cockamamie fairy tale about how he was really a prince in disguise. And I will personally slice the head off anyone who says anything different!" She unbuckled her swordbelt, let it fall to the floor, and gave it a savage kick before stalking out.

A short silence followed this scene. At last Talona remarked, "Well! I suppose the rest of you are going to follow *that* pathetic example." Her eyes swept her remaining students, including Gethina, who was still standing in the middle of the floor, breathing hard.

"Not bloody likely," Amaryllis muttered.

"What was that?" Once more Talona sprang—this time in the purely figurative sense. "Speak up, young lady! If you have something to say, say it so that the whole class can hear."

For an instant, Amaryllis toyed with the idea of making up another lie. Then she dropped it. The one about Rushy Glen hadn't worked worth spit. She knew she was a poor liar, and besides, she was angry. Why shouldn't she be able to come late to class because she'd stopped to browse at Hamid's? Why couldn't she indulge in her favorite occupation anymore, simply because it wasn't proper for a swordmaiden? She opened her mouth to speak and what came out of it was as honest as her heart could make it:

"I said *not bloody likely*! And you know *why* it's not bloody likely as well as we all do. Santorma's father is the richest king for leagues around and she's his only child! If any one of our fathers had half his money and if any of us were our kingdom's only heir, we'd be out of this place so fast it would melt your buckler! But we're not rich and we're not sole heirs, so we can't marry swineherds and turn them into princes. *That* would be a picnic. But, oh no, *we've* got to marry princes, only there are hardly enough of them to go around since the Witches' Auxiliary turned so cursed many of them into frogs!"

"It wouldn't be so bad if they'd just left it at turning them into frogs," Pucina sighed. "Then we could kiss them, break the spell, and they'd have to marry us. But as soon as they become frogs, those odious witches nab them for the brewing of their triply-damned Vorn's Sovereign Essence! You can't kiss a cup of frog consommé."

"You can," Amaryllis corrected her. "But you don't get bang-all for your trouble."

"I blame the government," said Princess Rika of Yellowcrag. "If the Interkingdom Alliance hadn't cut off all funding for the black arts, the Council Sorcerous wouldn't have slashed the budget for the Witches' Auxiliary and they never would have needed to start such an aggressive fund-raising project in the first place."

Talona held up a chiding finger. "No politics in class," she said. Then she returned her attention to Amaryllis. "Whining never helps, whether you're princess or swordswoman. In a free market economy, the laws of supply and demand become the facts of life.

Our remaining princes know they can afford to be picky; you can not. Not if you want to become a bride. At the moment, it strikes their fancy to marry only swordmaidens. It's become a bit of a status symbol with the boys, really. We ought to be pleased that they're no longer afraid of strong women. Now as I see it, you have three choices: Wait for princess brides to come back into style—" (Amaryllis looked dubious) "—leave this school and accept a life of single cursedness—" (Amaryllis looked aghast) "—or sit down, shut up, and *do your work!*"

Amaryllis sat down and shut up, but that was as far as she was going to go. While the other ladies scribbled their evaluations of the recent combat and Gethma helped herself to the contents of the first aid kit, Amaryllis sat idly in her place until Talona noticed her lack of industry.

"Why aren't you writing?"

"I can't. I didn't get to see the fight. I was still pretty groggy for most of it."

Talona shook her head. "Tsk-tsk. What did I say about whining?"

The veteran swordswoman's condescending tone was just too much for Amaryllis to bear. She leaped to her feet and shouted, "I quit *too!*"

"Fine." Talona was unperturbed. "No refunds on the remainder of this semester's tuition and good luck to you." Without further ado she turned her back on the simmering student swordmaiden and told the rest of the class to hurry up and finish their reports.

"I'll show you!" The princess' cheeks were flushed with anger, her dainty hands were fists. "I'll find a prince and I'll convince him that I'm a real swordmaiden without any more of your stupid schooling *and* I'll marry him! So there! Nyah! What do you think of that?"

Talona's head slowly came around. "Fine," she said quietly. "You try that. May I suggest the kingdom of Egrel as the best place to start? It's most conveniently

located. Their prince Destino is reputed to be handsome enough, and he's an only child, so you can be
fairly well assured of becoming queen in time."

Amaryllis frowned. "Why are you telling me all
this? Why do you want to help me?"

"Because no matter how much information I give
you, you won't succeed. You'll be found out first, and
the news will echo throughout every civilized land. In
that way, you shall serve as an object lesson for the
rest of your classmates and I shall never be troubled
to maintain discipline again. I ought to thank you for
services rendered."

The princess' lily brow creased even more. "What
if I'm *not* found out?"

"*Not* found out? *You?*" Talona's laugh was like the
carking of a gore-crow. "Dear child, even the most
pudding-brained of princes can tell when a swordmaiden is faking it."

Amaryllis stalked out of Talona's School for Swordswomen while her erstwhile teacher passed down the
rows of benches and trestle tables, collecting papers.
She was so furious that she went about a mile past
Rushy Glen before she realized that she now had all
the time in the world for shopping.

"Damn," she muttered. "Now what? I can't go back
home. Daddy will be a bear when he hears about the
tuition, and my soppy half-sister Villanella will start
yapping again about how *she* should've been the one
sent to school. As if she'd ever land a prince, swordmaiden or not! With the face that old camel's got,
she'd better pray I do marry Prince Destino, because
the only way she'll ever get a man is if I'm queen of
somewhere-or-other and I can order some poor soul
to wed her on pain of death. And even *then* I'll have
to persuade him!"

With these and similarly charitable observations
falling constantly from her lips, Amaryllis walked some
five miles before reaching a major road, flagging down
a passing haywain, and hitching a ride. As she jounced

along on the seat beside a driver who smelled marginally fouler than the school pigs, Amaryllis had time
enough to reflect upon her situation, as well as to get
the hang of sitting so that her sword did not smack
her thigh black and blue. She gave thanks when she
learned from the lout that it was as Talona had said:
The kingdom of Egrel was not too far away. In fact,
they would reach the royal castle-town by sunset.

"What business ye got there, arh?" the fellow
inquired.

Amaryllis decided that if she were going to imper-
sonate a woman warrior, there was no time like the
present to begin the charade. She put on Talona's
grimmest face and replied frostily, "My business is
mine own, and doom perhaps to he who pries into it
too closely, unbidden."

"To *him*," said the driver.

"I beg your pardon?" Amaryllis' mask of cold pride
not only dropped, it shattered, and she almost slid off
the seat.

" 'Sdoom perhaps to *him* who pries into it too
closely unbidden. Damn and blast, but ye swords-
wenches otter know yer grammar better'n that, I'm
thinkin', arh."

Amaryllis suppressed a little thrill of delight. *He
thinks I'm a real swordmaiden!* Assuming a more
kindly tone, she said, "Your pardon, good churl. Per-
chance it will do no harm to make you privy to the
cause that brings me unto yon fair city. I am a poor
but honest sellsword, lately out of work since the per-
ishment of my last employer."

"Doesn't say much for yer skill wi' the blade then,
if ye let yer last boss die. Looks like carelessness."

"Uh, mmm, er—he did not die through any lack of
vigilance on my part," Amaryllis said swiftly. "His
wife poisoned him whilst they were, uh—"

"Say no more." The driver nodded knowingly.
"Well, no fear: Ye'll find work aplenty once we reach
the town. What'd ye say yer name was?"

"I am Amar—Amar—" Suddenly the princess realized that her given name sounded too soft and mooshy to be associated with a swordmaiden of her supposed redoubtability. "I am Amar the—the *Amazing*," she said, making a fast judgement call that sounded only a little lame.

The bumpkin, however, accepted it without demur and even remarked, "Aye, an' amazing ye are, that's for certain, arrh." Unfortunately he was staring at her chainmail-cupped breasts, not her swordarm, when he said it.

He was making his fifteenth try at steering the conversation back to the subject of how she managed to stand up straight with those things when they passed beneath the city gate—

—and were nearly swept right out again in a floodtide of thundering, screaming, terrified citizens. The haywain was an island in a human sea, the oxen tossing their heavy heads as panic whitened their eyes, the driver standing up on the footboard, whip in hand, unsuccessfully trying to make the stampeding crowd keep their distance from his beasts.

And then it was over. They were all alone on the inner side of the city gate, staring down a desolate street to the castle mount. Amaryllis gaped. "What was all *that* about?"

Before the driver could answer, the princess heard the sound of approaching hoofbeats. Out of a sidestreet came a white stallion and mounted on his back was the handsomest man Amaryllis had ever seen. Early training had stressed the importance of self-control in royal maidens, but this was an exceptional case. Amaryllis did not know *how* exceptional until she felt a tiny drop of something warm and wet on the back of her hand and realized that she was drooling. She hastily wiped her mouth and prayed that the glorious young man had seen nothing.

Her prayers went unanswered: He had seen her. He was doing a fair amount of drooling himself.

"If this kingdom survives the horror presently upon us," he said in one of those deep, resonant voices that command respect and carry for miles, "then when it is over I shall order a special thanksgiving service to praise whatever power has brought a creature such as you into my realm." He slid gracefully from the saddle and knelt in the dust beside Amaryllis' side of the haywain.

She scrambled from her place to urge him back to his feet. "Noble sir, do not abase yourself before me. I am but a humble swordmaiden, Amar the Armigerous."

"Thought ye said 'Amazing,' " the driver grumbled. No one paid him any mind.

"A swordmaiden!" The young man's eyes lit up. He clasped her hands to his breast in exultation. "This is a deliverance! Know, fair warrioress, that I am Prince Destino. Know too that I have fallen in love with you at first sight. Know likewise that if you will have me, I would make you my bride. Know besides all of the above that whether or not you accept my offer of matrimony—"

"Oh I do! I do!" Amaryllis cried.

"—that I would still offer you a lucrative dragon-slaying contract to—you do? I mean, you *will* marry me?" Amaryllis nodded hard enough to snap the neck of a lesser woman. "Ah, joy! Then I shall ride back to the castle to bring my parents the happy news while you ride forth to slay the wicked monster who—"

"What?" said Amaryllis. And also: "Monster? Slay?" And last but not least: "Huh?"

"Why yes, my beloved." Prince Destino gave her a melting look. "The dragon. I'm sure I mentioned it. It appeared sometime this afternoon in the castle courtyard where I was entertaining my fiancée, the Princess Dimity of Yither."

For a reason known best to herself, Amaryllis heard

only one word of the prince's last sentence: "*Fiancée?*"

Destino sighed. "An alliance contracted when we were both in our cradles. We were not supposed to wed for another two years, but what with the recent upheavals affecting eligible princes, her father insisted we rush ahead with the marriage; 'Before you give me a grandchild that's a damned tadpole,' was the way he put it. Princess Dimity of Yither is a very—"

"Don't tell me about Dimity!" Amaryllis looked hot enough to set the whole haywain ablaze. "Dimity is my stupid cousin, and a more graceless, stubborn, overbearing girl you've never seen!"

"Your . . . cousin?" The prince chewed this over. "But she's a princess, and you—"

"My father lost his throne to barbarian hordes from the north," Amaryllis said rapidly. "He and all my kin perished in the assault. I alone survived, an infant, rescued by my aged nurse. She's dead now too. There's no one left to tell you any different, so don't bother asking around."

"A swordmaiden, a disinherited princess, and the chosen of my heart!" Prince Destino was in ecstasies. "And once you've rescued her, I am sure that the princess Dimity's father will make no trouble about annulling the old contract, out of gratitude for his child's life. Oh, this couldn't be better! All you have to do now is slay the dragon."

"I'm honored that you consented to let me come along to watch you at work," Prince Destino said as he and Amaryllis rode towards the mountains.

"It was my pleasure, my lord," Amaryllis replied. *Curse it anyway!* she thought. *If I'm going to die, I might as well take him with me. I refuse to let that cow Dimity get her claws back into him!* She sat a little taller in the saddle and tried not to think of how dragon fire was going to feel on the vast

expanses of skin her scanty-though-spectacular
armor left unprotected.

"Yonder lies the dragon's lair," said the prince,
pointing to a yawning cavern at the foot of a mountain
that was much too close for Amaryllis' peace of mind.

She knew she was going to die—she had told herself so over and over, in hopes that repetition would
numb her to the awful fact—but somehow, now that
the fact was becoming more and more irrefutable with
every step her horse took, she simply could not face
it. Maybe it was the fast-fading smudge of smoke she
saw emanating from the cavern; maybe it was the
sight of bleached bones and human skulls strewn at
all-too-frequent intervals along the path; maybe it was
the stench of carrion and cold, old reptile that clung
in an ever-thickening cloud around this whole unhal-
lowed place. Whatever it was, she could not bear it.

She felt another tiny drop of something warm and
wet on the back of her hand. She knew that this time
it was not drool, but a tear. It was joined by others,
and others still, until by the time she and Prince Destino were within shouting distance of the dragon's lair
her eyes were streaming while she fought to swallow
her sobs.

She very nearly succeeded. Only one escaped. The
prince turned at the sound and his eyes grew wide.
"Why—why Amar, you're—you're *crying?*"

That was it. That was a word too much. Every single sob and moan and bleat of despair that the princess had been bottling up inside her demanded its
freedom. What's more, every single one of them got
it.

"Oh my goodness!" The prince was frantic. He
pulled his horse up alongside of hers and with a
great deal of fuss managed to haul her from the
saddle to sit sideways across his lap. She buried her
face against his shoulder and bawled. He regarded
her dumbstruck for a while, then carefully pronounced, "I see it all, now. Oh, my dearest, how could

I have been so blind? Not only are you bold of mien and strong of arm, you are also tender of heart. You fear that while you are in the process of slaying yon beast, some fatal harm might come to me before you had convinced it to be entirely dead. Such is the epic scope of your love! Well, don't you worry your pretty little head about it." He set her on her feet and reined his horse several paces away. "You go ahead and take care of business; I'll wait over here."

Still snivelling and wiping her nose on the back of her hand, Amaryllis went back to her horse to fetch her sword. She was no longer afraid of dying. At this moment the strongest emotion filling her bosom was the bitter realization that her old teacher, Talona the Terrible, had been right: It didn't pay to fake it. Thus armed with an unshakable who-gives-a-damn attitude, she entered the lair of the beast.

The dragon's cave stank worse on the inside; that was logical. The bones were thicker too. Amaryllis had not come away from Talona's school entirely ignorant; she knew how to hold her sword as she picked her way through the mounds of ribs and skulls and femurs. She tried to stalk her prey quietly, but the bones *would* rattle so, and whenever her sandalled foot touched one she could not restrain a little *Ick!* of disgust.

She thought she was finally getting used to stepping on the horrid things when she missed her footing on a particularly steep mound of skulls and fell flat on her rump in the midst of them. This time her reaction was no genteel, maidenly *Ick!*; it was a scream that dislodged several quarts of bats from the cavern roof.

The echoes of that shriek had not died down before Amaryllis heard a familiar voice inquire, "Are you *quite* done?" She blinked her eyes in the murk. Could it be—?

"Over here, stupid," came a second voice, also no stranger. Amaryllis could hardly believe what she saw. There on the cave floor, basking on a pile of gold and jewels fit to choke a basilisk, was her cousin Dimity. Not a sword's-length away lay the dragon. The dragon's *body*, that is. The monster's severed head was elsewhere, dangling from the hand of Talona the Terrible.

"What took you so long?" Dimity asked, tossing rubies into the air and letting them patter down on her satin skirts like a very expensive rain.

"You saved her!" Amaryllis cried. She ignored her cousin, focusing all her surprise (and a good measure of pique besides) on Talona. "You want the prince for yourself!"

"Hardly, child," the swordswoman replied, setting the grisly trophy aside. "You see, when you left my school, I realized that your father made me insert a rather nit-picky clause into our contract, stating that in case of the student's death, a pro rata share of the semester's tuition must be refunded. It never said a thing about whether you died at school or away. Since I'd told you to try your luck here in Egrel, I gave the girls a long weekend and came after you. Well, no sooner did I reach the capitol than I heard of the dragon."

"And she knew you'd head right for it, like a fly to—"

"Shush, Dimity."

Princess Dimity shrugged. "Truth is truth. Everyone in the family knows that Amaryllis is desperate to get married, don't ask me why."

"I happen to like children," Amaryllis snapped. "I'd like to have several. Do you mind?"

"You can have all of mine, while you're at it," Dimity replied. "I don't much care for the sticky little things. In fact, that was the one part of marriage I was dreading. Oh, and the royal ceremonies, and dressing up all the time, and organizing banquets, and redecorating the castle, and—"

"We get the idea, my dear," Talona said. She turned to Amaryllis once more. "As I was saying, once

I knew there was a dragon in the case, I was certain you'd go after it, whether or not you had a hope of killing it. You'd do it just to show me, wouldn't you?"

Amaryllis' head drooped. She nodded.

"I thought so." Talona was satisfied. "You have spirit, child; keep it. Just don't go letting it shove you into situations you lack the training to handle."

"I owe you my life," Amaryllis said. She didn't sound very happy about it.

"Pshaw!" said Talona. "By the time I found the dragon's lair, the hard work was done for me: The dragon lay steeped in a sleep so deep that it never knew when my sword came down on its neck. Just look at the size of the monster! If I had met it when it was fully awake, it might have been another story altogether; and not one I would have liked, I can tell you!"

"It . . . slept?" Amaryllis was puzzled. "But—"

"I did it," Dimity announced casually, standing up amid the heaps of treasure. "First I pretended to be the typical fraidy-cat princess and then, when the dumb beast thought it had nothing to fear from me, I managed to mix a little of Vorn's Sovereign Essence into its last meal." She reached into the silk pouch at her belt and withdrew the familiar yellow bottle. "Sent the monster straight to dreamland. Great stuff. A hundred and one uses. I never leave home without it."

Amaryllis didn't know whether to be appalled or revolted. "You *touched* the dragon's last meal? But it eats—it eats—"

"Hey, if I hadn't done it, I'd have been the dragon's *next* meal," Dimity responded hotly. "I'd rather be alive than dainty any day!"

Amaryllis dropped her sword, covered her eyes, and began to cry. Talona and Dimity rallied 'round, patting her on the back and making comforting noises. Amaryllis shrugged them off violently. "Stop it!" she

cried. "Leave me alone! You ruined my life, the pair
of you!"

"Stopped you from getting killed, yes, I can see
how that would ruin your life," Talona said dryly.

"Don't you *see?*" Amaryllis wailed. "Now Prince
Destino will know I'm not a real swordmaiden and
he'll marry Dimity!"

"No, he won't," said Dimity and Talona in perfect
harmony.

The ride back to Talona's School for Swordswomen
was a pleasant one. The ladies, mounted on fine
steeds that were the gifts of a grateful prince, enjoyed
the scenery and each other's company. When they
reached a likely spot, they dismounted to have lunch.
Unpacking their panniers, well packed with the leav-
ings of the wedding banquet, they licked their lips in
anticipation over the fine feast before them.

It did not take them long to devour it almost to
the crumb. Sated, Talona leaned her back against an
oak and sleepily said, "You know, my dear, if this *is*
the career for you, you must allow me to help you
pick out a nice suit of armor."

Dimity laughed and patted her satin skirts. "Not a
chance! I get more protection wearing a gown than
I'd ever get from that silly chainmail kilt and halter
you wear."

"It's traditional," Talona said. "People expect
swordswomen to dress like this."

"Well, thank goodness for tradition! It was all that
kept Prince Destino from believing that I'd done for
the dragon. Of course *I* could never overcome any
sort of monster; just look at the way I dress!" She
laughed louder.

Talona clicked her tongue. "Men."

"People," Dimity corrected her. "Men don't have
the market cornered on ridiculous assumptions. I
don't mind; it makes life interesting. So—" She

shifted to a more comfortable position "—how long do you think it'll take me to master the sword?"

"Are you sure you want to, dear?" Talona cautioned.

"If I'm going to follow a career as a fighting woman, I want to be prepared for it, and I *don't* want to depend on the swords of strangers when I need a little backup," Dimity replied.

Before Talona could speak, they heard a rustling sound from the thicket. "Merciful heavens!" the swordswoman exclaimed. "What have we done, stopping here? Do you know what this place is, child?" Dimity shook her head. "It's called Rushy Glen, and that means—that means—"

"Rushy Glen? I know what *that* means! Amaryllis told me. YeeHA!" Dimity sprang from the grass and vaulted into the saddle. She felt a brave and defiant battle cry rising to her lips. With a wild howl she made her horse rear and paw the air as the bold words rang from her lips: "A Hamid! A Hamid! Let's . . . go . . . *shopping!*"

And the realms rejoiced as their new protector galloped on into legend, her boon companion Talona the Terrible at her side, and a short stop at Hamid's Caravan of Discounts on the way.

Angels and ministers of grace defend us in the strangest ways.

WHOOPS!

Nancy Springer

The day her client took a commuting job, Opal Grumbridge was issued new equipment: a breastplate, a crested helm, a large but lightweight curved sword, and a big horse, white of course. She was told to wear the helm and breastplate, brandish the sword in her hand, carry her wings smartly above her head, and ride the horse. It's ridiculous for me to wear armor, she protested. I'm already dead; what's the use of armor? It's ridiculous for me to ride a horse; I can fly. But she could complain all she liked and get nowhere. It was all up to the client. In Christian iconography, armor meant defense against sin, and somewhere or other Meg, the client, had seen a statue or something, sort of an angel-cum-Joan-of-Arc, including a horse of course because the horse signified war, and now Meg was imagining her guardian angel this way.

Merciful heavens, Opal sighed.

Opal Grumbridge, guardian angel, had been a schoolteacher who had died a virgin, of stomach cancer, at the age of forty-eight; she had gotten through her genteel life without once straddling a horse, and she did not much care for the idea of getting on top of one now. But the needs of the client came first. Therefore it was on a white charger, with sword in

233

hand and eyes rolling toward the sunrise, that Opal sallied forth to oversee Meggie's first day on the freeway.

Meggie drove a raisin-colored Saab and drove it hesitantly. Meggie was one of the most inoffensive persons on the face of the earth; most of the time Opal wanted to take her and shake some starch into her, but this was of course not possible. Opal could not give Meggie a good talking-to, could not even attempt communication with Meggie unless Meggie addressed her first. Almost everything depended on the client. Meggie was not a difficult client, but often a frustrating one. When would she ever take hold? There she was right now, inching down the entrance ramp toward morning rush hour on the beltway, just inching along. Turning her thin young face skyward, closing her eyes behind their thick lenses when she should have been watching what she was doing. Praying.

Meggie's prayer sounded right inside Opal's incorporeal head: "Sir or ma'am, if you're up there, please help me."

Open your eyes, sit up straight, girl, and think what you're doing. Now. Velocity times mass equals—something or other. Floor it, floor it! There you go.

Meggie bumbled onto the six-lane. Upon her white destrier, Opal galloped above and slightly behind Meggie's Saab, or to one side, keeping an eye on her. The horse, blessedly, having been imagined by a person (Meggie) who knew nothing whatsoever about horses, was a paragon of superequine good behavior, cantering along smoothly on nothing but air, and Opal actually began to enjoy her ride. Up there on that magnificent curveting steed with impeccable skyward-position wing posture and her cerulean blue gown flowing to her riding-booted feet and her breastplate shining to match her halo just so and with her sword flashing in her hand, Opal was sure she looked just smashing if anyone could have seen her, which of course no one could.

Then, just as she began to relax and enjoy, Opal felt the most astonishing, upsetting, disturbing, never-before-experienced sensation in the region of her nethers.

Simultaneously a horn sounded from the bumper-to-bumper multi-lane traffic whizzing below her. Meggie had perturbed someone.

More about Meggie, quickly: her belief in angels was sincere (necessarily so, in order for Opal to have taken her on as a client), creative, non-denominational and rather poorly thought-out, being somehow syncretized with her vegetarianism. On her Saab's bumper rode a large green-and-white sticker which admonished, "Do Not Drive Faster Than Your Angel Can Fly," but apparently Meggie had not considered how fast angels must travel to get where they have to go. Meggie drove under the speed limit. Always.

Once more Opal felt the astonishing WHOOPS! in that part of her most closely approximated to the horse's back, and simultaneously she saw someone thrust his shaking hand out of his car window and make a most exceedingly vulgar gesture at Meggie.

Oh, for heaven's sake.

Traffic was lumping up all around Meggie. Driving in the middle lane, with commuters rocketing past her on the left and the right then swerving in from opposite directions to claim the space in front of her, with other, more trepid drivers trapped behind her, Meggie was creating a massive, honking clot in the vehicular artery. *Meggie*, Opal urged, bending the rules a bit—well, Meggie had called upon her not long before—*please, Meggie, drive a little faster, that's a dear.*

But Meggie did not drive a little faster. Opal could see her in her pitiful little car, hunched over the wheel, her thin shoulders rigid—Meggie was scared. Moreover, while Opal always heard all too clearly

whatever Meggie had to say to her—or pray to her—
unfairly, communication the other way seemed to
work intermittently at best.

WHOOPS!

This was most unpleasant. Every time one of the
other drivers gave Meggie a single-fingered salute,
Opal felt it. Of course one of the rules was that truly
fervid prayer could be received by somebody else's
guardian angel; when it came to humankind's emotional extremes, angels played zone, not one-on-one.
But certainly Opal had never before thought that this,
ah, this particular non-verbal message could be con-
strued as prayer.

Evidently it could.

WHOOPS! How disgusting.

Meggie, drive faster!

But Meggie didn't. Knowing Meggie—as Opal had
known Meggie since her conception twenty-two years
before—Meggie quite simply couldn't.

Focused straight ahead through the windshield and
those awful glasses of hers, Meggie might be largely
unaware of the impression she was making on her
fellow commuters. Opal hoped so.

WHOOPS!

Oh, dear, another unfriendly hand was projecting
out of another window. There was certainly a lot of
traffic on the beltway this morning. Aggressive traffic.
Luckily, Meggie's exit was coming up in a few miles.

A leadfoot Meggie was not. Creative thought pro-
cesses, though, Meggie could handle quite well.

Meggie, Opal entreated earnestly, *imagine me in
full armor from now on. Do you understand, dear?
Meggie? I am feeling the need of some, ah, posterior
protection, Meggie. Full armor, Meggie, please.*

Meggie responded quite well, as it turned out. But
full armor didn't help. Opal found that out on Meggie's way to work the next day.

"Sir or ma'am, help me, I am going to die."

Just drive a little faster! WHOOPS!

In Opal's wishful imaginings, the shiny surface of the ineffable metal would deflect certain sorts of, ah, nether prayer and turn them back upon the senders in the most netherly appropriate manner—but in actuality, nothing seemed to penetrate like this kind of prayer. Except, possibly, that which it symbolized. However, Opal couldn't say. And she certainly didn't care to think about it.

Part of the problem, she decided, might be the horse. Or, rather, the regrettable horseback-riding position, in which one was spread in such an unseemly manner, carried along in such a, uh, pelvically rhythmic way.

WHOOPS! Another fervid single-fingered prayer had just issued from a frustrated auto parts clerk in a high-rider pickup. Meggie was driving forty-five precisely. It was hard for the supernatural horse to gallop slowly enough to follow her, Opal opined, knowing it would have been hard for her, the guardian angel, to fly slowly enough. Contrary to Meggie's bumper sticker, angels preferred flying at approximately the speed of light, which was why they sometimes appeared to be made of that whitely colorful insubstance. While ubiquity was a theological attribute of deity and only the deity, nevertheless an angel, when properly motivated, could fly so fast it was very nearly in two places at once. Opal almost knew how the drivers trapped behind Meggie felt; she would have found flying behind Meggie insufferably boring. But at least she would have been able to position her legs decently together.

WHOOPS!

Meggie, Opal requested firmly, *I want you to eschew this horse.*

"Aaaaaaaaah!"

Meggie's uncouth petition was not a reply to Opal's attempted message, but a yawp of terror. "Aaaaaaaah, what's he doing?"

He was running her off the road, was what he was doing.

A bandanna-headed guy in a grotty old maggot-mobile panel van. He didn't care if he hurt it. He forced her off onto the shoulder, and it was to Meggie's credit that she didn't lose control of either the car or her bladder. With not a clue what else to do she bumped to a stop, and the man in the van slewed to a gravel-spraying movie-maneuver halt diagonally across her front left fender, trapping her where she was. He got out. He had a strong, unpleasant smell, and there was an even stronger, more unpleasant emotion contorting his face.

And he had a gun.

Opal had never materialized before. Materializing was considered a most unwise last resort.

But there wasn't time to think. She plummeted straight down off the horse, landing between Meggie and the bandanna-man in an instant, in less than an eyeblink, landing THUMP on her solid and exceedingly visible booted feet, five fearsome feet tall and shinily armored from her ankles to her neck, a crested helm on her poodle-permed head, wings upswept at the optimal forty-five degree angle, sword upraised, fists and jaw clenched, eyes steely as only a lifetime of teaching sixth graders can make them. Sheltering Meggie and the Saab between her upspread wings, she confronted the man with the gun. What in heaven's name did he think he was doing, frightening Meggie that way? "You put that down *right now*," she told him.

Instead he waved it about in an ineffectual manner. Perhaps he was not too bright. The expression on his face indicated mental incapacity.

"Young man, I said put that nasty thing down!"

To her annoyance he did not obey her. He turned and ran away from her, lunging into his van in a blundering hurry. Too late for her to do anything about it, he lifted a reflexive finger as he roared away.

WHOOPsie. "Stop that!" She turned to face Meggie. "Why must they all do that!"

Meggie's expression was no more astute than the uncharming gentleman's had been, which was exasperating, because Opal knew Meggie to be an intelligent girl.

"Heavens, close your mouth before something flies in. Shake your mind into some sort of order, child." Opal felt a borderless buzz, a distancing rather like the deathbed experience of leaving the body behind, and realized that she was starting to fade. She spoke rapidly. "Listen, Meggie, we must do away with the horse, do you understand? I shall ride on your roof from now on." Indeed, the horse had galloped off somewhere. Opal could have flown, of course. But as slowly as Meggie drove, it would be a great deal less taxing to ride.

With a single downward stroke of her wings Opal swooped up and settled herself above the windshield, scraping and clunking unpleasantly against the metal of the Saab's roof, legs crossed in a ladylike fashion insofar as she was able to cross them at all. Armor certainly was a nuisance. *Now sit up straight, Meggie, pay attention to what you're doing—floor it, floor it! Very good.*

Back on the freeway, Meggie drove, if possible, even more timidly than usual. The trouble with Meggie, Opal mused with a sigh, was that those parents of hers had potty-trained her way too early. They were loving, fussy people, Meggie was their only child, and they had painstakingly raised her to be a quintessential victim, just the sort of person to attract a ne'er-do-well with a gun. In sixth grade Meggie had been the class scapegoat. Thereafter, the school nerd. She had gone to community college and lived at home. Her mouse-colored hair fluffed baby-fine around her thin face and her thick glasses. She peered. She had nice manners, yes, ma'am, yes, sir. She had found a job as the research assistant of an elderly expert on chalk dust by-products.

Horns blared constantly, their cacophony almost as distressing as—WHOOPS! Opal tried a different position, though she knew in her sinking incorporeal heart that it wouldn't help.

What Meggie needed was some backbone. Opal had instructed Meggie in the womb, and felt certain Meggie had had some backbone then. She ought to have it still if she could only locate it.

"G-g-g-guardian angel?" Meggie whispered a few feet below.

Yes?

"Are—are you really there, guardian angel? I saw you—I mean, at least I think I saw you—and I can hear you, I mean I think I hear you, but just barely."

I am most certainly here. My name is Opal. Opal Grumbridge.

"O—O—Opal?"

That's right.

"You're on top of my car?"

Yes, dear. Why are you calling me? What do you want?

"I—I don't know. They're going to say I'm crazy."

The meek shall inherit—WHOOPS! This was getting most excessively tiresome. Opal dropped all thoughts of meekness and communicated to her charge with considerable force, *Meggie, you really could drive faster.*

"Yes, ma'am. But I—I don't feel good. That man s-s-s-scared me. People are so mean." So Meggie had noticed at least some of what was going on.

Poor Meggie. Opal's tone of mind softened. *Sweetie, you need to toughen up.* Poor dear, it was a blessing that she could hear her now, it was a blessing to be able to talk with her even though Opal knew she would get the very dickens from her supervisor when she reported that she had materialized, however briefly. *You need to stand up for yourself. Chin up, shoulders back, chest out.* On the car roof Opal demonstrated, sure that if anyone could see her she would look quite stunning with her helm shining to match her sword and her face to the wind and a simply divine wingspread—

Beep. Honk. WHOOPS.

Aaaaaaaugh! Opal had just been whoopsed once too often.

The offending hand protruded from a Pontiac LeMans just then passing Meggie on the right. Without even thinking about it, in pure-hearted vexation, Opal swept her sword down. Being a fully motivated angel, she moved quite fast.

It really was a very nice sharp sword.

Meggie doggedly progressed onward, eyes upon her exit sign, that green gate of heaven standing half a mile ahead, oblivious to the way the cars behind her were swerving to avoid the freshly-severed hand lying on the pavement.

Oh, dear. Opal wondered whether that had been the wise thing to do.

But on the other hand—excuse the expression—why had they given her a sword if they didn't want her to use it?

And an angel with a mission really could move very, very fast. Maybe even fast enough to—forestall them? Do unto them before they could—do unto her?

Opal Grumbridge smiled. Chin up. Chest out. Halo tucked tidily under her helm.

On her way home with Meggie that evening, Opal left eight hands strewn on the beltway and didn't get whoopsed once.

"Someone took your license number, miss. And we have quite a few witnesses who accurately described your car. You seem to have achieved a certain degree of notoriety among the beltway populace within the past couple of days, miss."

In the little grubby room at the police station

Meggie sat as if her bones were spaghetti noodles, head practically invading her navel; frizzy-haired, she resembled a large piece of dryer lint. Overhead Opal hovered, blessedly out of armor for the evening—for some reason Meggie was imagining her in a crimson robe. Although she felt very anxious, Opal made herself stay quiet. It would not do to have Meggie addressing her under these circumstances; Opal knew that law enforcers throughout the centuries have taken a jaundiced view of those who talk to angels. Meggie's parents, thank goodness, were not present. They had accompanied Meggie to the station but were obliged to confine their hysterics to the waiting area. Thank heavens. It was too bad Meggie was being questioned this way, but it would have been even worse with her parents answering for her.

"Miss?"

"Yes, sir."

"You admit that you were driving your car on the beltway at the time of the incidents?"

"Yes, sir," Meggie said to her navel. "I was coming home from work."

"Were you present at the scenes of any of the reported incidents?"

"I—I guess so, sir. After a while I began to notice that cars were swerving away from me."

"Cars swerving? Did you see anything else?"

"No, sir. I was concentrating on my driving."

"We found a few scratches on your roof. Any idea how they got there?"

"No, sir."

"You sure? It looks like you might have had some sort of mechanism stuck up there. Something with a magnetic base, maybe."

Meggie just sat, spaghetti topped with dryer lint.

"Miss," the police officer said in condescending tones, "you might as well tell us about it. What sort of weapon or device did you have sitting on top of your car?"

Meggie's head came up. With astonishment and pleasure Opal noted the firm thrust of Meggie's chin. Meggie said, "Did your witnesses see something on my roof?"

"I asked you a question, miss."

Meggie straightened. Meggie sat with chest out, shoulders back. Meggie said, "I think you're crazy."

Very good! Opal blurted.

"If you think there was something on my roof," Meggie said, "you go find it."

Excellent! Nobody could have seen Opal, and she hoped Meggie knew it.

"Meanwhile," Meggie said, "you have no reason to keep me here, because *I didn't do anything.*" Meggie stood up. "I'm going home."

"Sit down, miss."

"Arrest me if you think I did anything," Meggie said, and she walked out.

Before rejoining her parents, however, Meggie detoured into a ladies' room, where she sat in a stall and shook.

Meggie, you were wonderful! Magnificent! Such starch. Such backbone. And with an exalted heart Opal knew that the girl had done it to protect her. *I am so proud of you.*

"Opal," the girl whispered, huge-eyed, "I don't think you'd better, uh, you know what, anymore."

Opal had come to the same conclusion, but did not say so. *All you have to do is imagine me without the sword.* There was a definite risk in explaining these things to the child—suppose Meggie got angry at her some day and imagined her away altogether? Still, Meggie was—not a child. A young woman. And needed to know so. *All you have to do is take control, Meggie,* Opal told her. *You're the one in charge.*

The next morning, joining Meggie for her commute, Opal sat like a figurehead just above her windshield again, wings lifted in a smart vee—but this time

Meggie had imagined her, bless the sweet girl, in a very comfortable gold brocade robe with rich blue velvet trim, very flattering. No more armor for the time being. Not that the armor was unattractive—certainly its golden sheen had been rather distinguished—but it was so stiff and ungainly, Opal certainly did not miss it. It had not protected her from anything.

Least of all from the wretched hand gestures. If only Meggie would drive a little faster.

"Floor it, floor it," Meggie whispered to herself, getting onto the beltway.

The youngster was learning.

However, once having achieved the center lane, Meggie did not drive an iota faster than forty-five. Opal sighed and sat waiting with clenched fundament.

After a few minutes, however, she sat more airily erect and looked around, pleasantly realizing: today was different. Nobody was passing Meggie. The nearest vehicles were trailing a cautious six car lengths behind her, and behind them traffic was backing up for miles, all those shiny—it suddenly occurred to Opal that a car is nothing more than armor on wheels—all those commuters in shining armor ranked like a monarch's entourage. A few shoulder-riders came veering crazily along the edges, then slowed abruptly when they saw Meggie and hung back like the others, joining the dignified procession. And through all of this no horns traumatized the dawn; a thousand vehicles moved along in an almost holy silence. Apparently nobody wanted to take any chances with anybody after what the nice anchor-persons had been saying on the news. Nobody, not even the shoulder-riders, seemed to be giving anyone the single-fingered salute today.

Far back in the metallic cavalcade one rash horn sounded. "Aaaaah, give it a rest, cabbagehead," Meggie muttered.

Opal blinked. She had never heard Meggie say anything so harsh.

Quite suddenly Opal felt her outfit transmogrifying right on her insubstantial body. She glanced down; over her robe she was wearing a breastplate now. On her head she felt her golden helm—good; she considered that she looked quite fetching in the helm. If anyone could see.

In her hand she held her sword.

"Opal?" Meggie asked.

Yes, dear.

"Hi! Good morning!"

Good morning to you too, dear. Ah, Meggie, did you just decide you wanted me carrying this sword after all?

"Yepperooni. I think I like you that way. Beautiful day, isn't it? And traffic is really light."

There seems to be nothing at all for miles in front of us, Opal agreed.

Meggie certainly seemed full of herself. Meggie continued to chatter. "I've been thinking," Meggie said, "and I've decided I'm going to ask people to start calling me Megan. 'Meggie' sounds too much like a high-cholesterol breakfast dish."

My goodness. I mean—that sounds like a very good idea, sweetheart. Uh, Megan.

"I think so," Megan said. "You want to go a little faster? Hang on. Whoops!" With a surprised lurch the Saab surged forward as Meggie—Megan—pushed it up to fifty.

It doesn't matter how important your job is, young lady, you should still write home.

THE GUARDSWOMAN

Lawrence Watt-Evans

Dear Mother,

Well, I made it. I'm a soldier in the City Guard of Ethshar of the Sands, in the service of the overlord, Ederd IV.

It wasn't easy!

Getting here wasn't really any trouble. I know you were worried about bandits and . . . well, and other problems on the highway, but I didn't see any. The people I *did* see didn't bother me at all, unless you count a rude remark one caravan driver made about my size.

He apologized nicely after I stuffed him headfirst into a barrel of salted fish.

After that everything went just fine, right up until I reached the city gates. I asked one of the guards about joining up, and *he* made a rude remark, but I couldn't stuff *him* into a fish barrel—for one thing, he had a sword, and I didn't, and he had friends around, and I didn't, and there weren't any barrels right nearby anyway. So I just smiled sweetly and repeated my question, and he sent me to a lieutenant in the north middle tower. . . .

I should explain, I guess. Grandgate is very complicated—it's actually three gates, one after another, with towers on both sides of each gate, so there are

246

six gate-towers, three on the north and three on the south. And each of those towers is connected by a wall to a really *big* tower, and then the city wall itself starts on the other side of each of the *big* towers, which are the North Barracks and the South Barracks. Everything right along the highway, out to the width of the outer gate, which is the widest one, is part of Grandgate Market, and everyone just walks right through if they want to and if the guards don't decide they shouldn't. Everything between the inner towers and the barracks towers, though, is sort of private territory for us guards—that's where we train, and march, and so on.

Anyway, the gateman sent me to a lieutenant in the north middle tower, and *he* sent me to Captain Dabran in the North Barracks, and he sent me back to another lieutenant, Lieutenant Gerath, in the north outer tower, to see whether I could qualify.

I had to do all kinds of things to show I was strong and fast enough—most women aren't, after all, so I guess it was fair. I had a foot race with a man named Lador, and then after I beat him I had to catch him and throw him over a fence rail, and then I had to pick up this fellow named Talden who's just about the fattest man you ever saw, Mother, I mean he's even fatter than Parl the Smith, and throw *him* over the fence rail. I tried to find nice soft mud for them to land in, but I'm not sure if they appreciated it. The lieutenant did, though.

And then I had to climb a rope to the top of the tower, and throw a spear, and on and on.

The worst part was the swordsmanship test. Mother, no one in the village knows how to use a sword properly, not the way these people do! Lieutenant Gerath says I'll need to really work on using a sword. That prompted some rude remarks from the other soldiers about women knowing what to do with swords, only they didn't mean *sword* swords, of course, but they all shut up when I glared at them and then looked meaningfully at the fence rail and the mud.

By the time I finished all the tests, though, a whole crowd had gathered to watch, and they were laughing and cheering—I never *saw* so many people! There were more people there than there are in our entire village!

And I was exhausted, too—but Lieutenant Gerath was really impressed, and he vouched for me to Captain Dabran, and here I am! I'm a soldier! They've given me my yellow tunic and everything.

I don't have a red skirt yet, though—all they had on hand were kilts, and of course I want to wear something decent, not walk around with my legs bare. It must be cold in the winter, going around like that.

Anyway, they didn't have any proper skirts; they're going to give me the fabric and let me make my own. And they didn't have any breastplates that fit—naturally, one that was meant for a man isn't going to fit *me*. I'm not shaped like that. The armorer is working on making me one.

I asked why they didn't have any for women, and everyone kind of looked embarrassed, so I kept asking, and . . .

Well, Mother, you know we've always heard that the City Guard is open to anyone over sixteen who can handle the job, man or woman, and everyone here swears that's true, so I asked how many women there are in the Guard right now, and everyone got even *more* embarrassed, but finally Captain Dabran answered me.

One.

Me.

There have been others in the past, though not for several years, and they wouldn't mind more in the future, but right now, there's just me.

I guess it's a great honor, but I wonder whether it might get a bit *lonely*. It's going to be hard to fit in. I mean, right now, I'm writing this while sitting alone in the North Barracks. I have my own room here, since I'm the only woman in the Guard, but even if I didn't, I'd be alone. Everyone else who's off duty went out. I asked where they were going, you know, hinting that I'd like to come along, but when I found out where they were going I decided I'd stay here and write this letter.

They're going down to the part of the city called Soldiertown, where all the tradespeople who supply the Guard are. I've been down there—to Tavern Street, and Sword Street, and Armorer Street, and Gambler Street.

Except tonight, they're all going to Whore Street.

Somehow I figured it would be better if I didn't go along.

Well, I guess that's about everything I had to say. I'm a soldier now, and I'm fine, and I hope everything's fine back home. Say hello to Thira and Kara for me.

Your loving daughter,
Shennar

Dear Mother,

I'm sorry I haven't written sooner, but I've been pretty busy. The work isn't all that hard, but we don't get much time off.

Well, I *could* have written sooner, but . . .

Well, anyway, I'm writing *now*.

Everything's fine here. I got my uniform completed—the armorer had a lot of trouble with the breastplate, but he got it right eventually. Or almost right; it's still a bit snug.

I've been here for two months now, and mostly it's been fine. I don't mind standing guard at the gate, or walking the top of the wall, or patrolling the market, and so far I haven't had to arrest anyone or break up any fights. Not any *real* fights, anyway—nothing where picking someone up and throwing him away didn't solve the problem.

And my time off duty has been all right; most of the men treat me well, though they're a lot rougher than I'm used to. I don't mind that; I can be rough right back without worrying about hurting anyone.

But I'm not sure I'm really fitting in. I mean, everyone's nice to me, and they all say they like having me here, but I don't really feel like I'm part of the company yet, if you know what I mean. I'm still the new kid.

And it doesn't help any that once every sixnight, all the men in my barracks hall go down to Whore Street, and the whole place is empty, and I can't go along.

The first time they did that I just sat here and wrote to you, and then tidied up the place, and kept busy like that, but the second time I was determined to do something.

So I tried going downstairs to one of the other barracks halls—I'm on the fourth floor of the North Barracks—but I didn't know anybody there, and they were all busy with their regular off-duty stuff. The only way I could see to get in on anything would be to join the game of three-bone going on in the corner, and I'm not very good at dice, so I didn't.

Then I tried going into the city, but I went in uniform, and the minute I walked into a tavern everyone shut up and stared at me. That wasn't very comfortable.

I thought maybe they'd get over it, so I bought an ale and sat down at an empty table and waited for someone to come over and join me, but no one did.

It wasn't much fun.

When I finished my ale I came back here and sat around being utterly miserable. I felt completely left out; it was as bad as when the village kids wouldn't play with me because I was so big and strong. I didn't exactly cry myself to sleep, but I sniffled a little.

The next day all my barracks mates were back, laughing and joking and feeling good. I made some remarks, and Kelder Arl's son said, "Well, Shennar,

at some of the houses there are boys for rent, too."
And everyone laughed.

I didn't think it was very funny, myself. And I certainly didn't take it seriously. I don't understand why the men all go to the brothels, anyway—they're mostly decent people, and could find women elsewhere. Some of them *have* women elsewhere, but they go to Whore Street anyway.

Men are strange.

But it did get me thinking that what I needed was some nice young man I could visit every sixnight. It wouldn't really do to bed with one of my fellow soldiers; I wouldn't feel right about that. And besides, most of them aren't *that* nice. I wanted a civilian.

So I started looking for one. I wore my civilian clothes and went to the most respectable inns and shops and tried to act like a lady.

Honestly, Mother, you'd think that in a city this size, it wouldn't be hard to find a good man, but I certainly didn't manage it. For sixnight after sixnight I looked, and I found plenty of drunkards and foul-smelling wretches, and big stupid oxen, and men who might have been all right if they weren't so small I was afraid that I'd break them in half if I ever hugged them.

And, well, I gave up, and here I am writing this letter while the men are at the brothels again.

What *is* it that makes them so eager to spend all their money there?

Mother, you know what I'm going to do? I'm going to seal this up for the messenger, and then I'm going to go down to Whore Street and *ask* someone. Not one of my barracks mates, but someone who works there. I'll just *ask* why the men all go there every sixnight.

Maybe if I can figure *that* out, it'll give me some idea what I should do!

Love,
Shennar

Dear Mother,

I met the most wonderful man! And you'll never guess where.

I'd gone down to Whore Street, the way I told you I was planning to, and at first I just walked up and down the street—it's only seven blocks long—just looking at the brothels and listening to the people. But after a while that wasn't getting me anywhere, so I got up my nerve and went up to one of the doors and knocked.

This woman who wasn't wearing anything but a chiffon skirt and a feather in her hair answered, and took one look at me, and said, "I'm sorry, but you must have the wrong place." And she tried to shut the door.

Well, I wasn't going to give up that easily; I was afraid that I'd never be able to get up the nerve to try again if I once backed down. So I put my foot in the door and pushed back.

I tried to tell her I just wanted to talk to someone, but she wasn't listening; instead she was calling, "Tabar! Tabar, quick!"

I pushed in through the door and I tried to catch her by the arm, since she wasn't wearing any tunic I could grab, but I couldn't get a solid hold, and then this voice deep as distant thunder said, "Is there a problem?"

And I looked up—really *up*, Mother! And there was this face looking down at me with the most spectacular mustache and big dark eyes.

"She wouldn't let me in," I said, and I let the woman go. She ran off and left me face-to-face with this *huge* man—we'd have been nose to nose if he hadn't been so tall.

"We don't accept women as customers here," he said. "You could try Beautiful Phera's Place, two doors down."

"I'm not a customer," I told him.

"If you have a complaint you can tell *me*," he said. "Though I don't promise we'll do anything about it."

"It's not a complaint, exactly," I said, "but I'd like to talk to you."

He nodded, and led the way to a little room off to one side.

And while we were walking there I got a good look at two things.

One was the front room. It was amazing. Silk and velvet everywhere, and beads, and colored glass, all in reds and pinks and yellows.

And the other was the man I was talking to. Mother, he was taller than Father! And *much* broader. I'd never seen anyone *close* to that size before! He had lovely long black hair, and these long fingers, and that *wonderful* mustache. He was wearing a black velvet tunic worked with gold, and a black kilt, and he moved like a giant *cat*, Mother, it was just gorgeous.

Anyway, we went into this little room, which was very small, and pretty ordinary, with a little table and a couple of chairs, and we sat down, and he looked at me, didn't say anything.

I couldn't help asking, "Why aren't you in the *Guard*?"

He smiled at me. "You must be new around here," he said. "Think about it. A guardsman—or guardswoman—has to be big and strong enough to stop a fight, preferably before it starts. You've probably seen a guardsman stop trouble just by standing up and frowning, or by walking in the door and shouting—guards hardly ever have to draw their swords."

"I've done it myself," I admitted.

"Well," he said, "this is Soldiertown. Most of the customers here are guardsmen. If *they* start trouble, Rudhira wants to have someone around who can stop guardsmen the way guardsmen stop ordinary tavern brawls. So she hired me."

He wasn't bragging, Mother. He turned up a palm, you know what I mean. He was just stating a fact.

"But wouldn't you rather be in the Guard?" I asked.

He looked at me as if I had gone mad, then laughed.

"Rudhira pays better," he said. "And there are extras."

"Oh," I said, and then I realized what the extras probably were, and I blushed and said, "Oh," again.

"Some houses use magicians to handle trouble," he said conversationally. "After all, we all need to have the magicians in sometimes to make sure nobody catches anything, and some of the girls want magic to be sure they don't get pregnant, so why not use them to keep things peaceful? But if a customer's drunk enough he might not notice a magician right away, and magic takes time, and can go wrong—and besides, I cost more than a guardsman, but not as much as a wizard! So Rudhira keeps my brother and me around, and we make sure everything stays quiet and friendly and no one gets rough." He leaned back, and asked, "So why are you here?"

So I explained about how all my barracks mates would disappear every sixnight, and how tired I was of being left with nothing to do, and I asked why they all came *here*, instead of finding themselves women . . . I mean, finding women who aren't professionals.

"Oh, it's all part of showing off to each other that they're real men," Tabar said. "They all come here because they can do it *together*, and show how loyal they all are to each other. The more stuff they do together, the more they trust each other when there's trouble."

I had to think about that for a while, but eventually I decided he was right. If one of the men went off with his own woman, he wouldn't be as much a part of the company.

But of course, that meant that *I* wasn't as much a part of the company.

I'd sort of noticed that, as I guess I told you, but I thought it was just because I was new, and not from the city, and of course partly because I was the only woman. I tried to fit in, and I did everything that everyone else did back at the barracks, all the jokes and games and arm wrestling and so on, and mostly it was okay, but I could feel that I wasn't *really* accepted yet, and I thought it was just going to be a matter of time—but when Tabar explained that I realized that it wasn't just that. The expeditions down to Whore Street were part of fitting in, and I wasn't doing it.

I *couldn't*, unless I wanted to go to someplace like Beautiful Phera's, which I didn't, and besides, none of my company went to places like that—they all liked women, or at least pretended to when they went to Whore Street, and the specialty places charged extra.

Even before I asked Tabar about it, I knew that didn't really make any difference that I couldn't.

Anyway, I got talking to Tabar about it all, and we talked and talked, and by the time I headed back to the barracks it was just about midnight.

And the next sixnight, when the men were getting ready to go, I had an idea. I said, "Hey, wait for me!" and I went along with them.

Some of them were kind of nervous about it; I could see that in the way they looked at me, and they weren't as noisy as usual. One man—you don't know him, but his name's Kelder Arl's son—asked where I thought I was going, and I said, "Rudhira's." And everyone laughed.

"You like women?" someone asked, and someone else said, "Or are you trying to pick up a few extra silvers?" And I didn't get mad or anything, I just laughed and said no.

I didn't get mad because I knew Tabar would be there.

As soon as we set foot in the door I called, "Tabar!" And there he was, and he stopped dead in his tracks when he saw me, and this big grin spread all over his face.

"Shennar," he said, "what are *you* doing here?"

"The boys and I are just here for our regular fun," I said, and everyone laughed, and we had a fine time. I talked to some of the girls, and joked with the men, and then when the men went upstairs Tabar and I went back to his room. . . .

He's wonderful, Mother. If you ever come down to visit you'll have to meet him.

Love,
Shennar

Dear Mother,

What's wrong with a whorehouse bouncer? It's honest work.

Mother, I'm not a delicate little flower. I'm a hundred and eighty pounds of bone and muscle. And Tabar is two hundred and fifty pounds of bone and muscle. I like him.

And seeing him has really helped. I'm fitting in better than ever. I love my job, Mother, and going to Whore Street every sixnight is helping me with it.

Besides, I like Tabar a *lot*, Mother. And it's not as if it costs me anything, the way it does everyone else. Tabar and I joke sometimes about which of us should be charging.

The only thing is . . .

Well, it looks as if Tabar and I will be married, at least for a while. We hadn't really planned on it, but it's happened. The lieutenant says I can get leave when I need it, and I've been saving up what the men use as brothel money so I won't starve while I'm on leave, but I'm not sure how it's going to go over with the rest of the company having a baby around here.

I think they'll get used to it. But it's driving the armorer crazy enlarging my breastplate every sixnight or so!

Love,
Shennar

Sometimes those who *can* do, teach.

TEACHER'S PET

Josepha Sherman

Vassilia reined in her horse, settling her helm mo:
comfortably on its cushion of coiled-up yellow hair
and biting back a very unknightly oath. She had been
following the tracks of the child-stealers through the
forest all day, praying that the on-and-off again rain
wasn't going to come down heavily enough to wash
all those tracks away, but now—akh, why this? Here
she was on the only road through these tangled *versts*
of forest, at the only spot where that road was trapped
between two tall outcroppings of stone leaving no way
to go around—and of course this was exactly where
the wagon, the covered sort most merchants used,
had gotten stuck, one wheel sunk in a hole, completely blocking the way.

Damnation.

Judging from the wagon's shabbiness, Vassilia
thought, the merchant must be down on his luck.
Very much down on his luck, she amended, watching
the tall figure in a threadbare brown cloak struggling
with a sweaty, nervous, very reluctant horse, trying to
convince the animal that yes, leaning *this* way and
pulling would get the wheel out of the hole. For all
her impatience, Vassilia found herself listening in
bemused wonder as the man cursed the horse in a
surprisingly cultured voice and incredibly inventive

profanity. "Sweepings of a triply-cursed *leshy's* sorcerous litter," indeed! Original!

"I don't think he's getting the point," Vassilia said, leaning on her saddle's pommel.

The man whirled in almost comical surprise, revealing a lean, long-featured, harried-looking face with startlingly blue eyes, and snapped, "If my lord *bogatyr* thinks that he could do better, he is welcome to—ah, she, that is . . ." He stopped, clearly flustered. Vassilia, who'd been thinking, *Nice. Not at all handsome, but nice,* grinned.

"Never saw a woman warrior before, I take it."

"Ah, no. I knew that such existed, but—no, I haven't." The bright blue eyes were alive with curiosity as he gave her a quick, surprisingly graceful bow. "You're not at all the way I'd pictured them. All scarred and manly—I mean you're definitely *not* all scarred and manly—forgive me," he added, reddening, "I'm making a bit of a fool of myself. Your pardon, ah . . ."

"Vassilia," she supplied, amused. "Vassilia Vassilovna, *bogatyr.* And you are?"

"Semyan of . . . well . . . no particular lineage."

"Ah." There were plenty of folks not recognized by their fathers; that didn't make them better or worse than others. "And you are what?" Glancing at the wagon, seeing the edge of a bronze-strung gusla, she hazarded, "A *skomorokh?*"

He laughed. "I'm afraid I'm not any sort of a minstrel. No, I'm a teacher."

"Of what?"

Semyan shrugged. "A little of this, a little of that, art, music, whatever folks wish to pay to learn. I've been doing well enough going from town to estate, estate to town. Till now," he added gloomily. "Idiots came galloping by as if devils were chasing them and almost ran me into the rocks."

Vassilia fought to keep her face impassive. "Did you get a good look at them?"

"Not much. I was too busy trying to keep Brownie here from breaking a leg. Might have been three of them, or four."

"Did they . . . have a child with them? A boy?"

Semyan looked at her with sudden sharp interest. "I think so. Why?"

"Just guessing," she said, knowing it sounded inane. But she wasn't about to discuss Duke Feodor's missing son with a stranger. Trying to cover, Vassilia added, "The wagon doesn't look too badly stuck," and hopped down from her horse in a tiny clanging of mail, letting the reins trail so the animal wouldn't stray. *The sooner I get the wagon out of the way, the sooner I can go on.* "If you push against the wagon *that* way, I'll see if I can't get Brownie here moving."

Semyan threw up his hands. "It's worth a try. The good Lord knows I've tried everything else."

Vassilia climbed up onto the wagon seat and took up the reins. "Ready?" At Semyan's nod, she yelled a savage war cry into the horse's ear. The startled animal jumped forward—and the wagon lurched forward with him.

"That does it!" Semyan yelled and came running around to the wagon's head as Vassilia reined Brownie in. "We're free. My thanks, *bogatyr!* I had pictures of being stuck here till I took root." As he climbed up onto the wagon seat and Vassilia climbed down, he grinned at her in passing. "Not a nice idea, being stuck forever. Particularly not with the weather turning so nasty. Ha, yes, here comes the rain again."

Rain? Deluge, rather. Vassilia hastily pulled the hood of her cloak over herself and her mail shirt, swearing under her breath. Just what she didn't want! This downpour was going to wash away the tracks completely.

"You're welcome back up here in the wagon," Semyan said. "You don't want to—ah—rust."

Still muttering to herself, Vassilia tied her horse's reins to the wagon, then scrambled up under cover.

Akh, crowded in here, with chests and the gusla and more books than she'd ever seen at one time. She made her careful way through the jumble and came out on the wagon seat beside Semyan.

He gave her a wary glance as he slapped the reins, starting Brownie into a plodding walk. "You're tracking them, aren't you? The louts who forced me off the road."

Clever of him. And no use denying it now. "Yes."

"Might I ask why?"

She shrugged and said nothing, but after a silent moment Semyan continued slowly, "It's the boy you're after, isn't it? The one you asked me if I'd seen. Who is he? Your son?"

"Hardly." Vassilia sighed and admitted, "His name is Alesha, and he's the son of my liege lord, Duke Feodor. I was sent out, along with the rest of his knights, to recover the boy." She left out the fact that she, the only woman among them, had also been the only one sent out without helpers of any sort. *But I'm also the only one who actually found the child-stealers' track.* Looking darkly out at the downpour, she added, *For what that's worth!*

"Don't worry," Semyan said softly. "We'll find them."

" We?' "

"Why not? I've—I—well, let's just say that I don't like those who hurt children."

Vassilia grunted. She could guess he'd be sensitive on that point, being the nameless fellow he was; children without family protection were generally considered fair game by the cruel. "Besides," Semyan added with a sudden grin, "it's not as if I had some pressing appointment elsewhere! And I do owe you something for getting my wagon free. Is there anything you'd care to learn?"

"Such as what? I already know weaponry."

"Well, yes, of course. And I'm not belittling that

knowledge. But there's so much more! History and art and music—surely you know something of those as well."

"Something." Her *bogatyr* father had had little patience with any type of learning other than that pertaining directly to the art of the warrior. "History's fine where it is: in the dull, dead past."·

"It's not dull!" Semyan said indignantly. "It's about people, and what's a more fascinating subject than that? Wait, I'll prove it to you." Eagerly, he began telling her tales of scandal and intrigue, warfare and political maneuverings, skillfully as any *skomorokh*, his long face so animated it was almost handsome, his blue eyes bright. In the middle of telling how a certain queen—the name meant nothing to Vassilia—had, together with her paramour, murdered her husband, who had earlier slain their daughter, Semyan stopped short. "Now, does that sound dull?"

Fighting down the urge to yell a childish, *but what comes next?* Vassilia admitted, "No. Not at all."

"Ha, and that's just a bare sample of what's out there waiting to be learned! What about art and music? Can't show you how to paint, not here in the rain, but there's still music—here, hold these." He handed her the reins, then reached back into the wagon for the gusla, running a hand over its strings then wincing. "Out of tune. Damp gets into it, even though—" he glanced up "—it seems to have stopped raining again."

"Right. The damage has already been done."

"Mmm?" Bent over his gusla again, Semyan missed her glare at the muddy road. The now totally trackless road. "No, no, I can always retune this. Wait a minute . . . there . . . ah. Better." He glanced up, and a flicker of sympathy in his eyes showed that he had, indeed, understood what she'd meant. But without another word, Semyan burst into song, his voice a clear, light baritone:

"On an oak tree sat two doves
And billed and cooed close heart to heart
Tenderly they showed their love
And vowed that they should never—

"What is it?" he asked suddenly.

"Bandits," was all Vassilia had time to say before the wet, desperate men burst out at them. Akh, no, these weren't bandits, these were too nicely dressed for bandits—

No time to worry about it. She whipped out her sword, dimly aware that Semyan was shouting out weird words that sounded like:

"Sharp of claw
And keen of eye
Cunning, savage, daring, sly,
Deadly foe of vole or mice—
Let it be at my device!"

Suddenly the sword, all at once far too heavy, dropped from her hands. Suddenly Vassilia *had* no hands. She was down on all fours on the forest floor, and she had paws and fur, dull yellow fur, and her vision was so very changed and her sense of smell alarmingly keen—

"A *cat!*" she yelled, hearing her voice sound eerily shrill and mewly. "You've turned us both to *cats!*"

Semyan had become a lean, shaggy brown tom. "Never mind that now," he hissed—it sounded more like *"Ne'min' tha' neow—*"Run!"

Fortunately her body seemed to have instantly adjusted to its new shape. Four legs were far quicker than two. As the frightened bandits—or whatever they were—yelled and cursed and tried to cut down the "demon cats," those cats dove into hiding in the underbrush.

"My wagon," Semyan moaned. "My books."

"Yes, yes, and my sword and mail coat, curse it."

This cat mouth and throat was *not* meant for human speech, and the words were coming out sounding weird indeed, but Vassilia persisted fiercely, "Never mind that now—we're *cats*, dammit! Get us out of this! You . . . can get us back, can't you?"

"Of course." But he didn't sound quite as sure as Vassilia would have liked. "The only thing is," he admitted, "it was the *bandits* I was trying to transform. Akh, don't worry. It's not really a catastrophe or cataclysm."

Vassilia groaned. "Not only is he an inept sorcerer, he makes puns as well. And what the *hell* is a teacher doing working spells?"

"I *said* I taught a little this, a little that."

"A little magic. Wonderful, Heh, the bandits are leaving—no, they're not bandits, I was right! That's Duke Feodor's son with them! Those are the child-stealers—turn me back, quickly!"

"I have to think of the right—"

"Hurry, dammit, they're getting away!"

"Will you be still a moment and let me *think?*"

"For a change, you mean? All right, all right, I'll be quiet."

"Mm—hmm . . . yes . . . I have it. I hope." He shrugged, an odd thing for a cat to do, then began:

"No longer cat,
    In shape or soul,
    No longer cat, but—"

"Akh, hurry. I'm getting this horrible urge to pounce on that—"

". . . turned to—"

". . . vole—oh no, I didn't—"

The world blurred and grew. She was still four-pawed, but smaller now, much smaller, and her nose was sharp and pointed. "Oh no," she repeated helplessly, her voice now so high-pitched it made her wince.

"Oh yes," Semyan snapped. "Thank you *so* much for the interference, *bogatyr*."

"We—we're *voles!*"

"So we are."

"Look, I'm sorry, I didn't mean it, I offer a hundred apologies. But meanwhile the child-stealers are getting away, and I can hardly chase after them like this, yelling, 'Surrender or I'll nip you!'"

He laughed wearily at that. "Not exactly an awesome image, I agree."

"Then get us out of this!"

"I don't know if I can." He gave a long sigh. "And don't glare at me like that. Yes, I am tired, very much so. Shape-shifting's not the sort of thing I do all the time—most certainly not twice in a row like this."

Vassilia licked suddenly dry lips with a tongue that seemed abnormally long. "Are you saying . . . you're not saying we're . . . stuck, are you?"

"No, of course not. I just don't know if I can manage another transformation right away. I definitely don't know what we'd end up becoming."

"Then don't try anything! It won't hurt us a bit to wait till you're rested."

"Mm." He curled up in a little heap. Vassilia paced restlessly in the ever-increasing darkness, hardly appreciating her improved night vision, aching to go after the child-stealers. *And wouldn't that look ridiculous? Just as I said to Semyan, a vole scurrying after several grown men isn't exactly going to send them shivering into surrender.* She froze, listening. No. Oh, no. "Semyan."

"Mm?"

"Semyan, I think you'd better wake up. Semyan!"

He sprang to his feet, glancing wildly about. "What? What?"

"There's a wolf prowling about. Wolves eat voles, don't they?"

"Yes. One of the things I've taught is Natural History. And let's just—aie!"

A sharp-fanged muzzle snapped shut where he'd been a moment before. "Run!" Semyan yelped.

They raced in opposite directions; Vassilia ricocheted off a tree, heard Semyan crash into another, turned, crashed right into him. They both fell backwards, and the wolf's second snap shut on empty air between them. They scrabbled to their feet, crashed into each other again, scurried off side to side, then made a frantic right turn as the wolf sprang forward to block them.

"Adolescent," Semyan panted. "Hungry as a human boy."

"I'm not going to be his snack!" Vassilia snapped, and charged the wolf. Startled (*As if a man had seen his lamb chop leap off the plate!*), he leaped back, then let out a very doggish yip. *Oh, wonderful. Now he thinks I'm a toy!* She dodged a playful paw that would have sent her flying, dodged a playful snap that would have crushed her. "Semyan! *Do* something!"

He was already chanting a plainly improvised verse:

> "Taller, stronger, vole no more,
> Bold and daring as can be,
> Quick and deadly, fierce and sure,
> As I call this, let it be!"

"Damnably poor verse," Semyan began to add. But then the world swirled about them yet again. Vassilia felt herself growing and thought, *Human, let me be human.*

Not human. She still had inhumanly keen night vision and sense of smell, four paws, fur—and sharp, predatory fangs. Vassilia groaned as she realized what she'd become and heard it come out as a growl. "I've been called a bitch before, but this is ridiculous."

The adolescent wolf yelped in alarm at the sudden appearance of two adults. He sniffed once, loudly, as if trying to puzzle out their not-quite lupine scents, made an abortive attempt at proper canine belly-to-ground submission, then gave up and raced away.

"That's it," Semyan said flatly. "I felt the magic stop. I can*not* manage any more changes."

"At *all?*"

"It's not that. I don't know if I can get us back to what we were! Look at what's been happening: we've gone from cat to vole to wolf—never back to human, not even for an instant."

Vassilia sighed. "It could be worse. If I have to be stuck in a form other than my own, I'd much rather be a wolf bitch than a vole."

"And at least in this shape we don't have to be afraid of anything much. Except, maybe, for hunters."

"Hunters," Vassilia echoed thoughtfully. "Semyan, listen to me. We'll worry about getting out of this mess later. Right now, since we're stuck in these wolf shapes, let's use them." Quickly she told him her hasty plan. "Well? What do you think?"

Semyan grinned a toothy lupine grin. "Yes. If we've got to be wolves, let's be superwolves!"

Keen wolf noses easily picked out the scent of the child-stealers and their horses. Ignoring the little stab of hunger the thought of horse brought her, Vassilia bounded forward, Semyan at her side. And oh, it was wonderful, leaping with almost magical ease through the dark forest, hearing, smelling a whole new world, feeling smooth lupine muscles propelling her forward with inhuman grace.

Smoke, burning her nostrils. Flame, searing at her eyes—

Campfire, her human mind remembered. *There they are, and little Alesha, too.*

The boy hadn't been badly harmed; he was too valuable a prize for that. But he was bruised and disheveled, blond hair full of leaves and twigs, and trying very hard not to look scared. And at the sight of him, something deep within Vassilia said, *No.* She had sharp fangs, sharp enough to tear the throats from the men before they could so much as move, and from the glint in Semyan's eyes she knew he was thinking the same. They would lunge and tear and feel the hot blood fill their mouths—

No! God, no! Horrified at what she'd been about to do, Vassilia remembered, *I'm not a wolf, dammit, I won't act like a wolf!*

Instead, hoping Semyan would follow her lead, she stepped boldly out into the open. Ha, yes, Semyan was here at her side, staring coldly at the men grabbing frantically for weapons.

"Your weapons are useless," Vassilia said, delighted for the first time at how distorted wolf form made her voice.

"Strike at us," Semyan continued, "and your weapons will turn in your hands. We are not to be wounded by mortal men."

"Oh, nice touch," Vassilia whispered, and caught a quick flash of a lupine smile.

"W-who are you?" one of the men asked.

"Messengers," Vassilia told him, improvising hastily.

"Messengers of the Deepest Forest," Semyan added, "come with a warning."

"What warning?" another man asked, just a touch of wary skepticism in his voice.

Semyan glanced hastily at Vassilia, who thought, *Right. Leave the tricky part to me.* "A warning," she agreed. Continuing in as eerie a voice as she could muster, hearing it ring out with something of the wolf's icy call, Vassilia intoned, "You have passed out of the human Realm. You have trampled into where you should not be."

"This is not a place for mortal men." Semyan's voice was every bit as chill. "You must leave. If you would live, you must leave—now! The Forest," he added portentously, "commands it."

By God, it was working! The men, ruthless creatures though they were, were actually getting nervously to their feet, backing slowly away. "Wait!"

Vassilia snapped. "Do not take the small one. You should not have brought the cub-who-is-not-yours."

"Clever!" Semyan said out of the corner of his mouth. "Heed our words. The human cub may stay. The human cub *must* stay. Your souls are stained and torn. His is clean as the forest's heart."

"He *must* stay," Vassilia echoed. "Do not seek to argue!" Beside her, Semyan gave the most bloodcurdling of snarls, and the men flinched. She smiled and watched them recoil from the glint of her fangs. *Big, brave child-stealers, scared like little boys of the big, mean wolves. The magical, talking wolves.* "The forest claims his innocent soul for its own. It does not wish yours. Not now. Not unless you stay to be the forest's prey!"

She threw back her head and howled, and Semyan howled with her. It was too much for the men. Ordinary wolves would never have frightened them—but talking, sentient, threatening-with-unknown-power wolves was something else. Yelling in panic, they turned and ran. Vassilia fought down the lupine instinct screaming at her *The prey is escaping!* and turned to little Alesha, who was staring at her, wide-eyed, his hands gripping a branch so hard she could see the blood leave his fingers. "Don't be afraid," she said gently. "I know I look frightening to you, but it's just me, *Bogatyr* Vassilia, in a different shape."

"V-vassilia? And who's that?"

Semyan bowed, forelegs bent. "No one more alarming than a teacher." He straightened. "Too bad those scoundrels got away. I really wanted to chase them."

"So did I," Vassilia agreed. "No matter. They're on foot, with no supplies. Either one of Duke Feodor's men comes on them, or the forest really *does* take them as prey. Young Master Alesha here is safe, and that's the main thing."

"Not the only main thing," Semyan said sadly. "I

mean, look at us. Wolves. And I—hate to tell you this, Vassilia, but *I don't know how to turn us back!*"

"A spell?" Alesha squirmed in excitement. "You're both under a spell? Like the one in my storybook, the one where the prince is a stag and the princess is a doe."

"Something like that, yes. Vassilia, forgive me. I didn't mean to—"

"But that's *easy!*" the little boy burst out. "Do what *they* did!"

"It was just a story," Vassilia said, but Alesha insisted, "Do what they did! Do what they did!"

Semyan looked at Vassilia blankly. "What did they do?"

She shrugged. "This."

And she kissed him. For a moment it was uncomfortable muzzle against muzzle, but then . . .

. . . it was her human lips against his human lips and there was nothing they could do but go right on kissing.

"I told you so!" Alesha crowed. "I told you it would work!"

Vassilia and Semyan broke apart, panting, hastily wrapping themselves in the child-stealers' discarded cloaks. "It worked, all right," Vassilia said when she could get her voice back under control. "W-we'll have to stay here till morning. Then we'll go look for your wagon, Semyan, and my sword, and get you home," she added to Alesha, ruffling his tangled hair.

"And then?" Semyan asked carefully, his blue eyes bright.

Vassilia shrugged. "And then, Duke Feodor will always welcome a good teacher. Particularly one who's helped rescue his son."

"And . . . you? How do you feel about it?"

She stood silent for a moment, studying him. He really wasn't anywhere near handsome, and who knew what other sorcerous surprise he might pull. And yet, and yet . . .

Vassilia felt herself starting to grin. "Well, we made a pretty good team just now."

"We did, that."

"Akh, I think I would welcome a good teacher, too. In fact, I suspect that, if things go the way they might—and there aren't any more startling transformations!—I just might enjoy becoming . . . teacher's pet."

He laughed. "I just might enjoy that, too. And yes, I promise you this: Both teacher's pet and teacher shall remain most truly, thoroughly human!"

And you thought *you'd* seen someone have an identity crisis!

This is Janet's first professional sale.

WERE-WENCH

Jan Stirling

Terion readjusted the heavy pack on her back with a grunt and a clunk of tight packed metal. All her armor except the mail shirt she wore was bound onto it and all her weapons too, except the sword whose familiar weight hung from her waist.

The sun beat down with merciless late-summer strength, turning the packed dirt of the high road to a white blaze before her. Little dry puffs rose around her boots; drops of sweat trickled down her nose and left dark spots on the ground and a taste of salt on her lips. Bars of shade from the roadside trees made cool strokes across her face as she trudged. She hated returning to her home village without a horse under her. It made her feel poor.

She'd a fine animal until yesterday, when the stupid beast had broken its stupid leg in the stupidest way possible. Turned out to graze, the thrice-cursed quadruped (it didn't deserve the name horse) had taken a mind to romp like a colt. Racing around, it frisked and bucked until it found a hole with its right forehoof and snapped its leg like a twig.

Terion wiped the sweat from her face with her sleeve, then stepped off the high road and onto a narrow path. It wound past fields of reaped barley, by an orchard, then down between hedges into blessed shade and gloom; sensible people were at their naps. She could hear an occasional sleepy bleat and smell the sheep in one of the village pens. This was the outskirt of the village, with cottages set back from the laneway in their kitchen gardens and home fields.

She paused with her hand on the gate of Feric the Fey, the closest thing to a wizard the village held.

He popped up from behind the gate like a wild-haired jack-in-the-box and she jumped backwards with a little whoop of surprise, her hand falling to her sword.

"Come in," he said, opening the gate and bowing gallantly.

Glaring at him as she went by, Terion marched up the path to his cottage door. Looking over her shoulder she asked, "May we go in? I need to talk to you."

"Of course," he said, quite amazed. He rushed down the path to follow her indoors. "Uh, would you like some tea?"

She eyed him coolly. "No. I want to hire you."

"You *are* Terion?"

"So," she said, dropping the heavy pack, making a dull clank on the packed clay floor. The chafe marks on her shoulders gave an internal whimper of relief. "You do remember me."

"As if I would forget you." Feric laughed, bustling around the untidy interior of the two-room hut. Instead of the tea, he pulled an earthenware crock of buttermilk from a bucket of water beside the hearth and poured two mugs. He handed her one.

"The first time you speak to me in ten years and you want your fortune told." He chuckled nervously. "Well, let's see now. You won't marry your first love...."

She sank wearily onto a stool. "I would've, if he hadn't left me standing alone on the dancing ground—the night of our betrothal—to walk off with something no one else could see."

"Someone, my dear, someone." He smiled in fond remembrance. "She had red-gold hair, almost the same color as yours, but her eyes were violet instead of plain blue."

Terion snorted. The buttermilk was cool and fresh, cutting the dust in her mouth. Feric refilled her mug and went on:

"Fairies are mischievous folk, you know. She had her eye on me for quite a while, but chose that moment to ensnare me simply to annoy you."

"Hunh! She must've been something wonderful to bring that smile to your face after all these years. Or do you still see her?"

"Oh no. I'm not so young and handsome anymore, after all." Terion snorted again. "Nor so old that my venerable wisdom would be sought out. And I'm afraid I'm not very interesting all by myself."

"Do you ever regret it?" she asked.

"No," he said still smiling. "I could never do that. Because of my small gifts, Terion, you and I would never have been happy. Half my sight looks into another world and half my heart is there. It would have made me a poor farmer. As it is, I can barely provide for myself, let alone a wife and children." He grinned at her suddenly. "Imagine having children with the sight."

Terion raised her brows, then shuddered.

"No thank you, and that's to having children at all. Give me a battle to fight any day." She smiled weakly at him and sighed. "Ah well. I need your help, Feric."

"Tell me about it," he said, placing a bowl of berries by her hand. Then he sat on a stool beside her.

There was silence while she turned the mug in her hands. Then she blurted, "I've been cursed."

Feric blinked and sat up straight. "Cursed? Are you sure?"

She glared at him. "Of course I'm sure. I was there when he did it."

Holding up a placating hand, he asked earnestly, "Who did, and when and what, *exactly*, did he say?"

"It was Rarik the Red, and it was the dark of the moon just past."

"The moon's full tomorrow, so that's about sixteen days. Well, go on. What did he say?"

She licked her lips and closing her eyes began to chant:

"The bound shall dance in the full moon's light,
The hidden show, when the moon is bright.
Brazen harlot, scarlet whore,
The meanest men she shall adore.
Whilst bound and hidden is despised,
be the merry slut in all men's eyes."

"Oh," Feric said with consternation. "I don't think I like the sound of that! What did you do to make him curse you?"

"I put a sword through his gut." She looked like she wanted to do it again.

"Ah! I'd probably want to curse you myself under those circumstances." He dragged a long-fingered hand through his unruly brown hair. "That's a very elaborate curse for a gut-stabbed man," he said doubtfully.

"Well, fortitude under extreme stress is a common trait among high-ranking sorcerers." Her eyes narrowed. "I'm not making this up, Feric."

"Terion," he bit his lip, "I don't know if I can help you. Now, wait," he said forestalling her, "I will if I can, I swear it, but it's very likely beyond my small gifts, and my even smaller store of knowledge. I make charms and brew potions, I help farmers get along with the small folk. But this," he waved his hands helplessly, "is true magic, and for that you need a real sorcerer, with a library to consult. Not a dabbler like myself."

"You don't plan to charge me for that advice, I hope. You do realize I'm unlikely to gain the cooperation of a *real* sorcerer after skewering one of them. That's a privilege they reserve for themselves."

He tapped his chin thoughtfully, ignoring her sarcasm.

Terion got up and went to her gear, released the rope binding on her armor, which she laid on the floor. Then she opened the pack and reaching deep, pulled out two large leather-bound volumes locked with metal clasps. She slammed them down before him on the table.

"These belonged to Rarik the Red," she told him. "I thought of you, old friend, when I saw them." She reached into the neck of her tunic and drew out a leather thong with two small keys strung on it. "This was around his neck."

Feric gazed at the two books, his fine brown eyes taking on a wistful, hungry look.

Terion grinned, waved the keys. "Do you want them?"

He swallowed hard. "Teri, there may be nothing in either of them that will help you. Yes, I want them," he said with calm dignity, "but I won't lie to you. Sit down and hear me out."

Terion sat. Her hand jerked sharply and, shame-faced, she laid the keys before him.

"The curse mentions the full moon twice. It demands no great wisdom to assume it takes effect then. Stay here with me until we at least know what's going to happen. I'll study these books and see if they can help. If there's nothing in them of aid to you," he took a deep breath, "I won't keep them. Moreover, I'll try to find out who can help you. I fancy these books would be sufficient payment for their efforts." He spread his hands. "That's all I can offer."

Terion nodded miserably, clenching her hands together until the knuckles turned white.

He placed his hand over hers. "I owe you at least this much."

She turned her hands to take his. "Thank you." After a moment, she shifted awkwardly and asked, "Is that clearwater pond still out back? I'd like to wash off some of the road."

"Yes, everything's still the same."

"Um, do you suppose I could borrow something clean? I'm a little behind in my laundry."

He laughed. "Weren't you always? I've something of my mother's that might fit you, and good soap besides." He dug into a chest smelling of lemongrass and gave her a soft, blue robe with loose sleeves. Handing her a fragrant square of soap, he said, "Off you go. Supper will be ready when you come back."

She returned just at moonrise, looking like a different woman. Feric turned to find her leaning languidly against the doorframe, studying him with heavy-lidded eyes. The blue dress, which had hung modestly loose on his mother's gaunt frame, hugged Terion's curves like a lover. Her red-gold hair, loosed from its tight braids, curled halfway to her slender waist, glittering in the lamplight like a fairy ornament. She smiled at him and suddenly he felt as though his veins were filled with melted butter.

"Ferrric," she purred, "let's go down to the inn and see who's there."

He forced the grin from his face and answered, "But you know who's there, the same folk as always. As I said, nothing's changed."

She pouted and Feric felt as though he'd been punched in the stomach. First, because this glowing beauty was displeased with him and second, because this was *Terion* pouting at him.

"Well, then," she said with a toss of her head, "I'll

go by myself. Don't wait up for me." She turned and flounced off.

Feric covered his mouth in horror. Teri, pouting and flouncing?

"The curse," he whispered. "It's working."

Terion stood quivering outside Mother Guid's tavern. Half her muscles pushing to go in and have a good time, half shoving back, urging her to go home and lie down till the feeling passed.

She hadn't been inside this building since Mother Guid had turned it into a disgrace. And now, though she knew in her bones that an exciting time lay before her, painful images of "What Mum would have said" and "How her poor father would have felt" paralyzed her.

Mother Guid, by the way, was nobody's mommy, certainly not her hard-eyed hostess's. Mother being an honorary name given female innkeepers in this part of the country and not an honor that the fairly young and very buxom Guid appreciated.

The moon rose another notch in the sky and Teri's spirit wavered. The scent of beer swelled from the doorway, a scent rich and wet and cool; it hooked her by the nose and drew her in to warm light and raucous laughter.

She entered the tavern slowly, one might almost say shyly. If one could overlook a walk that would have put a less flexible spine in traction.

The girls working the room seemed to feel her enter and bristled like cats. Hands smoothed hips, heads lifted, shoulders were thrown back to bring nearly exposed bosoms into more prominent display, lips were licked to induce a tempting shine.

All to no avail. The male members of the company turned as one to the lush figure in the doorway.

Teri stood just inside, hands clasped behind her back, smiling delightedly at her male admirers. She took a deep breath in satisfaction. Around the room

male eyes widened and narrowed in respectful tribute
to the effects of her respiration. She ignored Mother
Guid's girls as though they'd been transformed into
the toast racks they frankly resembled next to her own
glowing femininity.

Over the years Mother Guid had developed an
extreme sensitivity to atmosphere and she sensed the
emotional temperature of the room racing towards
ignition. She poked her blond head out of her alcove
to see what was going on.

Terion was just accepting an invitation from a red-
faced old duffer to join him in a mug. She placed
herself in her seat with a saucy precision that stopped
the breath of more than a few of the men present.

Mother Guid raised her brows. She wasn't too
happy about having a free-lancer working her place.
Especially one that made her girls look so shopworn.
Though, to be fair, this one could make a maiden of
sixteen look "past it." She weighed the matter. On
the one hand the girl could be trouble. On the other,
they couldn't all have her and that might inspire a
rush of business. She decided to wait and see.

Terion preened, giddy with the attention she was
getting. More than one fellow had caught her eye,
and she was thrilled to know that she could kiss any
one of them and they would say thank you and
mean it.

A sweaty lout with breath that would peel paint
sat down beside her and plopped a meaty hand on
her thigh.

"Hello, sweetheart," he said smoothly, "care for a
toss?"

A low growl emerged from her throat and they both
looked startled at the sound.

He laughed at her.

"I take it that's yes?" and he dug a finger into
her ribs.

She returned him an expression whose only relation
to a smile was that her teeth were bared.

"Take your hand off my leg," she said sweetly, "or I'll hurt you."

He laughed uproariously and slapped his own thigh with his free hand.

"Oh, sweetheart, you are a one!"

She reached out for him and there was a nasty little crunch.

He leapt to his feet howling and pranced around with his hands cupped to his chest.

Indeed, Terion would break many hearts this night. And nearly as many fingers.

The moon rose another notch and the smug smile with which she'd been watching her erstwhile swain's caperings smoothed out and vanished. Terion rose to find other adventures.

She was playing dice for kisses when she briefly returned to herself. Opening her eyes she found herself looking into the bloodshot eyes of the fellow she was kissing. Their breath mingled, their lips were smooshed together, yet, the moment had something in common with those conversations where you've exhausted everything you have to say to each other but simply walking away would be rude and trying to go on is pointless. Terion blushed. Fortunately, at that moment an enthusiastic drunk tried to join them, throwing his arms around Teri and wetly kissing her cheek. It was with some relief that she broke his nose.

She was shaking out her hand when the moon rose higher and she winked at her woozy victim.

Her fellow carousers grew uneasy with the mixed signals she was sending. One moment she was soft and cuddly as an adolescent dream, next she had the harsh reality of a hangover.

She hunched her shoulders forward adorably and said, "I can do a sword dance."

The men laughed nervously. They didn't really believe that such a dainty creature could do anything so martial, though many of them bore wounds from wooing her. Still, they gamely hoisted her onto a table and one of them fiddled a tune.

Her eyes met those of a man she liked, while her hips carved extravagant figure eights in the air.

"Loan me your 'sword so that I can dance," she demanded coyly.

He laughed. "Ah, lass, it's very sharp, you'd cut yourself sure."

She pouted and looked at him from the corner of her eyes.

"What's the matter," she teased, her eyes dropping to his hips, "don't you want me to touch it?"

In an instant the sword was in her hand.

They began to clap and cheer and she began to dance. At first, she merely held the sword and danced a wild hootchie cootchie around it, accompanied by hoots and howls of appreciation. Then, slowly, it became a perfectly traditional sword dance, except for the bumps and grinds that at times threatened the more undulant portions of her anatomy with being lopped off.

Her admirers' appreciation began to level off as they recognized the skill with which she handled the sword. Those, admittedly few, not riveted by the parts of her that jiggled took note of the thickness of her wrists and the muscles rippling along her arms and resolved to seek commercial companionship instead.

Mother Guid pursed her lips as the dance ended in wild applause and everyone shouted for beer. If most of her girls were getting the night off, at least she was doing well selling drinks. She watched one of the men make the move she'd been expecting all evening.

A handsome young fellow with a black beard leaned close and whispered in the girl's ear, then lifted his chin to indicate upstairs.

"Noooo!" Terion said, her eyes wide. "Save your money. Why do you think the Lady created bushes?"

Mother Guid was behind her in a flash.

"Excuse me, dearie, would you mind coming with me for a moment?"

When they reached an uninhabited corner of the room, Mother Guid spun round.

"What's your name, dearie?"

"Terion." She blinked at Mother Guid and raised her arms to lift her long hair off the back of her neck.

The men breathed a collective sigh.

Terion hoisted a shoulder and peeked coyly over it at them. Then she turned back to Mother Guid, managing to put some hip action into the motion.

The room moaned.

Something clicked into place in Mother Guid's mind.

"Terion? Not the Terion who went for a soldier?"

The strangest expression came over the girl's face and she glanced around as though puzzled to find herself here. When she looked back at the older woman her eyes narrowed and her mouth hardened.

Mother Guid was suddenly aware of the hard muscle beneath Terion's curves, and she smiled nervously.

"It's so nice to see you again, Terion, dear."

The moon rose to mid-heaven and Terion's smile returned, her eyes went soft and vacuous once more.

"You can call me Teri!" she chirped.

And Mother Guid nodded, smiling, nervously aware that something very strange was going on. The Terion she remembered was an out-and-out prig. She shuddered as she watched the girl prance back to her boyfriends and thought, *Now, Guid, if you don't ask questions, then you don't have to worry about the answers*.

She snagged Teri's arm and drew her back. "Well, dear, it's nice to see you again—but not if you spoil my girls' custom, you understand. What with my overheads and expenses and the rent . . ."

Teri pouted, then clapped her hands together and giggled. "Oh, I understand!" she trilled, wrinkling her nose.

Mother Guid blinked.

Teri leaped up onto a table. "You wonderful men," she called out in a voice like heated honey. "We've been having such a wonderful time, haven't we?"

Roars of agreement, some of them through swollen, bruised lips.

"But we've been neglecting poor Mother Guid and her girls," Terri went on. "And we shouldn't do that. So we're going to play a *game*."

Eyes glittered as Teri clapped her hands and bounced up and down.

"First we'll have an *auction*, and then we'll have a *contest*, and it'll be such a wonderful—"

Several hours later Mother Guid looked down dazedly at the little chamois leather sack of coins one of her girls—known as Enna Ironthighs—slapped down on the table in front of her.

"I don't care!" Enna blurted. "I give up. *I'm* not a python with insides made out of old saddle leather. She's not *human*."

A roar rose from the taproom beyond. A table broke.

"This has got to stop," Mother Guid said. Too much furniture was being lost; and besides, she *had* all their money.

Terion woke next morning to a body drained and aching, her head pounding like a battle ram and a taste in her mouth best not thought about with her stomach in this condition.

"Terion?" a timid voice whispered.

Cautiously, she slitted her eyes open. Daylight pierced them clear to the back of her skull. She recoiled, then sang out, "Ah!" for the pain movement caused. "Close the door," she whispered.

Feric obeyed and stomped over to her. "Drink this," he ordered.

"Can't."

"Drink! It will help."

It tasted vile, but not as bad as it smelled. Almost instantly, the crushing pain in her skull began to recede, the ache in her limbs as well. She sighed with relief.

"Thank you," she said, looking at him gratefully. There was an oddly pinched look about him. "What's the matter?"

"Do you remember anything of last night?"

Terion frowned. "I seem to remember . . . sitting on Gaffy Swanthold's knee . . ." she said in shocked disbelief, "and letting him tickle me as he would." Then she chuckled. "What a nightmare!"

Feric was shaking his head. "That was at the start of the evening. Mother Guid came over to complain about you. 'I'm not one to mind a frolic,' she said, 'my girls have been known to kick up their heels, but that Terion of yours is a whole other matter!'" He looked at Terion with concern.

"Kick up their heels! Ha! Is that what she calls it?" Her grin faded at the expression on his face. "You're telling me the local madam thinks I'm too wanton? You're not serious!"

Feric's lips compressed. "They carried you home last night, Teri. Singing. You attacked me when I put you to bed. You tried to rape me. I barely got away from you and then only because you were so drunk."

"I never did!"

"I've got bruises to prove it."

Her hands clenched the blanket and her eyes pleaded with him. "I don't remember any of it," she said plaintively.

"It's the curse," he said, his face grim. "When the moon is full, you become . . . a wench."

"A wench!"

He nodded. "A low tavern wench—more of a slut, really."

Terion gave him a look that had turned many a fierce man's bowels to water.

Feric merely sighed. "I expected something like

that. It's a very clearly worded curse, you know. Most unusual."

"Still," she said, dazed, "for a spur-of-the-moment effort it's apparently quite effective."

"Well, the cure is also clear." He smiled wryly and patted her hand. "And it's entirely up to you."

Terion eyed him apprehensively, but he remained silent, gazing at her with those understanding brown eyes of his. She licked dry lips nervously.

"Are you going to tell me?" she asked.

He looked away embarrassed.

"Terion, are you celibate?"

"Well of course. It's only sense if you're a woman mercenary. It simplifies things and it's the most effective contraceptive there is." She shrugged. "Why do you ask?"

"It's suggested by the structure of the curse. Obviously, Rarik knew you well."

"Not as well as he wanted to," she snarled. "My captain took service with him six months ago. Easy duty, he said, soft as a kitten, he said. But Rarik wouldn't leave me alone. *I* had to go riding with him, *I* had to guard his quarters late at night. He'd stare at me and stand close to me and touch me." Her eyes were bright with fury. "He magicked me, Feric. One night he kissed me." Terion was blushing furiously. "And I . . . kissed him back. All the while I knew what I was doing and I couldn't help myself. The moment his control slipped, I took up my sword and I struck him." She was shaking with rage at the memory. "He cursed me with his dying breath. I fled. Because I knew the captain would have to hang me when he saw what I'd done."

Feric stared at her in a kind of pitying horror. Not quite able to believe that his friend had killed a man because she felt herself responding to his overtures.

Terion calmed herself with an effort. "What do I have to do to break the curses?"

Feric bit his lip. "You have to accept . . . even revel in . . . your, um, sensuality."

She blinked. "I'm a soldier."

"And a human being."

"But I have a reputation for prudence and sobriety," she said indignantly.

"Modify it."

"You don't . . . I just . . . I like to keep myself to myself," she muttered.

"You like to be in control, Teri. But to break this curse your feelings must sometimes rule." He sighed. "It's my fault. You weren't like this once."

"Oh, true. There you went, off with your fairy lover, blissful as a pig in clover, never a thought to me." She'd begun in a light, mocking tone, but finished almost viciously, "I've had wounds that cut to the bone and not one of 'em hurt as much as that." She turned over in the bed, facing the wall.

He winced, but gamely carried on.

"Terion, either you accept this part of yourself and allow it a place in your life, or three days a month it will control you completely. And soon you'll have quite a different reputation."

She sniffed. Feric thought it was in contempt, but she might have been weeping. He gave her privacy, to think or cry as she saw fit.

Feric wondered what he was going to do with her tonight. He could put her in the shed and nail the door shut. No, she'd probably tunnel her way out.

He didn't want to confront her in her wench persona. When Terion had stood over his bed, reeking of sensuality and beer, she'd frankly terrified him. Feric sighed. He'd see her through this. Somehow, he'd help her.

When he returned with water from the well she was sitting glumly in the doorway.

"Even if I wanted to become . . . to appreciate . . ."

She sighed. "Well, I couldn't do it by moonrise, now could I?"

He sat down beside her, placing the bucket between his feet. "Why not? That's the way it is sometimes. You change your life all in a moment. One summer evening we were going to be farmers and married. The next morning, you were a mercenary and I was Feric the Fey. You just have to make up your mind and believe in your decision."

She leaned her head wearily against the doorframe. "It's hopeless," she said.

Feric reached for her and guided her head to his shoulder. He stroked her hair and kissed her brow. "It is not. It's a change, that's all."

She sat up abruptly. "I have to leave."

"What, now?"

"Now."

"But why?" He was torn between being put out and quite leery.

If she felt herself responding to him there was no telling what she might do.

She didn't *appear* to be wearing weapons.

"Oh, for the Lady's sweet sake, Feric. Unclench yourself. I can almost hear you thinking I'm going to attack you!" She *tsked* and shook her head. "Since you don't know, I'll tell you. Sorcerers are not romantic. Not one of them would waste energy in a merely *human* endeavor like love. Rarik's interest boded ill from the start." She shrugged. "Perhaps he assumed I was a virgin, since I had no lover. His ilk set great store by virgins . . . and their blood, and their souls." She raised one brow significantly.

"I have to leave because the captain probably sent someone after me," she said, rising. "It's serious business; the company had a contract to protect Rarik and one of us killed him. He *has* to clear the company's name. I think I've been enough trouble to you without that."

"A bad time to be the talk of the town," Feric

agreed. He snatched her hand as she turned to go. "Stay. If they catch you on the road when the moon is up you won't be able to defend yourself. Far from it! You'll be doing your best to make their dreams come true."

Her lips quirked in a smile. "Then they may die of shock."

He laughed and rose, tried to take her in his arms. She quickly and calmly twisted him into a complex and uncomfortable hold.

"What were you doing?" she asked, letting him go.

He shook his arm, which felt as though it had added an elbow.

"Ah . . . trying to persuade you to stay."

Her eyes widened and her lips quirked in the lopsided smile that meant she was taken by surprise. Feric stretched to his full height, trying to look manly and commanding.

Terion patted his cheek kindly, and laughing, asked, "What *is* this fatal attraction I have for sorcerers?" She turned to go indoors, still chuckling.

"I'm not a sorcerer," Feric protested, pretending he hadn't heard the word "fatal." "And you still need my help. Besides," he exclaimed triumphantly, "you won't get far on foot! Let me hunt up a good horse for you."

Terion was glad she'd let Feric persuade her to stay another night. By the time she'd bargained for a decent horse and a good mule to carry her gear it had been close to sunset.

She'd agreed to let him tie her to the bed before the moon rose and she'd still been there this morning.

When Feric came into the house picking leaves out of his hair and dripping with dew, she asked what had happened. He only blushed and said, "Your other self has an interesting imagination and a vivid gift of description."

Terion sighed; she was definitely going to miss him.

After breakfast she'd packed, given him a sisterly kiss and left, refusing to look back at his worried face. She'd left the books as well, though he'd tried to force them on her.

"The extra weight will slow me down," she'd told him. "Do you want to get me killed?"

His eyes had gotten very big.

She'd always loved his eyes.

A flash at the wood's edge just ahead drew her from her reverie. Her heart froze. Not a hundred feet from her stood Kesel, one of her former comrades in arms.

He saw her, no question of it. He'd seen her first, in fact, letting her know it by allowing the sun to flash on his helmet one more time. Then he grinned and, elaborately casual, led his horse back under the trees.

Terion smiled grimly as she rode into the shelter of the woods. Kesel was still a friend, then. At least enough of one to give her fair warning. Good enough. With care and speed on her part and the search party doing their best not to catch her she should be able to elude the captain's grasp.

She was well into the woods when it struck her. Friendship for her wouldn't extend to Feric.

The villagers knew where she'd been staying and would doubtless send the mercenaries right to his door. They'd find her gone and start to question him, dragging it out to give her ample time to leave the area.

Sweet Lady. She knew all too well the casual brutality of which her comrades were capable. Of which she had become capable in her years with them. She had to go back.

Terion left the horse and mule a good half mile from Feric's cottage, then spent a cautious hour creeping towards the little clearing that surrounded his home.

She could have spared herself the effort.

Kesel and the rest of the posse had spent the morning getting roaring drunk. Most likely on Mother Guid's strong beer. Terion could have danced naked out of the woods and covered with bells and they'd have thought the ringing was in their ears.

Feric drooped between two men who could barely stand up themselves. Kesel slammed a punch into Feric's stomach that knocked all three men down, the momentum of his swing bringing him down on top of them. The men rolled and cursed and kicked, and when they dragged themselves off the ground at last, Feric stayed down.

If it were anyone but her friend she'd probably be laughing. As it was, fury boiled in her middle; she held back a scream of rage by sheer will. The desire to strike them, to hurt them, almost lifted her off the ground.

Prudence held her back. Good as she was with a sword, five to one were impossible odds. Even drunk they had advantages of reach and weight. Not to mention the fact that she genuinely didn't want to kill them. Box their ears, kick their butts, yes, kill, no.

She slipped up to where the horses were picketed and patiently cut their reins. The horses knew her and remained silent—as they'd been trained to when nothing troubled them. That same training was the reason she couldn't steal them, for they'd respond to their masters' whistles before taking notice of her pounding heels or shouts.

So her plan was to spook them and get them milling about. They wouldn't go anywhere, but it would take their drunken masters a while to get them sorted out. By then she should be a safe distance away from Feric and ready to lead them a merry chase.

Laughing uproariously the men kicked Feric, but with no result.

Then Kesel shouted, "She's a hen i'nt she? Let's look for her in the henhouse." And all five stumbled off to massacre chickens.

Exasperated and relieved at once, Teriòn crawled through the grass towards Feric, needing to know if he was all right.

The scent of weeds and moist earth was strong in her nostrils. Grasshoppers flicked through the warm grass, disturbed by her approach.

She knew where the posse was by their hoots and guffaws and the mad squawking of chickens, but still, her back felt terribly vulnerable. The sense that someone was going to leap onto her and pin her to the ground was almost overwhelming.

Just as she reached him Feric rolled over onto his elbows, groaning.

"Feric," she whispered.

He lifted a bloody face to her, his unswollen eye wide with shock. "Go away," he said, dazed.

"Come with me. You can ride the mule, I left the animals not half a mile from here." She reached for his hand, but he pulled it away.

"Their horses . . ." he began.

"I've already cut their reins, one good wallop will stir them up. But they won't run away and they won't carry us, especially not you."

He grinned and whispered a word to her. "Say that to them. They'll run alright. Go to your horse, Teri, I'll meet you there."

"What do you mean you'll meet me? I'm not leaving you here!"

"I have to get the books."

"The books! Are you crazy?"

"Trust me Teri. I know what I'm doing." He looked at her fearlessly and nodded. His lip was visibly more swollen.

She sensed his confidence was unfeigned, but her experience and instincts screamed that whatever he planned couldn't possibly succeed. Yet she also knew that, even if she could bring herself to add a lump to his collection, she couldn't drag his unconscious body half a mile through the woods without getting caught herself.

"Listen," she said, tears in her eyes, "just lie here and let me lead them off. It's me they want. You don't have to do anything."

Feric smiled crookedly and kissed her, leaving blood on her lips.

"Wait till I'm inside the cottage before you say that word to the horses. Then go and wait for me. I'll be there, I promise." He turned, and began dragging himself towards the cottage.

Biting her lip Terion turned and crawled the other way.

Through the horses' legs she watched him pull himself painfully up on the doorframe and enter the darkness within. Then she quietly spoke the word he'd given her.

The effect was astounding. Five well-trained horses went completely mad. They bucked and screamed and whirled about. Terion barely scrambled out of their way in time as they turned and tore down the path, leaping the gate to run screaming down the road.

The five drunken mercenaries came running in a cloud of chicken feathers to find an empty yard. They stood dumbfounded. Someone said, "Well, hey ... we'll never catch her now."

A sound made them turn. Feric stood in the cottage doorway, the two books of magic in his arms, his hair wild and matted with blood.

"You'll never find her," he shouted. "Never! I'll destroy her before I'll let you have her." Then he spoke a word like a crack of thunder and burst into flames.

Terion's horrified cry was lost in the amazed cries of the men.

The cottage itself began to blaze and Feric stumbled backwards into the inferno. Fire roared like an angry beast, burning too hot to smoke; in seconds the whole house was engulfed in flames.

Terion could feel the fire's heat where she was hiding, could feel it drying her tears.

She'd simply walked back to her horse, not bothering to hide, not caring if she was caught. Night was coming on now, and with it the curse, and she couldn't bring herself to care about that either.

A rustling brought her head up. But for the first time in many years she didn't bother to reach for her sword. If they found her, they found her.

Out of the growing darkness a man staggered; the scent of smoke clung to him and his face was black with soot.

"Feric!" she shrieked. Terror gripped her as she stared at her friend's ghost.

"Shhh," he said, lifting a finger to his lips. "They're still around somewhere."

"You're alive? You're *alive!*" Somehow she found herself plastered against him, kissing him passionately.

"Gently, Teri, gently," he pleaded around her lips. "Every inch of me has a burn or a bruise or a cut."

She laughed and rolled her eyes towards the darkening sky. "Get used to it—in an hour or so I won't be able to keep my hands off you. Not that I want to." Her tone gave the words two meanings. She hugged him again, but lightly. "How?" she asked, wonderingly. "How?"

"I didn't do it quite right," he said and shrugged off the pack that held the two books of magic. "It was supposed to be an illusion spell. I'm lucky I didn't roast myself."

"Poor Feric." She touched his cinderized hair. "What are you going to do now?"

"Well . . . you *said* I could ride the mule." He slapped the books and a cloud of ash erupted. He coughed. "Maybe I can find someone to teach me to use these."

"Of course." She nodded and spread her hands. "I owe you, it's the least . . ."

"Maybe you could help me find them," he suggested.

Terion blinked. "Why not? It beats farming." Then she slowly grinned. "But first, let's find a clearwater pond and you wash off that soot and I'll wash off the road. Then we'll have a nice . . . sleep."

They both blushed.

". . . and see how we feel in the morning. Hmmm?"

"I know the perfect spot," he said. And taking her hand he led her off into the gathering night.

This story deals with a very different sort of armor, family matters, and the importance of being able to improvise.

BLOOD CALLS TO BLOOD

Elisabeth Waters

Lucy arrived home from work wanting nothing more than a long hot bath and a quiet evening. It was good to be back on the streets after a rotation in Juvenile. Juvenile was a tough assignment, especially when you had children of your own; it made you only too aware of all the awful things that happened to children in this world. But walking a beat, or, in Lucy's case, bicycling it, was hot and physically tiring.

She could hear voices coming from the kitchen, presumably one or more of the children, but she didn't go that way. They knew that she had just come in; her home security system was the best that money could buy and thirteen-year-old hackers could improve upon, and she had passed three cameras already. But, by family custom, nobody spoke to Mom when she got home from work until after she'd had a bath and a chance to unwind. So Lucy continued unmolested upstairs to the master bedroom, took off her gunbelt, unloaded the gun and locked it away, shed her clothes and the bulletproof vest, and started filling the tub. The attached bathroom boasted a tub that would hold several people (assuming, of course, that they were very good friends). The tub also had a built-in Jacuzzi. Lucy climbed in, turned on the jets, and soaked until she had dishpan hands, feet, knees, and elbows.

Feeling considerably more human, she put on a robe and went downstairs to join the rest of the family for dinner. She found her husband George and their twin daughters, Diana and Cynthia, at the kitchen table. There was no sign of dinner. Piles of reference books surrounded them, and all three were busily reading. She picked up the nearest book. "*Elf Defense?*" she asked incredulously, noting the title.

Diana, who at age fifteen was already showing the makings of a fine reference librarian, looked up. "Well, hard data on this problem is a bit difficult to find. After all, Mom, not that many people really believe in elves these days. That's why we didn't call the police."

"When?" Lucy said hollowly. "And about what? And where's Michael? Is he spending the night at Jimmy's?"

Cynthia seemed totally engrossed in the book she was studying which, Lucy saw, reading upside down, was titled *Psychic Self-Defense*. Diana looked at her father, who also looked as if he would rather not answer that question.

"Maybe you should sit down, dear," he said.

Lucy grabbed the nearest chair and sat. "All right, I'm sitting down. Where's Michael?"

"He was kidnapped by elves this afternoon."

Lucy shot back to her feet. "Elves?"

"Now you can see why we didn't feel that calling the police would be appropriate," George said.

"We didn't want to be laughed at," Cynthia added, looking up from her book.

"I'm not laughing," Lucy pointed out. "Start talking."

"I wasn't here," Cynthia said quickly. "I was still at the hospital." She did volunteer work there three afternoons a week.

"And Daddy was writing," Diana said. This meant

that Daddy's brain had been in another universe at the time. "So I guess I'm your only witness, Mother."

"All right, then, Diana. What happened?"

"Do you remember Precious? That girl last month with datura poisoning?"

"How could I forget Precious Gift of the Goddess? It's not an easy name to fit on bureaucratic forms. But, as far as I know, she's in foster care now, so it's hard to see how she could have anything to do with this."

"Maybe you should see the note." Diana handed over a small parchment scroll. Lucy unrolled it. It was written in silver ink, real silver judging by the weight of it.

The handwriting was spiky and obviously intended to look elvish in origin, but Lucy had been born with the Sight. This note was written by a human, a very angry human.

"You took my last born from me," she read aloud, "so I have taken yours. The fair folk will not be cheated." She frowned at the signature. " 'Morgana.' Are we talking about Precious's grandmother here?"

"Is her name Morgana?" Diana asked in surprise. "I thought it was Janine."

"She calls herself Morgana," Lucy said, "and she's definitely a mortal. So where do the elves come in?"

"They took Michael," Diana said, "and they left this note."

"What makes you think they were elves?"

"They opened a gate," Diana pointed out into the yard, "right there, next to the hummingbird feeder." Lucy looked. There was definitely a gate in the backyard, a hole in the side of the hill with a silvery gray light coming from it. The light turned reddish at ground level, and Lucy, squinting, saw that the red area was just above one of her good cast-iron skillets. She could feel a faint pull through it as well, a tugging at the bond that stretched between her and each of her children. Since Diana and Cynthia were in the kitchen with her, Michael was obviously on the other side of that gate.

Diana continued with her story. "They came in here and grabbed Michael—we were sitting at the table. He broke his glass against the table and tried to slice them with the broken edges, but it was like it didn't touch them—"

"Are you sure it did?"

"—but I hit one of them in the face with the serving spoon I got at RenFaire, and the handle left a burn mark." She pointed to the spoon in question: a copper bowl riveted to a wrought-iron handle. "A human would have been marked by both the copper and iron, not just the iron, and he would have been cut or bruised, not burned." She shuddered. "And you should have heard him scream! They bolted back through the gate faster than I could move. I threw the skillet at them, but I missed. Mom, I'm sorry; I tried, I really did!" She burst into tears, and Lucy reached over and grabbed her in a hug.

"I know you did, honey, and this isn't your fault." She patted her sobbing daughter on the back. "Don't worry. We'll get Michael back." She looked out the window again. "Besides, you may not have hit them, but you appear to have locked their gate open. That will make going after them much easier."

"I found it!" Cynthia said suddenly, and Diana pulled away from Lucy and grabbed at the book. Diana had always been good at blocking her emotions with her intellect.

"Great!" She scanned the page quickly. "We'll need salt. Daddy, do we have any sea salt left?"

"Third cupboard from the left," George said automatically. "What did you find?"

"The formula for making holy water," Diana said. "According to my research, such as it is, iron and holy water are the main weapons against elves."

"Actually, Coke works, too," Cynthia said. "At least it did on Precious. She got a can of it while she was in the hospital and it really *did* make her drunk. And she says she's only part elf."

"Getting someone drunk isn't much of a weapon," Diana pointed out, pulling several two-liter soda bottles from the recycling bin. "And first you'd have to get all of them to drink Coke—and you can't count on their having watched enough TV advertising for that."

"Iron." Cindy stared into space, obviously trying to think of good sources of iron. "Would steel count?"

"I should think so," George said. "It's an alloy of iron."

"Are you going after them, Mom?" Cindy asked, eyeing Lucy as if measuring her.

"Yes, I am." *At least I've been Under the Hill before*, Lucy thought, *even if it was years and years ago. And the elves generally don't hurt children, so Michael should be okay for a while anyway.*

"Then I've got the perfect thing for you to wear," Cindy said. She ran from the room to fetch whatever it was. Diana had filled a large mixing bowl with water and was now casting salt into it, murmuring prayers as she did so. Lucy waited until she had finished the process and was pouring the water into the empty soda bottles.

"Diana, why did you say Morgana's name was Janine?"

Diana looked at her and bit her lip. "I did some research at the county courthouse, after Cindy first met Precious. I didn't mean to pry into your private life, Mother, but Precious said that she and Cindy had the same blood, and I was curious."

"The files at the courthouse are a matter of public record, Diana; it's hardly prying into my private life. Putting a camera in my bedroom is prying into my private life."

George smothered a laugh. "I think Michael understands that now."

"He had better," Lucy said. "So, Diana, what did you find out?"

"I started with Precious's birth certificate, which took a while to find because it was under 'Goddess, Precious G.' Her mother's name is Laurel, and for father it says 'unknown.' So I looked up Laurel's birth certificate, and it says father unknown, but the mother is Janine Kennedy. I had brought our family genealogy notebook with me, and when I checked your birth certificate the mother's name was the same and the age was right. So it looks as though Precious is our first cousin."

"As far as I know, that's correct," Lucy said. "You never met your grandmother; she didn't approve of my career choice or my choice of husband. As far as I'm concerned, she's no loss. Dad left her when I was ten, but I had to visit her until I turned eighteen."

"Do you think she might have Michael at her house?" Diana asked. "I've got a recent address for her."

"How recent?"

"Last summer. She changed her voter registration, to switch political parties. She's registered as Peace and Freedom at the moment. It looks like she changes every few years—her deleted registration wasn't very old either, but her address hasn't changed since Laurel was born."

"It hasn't changed since I was born," Lucy said. "Her father left her the house and a trust fund. It's too bad; if she'd ever had to work for a living she might have had to learn to interact with mundane reality. Then at least she might have told her granddaughter that datura is poisonous." She sighed. "But once she finished school and married, she sort of pulled away from the real world. She was more interested in elves than people for as long as I can remember. It drove Dad nuts, and Laurel's birth was the last straw."

"Laurel really isn't his, then," Diana said. "Is that why he divorced her?"

"Diana!" For the first time in this conversation

Lucy was shocked. "Of course he didn't divorce her! Divorce is wrong. You know that—or didn't they cover that in confirmation class?"

"Yes, they did, and I know it's wrong, but lots of Catholics still get divorced, and if she was committing adultery, that's a mortal sin." Diana giggled suddenly. "And if she had a child by an elf, that's miscegenation."

"What's miscegenation?" Cindy asked, coming into the room carrying a double handful of what looked like a pile of small metal rings.

"Mixing of races, in this case interbreeding between human and elf," Lucy replied briskly. "What do you have there?"

"So Precious really is part elf?" Cindy asked. Diana nodded. "Well I guess it's better to have an elf for a father than to have a mother so promiscuous that she can't say who fathered her child." She spread the metal out on the table. Lucy looked at it incredulously.

"You're joking, right?"

"No, Mom, really. It's stainless steel, and Dad says that counts as iron, and I'm sure it will fit you. We're pretty close to the same size."

George coughed. "I bet it would look great on you, dear."

Lucy glared at him. "I am not going anywhere in a chainmail bikini!" She turned on Cindy. "And where did you get this, young lady? I haven't seen it before."

"At the RenFaire."

"You wore *this* at the Renaissance Faire? I'm amazed you didn't get sunstroke."

"No, I got it at the RenFaire. I'm planning to wear it at a science fiction convention in May."

"We'll discuss it later," Lucy said. "But I assure you that I am not going outside the house in that. I'll wear my bulletproof vest; the breast and back plates in it are steel."

"But they're covered by fabric," Cindy protested.

"That doesn't matter as long as it's not silk," Diana said. "Silk insulates, but I don't think Kevlar does."

"I still think she'd be better off in this," Cindy said.

"Not if I have to come out by another gate somewhere else," Lucy pointed out. "I'd be arrested for indecent exposure, or at least picked up for psychiatric evaluation." She scooped up the chainmail. "Put this back in your room, Cindy."

Cindy took the bikini, but stood there frowning. "Maybe if you drink holy water it will help protect you."

"Salt water is an emetic," Lucy pointed out. "I don't think that throwing up would improve my efficiency."

"I can fix that," Cindy said. "I'll be right back." She dashed out of the room again.

Lucy sighed. "While Cindy has her next brilliant idea, I'll go get dressed." She went back to her room, dressed in blue jeans, sneakers, a T-shirt, her vest, and a sweatshirt. She stuffed her keys and ID into one pocket and looked at the gun drawer. *No*, she decided, *it probably won't help against elves, and if I shoot it I'll spend days doing paperwork. And it would be impossible to explain the circumstances to a review board.* She took the handcuffs off her belt and shoved them in another pocket and picked up her police issue flashlight, before returning to the kitchen.

In her absence the girls had gathered together Michael's water pistol collection and Diana and George were filling all of them with holy water. Cindy was mixing something in a pitcher. She sampled a spoonful of it, then nodded. "This is it." She poured a glass of the liquid and handed it to Lucy. "Here, Mom, drink this."

"What is it?" Lucy eyed the glass suspiciously.

"Oral rehydration fluid," Cindy explained. "It's what they give babies who've lost a lot of fluid. In addition to water and salt—holy water in this case—it has baking soda and sugar. It won't make you throw up, and it should help spread the holy water throughout your body."

"I don't believe this," Lucy said. "The scientific method as applied to search-and-rescue operations Under the Hill." She drank down the liquid in a long gulp.

"I think it's working," Cindy said, watching her. "You look brighter somehow, sort of a glow." She grabbed a sports bottle and filled it from the pitcher. "Take this with you, and give some to Michael when you find him."

It was working all right; Lucy could feel it and when she looked at her hands she saw that Cindy was right. Even in the daylight they glowed brightly. Also, she could feel a much stronger pull coming through the gate now. "Did Michael have any holy water with him?" she asked.

"Just one water pistol," Diana said. "He filled it at mass last Sunday. It was tucked in the back of his belt and his T-shirt covered it, so they may not have found it yet."

"Or wanted to handle it if they did find it," Lucy murmured.

Diana took a net tote bag out of the kitchen closet and started to load it. "Eight water pistols, filled. Two two-liter bottles of holy water as additional ammo. One sports bottle of potable holy water for defense. One flashlight. And the bag has both short and long handles so you can either carry it or sling it over your shoulder." She frowned anxiously. "Can anyone think of anything else?"

After a moment, three heads shook. "Okay, that's it then," Lucy said briskly, picking up the bag. "Wish me luck."

A ragged chorus of "good luck" followed her out the door.

She crossed the yard to the gate and stepped through, being careful not to touch the skillet. It seemed to be doing a fine job right where it was.

* * *

She paused just on the other side of the gate to give her eyes time to adjust to the difference in light. They were only half-adjusted when the groaning started.

"Oh, my head, my eyes!" Even through the groaning, the whispery voice was familiar, although it had been twenty-five years since Lucy had heard it.

"Moth?" she asked, bending over the slight gray figure lying at the side of the path. "What are you doing here?"

Moth whimpered and tried to shrink further into the ground. "Don't get so close! It hurts!"

"Sorry." Lucy backed off a bit. "Must be the holy water." Her eyesight was adjusting and she could see him more clearly now. He was obviously in pain, and he had a burn mark across his face. His hands were blistered as well. "What happened to your face?"

"Hit with cold iron I was," he said. Aside from the burn marks, his appearance hadn't changed since he had been one of Lucy's childhood playmates. "Do I know you, mortal?"

"I was Lucy O'Hara," she said briskly. "We used to play together when I was a child."

"And now you're a woman grown—no doubt with children of your own." Moth sighed. "You mortals grow so quickly." He looked at her and shook his head. "I remember you; you lived in the yard with the datura and the wisteria."

"Yes."

"Well, Lucy," he said in a persuasive tone only too familiar to the mother of teenagers, "could I trouble you to move that pan out of the gate?"

"The iron pan? The one that's holding the gate open?" Lucy asked in mock innocent tones.

"You always were a bright little thing," Moth admitted.

"Brighter than you, it would seem," Lucy said, "if

you got tricked into tangling with my children. Why did you do it?"

"Your children?" Moth looked horrified. "The boy is yours? I swear by the Queen's throne, I had no idea. Morgana said he was hers, that he'd been kidnapped and needed to be rescued."

"My *mother* talked you into this?" Lucy was incredulous. "Don't you know she's crazy?"

Moth groaned piteously again and touched a careful finger to the burn mark on his face. "I'm certainly getting the message now. I suppose the girl that hit me was your daughter?"

Lucy nodded.

"Didn't you teach your children any manners?" he asked sternly.

"Yes, I did," Lucy said. "I also taught them that if anyone ever tried to grab them they should fight like hell."

"They're a credit to your teaching," Moth said with feeling. "Now will you please move that wretched pan so I can get this gate closed?"

"Yes, of course I will, Moth," Lucy said promptly. "Just as soon as I get Michael back and home safe. Where is he?"

"What's it worth for me to tell you?"

Lucy smiled grimly. "I haven't forgotten what I learned as a child, Moth, and I am not in a good mood right now. *You* opened this gate—for the sole purpose of kidnapping my child—and you can't leave here until the gate is closed. Obviously," she gestured to his hands, "you can't grasp the pan long enough to move it yourself, so until I come back this way with Michael, you'll be stuck here. I should think that would be reason enough for you to tell me how to find Michael as quickly as possible."

Moth ground his teeth together. "He was taken to Lord Cedric. His chamber is just the other side of the Feasting Hall. The path leads right to it."

Any path Under the Hill led to the Feasting Hall.

Lucy didn't bother to ask about distance; distances Under the Hill tended to be arbitrary and changeable. "Thank you, Moth. I'll be back as quickly as I can." She hesitated slightly. "I'm sorry my children hurt you, but my world isn't a safe place, and my children have learned to fight when they are threatened. You should not have frightened them."

Moth didn't answer, and Lucy shrugged and hurried down the path.

As she approached the Feasting Hall, she heard angry voices, punctuated with occasional screams. "Get that gun away from him!" someone cried out. Lucy pulled two water pistols out of the tote bag and slung it over her shoulder. With a pistol in each hand she stepped into the doorway.

"Freeze!" she shouted. "Police!" Mentally she groaned. *As if they're going to be impressed by the police. Some habits are so hard to break.*

"Mom!" Michael was struggling in the arms of a tall and rather beefy looking man, dressed in the silks the elf lords favored. "Shoot 'em in the face—it blinds them temporarily!" He twisted and squirted the man holding him. The man blinked and shook his head, glaring at the boy. Michael looked bewildered. Everyone else in the room froze, looking from them to Lucy and quickly back at them again.

"He's a mortal, Michael," Lucy said. "Holy water won't hurt him."

"That's right," the man said defiantly. "Nothing you can do will hurt me."

"This will hurt you plenty!" A shot rang out behind Lucy, and a bullet passed over her shoulder and buried itself in the wall above the man's head. "Let go of my brother or die!"

"Cynthia," Lucy spoke through gritted teeth, "give me the gun." She held out her right hand. Cindy, dressed in her chainmail bikini with her mother's gun belt over it, took the water pistol and replaced it with the gun.

"Mother," she spoke in an urgent whisper, "we called Precious right after you left, and she said her father is a mortal! That's why I came after you."

"And how did you get my gun and ammo?"

"Would you believe you forgot to lock it up?"

"Not for one second. We'll discuss this later, young lady."

She turned back to the man holding her child. He had pulled out a dagger and was holding it at Michael's throat. "I think we have a standoff here, cop," he said, sneering on the last word. "Drop your gun."

"Not while you're holding a knife on my child I won't," Lucy said promptly. "Besides, if I drop the gun, it might go off again, and someone could get hurt." Cynthia edged in to her mother's right side, squirt gun at the ready, obviously prepared to deal with anyone who tried to take the gun by force.

There was a tinkling of bells as someone came through the door to Lucy's right. Lucy risked a quick glance in that direction before returning her gaze to the man who held her son. As she had suspected from the sound, it was the Queen. "Hold your fire," she murmured to Cynthia. "Do *not* shoot at anyone unless I tell you to."

"Right," Cynthia gulped, suddenly noticing that she was in over her head.

Lucy remembered the Queen as capricious, but not actively malicious. And the elves did value children. But right now the Queen's main emotion seemed to be annoyance. "What is the meaning of this disturbance?" She looked at Michael and his captor. "Lord Cedric, whence comes this child?"

"I claim him as replacement for my daughter, taken away by the police."

"You can't keep me," Michael pointed out, "I've been baptized."

"You can't be a changeling, true," Lord Cedric acknowledged, "but I can hold you hostage until my daughter is returned home."

"But she nearly got killed there!" Cindy protested.

"Does he mean Precious?" Michael asked. He twisted to look up at the man who held him. Lucy held her breath waiting to see blood drip down his neck, but apparently the knife blade wasn't tight against his throat. "You want Precious returned to *Morgana?*" Michael continued. "Are you nuts?"

Cedric glared at him. "You think she's better off in foster care, boy? I was in foster care before I came here; I know what it's like!"

"So do I!" Michael snapped. "I've been visiting her. And *she* says she's a lot happier there than she was at home!" He looked at Lucy. "If I have to stay here to keep Precious away from Morgana, Mother, I'll do it. Precious deserves better than that."

"Anybody would," Cindy said from beside Lucy. "Morgana's a psycho. Did you know that she gave Precious drugs? And she's got Laurel addicted."

Lucy sighed. "I know, Cindy. That's why Precious is in foster care."

"Why isn't Morgana in jail?" Michael demanded.

"These things take time," Lucy reminded him.

"Yeah, the wheels of justice make the mills of God look like a fast food joint."

A cynic at thirteen, Lucy thought. *What a world we're raising our children in.*

"So I'll stay here," Michael continued. "I don't want Precious hurt again."

Cedric looked at him incredulously. The Queen looked on with faint interest. Lucy decided it was time to intervene.

"Your chivalry is noted, Michael—as is your willingness to miss next week's English exam," she added with a grin. Cindy giggled. "But I think we can work out a more reasonable solution." She turned to Lord

Cedric. "You don't want Precious in state-sponsored foster care, right?"

"Absolutely not. And that is non-negotiable."

"I understand. It's not an ideal solution, especially for a child with her unique heritage."

"But if he's mortal—" Michael began.

Lucy silenced him with a look. "My sister Laurel's father was not."

"That's true enough," the Queen said coldly.

Oh oh, Lucy thought. Cindy opened her mouth; Lucy stepped on her foot. Cindy hastily shut her mouth and tried to look like a statue. Michael caught on that this was not a good time to discuss Laurel's father and shut his mouth. "I am Precious's aunt," Lucy continued, "and this can be documented with our birth certificates. I can therefore petition the court for custody of Precious, and I see no reason why the petition should not be granted. Once Precious is living in my household, you," she addressed Lord Cedric, "will be able to visit her and see for yourself that she is well and happy."

"And I suppose you want your son back now." Lord Cedric looked her straight in the eyes.

Lucy returned his stare. "Yes."

"What guarantee do I have that you will do as you say?" he asked distrustfully.

"My word of honor," Lucy said firmly, meeting his eyes unflinchingly.

"Why should I trust your word?" he asked.

"Because I say so!" Both Cedric and Lucy turned in surprise at the Queen's words. "She and her children are free to leave and are to do so immediately." Cedric looked bewildered by the Queen's decision, but Lucy noticed that the Queen squinted slightly when she looked toward Lucy and Cynthia, and that the other elves were all looking elsewhere. She looked straight at Cynthia for the first time since the girl had joined them and noticed that her skin had a bright glow to it. And there was quite a lot of skin exposed.

You could light the hall with her, Lucy realized, *and I'll bet that she's hurting their eyes. That's why the Queen wants us gone. Her idea about drinking holy water is really paying off.*

Cedric released Michael and shoved him toward Lucy. "Go then," he said, "but remember—I know where you live."

"Good," Lucy said, smiling sweetly. "Then you'll know where to visit your daughter." She slipped her gun carefully into its holster on Cindy's hip, put her arms around her children, and herded them up the path, back to the mortal world and home, pausing only long enough at the gate to retrieve her cast-iron skillet and say goodbye to Moth.

Lucy came home from work feeling pretty good. It had been a beautiful day, nothing had gone wrong during her shift, and life was going well at home. George had just sold another book, her children were all doing well in school, and Precious had settled into the family and was catching up on the things she had missed, like ice cream and television. Precious had also proved to have quite a green thumb (or maybe a bit of outside help) and the garden was in full bloom. Lucy walked around the house, admiring the wisteria that covered the back arbor with purple flowers.

The wisteria, however, was not the only thing in the backyard. Michael and Precious sat at the picnic table, talking with Moth. All of them got up when they saw her, and Precious ran to give her a hug. Michael and Moth followed behind her.

"Aunt Lucy, may we go visit my father for a while?" Precious asked.

"I've done all my homework," Michael said, answering Lucy's next question before she could ask it. "And Moth says he'll take us through the gate and bring us back."

Lucy looked at Moth. "I'll take good care of them," he assured her.

"I want them back by dinnertime," she said. "*Our* dinnertime, *today*, in two of our hours."

"Very well," Moth agreed.

As they started across the yard to the gate, Lucy added, "And if they're not back by then, I'm coming after them."

"They'll be back on time, Lucy," Moth said fervently. "You have my word."

Maybe she's not the Original swordswoman, but Maureen Birnbaum has got my vote for being—now and forever—the Greatest.

MAUREEN BIRNBAUM IN THE MUD

E. T. Spiegelman
(As told to George Alec Effinger)

So picture this:

I'm like sitting on the edge of the upstairs bathtub, which in Mums and Daddy's house is half-sunken so my knees are jammed up under my chin, and I'm watching my dear, dear friend, Maureen Birnbaum the Interplanetary Adventuress, apply eye shadow. Maureen is, you know, very finicky about makeup when she uses it, which isn't often these days because she's mostly a barbarian swordsperson who only rarely bothers with normal stuff.

Her style of dress begins and ends with her solid gold-and-jewel brassiere and G-string, and her grooming habits have likewise been put on hiatus in favor of perpetual vigilance. Muffy—that was her old nickname back in the Greenberg School days, but you should know how much she hates it now—spends her waking hours hacking and hewing villains and monsters. She is, she tells me, a very good hacker and hewer indeed, and I should doubt her? Well, okay, entre nous sometimes I have just these little teeny suspicions that Muffy's narrations are how-shall-I-say preposterous.

Be that as it may. Muffy applied the eye makeup

*in layers of several different but carefully chosen
shades. In the olden days, sometimes she'd end up
looking like a surprised raccoon north of her nose.
She's gotten more skillful since then—though like I
still wouldn't want to call the results tasteful. It
seemed to me that she was aiming at a kind of Monet-
at-Giverny waterlilies effect between her brows and
eyelids.*

*The color she was, well, slathering is a good verb,
was called Azul Jacinto. Muffy was vigorously but like
inexpertly blending this weird purple eye shadow with
the previous tinctorial stratum, which if I remember
correctly was Caramel Smoke. They should've put a
Kids:* Don't Try This At Home *warning on the
containers.*

*She goes, "Finally, finally, I've found a way to get
back to Mars and my own true beloved, Prince Van.
And like I want to look just absolutely devastating.
So be cruel, Bitsy. Tell me what you really think.
Honestly, now."*

*"You look terrific, sweetie," I go. Let her find out
the hard way. That's what she gets for calling me
Bitsy. I've told her a million times that if she can't
stand being called Muffy, I can't stand being called
Bitsy. I'm not seventeen anymore. I'm a grown-up
divorced mother with responsibilities, and I want to
be treated with respect every bit as much as Muffy—
Maureen—does.*

*She smiled at herself in the mirror. "Great," she
goes. "I'll only be a little longer." She'd said that an
hour ago.*

*"Should I go out and tell the cab driver? Take him
a Coke or some coffee or something?"*

*Maureen just shrugged. "I'll give him a big tip. He'd
rather have that than coffee anyway, for sure. Cab
drivers wait for me all the time."*

"Whatever."

"So," she goes, making her mouth into a big open

O and stretching her right eyebrow upward with her pinkie, "where was I?"

Damn it. *I was, you know, praying that she'd forget about telling me the rest of her most recent thrilling exploit. "You whooshed out of New Orleans and wound up in this bitty little medieval village."*

"Uh huh," *she goes, hastily daubing Azul Jacinto like a muralist rushing to met the NEA grant deadline.* "Well, be a darling and open that other box of Frango chocolates, the raspberry ones, and I'll just finish up here."

Comment dîtes-vous en français *"Yeah. Right." What follows, I swear, I am not making up. I should only be so clever.*

I shouldn't even be like *talking* to you anymore, Bitsy, the way you left me standing there on the sidewalk in New Orleans. Do you mind if I tell you that I thought you were just too *R-U-D-E* for words? Still, all that's forgiven, because we've been best friends *forever* and I can see what a wretched life you've carved out for yourself, but didn't I *warn* you about Josh? And didn't I point out—

All right. Never mind. I'm sorry I brought it up. So there I was, like simply *abandoned* in a strange city, thank you very much. They call New Orleans "The City That Care Forgot," but they've forgotten other things, too. Like the past participle. All over town, I kept running into "ice tea" and "boil shrimp" and "smoke sausage." I really wanted to sample that smoke sausage, just to see if it was like my Nanny's shadow soup. She said when they were too poor to buy a chicken, she'd, you know, *borrow* someone else's and hold it over her pot of boiling water. That's how you make shadow soup. *Cossacks* were involved in that story somehow, but I can't exactly remember how.

I've lost my train of thought, I must be getting old. Oh, for sure, the *village.* You know that I can whoosh through time and space with ease, but that I don't always end up exactly where I planned. *Believe* me, sweetie, I hadn't planned to visit this—well, I hate to call it a *town*, exactly, because it was made up of just five horrible tiny shops and no houses at all. Don't you think that's a little odd?

Sure, the merchants must've lived in the back of their shops, except I didn't *see* any backs. Just these one-room huts made out of sticks. They could've learned some important and useful things about architecture from a Neolithic tribe in New Guinea or somewhere.

So here's Maureen Birnbaum, Protector of the Weak, ankling into this dinky place. It looked like a strip mall of outlet stores during the reign of King Albert.

Albert. *King Albert*. The one who burned the cakes. *You* remember. No, that wasn't Charlemagne. It was King Albert the Great. Or somebody. Hey, Bitsy, it's not even *important*, all right? Jeez!

So guess what the name of this village was? No, not Brooklyn. Ha ha, too amusing for words, Bits. No, they called the place Mudville. As in "There is no joy in." I thought, "Like wow, I've traipsed into another literary allusion." I was all set for Casey at the Bat and baseball. Girlfriend, was I ever *wrong*.

Imagine, if you will, Our Hero entering the first of the five shops of sticks. A tinkling bell announced my arrival—further oddness, on account of there was no actual door for the bell to tinkle on. I turned around and saw what was probably the shopkeeper's teenage son, a gawky kid with a face so broken out it looked like a Hayden Planetarium sky show in Technicolor. He was crouched beside the entrance with a little bell and a little hammer. Hey, what the hell, he was learning the trade and you got to start *someplace*, I guess.

The guy behind the counter goes, "Welcome to Scrupulously Honest and Fair Fred's Armor Emporium. May I help you?"

"Are you Scrupulously Honest and Fair Fred?"

"No, he's sick today. I'm his brother, Aethelraed, but never fear, dear lady, I am also scrupulously honest and fair. Pretty much."

"Uh huh," I go, "and don't call me 'dear lady.' "

"May I show you our wares? We just got in a very nice tarnhelm, nearly mint condition. Its previous owner came to a sorry end guarding a hoard."

"Bummer," I go. "So like it didn't do *that* owner a hell of a lot of good. Not a terrific recommendation for the tarnhelm. Still, let me take a look. How much are you asking for it?"

The merchant smiled broadly. "Just three thousand pieces of gold. A wonderful deal. Shall I wrap it for you or will you wear it?"

Well, Bitsy, I had a twenty-dollar bill stuffed in my right bra cup and a one-dollar bill stuffed in the left. Of course, for emergencies I had a charge card tucked in my G-string. I thought three thousand pieces of gold sounded kind of steep for a tarnhelm—it's *magic*, Bitsy, it turns you into whatever shape you want. I see 'em *all* the time—and I didn't know if this gonif could relate to Daddy's AmEx plastic. Sure, no matter where I go in the Known Universe, they speak English—isn't that neat?—but sometimes their medium of exchange is edible roots and not dollars.

So like anyway, just as I was about to make a totally *withering* reply, what do I hear but—wait for it—my *mother's* voice behind me—not Pammy, Daddy's babe/wife, but like my actual *mother*, who I haven't heard from in *months*. Okay, so I haven't been around much myself, but I'd just assumed Mom had disappeared under a mountain of mah-jongg tiles in Miami Beach or someplace. And she goes, "So is that worthless piece-of-trash tarnhelm still under warranty, Miss Buy-The-First-Thing-You-See?"

I turned around and just stood there, blinking like an idiot. I didn't know what to say to her. I go, "*Mom?* What are you doing here?"

She shrugged. "Shopping. That's a crime now?"

I opened my mouth and closed it again, you know, like dumbfounded. Finally I go, "You're in the market for chainmail today?"

She gave me one of her little *tsk* noises. "What, I can't go into a store and browse around a little? Where does it say I can't just look at prices?"

She picked up a Cloak of Invisibility that she couldn't have paid for if she had all the money Daddy made when he sold his silver to the Hunt brothers. "You don't find quality like this even on Seventh Avenue," she goes, and she tossed the cloak aside like it was some horrible thing I'd given her for her birthday.

That's when I guessed it wasn't really Mom. My *real* Mom would've tossed the cloak aside, all right, but then she'd have given it a disdainful look and told the shopkeeper, "You'll accept ten dollars, I *might* take it off your hands." This near-Mom hadn't even *tried* to bargain.

"Hey," I go, "who are you *really?*"

She took a breath and heaved a sigh. It was very authentic. "My name, Maureen, is Glorian. I am called Glorian of the Knowledge by some, yet I have other names, many other names. I am a supernatural personage of ancient power and wisdom, here to guide you on your appointed quest."

"I *hate* these goddamn quests," I go. And I *do*, too. Like why can't I accidentally whoosh myself to a nice beach with clean white sand and warm water and a few eager Brad Pitt types and a pitcher of strawberry daiquiris and, you know, no one expecting me to defend or rescue anybody at all for a couple of weeks. That doesn't seem to be in the cards for good old Maureen.

"No one enjoys quests," Glorian goes. "It wouldn't be much of a trial if it was all fun and laughter."

I turn on my Number Three Frown—you know: I Really Don't Have Time For This. And I'm like, "No way I can just whoosh on out of here and bag this whole quest thing, huh?"

Glorian-Mom smiled. "I'm sorry."

So I shrugged. A warrior-woman's work is never done. "Then let's rally," I go.

"Cool." Like my Mom would *never* say "Cool." Like anybody called "Glorian of the Knowledge" would ever say "Cool," either. Yet, Bitsy, it *happened*: I was there.

Now here's a secret Maureen Birnbaum makeup tip for you. After you put on the darker shade of eye shadow, you want to dab on just an eensy amount of the under-color right in the middle of the eyelid—where did that Caramel Smoke go?—okay, here. Watch. Now, if Prince Van was the disco type, I'd put some gold glitter there instead. But he's not, and I'm not, and you probably wouldn't even *have*—

You *do*? Well, get *rid* of it.

So then this Glorian goes, "There are a number of ground rules, of course, but I'll explain them as we go along. The first thing you must know is that you'll need certain supplies: armor, weapons, magical scrolls and texts, potions and wands, as well as sufficient food and water. By its nature, the quest places certain limitations on you. For instance, you may carry a total of only twenty objects."

"I don't see why—"

Glorian raised a hand. "Twenty objects, regardless of their combined weight. Please believe me. The Powers That Be will not permit you to carry more. If you have twenty objects, and you find something more that you wish to take, you must drop one of the other items."

"What about *you*?" I go. "Your arms are broken, or are you too, you know, *special* to give me a hand? Or don't you mythical types schlep like normal people?"

Glorian looked at me for a moment. "I *will* carry

your treasures for you, but not your weapons and your other, shall we say, impedimenta."

The word *treasures* I liked. "Great. I can deal with that, then. One thing I *would* like, honey, is could you please *stop looking like my Mom*? And like right now! It's driving me crazy."

There was this little wibbly blur in the air where Glorian was standing, and then my Mom sort of turned into—this is going to sound omigod weird— *Brad Pitt*. Like that Glorian character had *read my mind* about the white sand beach and the daiquiris and everything. And now I was going to have to spend this entire exploit with a semi-real know-it-all who looked just like *Brad Pitt*.

I truly felt that I was up to the challenge.

"The second important rule is that you begin the quest with five hundred pieces of gold. That's all you have. You must decide how to spend it here in the town. You may purchase anything you like, of course, but what you choose may seriously affect your chances of survival."

"*Ha*," I go. "I've survived *this* long, haven't I? I think that shows that I can manage for myself, thank you very much."

"Maureen, everyone alive today has survived this long. None of them seriously believes he'll live forever."

Well, I wasn't about to tell him that I suspected that I was immortal. Bitsy, it's *true*. I *mean* it. I think I *am* immortal. All right, stop laughing. You just don't know what I know.

Blusher. What do you have in the way of blushers? These aren't *my* tones, after all, but you're seeing the real Maureen pioneering spirit at work here. I guess I can fake it with a layer of Vent du Désert and some Pêche aux Chandelles smushed around on top. That'll look tuf on my nipples, too, huh? Oh, grow *up*, Bitsy. Hey, you don't have one of those big Ping-Pong ball–shaped sable brushes? Never mind, I'll use my thumb. *Resourceful*, sweetie, fighting women are *always* resourceful.

Anyway, I decided to peek around in all five of the shops before I shelled out a single gold piece. I started making up a shopping list. It was pretty tough, though. I saw a *million* things I wanted—it was like, oh, say your mother gives you a thousand-dollar gift certificate to Tiffany's, and you go in there all excited and everything, and you find out that all you can afford are two silver cigarette cases or *half* a pair of the earrings you *really* want. See what I mean? Perspicuously bogus, huh?

Fortunately, it turned out that the major expense for your average hero-trainee is the weapon. Most begin with a puny dagger and hope to trip over something better during the quest itself. I, of course, came pre-armed with my *most fab* broadsword, Old Betsy, so that meant I could spend more on other things.

I took Glorian's advice and bought food and water and a lamp. Evidently it was dark where we were going. The lamp was this cheesy brass Aladdin-looking thing. It *burned* all right, and it gave off a bright enough light, but when I shook it, nothing sloshed inside. I checked it out, and you know I couldn't even find a place where you'd put oil into the damn thing. "Magic," Glorian goes. I figured *what the hell*.

Finally, I've got about four hundred pieces of gold left. I was going to invest it all in a nice suit of steel plate armor, but Scrupulously Honest and Fair Aethelraed wanted two thousand for it, and I couldn't haggle him down any lower than seventeen five. I finally walked out of his crummy shop wearing a hard leather outfit studded with metal points—I mean, wow, I would've been a big hit back in the French Quarter bars, but *oh no!* like I wasn't *there* anymore. And I didn't have a whole lot of confidence in the leather gear, not when it came to protecting me from scrabbling claws and gnashing teeth.

So this is how I began my adventure: with the swell

groovy kicky bitchin' North Beach Leather ensemble—but nothing much in the way of special hand, foot, or head protection—and a small shield, also leather, but brown. Brown! Who wears *brown* leather?

Oh. Well. On *you* it looks good, honey.

I had the stupid genieless lamp and Old Betsy and five portions of food—Glorian chose them for me, on the basis of nutritional value, wholesome ingredients, and his own idea of a cost/benefit ratio. I asked him, "What *kind* of food is in those packages?" He goes, "It's *food.* Just *food.* The kind you get at a wayside inn. You know, you sit down at a big table and they bring you *food.*" I also had a wooden canteen filled with drink—"Just *drink*," he goes—and a modest selection of magical items.

I hadn't wanted to spend money on magic. I figured me 'n' Old Betsy ought to be a match for any kind of monster we were likely to meet. Glorian disagreed. I could *always* count on him to disagree. What a *feeb*.

We book it on out of town—the place was five huts big, so *out of town* was maybe a hundred yards down the road—and Glorian goes, "Close your eyes. Please don't ask, just do it."

I closed my eyes like a good girl.

"Fine," he goes. "Now you can open them."

Well, I look and suddenly there's a *cave* beside the road. There hadn't been a cave there before. There hadn't even been rocks for a cave to be *in*. Now there was a bunch of rocks and this like danksome cave. "And this is?"

Brad Pitt looked all blond and solemn. "Caverns measureless to man," he goes.

"Down to a sunless sea," I go. Wow, one of those days I was awake in Mr. Salomon's class finally paid off in The Real World. Anyway, Glorian's eyebrows raised a little. Score one for the Muffster—and don't you *ever* call me that!

"Please, Maureen," Glorian goes, "after you." So,

with Old Betsy in one hand and the lamp in the other, I ducked into the cave and started down a long, winding staircase *hewed from the living rock* and like all covered with this funky wet green gunk.

"What *is* this place?" I go.

"It's a MUD, Maureen."

"Hey, it's got water dripping down the walls and the place *reeks*, but at least there's no mud. I don't *see* any mud."

"No, not *mud*. MUD. An acronym meaning Multi-User Dungeon. It's a term used by people involved in online computer role-playing games."

Bitsy, I was steamed. "*Games?* Is this a *game?* I don't have time for *games*, Glorian! There are poor, suffering women and children out there who need my help!"

Glorian-Brad frowned. "You'll soon find out that this is no game. This is very serious. *Deadly* serious."

"Good," I go. "I don't want to waste valuable killing time on pretend enemies. I haven't even *seen* any monsters yet."

"Soon."

"No *treasures*, either, pal." Hardly had I gotten those words out of my mouth, when I followed a sharp turn in the passageway and entered a big, high-vaulted subterranean chamber. Overhead there were stalactites in every goddamn color you could think of—*stalactites*, Bitsy. No, you're wrong. I made up a mnemonic like fully *years* ago. Stalactite comes alphabetically before stalagmite in the dictionary, and you read from the top to the bottom. Stalactites hang. *Trust* me.

Well, just *forget* it, then, honey. The *important* thing is the chamber wasn't entirely empty. There was this gooey thing in one corner, radiating a kind of sick pink glow. In a horrible way, it reminded me of those pink marshmallow Peeps you see around Easter time. You know, the ones you let get stale and then you microwave 'em. That's what we always did. I'm sorry,

Bitsy, I guess you just missed out on *whole lots* when you were a kid.

I looked more closely at the monster. *"Yuck,"* I go. "What *is* that thing?"

"It's a Pink Gooey Thing," Glorian goes. I *know*, Bitsy. He was just *terribly* helpful like that through the whole miserable adventure. I asked him what I should do, and he goes, "You could kill it."

Aw, don't give me that, Bitsy. It looked like it really *needed* killing. Besides, it would probably have shot me full of monster death rays in another few seconds. This was like nothing that zoo lady ever brought out to show Johnny Carson.

Johnny Carson. You know, the theoretically funny guy who comes on right before David Letterman. *Huh?* You're *kidding.* I can't keep up with all that stuff. It's a good thing that like I really *don't care.*

Anyway, I started walking forward, wielding Old Betsy, but then I decided to try out one of my magical weapons. I figured it would be good to get familiar with them before I faced, you know, the evil, terrible Nightmare Critter that guarded the Treasure Beyond Counting. That was my ultimate goal, Glorian had told me. If I lived that long.

I had several scrolls and one magic wand. I felt kind of, oh, *stupid* waving the wand. I heard these little mouse-voices in my mind singing "Bibbity-Bobbity-Boo," but I did it anyway. It was a Wand of Basic Blast, the poosliest magic weapon in the shop, but also the only one I could afford.

The wand made pretty Tinkerbell dust in the air, and then there was a distinct *zapping* sound and I smelled something awful like the time Daddy's fan belt broke on I-95 but he didn't realize it for a few miles. Where the Pink Gooey Thing had been, there was now nothing much except a few pretty red stones.

"Well done, Maureen!" Glorian goes. "You've slain the Pink Gooey Thing. You've gained five Experience

Points, and you find two hundred and fifty gold pieces worth of rubies."

"Tremendous," I go. "Let's hurry back up to the town and buy some more of this delicious *drink*, I'm so sure."

"Ha ha. Your Wand of Basic Blast has nine charges left."

"*Say What?*" I go. "Nine charges? You mean these things have to be *reloaded?* What kind of magic is *that?*"

"I forgot to tell you."

"And what's an Experience Point when it's at home?"

"You wouldn't understand."

I stopped in my tracks. I almost Basic Blasted his supernatural ass right into my next adventure. "Glorian," I go, in my Dangerous Voice, "did I hear you correctly?"

"Um," he goes, doing a speedy reconsider. "When you collect enough Experience Points, you're promoted to the next level and you're rewarded with a greater Hit Point quotient and a larger Hex reserve. Hex Points are what you use to cast a spell without a wand."

"I don't know any spells, Glorian."

"You will," he goes. "Let's just move along now. There's probably another supernatural guide with another hero up on the surface, waiting for us to clear out of here."

I shook my head. "You make this sound like Disneyworld."

He nodded. "A lot of the same people worked on it."

"Uh huh. Well, I just hope I won't have to chop an Abraham Lincoln animatronic to pieces down here. That would be just so *ill*."

We followed the underground path a little further, into the second vaulted chamber—Glorian preferred to call them "rooms." It was a lot like the first one, complete with a monster waiting for me. *Jeez*, Bitsy, if they really wanted to kill me, you'd think they'd get together and jump on me all at once, instead of spreading themselves so thin. Hey, it was okay by *me* if they were too dumb to live.

This one was a Giant Flaming Grasshopper. Try to imagine it for yourself, because I'm having trouble with these false eyelashes of yours. Where do you buy your accoutrements, honey? Lamston's? I mean, *hell*. I've found better makeup on worlds that hadn't made it into the Industrial Revolution yet. No offense. Hand me those little bitty scissors, okay? I have to trim the ends of these lashes or they poke me in the corner of my eye and *drive me crazy!* Thanks, Bits.

The Grasshopper? Easy, I took Old Betsy to it. Three whacks, that's all. Without sweat. And when I slew the sucker, it disappeared, and there was a curled-up parchment scroll on the ground. I picked it up. "What's this?" I go.

Glorian took a peek. "You have a Scroll of Locate Bathroom. Save that one—you'll want it later."

"Gotcha."

"And you have seven more Experience Points."

"That's just *so* exciting, Glorian. Now c'mon."

In the next dozen rooms, I killed a dozen more monsters: an Inedible Lump, a Hound From Hell, a Blue Blob, a Magenta Blob, three or four more giant insects, a couple of Spooks—one Quilted and one Plaid—and finally the most unspeakable—a Zombie Mallwalker. In return, I scored about fifteen pounds of precious and semi-precious stones, one of the worthless daggers, and a Wand of Shrieking. I also found three other magical items: a Scroll of Gain Weight, a Scroll of Blindness, and a Tonic of Cure Poison.

I dropped the Scrolls of Gain Weight—don't say a *word*, Bitsy—and Blindness. Glorian said there were a lot of booby prizes around in these caverns, mixed in with the valuable stuff. He also said that sometimes

what looked at first like a booby prize could turn out
to be worth keeping. I thought about what he said
for a few seconds, and then I dropped the dagger and
the Wand of Shrieking also. It turned out later that
he'd been right—aw hell, he was *always* right—and
that the Wand of Shrieking would've been very useful
against two or three monsters I came across further
along.

I also accumulated a hundred Experience Points,
and got my first promotion. I became Maureen Birnbaum, Stalwart 1st Grade. You know, oddly enough,
I didn't feel *the least bit* different.

From then on, it was one room after another, one
monster after another. There were more Gooey
Things, Lumps, Blobs, and Spooks, all in rainbow colors, and giant insects of all kinds, and then I started
running into rodents, which didn't please me—Giant
Glowing Rats, Ravenous Mice, and Lust-Crazed Ham-
sters. That's what Glorian called 'em, anyway.

In one room I found a Baby Green Gremlin, and
I sort of hated to, you know, *slaughter* the poor thing
except it leaped right for my goddamn *throat*. And in
the next room was a Mommy Green Gremlin, followed by the Daddy Green Gremlin. That Daddy
gave me a *real* battle. I used Old Betsy like she'd
never been used before, and every bit of magic stuff
I had with me. Finally, though, the Daddy Green
Gremlin disappeared in a noxious cloud of avocado-
colored smoke, leaving behind about a thousand
pieces of gold, some scrolls, two wands, and, best of
all, a complete suit of really neat chainmail.

Really neat chainmail in, God help me, Size 6.

What kind of Size 6 heroes were they expecting
around there? Maybe some eleven-year-old girl gym-
nasts had passed through the week before or something. "Glorian," I go, "how about a Wand of Expand
Armor? A Scroll of A Slimmer, Shapelier You? I can't
even fit my *hand* into this sleeve."

"Very sorry, Maureen," he goes. "I have no control

over what appears after you extinguish a monster. You have to take the trash with the treasures."

I've always felt that the world could get along very well without people smaller than a Size 10. Oh, yeah? Name *one*. Bitsy, Meg Ryan is an *actor*. They're not even *real*.

After I killed a Red Wriggler—giving me a Half-Strength Healing Potion and two hundred pieces of gold—it looked like the corridor had come to a dead end.

Glorian goes, "Just a moment." He went to a blank wall, bent over—Brad Pitt's buns in tight cutoff jeans—and pressed *something*. I don't know exactly what he did, but the wall sort of swiveled, revealing another down staircase cut into the speckled gray granite. Down we went to the next level.

"What's down here?" I go.

"It gets more difficult the further we descend, but the rewards are comparably greater as well."

In the first room, there was not one but two monsters waiting for me. I wondered what they did between heroes. You couldn't even get up a good game of "I Spy." There was really nothing to look at.

The first monster was a Furry Fungoid, according to Glorian, and the other was a plain old Werewolf. They came at me together, and I worked up a pretty good sweat before I managed to kill them. When I did, more gold and jewels appeared, along with a Wand of Fireballs and a Magic Parchment.

Just as I thought that Glorian would need a shopping bag to carry all the treasure, damned if he didn't pull a Bloomingdale's shopping bag out of the air somehow. Don't ask *me*. It was just one of his supernatural talents. It was very practical—better than, say, spinning oats into molybdenum.

Now, though, I had to make some decisions. I had gathered twenty-two items, and I'd have to drop a couple. I asked Glorian's advice. He goes, "The Wand of Fireballs is a much more potent weapon than Basic Blast."

"Okay." I dropped the Wand of Basic Blast.

"You'll want to keep the Magic Parchment. When you learn a new spell, you have to write it on the Parchment before you can use it."

After a lot of thought, I dropped a Ring of Increased Stamina. I hated to lose it, but I had enough confidence in my natural abilities. We went on.

Before we entered the next room, Glorian touched my arm. "If you successfully defeat this next monster, you'll be promoted to Stalwart 2nd Grade. Then you may choose one magic spell to learn."

"I'll be successful," I go. "Do *you* have some doubt?"

He gave me that full-lipped Brad Pitt smile. I just sort of, you know, *dissolved* inside. And he goes, "It would be a good idea to save now and then. Especially before this important battle."

That one soared right over my head. "What do you mean, 'save'?"

"It's a long and tedious process, Maureen, but when you're killed, I'll be able to resurrect you at precisely the moment when the save was done."

I didn't buy into this getting-killed thing. Glorian mentioned it with absolute certainty, and I didn't appreciate his lack of confidence. I'm like, "You can *resurrect* me? How do our community's spiritual leaders feel about that?"

He sort of let that one pass. "Do you wish to save now?"

"Sure," I go. "I'm easy to get along with."

The procedure *was* boring, just as he'd warned. I thought there would be some colorful magic involved, maybe a lot of chanting and incantation and some nice incense and stuff. Afraid not. Mostly Glorian just sat down on the cold granite floor and typed.

He *typed*, Bitsy. I don't know on what. Suddenly

he had this *keyboard* that like wasn't connected to anything, and he typed. For ten or fifteen minutes. When he was done, he stood up. The keyboard seemed to have gone away again. "All right," he goes. "Now you can enter fearlessly into that room."

I go, *"Hey!* Like I didn't need you to transcribe your thoughts for a quarter of an hour to go fearlessly into the next room. I was fearless before I met you, and I'll be fearless long after you've gone back to ... wherever."

"As you say."

The next room was like most of the others except for one detail: I didn't see a single monster. "Am I supposed to wait around here or what?" I go. "Jeez, some monster missed its cue, and I have to hold up my whole quest until it feels like showing up?"

Glorian spoke to me in Brad Pitt's soft, low voice. Have you ever noticed how *blue* his eyes are? Anyway, he goes, "Have patience, Maureen. No time is passing in the real world while we're down here. When you return—*if* you return—it will not be a moment later than when you first arrived in the village of Mudville."

"That's okay, but I still want to get on with it. I have more imp—" Something whacked me a good one on the back of my head. I almost fell on my face. Instead, I spun around and saw—

—nothing. There was nothing there. That didn't seem to matter, because it hit me so hard just below my breastbone that I doubled over and almost barfed.

"It's an Invisible Gooey Thing," Glorian informed me.

I wanted to make a crushingly sarcastic reply, but it was all I could do to force air into my lungs. When I could breathe again, I started poking around with Old Betsy, trying to find the goddamn monster. *Blammo!* It hit me again. I was getting furious.

And like Glorian is yelling, "Put your back against a wall!"

Good thought. That would keep the Invisible

Gooey Thing from sneaking up behind me. I went to one of the room's corners. When the monster came after me again, I'd be able to find it and kick its see-through ass into Monster Heaven.

It didn't take long. I collected a pretty good jab to the stomach, and then I lashed out with Old Betsy. I swung with all my strength at what looked to me like thin air.

I hit something. There was a tiny, shrill scream, and I saw a puddle of Gooey Thing blood form on the floor, and from out of nowhere a double handful of diamonds and a scroll appeared.

Glorian goes, "Very well done, Maureen! You killed it!"

I just, you know, played humble. I go, "You don't have to *see* 'em to *whack* 'em." Glorian scooped up the diamonds and added them to my treasure. I took the scroll and opened it. The writing was very decorative in a Metropolitan Museum of Art kind of way. Across the top was lettered *A Scroll of Glass Breaking*. I sure didn't want to trade off one of my twenty items to carry that worthless piece of magic, so I just dropped it and went on toward the next room. Glorian followed faithfully.

"See?" I go. "I *told* you I wasn't going to be killed."

"Yes, you did, Maureen. Saving is still a good idea, though. A hero must have more than courage. There is a time for prudence as well."

"Maybe. Now, you said something about a promotion?"

"Yes. The Invisible Gooey Thing was worth a hundred and twelve points to a Stalwart 1st Grade. You are now a Stalwart 2nd Grade, with all the perquisites and privileges appertaining thereto. I offer you my heartiest congratulations, Maureen. Both your Hit Points and your Hex reserve have been increased, making you more difficult to defeat in battle. Also, you may learn one of these magic spells: Fireballs, Light, Jump, or Paralyze Monster."

I have this habit of chewing my lip when I have serious thinking to do. "I've already got a wand for Fireballs," I go.

"Yes, but the Fireballs will be more powerful if they're cast by a spell than by a wand. And if you learned that spell, you could drop the wand and take another object in its place."

"That's cool. What do the other spells do?"

"Light illuminates an entire chamber regardless of size, far better than the beams thrown by your lamp. Jump will teleport you a short distance—it could save your life if you find yourself trapped somehow. And Paralyze Monster does just that, except it doesn't work on all monsters, and on the monsters it *does* affect, it works only eighty percent of the time."

"Hmm." I could hear the thinking music from "Jeopardy" tinkling in my mind. "Okay, make it Paralyze Monster, then. No, wait a minute. Jump. Yeah, Jump."

"Are you sure?"

Of course I wasn't sure. I'm like, "Give me another minute!" I thought about this real hard. I wanted to drop the Wand of Fireballs so I could pick up the next good object I found. I also liked the idea of Jumping out of tight situations. And Paralyze Monster sounded pretty handy, too. I didn't think I needed Light, so at least I'd eliminated one out of four.

"Maureen?" he goes.

"I'm *working* on it! *Jeez*, Brad! I mean, Glorian!" I debated with myself a little more. It was a tough call, like would you rather spend an entire week all alone with no money in Paris, or eight hours in Paramus, New Jersey, with Mel Gibson.

I went with Paralyze Monster. So shoot me. Glorian showed me how to write the spell on the Magic Parchment.

After that, the path got more complicated. The rooms didn't lead off each other in a nice straight line anymore. We were in a huge, confusing maze. I hoped Glorian was leaving a trail of bread crumbs or something, because if we were depending on my Girl Scout training to find the way back up to The Real World, well, I was going to get like real sick of *food* and *drink* a few days before I starved to death in this subterranean playground.

And I'd like to have a few words with whoever designed those monsters. I mean, except for the fact that any one of them could've, you know, *killed* me— if I'd let it have the chance—they were all pretty ridiculous. I would've laughed in their faces if *one:* they *had* faces, and *two:* they weren't trying to, you know, *kill* me. When you hear the word "monster," Bitsy, what do you think of?

Well, okay, either the alien from *Alien* or whatever it was that lived in the back of my bedroom closet. *I* could've come up with better monsters than the ones I had to fight. Probably somebody thought them up real quick at the very last minute during a lunch break.

You should've seen the next one I ran into. Glorian and I came to a fork in the tunnel and he goes, "Which way, Maureen? Choose, and choose carefully!"

"Does it really, really make *any* difference at all?"

"Well, truthfully, no."

So I go, "Then we'll turn left." That brought us to a small room. I could see a large metal shield in one corner, and a magic wand in another. Wow, like free gifts from the management! I took maybe three steps toward the shield, when the monster attacked. "Glorian—"

He goes, "It's an Un-Dead Elvis."

"Thank you very much," the monster goes. It executed a little hip swivel and then did this Flying Mare from all the way across the room. That's a *wrestling* term, sweetie. You should watch wrestling sometime. It's got to be *at least* as realistic as those soap operas of yours.

Well, at first I hesitated to lift my sword in anger against like *The King*, but this wasn't the *real* Elvis—I don't think. With consummate grace and speed I sidestepped, and the Un-Dead Elvis fell to the ground. I graciously waited until it got to its feet again, and then I chopped it into little tiny gory pieces. It looked at me as its life ebbed slowly away. In a tiny, weak voice, it gasped, "Thank you very much." And then it died.

Aw, *Bitsy*! C'mon! You're crying for a *monster*! Jeez, okay, pretend it wasn't an Un-Dead Elvis. Pretend it was, oh, an Un-Dead Vanilla Ice, if it makes you feel better.

Try *real* hard. You'll remember.

So now there was a wand and a shield in the room, and some sapphires and a new scroll and a package of *food*. Glorian got a second shopping bag and put the jewels in it. He told me I could take the *food* and it wouldn't count toward my total of items. The scroll was a Spell of Flatulence, and I went "Ew!" and dropped it.

Just as I was going to pick up the shield, something attacked me from behind. I never saw what it was, because I fell facedown on the filthy, cold floor, and Old Betsy went flying out of my hand. I got to my knees, but before I could stand up again, the monster killed me.

It *killed* me. Bitsy, I'm not trying to be funny. I was like, you know, way *dead*.

Honestly, honey, I don't really remember much about it. It was pretty vague—being dead, I mean. It was a lot like homeroom would be on the first day at a new school. You know, you're just sort of sitting around waiting for things to start, but you don't know anybody to talk to and you don't really know what's going on.

Thank *God* I let Glorian talk me into saving. He sure rescued my fabulous butt that time. The next thing I knew, I'm like, "You can *resurrect* me? How do our community's spiritual leaders feel about that?"

"All right," he goes. "Now you can enter fearlessly into that room."

I go, "*Wow!* Like déjà vu!" I was back in time, right before I went into the chamber with the Invisible Gooey Thing. Which was, let's face it, kind of a *drag* because I had to fight it all over again, and then the Un-Dead Elvis.

The second time around, though, I was ready for whatever had made that dastardly and unprovoked attack on my unguarded behind. It turned out to be a Golden Elf Gone Bad. That's what Glorian called it. It didn't look much like an elf to me. Not one of your *Tolkien* elves, anyway. It looked a lot like the lead singer from some Seattle grunge band. I almost hated to get its dirty guck on Old Betsy, but I really wanted to teach it a lesson.

It was dead soon. And it was pretty chintzy with its treasures, too. One stone, not even a jewel, and a small package of Kleenex which I didn't bother to pick up. I did take the metal shield that was sitting in one corner, and swapped it for my leather one. The wand was a Wand of Summon Demon, and I figured I didn't need that one at the moment, thanks anyway.

My eyes are *done*, and forgive me for saying so myself, but they are little short of legendary. Next, lips. I have a couple of neat little lipstick tricks, too, Bitsy, you might want to take notes. Now, the first thing I'm going—

Sure. Fine by me. Live on in ignorance if you want to.

Well, after the Elf room there were dozens, *hundreds* of more rooms. They all looked pretty much the same. We went down more staircases, to the third, fourth, fifth, and sixth levels. The monsters got bigger and faster and smarter and meaner. By the time I confronted the Cookie Monster—no, dear, it wasn't the "Sesame Street" Cookie Monster. This one was huge and like *really* scary—I had to come up with a different strategy. What I did, see, was stop just inside the doorway and zap the monster with every charge in the Wand of Fireballs, just to soften it up. Then I closed in with Old Betsy. Even so, I was getting as much as I wanted to handle, and I knew that the monsters waiting further on weren't going to get any easier. I needed more weapons.

Visiting all those hundreds of rooms and killing all those monsters had given me a pretty spectacular haul of treasure. Glorian was loaded down with four or five Bloomie's bags full of gold and jewels—and, believe me, sweetie, gold gets heavy *fast*. Those must've been *magic* shopping bags, 'cause the handles never broke. In The Real World, handles tear loose if you put so much as a circle pin in the bag.

I'd been promoted up through Stalwart 3rd Grade, Valiant 1st, 2nd, and 3rd, and Paladin 1st and 2nd. I'd learned more spells, and my Magic Parchment was almost filled up. I had a magic Helmet of Farseeing, magic Gloves of Deftness, magic Boots of Savagery— they didn't help me *fight* any better, they just looked whoa nellie! *great*—and *finally*, at long last, I found a suit of magic Fire-Resistant Armor in my size. *Nearly* my size, but close enough. I made good ol' Brad turn around, and I stripped out of the studded leather outfit and climbed into the armor. I needed his help to fasten it up. I don't *know* if he peeked at me. I *hope* so.

My supernatural guide did his rock trick again, and revealed another staircase. I started to climb down, but Glorian stopped me by putting a hand on my arm. "Maureen," he goes, "however this turns out, I want you to know that it's been an honor and a pleasure to accompany you this far."

"Hey!" I go. "Like what does *that* mean? It sounds like you're bailing out on me now."

He shook his head. "No, I won't abandon you.

There is but one more room, and one more monster to battle."

"The Nightmare Critter. And the Treasure Beyond Counting."

"Yes," he goes. "Few heroes make it even this far. Even fewer make it beyond that final confrontation. I believe you are well prepared, Maureen. You are brave, true, and strong. You are fearless, cunning, and steadfast. You are shrewd, bold, and vital. You are clever, daring, and generous. You are undaunted, tenacious, and—"

All right, Bitsy, *all right*! That's what he said, can I help it? He also told me that I was the Platonic ideal of all womanly virtues. Who am I to argue with a spiritual being? So he goes, "I have every expectation that you will triumph. Good luck, and may God bless."

Then, believe it or not, he shook my hand. I took a deep breath, turned away, and went down the stairs into the Den of the Nightmare Critter. It was the biggest room I'd seen yet, so huge that even after I cast the Spell of Light I couldn't see the far corners or the ceiling. And, wow, did it echo! It smelled awful, too, like all the abandoned tires in the world were stacked up in the shadows and they were burning.

There were two things I *didn't* see. One was the Nightmare Critter, and the other was, you know, the Treasure Beyond Counting.

I turned back toward Glorian. "Say, pal," I go, "where the hell *is* this—"

It was the phenomenally deafening roar that gave me my first clue. I spun around again, and like at first I still didn't see the monster. Then I did. It was a *dragon*. It was blue and sparkly. And it was about the size of your average collie.

"Huh?" I go. Okay, not me at my most eloquent, I'll admit. It seemed appropriate at the time. The dragon was sparkly because it appeared to be made out of cobalt blue glass. It would've been kind of cute if it weren't roaring and blasting fire and smoke at me. The fire was very real, and there was a lot more of it than you'd think a doggie-sized dragon could produce.

I started at the top, with the Wand of Fireballs, which I emptied into the Nightmare Critter without so much as making it flinch. I tried absolutely everything else at my command, including the Spell of Light in case it was, whatyoucall, nocturnal or something. I may as well have been reciting the Pledge of Allegiance for all the good it did. Finally, all I had left was Old Betsy, but that was good enough for me.

I waded into that dragon with all my might. I hacked and hewed and slashed and chopped and cut for what seemed like *hours*, and I didn't make Dent One in the dragon's glass hide. In the meantime, it was crisping me up pretty good, even though I was wearing Fire-Resistant Armor. I had to dash back out of range now and then to slap at my smoldering boots and gloves.

Glorian goes, "None of the spells you know can defeat this creature, Maureen, even in concert. In any event, you are out of Hex Points."

"*Now* you tell me," I go.

"And the dragon is completely impervious to your swordplay."

"*Now* you tell me. Say, why don't you give me some *help*, for a change?"

His voice gets kind of sad. "Even if I were allowed, I am powerless against blue glass. And if the dragon kills you now, I won't be able to restore you."

Suddenly, I felt just the least bit, you know, like *doomed*.

Glorian goes, "You should've saved before you entered this room."

"*Now* you tell me. Got any like *useful* hints, pal?"

"Yes. Fortunately, you once had in your possession the single weapon that can destroy this monster, but you chose to drop it."

I thought hard, even while the Nightmare Critter was moving up on me, shrieking and fuming and bellowing and blasting me with fire. I realized that I had been slowly retreating, and I was almost pinned against the wall. "That scroll! The Scroll of Glass Breaking, the one that appeared when I killed the Invisible Gooey Thing."

"You'll have to find it, Maureen."

The goddamn scroll was all the way up on the first or second level. I started edging toward the door, and the blue glass dragon followed, shooting flames at me the whole time. I made it out of the chamber and started up the stairs. The dragon kept pace. I retraced my steps through all the rooms, up all the staircases, and one by one my Hit Points were dwindling. It was like *omigod!* am I going to make it in time, or will I die the *Real Death* down here? And then nobody, not even *my best friend* Bitsy Spiegelman will ever know what happened to poor old Maureen!

So I get to the room—the *right* room, the Invisible Gooey Thing room—and I can tell you my heart just started thudding when I saw the scroll lying on the floor. I hurried toward it, but the dragon was just behind me. I could even hear it take a big breath. I knew, I just *knew*, that it wasn't about to flambé me— it was going to incinerate that scroll, the only thing in this bargain-basement Wonderland that could hurt it.

I took this *wonderful* flying leap, Bitsy. You should've *seen* me! It was *great*, kind of a 9.6 for difficulty, 2.0 for technique dive, and I landed right on top of the scroll just as the dragon ignited. I felt the fire sizzle the armor on my back. Then it got very quiet, and I knelt and opened the scroll. The dragon was looking right into my eyes, drawing in another breath.

So I read the goddamn scroll, and the Nightmare Critter shattered all over the place into a billion little blue pieces, and from *somewhere*, maybe from hidden speakers up in the dim reaches above my head, I heard the "Ode to Joy." I go, "Give me a *break*, okay?"

So then Glorian comes up to me. He's smiling his Brad Pitt smile, and he's *just about* to say something.

I raised a hand and stopped him. I go, "I want to know *one thing*: Where the hell is this Treasure Beyond Counting I've been hearing about?"

"Here it is, Maureen, and it's all yours." He held out another scroll.

"It's a scroll," I go.

"Yes, it's a scroll. It's a special Scroll of Summon Taxi. With it, you can go anywhere you like. Anywhere at all, just tell the driver."

"*Anywhere?*" I go, my tiny little mind already racing.

"Yes, Maureen, anywhere in the Known Universe."

"Like, say, *Mars?*" You know, Bits, that my glorious, beloved Prince Van is never long out of my thoughts.

Glorian goes, "Certainly, Mars."

"Cool!" I took the scroll, opened it, and read it. Just like *that*, a magic Yellow Cab appeared. I was impressed. I didn't even have to leap out into traffic and throw my body in front of it.

Glorian opened the passenger door for me and loaded all my shopping bags filled with gold and jewels. I took off the armor—I didn't want to keep it, and it would look pretty dumb to Prince Van—and sheathed Old Betsy and slung her across my back.

Glorian goes, "Farewell, Maureen."

I go, "Farewell, Glorian. You have been a good and faithful guide. Thank you for all your help. Seeyabye." He was standing there, holding the door for me, so I took the dollar bill out of my brassiere and tipped him.

Hey, Bitsy, I *know* I had a twenty in the other cup, but, *jeez*, like I'm so sure Glorian didn't have change!

I got in the cab. The driver turned around and he goes, "Where to?"

"Mars," I go.

"You got it." And we were off.

We started driving away through gray, misty, unreal scenery, and after a few minutes I realized that I was filthy, scorched, and completely covered with blood and ichor. *"Feh,"* I go, and then I told the driver to stop first at your house so I could get cleaned up for my darling prince. And *that,* sweetie, is how my *very last* and *forever final* exploit came to an end.

I don't have any idea how long it took the cab driver to deliver Muffy to my doorstep, but Lord! it wasn't long enough. When she arrived, she shoved her way into the house—my son, Malachi Bret, and I are staying, you know, temporarily with my mother. Then Maureen started begging and pleading for help to transform her from a tough-as-nails macha maiden into a fully to-die-for elegant yet phenomenally sexy faux princess. She wanted to be the kind of woman her dearly beloved, the Martian Prince Van, would find like totally irresistible.

"And you know I don't carry cosmetics with me on my exploits," she goes. *"I suppose I'll just have to make do with what you've got."* *The way she said that, you'd think my makeup situation was only slightly less hopeless than death by lethal injection.*

I showed her what I had in my room and in the bathroom, and I told her she could borrow whatever she wanted. "Just don't touch my mother's things."

"For sure. They're probably not my style anyway. Let's just see what you've got." *From long experience I knew that absolutely nothing would be good enough for Maureen, even if I had brought Max Factor and Coco Chanel back from the dead to give her a hand. She rummaged around in several shoe boxes filled with my basic makeup arsenal, making these little disparaging non-word sounds.*

She looked at a plastic bottle of invigorating spruce elemental essence for the bath. "Aromatherapy, Bitsy?

*Like duh." That didn't stop her from dumping most
of it into the tub as it was filling.*

*"I have a chamomile after-bath gel for improving
the skin," I go. "I don't know how well spruce and
chamomile fragrances mix."*

*"Don't worry about it, Bits." She lowered herself
slowly and carefully into the steamy hot water. "My
skin's just fine, thank you very much."*

"How I envy you," I go, in like my flattest voice.

*"Loofah," she goes. I handed her the loofah.
"Pumice stone." I gave her the pumice stone. It was
like being on the set of* General Hospital.

*I'll skip the rest of the ritual, except to say that
Muffy spent half an hour soaking in the tub, then
another ten minutes washing her hair under the
shower, and the better part of another hour doing a
wax-on wax-off routine on every visible hair between
her nostrils and the floor.*

*Then she started in on the actual paint job. She
goes, "Bitsy, what is all this stuff? Don't you remember anything I taught you? Let me just say a few
magic words: Givenchy, Lancôme, Princess Marcella
Borghese. You've just got to stop buying your makeup
from door-to-door ladies."*

*I shut my eyes tighty-tight as I struggled to keep
from ripping her lungs out. I even helped her do her
nails. After all the coats of base, polish—Flame Scarlet, one of my own favorite shades—and clear varnish
had dried, I glued a small gold-foil Olde English "M"
on the nail of her left ring finger and a little rhinestone
on the right ring finger. If you ask me, I thought that
was just too much, but Muffy never asked my opinion
and I didn't volunteer it.*

*There was lots more, but the only real crisis came
while she shuffled through my perfume collection. She
picked up one bottle, sniffed it, and grimaced. "This
is just so drugstore," she goes. "Who in their right
mind would—" She stopped abruptly, and her expression changed. "It's just that no matter how long you*

hang on to this cute novelty bottle, sweetie, it's never going to be a collectible." She settled for Paloma Picasso's Satin de Parfum. Mums had given it to me and I'd forgotten I even had it.

By the time she was dressed and ready to rush into Prince Van's brawny yet tender embrace, she'd spent more than three hours getting made up. To tell the truth, though, she did look almost spectacular. "In a hurry," she goes. "Gotta run. Say hi to your mother for me. Thanks for everything, Bitsy. This may be the last time we ever see each other, but please don't grieve. Be happy for me instead, okay? I'll leave the shopping bags of gold and jewels with you—I can always come back from Mars if I need them. In the meantime, they're yours. Kiss kiss!"

I opened the front door for her. I heard birds singing, and the breeze smelled of freshly-cut grass. Three neighborhood boys were playing Pickle-In-The-Middle on the sidewalk. It was a gorgeous day, except that the cab was gone. Maureen just stared at the empty driveway for a long time.

"The driver said he'd take you anywhere you wanted," I go. "You should've gone straight to Mars and not stopped here. That used up your one magic-taxi wish."

"Oh hell." If I didn't know her so well, I could've sworn she was on the verge of tears. She let out a deep breath, shrugged, and turned to me. "Know any good restaurants that accept rubies?" she goes.

Grace under pressure. That's my pal, Muffy.